The Prince of Frogs

The Prince of Frogs

ANNALIESE EVANS

TOR®

historical paranormal romance

A TOM DOHERTY ASSOCIATES BOOK
NEW YORK

THE PRINCE OF FROGS

A Tor Book
Published by Tom Doherty Associates, LLC
175 Fifth Avenue
New York, NY 10010

www.tor-forge.com

Tor® is a registered trademark of Tom Doherty Associates, LLC.

ISBN 978-0-7653-6167-7

First Edition: September 2009

Printed in the United States of America

0 9 8 7 6 5 4 3 2 1

To my critique partner and friend, Stacia Kane.
Thanks so much for all you do.

Acknowledgments

A huge thank you to my agent, Caren Johnson, for her unfailing support. Thanks to my family for their love and patience, to my husband for going above and beyond as a partner and friend, and to all the people at Tor for their hard work on this project. And last, to my readers, without whom none of this would be possible.

The
Prince of
Frogs

"Take my heart, my hinny, my girl,
Take my heart, my own darling;
Remember the promise you made to me,
Down by the cold well, so weary."

And so the little princess did as she was asked,
Though she feared the frog most greatly."

—*THE WELL AT WORLD'S END*,
Scottish folktale

Once upon a time there was a princess who slept eighty
years away, and awoke to find none she had known among
the living, and her body violated while she walked the gray
mists of enchantment. This is not her story. This is my story. I
am the one called Briar Rose, the woman of many thorns.

—ROSEMARIE EDENBURG

CHAPTER ONE

May 15, 1750
Edenburg keep
The Kingdom of Myrdrean

Rosemaric was awakened by a knock at the pane, a rhythmic rapping far too calculated to be made by a bird or other creature haunting the black forest surrounding Edenburg keep. There was something else at the window, something capable of reason.

The knowledge would not have been alarming if the royal bedchamber weren't on the south side of the castle, where the wall outside plunged hundreds of feet into the valley below.

"Ambrose?" Rose clutched the sheets to her chest, squinting through the darkness toward the window.

Her former liaison among the Fey de la Nuit was the only resident of Myrdrean other than herself who was capable of flight. Though her pale gray wings were hardly worth mentioning when compared to the onyx glory of Master Minuit's, they accomplished the task they had been created for. The legacy of her quarter-fairy heritage had only been hers to claim for a very short time, but those small wings had already saved her life more than once.

And might very well do so again.

Her enemies were many among both the supernatural and human worlds. Other human royals demanded her allegiance and threatened her with violence, the vampire and Fey communities were on the verge of war, and somewhere the black elf who had nearly destroyed London still roamed the earth.

Ecanthar, in his madness, believed only Rose's blood could raise a giant buried beneath the Thames. She feared he would come for her blood again, and if the intelligence gathered by the Fey was to be trusted, he was capable of shifting his form to do so.

The black elf could very well have sprouted wings to fly up to her window and kidnap her from her bed this very night. If she crossed the room and pulled wide the curtains, she might see his burning red eyes floating in the blackness, peering through the tangle of his raven hair. Assuming he had recovered his usual speed and strength after his battle with the Fey de la Nuit, there would be no escape. He would be through the glass in seconds, large, cold hands wrapping around her throat, stifling her screams, stealing her—

The rapping came again, a teasing tattoo that made Rose's heart race.

"Ambrose, is that you?" Rose asked again, increasing her volume to be heard through the thick pane, no longer caring if she woke Gareth. In fact, a part of her hoped he might be roused from his sleep so easily, proving he was once again the skilled, ever alert warrior she had known.

But a glance at the pillow beside her revealed her

husband still slept the deep sleep of the wounded. Since the night he was nearly murdered for the blood he held in his belly—Rose's blood—he had yet to recover his strength. He was so desperately in need of rest he often took to his bed before the clock struck one, an hour he swore was even earlier than the curfew imposed upon him as a child.

After all, half-vampire children kept rather odd hours.

"Gareth? Are you awake?" His cat-green eyes remained closed, the shadows beneath them making Rose hesitate to ask again. Her husband was as striking as ever, but a graver figure than before. He simply hadn't been the same scandalous, merry rake since he'd become the king of Myrdrean.

It made her wonder if he regretted taking her to wife.

Perhaps he wished he had sought out another with fairy heritage instead of honoring the betrothal contract forged by their two families.

Isn't that why you refuse his request to journey to the enchanted Fey lands? You test his love, and begin to find it false. The fabric binding you weakens with every passing day. Soon the threads will snap, and you will learn to hate this creature, this weak shadow of a man, this—

Rose shook her head sharply, chastising herself for her thoughts. She loved her husband as he loved her. She had looked into Gareth's mind a dozen times. His heart was as true as any she had known. To doubt him simply because he found their present living situation difficult to bear was cruel.

How many men would relish the knowledge that their wife was intimately bound by magic to their half brother? Ambrose and Gareth had scarcely tolerated one another even before this, and her husband knew the black faerie had feelings for Rose that went beyond affection.

And what of your *feelings? Does your body not long for the touch of the faerie? To feel his bare skin against your own?*

The thought was even more frightening than the suspicion that Ecanthar might be lurking outside her window. She craved the body of her husband and no other. These thoughts were madness.

Though the knocking did not come again, Rose threw off the covers and reached for her robe. The spring nights were cool, and she preferred to be modestly covered when doing battle.

No, that wasn't quite true. She *preferred* to be dressed in boys' clothes, but since coming to Myrdrean she'd had little occasion to dress against her gender. The ogres had yet to recover from the losses they suffered in London, and the tribe's fear of the dread Briar Rose had returned with a vengeance. She hadn't heard a whisper of ogre activity in Myrdrean or the surrounding nations since returning to her home country.

But that didn't mean she'd grown careless. Her sword still sat in its place by her bed, clean and ready for battle.

The metal fairly sang with pleasure when she gripped the hilt, its blade stretching as it filled with faerie magic. Rose couldn't deny the excitement filling her own veins as she stalked toward the window. Her mind might insist she craved peace above all else, but her heart thirsted for the thrill of combat. One did not spend over a hundred years as an executioner to suddenly become content minding hearth and home.

A part of her still longed for the chance to face down a foe, to feel her arms burn with exertion as sword cleaved through flesh, to see blood flow like a font from the sundered halves of an enemy.

Yes, there is a lust even greater than that for flesh sliding against flesh. The lust for blood, for the power that comes from—

Rose stumbled, tripping over the hem of her nightdress.

Something wasn't right. She had never relished her role as death dealer to the tribe. In fact, she had often prayed the ogres would cease feeding upon innocent humans, thus making her work unnecessary.

The sudden lust for blood and the strange, seductive voice in her mind . . . she was certain they were not her own. Whatever visitor lurked in the darkness beyond her window, he or she must have the ability to alter the thoughts of others.

Rose did her best to firm her mental shields, ensuring she was defended from outside invasion. Her mental connection to Gareth after their blood exchange had necessitated learning the skill. There were some thoughts she wished not even her dear husband to overhear, and she certainly didn't relish the idea of Ambrose or other supernaturals eavesdropping on her innermost counsel.

"Ambrose," she called once more, though now that she was fully awake she knew it was not the faerie who waited outside her window.

Since the night he had filled her with his magic, banishing the virulent energy of the black elf, she had a way of sensing when he was near. She could feel him as if he were a part of her.

He is *a part of you, Rosemarie, and will only become*

*more so once you rid yourself of the vampire. Surely
you know this charade cannot go on. You are destined
for greater things, dearest daughter.*

"Maman?" Rose's hand froze before she could
grasp the curtains.

Her mother's spirit had spoken to her in Myrdrean
once before, but that had been months ago, when the
keep was still in ruins. Her grandfather Stephen, the
Seelie king, believed Marionette's soul had finally
left the earthly plane and journeyed on to the Summerland now that her daughter's life was no longer threatened by ancient Fey prophecy. Rose certainly hadn't
felt her mother in the way she once had. It was more
that her maman was a loving energy contained deep
within her heart than an entity outside herself.

But even when she *had* heard her mother whispering
in her ear, it had been nothing like this. Marionette had
always been a warm, loving light in the lives of others,
never the kind to call to the darkness within.

Laughter echoed through the room, as if there were
no drapes hung to cover the bare stone walls.

I do not call to the darkness, my dear. I am *the darkness. Your darkness.*

The blue curtains, which looked nearly black in the
darkened room, began to glow a deep, urgent red. It
was the red of freshly spilt blood, of an ill-omened sun-
set, as scarlet as the eyes of the black elf who haunted
her dreams.

Rose stumbled backward, tripping over her gown
again, as if she were an awkward girl of fourteen, not a
queen of nearly two hundred years gifted with the
grace of a goddess from her cradle. But she suddenly
felt very young and very small, not at all the fierce

woman whose profession had once forced her to be faster and more terrifying than the monsters who roamed the night. It was difficult to feel anything but small in the presence of the figure rising like a phoenix from the flaming red curtains, stretching and writhing as she grew as tall as the rafters.

Rich velvet fabric flowed into satin skin the color of a dove's wing, pale flesh draped in scarlet like the blood of a stag spilled on newly fallen snow. Slowly, a white face with deep red lips formed near the shadows of the ceiling, a woman's face framed by hair as black as night.

Even cloaked in darkness, Rose could see that the giant was beautiful.

And terrible. A terrible, wicked beauty so ancient it made her bones ache to be in the creature's presence.

"Please," Rose begged as she rolled onto her knees, pressing her forehead to the rich carpet in supplication. She wasn't certain what she pleaded for, only that she wished she had stayed abed, buried beneath the covers as she'd done as a child when nightmares came to call.

You cower before me, as they all have done from time immemorial. I expected . . . more.

Disappointment pressed down around Rose. She gasped, squeezing her eyes shut, pressing her fists into the floor, desperately wishing the Great Mother had found her pleasing.

So you know me. That is better. The pressure threatening to crush her bones abated a bit, allowing Rose to suck in a ragged breath. *Show me your face, dearest. I would look upon that which I have created.*

Rose trembled as she looked up, up, up into the face of the Mother. Part of her had known the woman's identity from the very instant she appeared, even if her logical mind insisted the Mother was simply a myth told to explain the creation of the first supernaturals.

The giant laughed as if she was privy to Rose's thoughts, which she certainly was. There were no shields strong enough to protect a three-quarter mortal's mind from this creature. The Mother had existed before the land emerged fully from the sea, before anything as fragile as humans or the supernaturals who fed upon them roamed the earth.

A giant hand with fingertips like flesh-covered claws reached down, catching Rose under the chin and urging her to tilt her head even farther back. Rose obeyed, knowing there was no sense in pulling away. The Mother could slice her throat open with the slightest motion of her finger. Her wrist was larger around than Rose's entire body.

Beautiful, as beautiful a thing as ever walked the earth. The Mother sounded pleased, as if she took credit for Rose's long golden hair and captivating blue eyes, and the ten faeries who had visited Rosemarie with gifts in her cradle had nothing at all to do with the matter.

But then, as mother of the Fey line, perhaps she simply took credit for the clever use of faery magic. Whatever the reason for her pleasure, Rose was tremendously grateful. Just as the Mother's displeasure stole her breath, her approval seemed to shoot her body full of sunlight.

No, not sunlight. The pleasure was too wicked to be compared to anything so pure. It was a euphoria that made her want to rip things apart, to put her sword to bloody use and dance in the spray.

Rose's fingers fisted around the hilt of her weapon,

which suddenly felt alive in her hands. The faery sword burned hot against her skin, as desperate for blood as its mistress. But what was there to kill? There was no one. Not a single creature within the castle walls had offended her . . . none, save the monster who slept in her bed, the vampire who had stolen her rightful husband's place with deceit and—

"No." Her chest grew tight with anguish at the mere thought of hurting her husband. She would rather die herself than harm a single hair on his head. The Mother was the one who hated Gareth. It was she who placed these horrible thoughts in Rose's mind.

Do not lie to yourself. It is your own soul that thirsts for the vampire's blood.

Rose swallowed against the metallic taste rising in her throat—the flavor of blood, made familiar from her husband's lips, but more intoxicating than it had ever been before. She'd never found the slightly bitter taste unpleasant, but neither had it made her moan with delight or tremble with anticipation.

Gareth's veins rushed with the essence he had stolen only hours before. It would be a simple matter to take what she craved from his sleeping body. Fangs were not required when one had a sharp sword at the ready. She would slit his throat and fall upon him with her eager mouth, lapping at the wound she had made as his life seeped away. She would laugh as his blood flowed hot and thick across her face, her hands, spilling onto the sheets like—

"No. No, no, no." Rose squeezed her eyes shut, struggling against the horrific images in her mind. A part of her was certain she would be violently ill, but still her belly cramped with the hunger for blood.

Frantically she tried to fling her sword from her

grasp, but it seemed her fingers would no longer obey her command. They were already committed to the task of slitting open the man she loved.

"I am human," she said, her voice breaking as invisible strings jerked her to her feet like a marionette. "I do not thirst for blood, I do not require—"

You have been too long without, dearest. There is no shame in your hunger. The Mother is both the creator and the destroyer. The womb that births in a rush of blood and the mouth that devours in—

"I am human! I'm not a monster." Rose sobbed as her body spun toward the bed.

Then you agree your husband is monstrous? That his hunger makes him so?

"No, I-I don't. Please!" Rose screamed the last word, panic clouding her mind as her sword lifted itself into the air of its own accord and her feet took the final few steps to her husband's side.

The vampires were the least of my children, but I loved them once. I loved them all—my beautiful and powerful Fey, my charming vampires, my clever elves, even the ever-hungry ogres. They were much like baby birds, always with their mouths open.

The Great Mother's laughter felt oily and thick upon Rose's skin, defiling her as surely as the murder she would soon commit.

"I beg of you, please. I love him! I *love* him." Tears flowed freely down Rose's face, and her heart raced from the sheer terror of looking down to see the shadow of her blade on her husband's sleeping face.

The time for love has past. Now there is only death. Death to the Fey, death to the vampires, death to all who would dare set themselves above the Mother!

There was no laughter in her voice now, only hatred. Each word that dropped into Rose's mind seemed to leave behind the taint of evil and disease, until the room swam before her eyes, a blur of black and gray.

Black, gray, and red.

She screamed, a raw sound of pure agony as her sword swept down, a ruthless bird of prey intent upon her husband's throat. Though she could not bring her eyes to look, Rose felt the hot splash as Gareth began to bleed.

And bleed, and bleed, until her nightclothes were soaked and sticking to her body, until the smell of death permeated the room and Rose fell to the floor in a desperate attempt to find some sweeter air.

But there was nothing sweet to be found. There was only the rage of the Mother pressing in around her, stealing her breath, stealing her life, consuming her whole until it was as though there had never been a Rosemarie Edenburg to begin with.

CHAPTER TWO

Rose bolted upright in bed, her breath coming in frantic gasps and her nightclothes stuck to her damp skin. With trembling hands, she pushed her hair from her face and turned to gaze down at the man sleeping peacefully beside her.

Gareth was just as he had been when she came to bed a few hours before, not a hair on his dear head out of place. Her entire body went limp with relief.

It had been a dream, a horrid nightmare.

Still, it was *only* to the Goddess that she directed a prayer of thanksgiving for her husband's life. It would be a great while before Rose would feel safe invoking the name of the Great Mother in prayer or anywhere else. Even knowing the giant who had spurred her toward murder was nothing more than a dream, she was hesitant to even *think* of the ancient legend alleged to have birthed each of the races of supernaturals.

In the Fey stories, the Mother was always a kindly

figure, the embodiment of mother love and the forces of creation—nothing like the demon who had invaded her sleep. But then, it hadn't been the *true* Mother in her dream; that horrid creature had been her own creation.

Understanding that she was hardly responsible for what dreams came to her sleeping mind did little to ease her troubled heart. What sickness of spirit would make a wife dream such a dream?

Rose shuddered. There would be no more sleep for her. She doubted her mind could bear another visit from the terrors that came in the night.

Moving slowly, so as not to wake Gareth from his much-needed rest, Rose eased from the bed, not bothering with the robe flung upon the chair nearby. The cool air felt good upon her damp skin, and she was hesitant to repeat any action she had taken in her dream. Therefore, she left both the robe and her faery blade in the chamber as she eased out the door.

There was no need for the sword in the spell-defended castle, and if she took a chill later she could always take something from Gareth's room. Her husband was only five or six inches taller than his petite wife and his robes were not too terribly large. He'd received his height from his vampire father, not his faery mother.

That state of being had rarely troubled him, as the man was supremely confident, but now that he was forced to look upon his half brother on a daily basis, Gareth had begun to resent his smaller stature. He loathed craning his neck to meet the eyes of the six-foot Ambrose. It wore on him, enough so that Rose caught glimpses of his frustration in his mind.

There was a time when Gareth's shields never fell,

when he maintained fierce control even in the most challenging conditions. Before he was wounded, it was only when they made love that he lost all vestiges of restraint, abandoning himself to pleasure so completely it often felt as if their very souls had merged.

"Think of something else," Rose muttered aloud as she took a lit sconce from the wall and padded toward her father's library, ignoring the tension curling low in her body.

The fact that she and her husband had done nothing but sleep in their marriage bed for the past month or more had begun to take its toll. Her body ached and burned for him. Night after night she dreamt of Gareth's hands smoothing along her feverish skin, his strong thighs cradled between her own as he entered her, filling the emptiness within, banishing the lust that threatened to drive her mad.

And then there were nights when it wasn't Gareth's hands in her dream, but another's. In those dreams golden magic floated through the air and gray eyes, not green, stared into her own as she reached the pinnacle, screaming Ambrose's name, lost in the bliss of the faerie's thick shaft plowing between her legs.

Rose's breath rushed from her parted lips and her nipples drew tight against the thin fabric of her gown.

"Should have taken the blasted robe." Goddess help her, but she was truly in a pathetic state. The woman who had once shunned the advances of men was now hopelessly addicted to pleasure and tormented by wanton fantasies.

She cursed a string of foulness she knew Ambrose would find appalling and pulled open the heavy door to what had once been her father's favorite room in the keep.

The ornate decorations beneath her hand spoke of the former king's love of knowledge. One would think the door guarded the entrance to the treasury or the throne room, not a windowless library, grand only in the sense that it housed hundreds of books in half a dozen languages—all of which her learned papa had read fluently.

Unfortunately, Rose had spent too much of her life engaged in the pursuit of ogres to learn anything but English, French, and German. Her Latin and Greek were no better than a child's. Even before her enchantment, she had preferred running wild through the forests to attending to her studies or any of the usual ladylike pursuits.

Thusly, the only thing more abominable than her Latin was her embroidery.

Rose sighed as the door closed behind her, sealing her in with the comforting smell of dust and books. There was nothing that smelled exactly like a library. It was a healing scent, one that banished both nightmares and lustful thoughts and aroused the wholesome inquisitiveness of an active mind.

"Or the curiosity of a terrible snoop." The words actually made her smile as she set the sconce into an empty bracket on the wall and walked toward the ladder on the far side of the room. On the very top shelf, she would find her father's own writings.

She'd finished her mother's journals nearly a fortnight past—all but the volume she feared had burned when her London home was attacked by members of the tribe—but she had yet to stick her nose into her father's private affairs.

A part of her was certain she would find nothing of interest in those solemn-looking little leather volumes.

She predicted dry accounts of royal life and ledgers tracking how much of the treasury went to the price of grain. Such memoirs would be the perfect foil to the writings of his wife, a half-Seelie princess who had filled her large journals with fanciful drawings, scraps of spells, and pressed flowers.

"And secrets, mustn't forget the secrets," Rose said, running her fingers along the spines of her father's books, wondering if she would feel one of them call to her as she had when she first viewed her mother's.

Several seconds passed in silence with no sign of supernatural life from the shelf. But then, she shouldn't be surprised. Her father had been a mortal, a human man through and through. He had married into the Fey and sired two children with royal Fey blood, but no magic flowed in his veins.

"What a lucky man." Rose felt her momentarily lifted spirits plummet.

Her father might have been fortunate to be mortal and thus spared the additional intrigue supernatural blood brought into one's life, but he was hardly lucky. After less than two years of happy marriage, his first-born child had been cursed in her cradle and he'd spent the next three years searching the world for a way to break the spell.

He and his beloved wife had been so distraught that it took nearly ten years for another child to be conceived. Misery and despair were not conducive to the creation of life, especially for a Seelie princess. The Seelie fed upon the joy of humanity, and there had been little of that in the kingdom of Myrdrean once the infant daughter of the royal couple had been cursed to prick her finger on the spindle of a spinning wheel and fall down dead upon her eighteenth birthday.

"Yet father was still hopeful, even before the betrothal," Rose mused aloud, plucking two of the older
volumes from the shelf and backing down the ladder.

When she was sixteen, Ambrose and Gareth's
mother, the faerie responsible for cursing Rose, had
offered her parents a way to save their daughter. The
curse would be amended from death to one hundred
years of sleep for all, in exchange for a betrothal between the two houses.

Of course, the evil woman knew the Edenburgs
would not live to see their daughter marry. She was
well acquainted with the Fey prophecy that foretold
Rosemarie's future as the scourge of the tribe, an ogre
executioner who would wander the earth seeking revenge for the death of her family. The royal couple
had seen the betrothal as a godsend, however, and had
never been happier than those last two years before
Rose's eighteenth birthday.

But her father had been optimistic from the moment
he returned to the castle after his many years of wandering. Rose still remembered meeting him for the first
time, how he'd swept her nearly four-year-old self into
his arms, a merry smile on his bearded face. He'd had a
secret. She remembered thinking as much, even then,
and that it must be a wonderful secret indeed to make
his eyes shine with such excitement.

But would he have written such a thing down? A
secret he hadn't shared even with his wife?

"Read the blasted journals and find out, you ninny,"
Rose said, comforted by the sound of her own voice.

Though the wraiths and ghosts who had haunted
Edenburg keep not too terribly long ago had been banished by a combination of faery magic and the merriment of people coming to inhabit the once-deserted

land, there were times when she still felt watched. As if the attention of the dead was upon her, their curiosity aroused by the return of the long-lost queen.

A queen. She truly *was* a queen. Even after eighteen years of human life, eighty years of sleep, and nearly one hundred years as an executioner for the Fey de la Nuit, she still felt too young and inexperienced to deserve such an important title. Yet there were hundreds of lives within the castle walls depending upon her to keep them safe.

For some reason, she sensed she would find help with assuring their safety in the past. Though many truths of her family's legacy had come to light, the dead still kept their share of secrets, secrets she must learn if she was ever to become the ruler she aspired to be.

Rose opened the oldest volume and began to read, swiftly drawn into her father's detailed accounts of everyday life as king of his small country. Many of the entries were as monotonous as she'd feared, but by the end of the first volume there was talk of his betrothal to a beautiful young woman of fifteen, a girl who swore she was a faery princess.

The only thing more fantastic than her claim is that I believe her. Though we have only met the once, that evening in Vienna, there was something about her . . . something indescribable, magical.

Rose smiled as she reached for the second volume, excited to see the romance between her parents unfold. But upon opening the book, she found it had been tampered with. After the first few entries describing the details of the wedding feast and the couple's tour of Myrdrean, there was a great gap in the center where the pages had been torn out.

She ran a finger over the jagged edges of paper. Could her father have plucked incriminating entries from the book? Though she supposed it possible, it didn't seem likely. From what she remembered of Papa, he had been a meticulous man, more inclined to dispose of the volume entirely rather than leave it disfigured.

It was hardly something she could confirm one way or the other, but the tears looked fresh, as if the pages had been removed recently, not nearly two hundred years before.

But who would have gone to the trouble of tampering with her father's memoirs? Who could possibly have something to gain from concealing the details of her past?

Even she herself suspected her fascination with her parents' journals stemmed more from a need to feel close to them than from anything else. The vague notion that there were still secrets to uncover was most likely nothing but an excuse to spend hours in the library, rifling through the intimate musings of those she had lost.

She had learned the truth behind her curse, Ambrose's betrayal, and the prophecy that had nearly led to her death in London. What more could there possibly be?

"Papa's secret." Rose thumbed through the pages at the back of the book, still hesitant to believe her instincts were correct.

But the entries picked up exactly where she had suspected, nearly a year after her father's return from his journey during which he had sought someone who might break the curse. Even her mother hadn't known where he had gone. Her memoirs from that time told mostly of her travels to Faerie with her newborn babe, and of her despair when not one among her high-ranking family would come to her aid. Even her father, the Seelie king, had sworn there was nothing he could do to help his new granddaughter.

Rose took the last three books down from the shelf and quickly skimmed their pages. They were all intact, and not one breathed a word of what her father had done with himself for those three years.

There was no doubt someone wanted to keep the details of his journey secret. But who?

"I suspected I would find you here. Does sleep elude you once more?" Gareth stood at the end of the table where she'd settled to read, his eyes glowing in the dim light.

He'd donned a robe before descending the steps and looked as handsome as ever in the crimson wrap. His soft brown hair, which now fell well below his shoulders, was loose about his face, making Rose imagine how it would fall around them if he pressed her to the ground and kissed her. She had never felt safer than when in the arms of her husband, knowing the passion flaring between them would soon consume them whole.

As the Mother had consumed her in the dream, smothered her, stolen her free will, her breath, her life, everything that—

Rose sucked in a swift breath as her arousal was tainted by the fear she'd felt in her dream. "I've slept quite well the past fortnight. It is you who tosses and turns in your sleep as though you do battle with the sheets." She slammed the book closed, surprised at the sharpness of her tone. She was troubled by her strange thoughts and the missing pages from her father's book, but that was no reason to lose her temper.

Gareth spoke before she could think how to apologize. "I beg to differ, my little shrew. I've heard you cry out in the night nearly every evening since we arrived in this wretched country."

"There is nothing wretched about my country, sir. I—"

"We reside in the capital, and yet have one, I repeat, *one* crowded tavern as the sum total of our options for an evening's entertainment. There are no coffeehouses, no theaters, no opera—though I daresay I don't regret missing the torture that is the London Opera's corpulent soprano caterwalling her way through Rousseau's *Les Muses galantes*—and your court consists of two elvish ladies-in-waiting and a handful of servants. There are no court musicians, no—"

"Pardon me, but I have had more pressing matters to attend to than your entertainment. Resurrecting a country the human world once thought damned is scarcely—"

"*My* entertainment? Surely you jest, my lady." He smiled, a wicked twist of the lips that made a thrill of awareness whisper across Rose's skin. "It is *you* who craves entertainment."

"I?" She crossed her arms over her chest, hiding the telltale signs of her arousal. Surely she was sick in mind for an argument with her husband to make her nipples bead tightly against her gown. "There are not enough hours in the day as it is. I have hundreds of matters that need attending to and—"

"And yet still you writhe upon your pillow, desperate for someone to exhaust you even more thoroughly,"

Gareth said, stalking around the table, his gait as sure and graceful as it had ever been. He looked stronger than he had even a day before, and she suddenly wondered if her husband had been honest with her about the slow rate of his recovery.

But then, why would he deceive her? Surely he had nothing to gain from playing the invalid.

"Oh, I think I have *much* to gain. Such as knowledge of the true longings of my wife's heart."

"I don't understand," Rose said, cursing herself for letting him hear her thoughts even as she firmed up her mental shields.

She should know better than to relax her control when her husband was in a foul mood or when she herself was so weak. Her thoughts had disturbed her spirit and she knew they would do much more than trouble her husband. If he knew she had even passing fancies involving his half brother he would be devastated—filled with rage and inclined to seek vengeance upon both his wife and Ambrose—but devastated nonetheless. It wouldn't matter to him that Rose had no intention of acting upon those brief flashes of weakness; he would still be cut to the core.

Hurting Gareth was the last thing she wanted. Even when he drove her to distraction, she still loved him—completely, desperately even.

So desperately, she couldn't fight the arousal that thrummed through her veins as he closed the distance between them. His eyes might be narrowed in anger and his tone far from that seductive whisper he employed when they were about the business of two married people, but her body cared little for such matters. Her flesh thrilled simply to be near him, to smell the scent of evergreen and salt and man that had become Gareth to her, to feel his strong hands gripping her shoulders—even if his fingers dug too deeply for the touch to be tender.

"Think on it, Rose. Think on your dreams, and see if you can't discern my meaning." He leaned closer, until his warm breath puffed against her mouth.

Rose met his glare, though truly she wanted nothing more than to close the distance between their lips. It had been far too long since she'd thoroughly tasted her husband, since she'd felt his tongue sliding into her mouth, stroking against her own, building the desire within her until she begged him to take her.

And sometimes he did make her beg. Such was Gareth's nature—an abundance of goodness and passion, mixed with the perfect degree of wickedness. He was not always as she would have him be, and she wouldn't have it any other way.

"Speak, Rose. Tell me with your lips what is in that mind of yours if you insist on keeping me from reading the truth there myself." His voice was brittle, completely lacking in his usual humor. He truly was enraged, a fact made even clearer as his grip on her shoulders grew so tight she winced in pain. "What are you afraid I will learn, sweet?"

"I am afraid of nothing," Rose said, struggling to keep her voice calm and even. "But I do have cause for anger."

"What cause?" He looked genuinely surprised.

"My husband has kept himself from my bed."

"I have been in your bed every night."

"You know that is not what I meant, just as you know you are not as unwell as you would have me believe, certainly not so weak that you lack the strength to . . . bed your wife." Rose blushed in spite of herself. She had been no virgin when they wed, but she had been innocent of the desire Gareth could arouse within her. The ferocity of her need for him made her ashamed at times.

Gareth's eyes flashed, catching the light and burning bright green for a moment. "Ahh . . . I see. So that is why you writhe upon your pillow? You're hungry for your husband's touch?"

His hands gentled on her shoulders, then slid slowly down her arms until his thumbs brushed against the aching tips of her breasts. Rose's breath rushed in with a quiet gasp as fire shot from her nipples to between her legs. Gareth, noting her response, swept across the needy flesh again and again, until her sex grew slick and ready and her entire body cried out for more.

"Is that so, wife?"

Rose's eyes slid closed on a moan.

"I will have an answer." His teasing touch became almost cruel as he captured her nipples between his fingertips and squeezed. Unfortunately, Rose had discovered the thrill of a hint of pain with her pleasure.

"Yes, it is so," she said, beyond the point of feeling shame.

Despite his anger, despite the lies, Rose knew she would do nothing to stop Gareth from taking her. There would be time to quarrel later, *after* she'd felt her husband buried deep inside her, claiming her until she screamed her pleasure to the wooden beams arching high above their heads.

"It is so, she says," Gareth whispered, gentling his ministrations just a bit, dulling the edge of pain and coaxing it back into the land of pure, carnal pleasure. "It. Is. So."

Rose's hands fisted in the fabric of his robe as she struggled to pull him close. But Gareth held himself away from her, reminding her that six inches and several stone could make quite a difference in strength when one was only five feet tall.

"But if that is so, my love." Gareth's mouth hovered above her lips, making her head spin. "Why is it that— when your hands roam over your body in the night and the sweet scent of your arousal fills the air—*why* is it not your husband's name you call?"

Between the drugging effects of his touch and the surprise of his words, she couldn't help herself. Her shields slipped ever so slightly as one name raced across her conscious mind.

Ambrose.

"Yes, *that* is the name." One of Gareth's hands moved to fist in her hair, tugging her head back so that she was forced to look him full in the face. "I had hoped I was mistaken, but I should have known better. It was always that damned faerie you wanted, wasn't it, Rose?"

"Never," she swore, praying he could read the truth in her eyes. "Never. There is only you in my heart."

"But we are not discussing your heart, dearest, but your eager little body." He pressed his hips forward, bringing the hard ridge of his arousal where she still ached for him. The gesture was meant to debase her, but only made the frustrated desire within her spiral even higher.

Damn Gareth. For his jealousy and his ability to weaken her with lust so profoundly.

"My dreams are not something I can control," she said, lifting her chin even higher, daring him to contradict her.

"And why would you wish to, when they are so very pleasing? You dream that which you *wish* to dream, what you wish to come to pass. Or perhaps it has already come to pass? Has he fucked you, Rosemarie? Has he—"

"Don't be ridiculous. You insult me and demean yourself," Rose said, continuing before he could argue. "Ambrose *watched* and did nothing as the ogre Benoit de Fournier took my maidenhead as I slept. How could I ever forgive something so—"

"A hundred years will dull the pain of betrayal, and you are a very forgiving soul, especially when it suits your desires."

"It was a dream, Gareth! I also dreamt tonight of a giant with claws for hands who pulled me within her flesh, smothering me until I knew I would die." Rose's voice grew high and thin, a product of the fear coursing through her veins simply from mentioning the dream aloud. "Is that also something I wish to come to pass?"

"You are a rather perverse chit," Gareth said as he dropped his hands to grip her around the waist. "I confess I have little idea what you crave."

"Another lie." Rose caught his eyes, daring him to deny the fire that burned between them. "You know precisely what I crave." She lifted one knee, slowly, deliberately, wrapping her leg around her husband's waist and squeezing, pulling him to where she was already hot and ready.

Gareth mumbled something, but Rose couldn't concentrate on his words when his hands were lifting her onto the table and roughly spreading her thighs wide. It was impossible to remain aware of anything but his lips crushing down upon hers, his body urging her to lie back on the heavy oak as he moved above her, revealing he did indeed know precisely what his wife desired.

CHAPTER THREE

Rose moaned into Gareth's mouth as his kiss grew even more brutal. She knew her lips would be as bruised as her bones by the next morning. Every place her body touched the wood beneath her ached from the combined weight bearing down upon her. She had lost what little padding she possessed in the past months—working such exhausting hours it was impossible to keep any meat on her bones—and she felt that lack of cushioning as Gareth pressed between her legs.

But the discomfort was banished by the thrill of anticipation. Even through his robe and her gown, she could feel the heat of him, how his cock fairly burned with the need to shove inside his wife, his love, the only woman who had ever possessed him so—

"Remove yourself from my mind, wife."

"Protect your thoughts if you do not wish me to hear them," Rose returned, smiling against his lips, her heart soaring from the brief glance into Gareth's. He loved her and forgave her for whispering another's name in her sleep. He knew she was without fault. Truly, no one could control what phantoms came to haunt her in the night.

"Of course you are forgiven, but I will not forget," he said, tugging at the tie holding his robe closed. "I will bed you every night and every morning until you are too exhausted and pleasure-drunk to dream of anything at all."

"What a fearsome threat, my lord."

"It is not a threat, but a promise." Gareth shrugged the robe from his shoulders. As it fell to the ground, Rose's breath caught. He was truly a perfect example of a man, every muscle clearly outlined beneath his pale skin, every part of him in complete harmony with the rest. He made her hurt with the beauty of him, made her sex ache and throb with the need to have him.

"And you *shall* have me." Gareth gripped the bottom of her gown and pulled it over her head in one swift motion. Rose was chilled from the cool night air yet burning alive at the same time. She reached for her husband, wanting his bare skin against hers, wanting to feel him burning alongside her.

But Gareth grasped her wrists and held her eager hands from his body. "No, not just yet. There is the matter of your punishment."

Rose arched a brow, smiling as Gareth's hands tightened around her wrists. "Punishment? Oh no, how very awful." She moved her lips closer to his, her words a seductive whisper. "Anything but a punishment, Your Grace."

Gareth laughed in spite of himself, but the dangerous glint returned to his eyes a moment later. "You think me a fool, do you? That I lack intimate knowledge of my wife?"

"Not at all, sir. I think you know your wife most intimately, and will perhaps know her even better before the morning comes." Rose tossed her long hair over her shoulders and arched her back, wantonly displaying what she knew were two of her husband's favorite parts of her body. He could spend hours at her breasts alone, teasing and tormenting, driving her to such pinnacles that she often achieved her pleasure without so much as a finger between her legs.

Gareth's eyes flicked to her chest and darkened with unmistakable lust. Still, he didn't move an inch closer, only smiled and slid his gaze back to her face. "A tempting offer, but hardly fitting. I believe you would enjoy such torment."

"And you intend me to suffer?" Rose asked, heart racing as Gareth forced her hands behind her back and reached to where her gown had fallen to the table beside her.

Slowly he wound the silk fabric around and around her wrists before tying a firm knot. Only when he was certain her hands were firmly bound did he give his reply. "Oh yes. You will suffer." His fingertips played up and down the outside of her thighs, making her tremble. "By the time we are finished here, you will be weeping most pitifully."

"I already weep, my lord," Rose said, knowing he understood her meaning when he brought one hand between her legs and plunged two fingers where she was so very slick and ready.

A muscle in Gareth's jaw leapt as he played between her legs, but he maintained strict control, using such a light touch that he offered her desperate body not an ounce of relief . . . only more frustration. He toyed with her for what felt like hours, until she squirmed upon the table, increasingly frantic for more than soft torment.

"You are a complete wanton." He leaned forward, breathing the words against her neck as his thumb slowly circled the nub at the top of her sex. "And I adore you for it."

Rose's head fell back with a moan as she pressed her throat closer to his mouth, part of her craving the feel of his teeth piercing her flesh. She'd made Gareth swear never to drink from her again after the night he was nearly killed for possessing her blood within him. But sometimes she regretted forcing such an oath from the vampire. Times like these, when she craved the erotic depravity of her husband drinking of her essence as he plowed between her thighs. Only a few short months ago the idea would have repulsed and terrified her, but that was before she knew she herself was more than human. Knowing it was impossible for her to be transformed into a blood woman had drastically altered her perspective.

Or perhaps it was simply experiencing the ecstasy of donation firsthand. She had become increasingly vulnerable to all the temptations of the flesh since her marriage. It was a weakness, no doubt, but one she was scarcely motivated to remedy . . . at least not anytime in the near future.

"Gareth." She sighed his name, hoping he heard her adoration in the word. She loved him more than her life, craved him as the patrons of an opium den craved the pipe, would gladly give up her throne and more for one night in his arms.

"No, you don't," he said, laughing as he pulled away from her neck and lifted her from the table. "You shall not deter me from my course by whispering sweet nothings into my mind."

With aching gentleness, he turned her and pressed her back down upon the table, his palm sure and firm between her shoulders as he urged her lower and lower, until her breasts flattened against the wood and her ass was presented to him like a bitch in heat. Rose trembled, not remembering when she had felt so exposed. It was a troubling position to find oneself in, but an incredibly arousing one as well.

"Though I must confess, being compared to an opium pipe is surely one of the most flattering things I have ever heard." His warm hands petted her, tracing the curve of her narrow waist to the swells of her buttocks. "Do I really intoxicate you so, love?"

"Yes, you—" Rose cried out, her words flying from her mind as Gareth delivered a sharp swat to her exposed bottom. He had threatened to turn her over his knee more than once, but the threats had never taken the form of action.

"Continue," Gareth said, urging her on with another swift slap.

"I-I don't remember, I—"

"Then you must think harder." He punished her lack of response with the flat of his hand, again and again, until Rose's breaths came in shallow pants and her tormented skin burned.

But the sweet stinging of her bottom flesh was nothing compared to the burning between her legs. The petals of her sex were swollen to the point of pain, and the evidence of her arousal leaked down her thighs.

Her pussy practically wept, so desperate for her husband's touch, for her husband's cock, that it was not long before tears came to her eyes as well.

"Please, God, please," she begged, her voice catching.

"I rather dislike hearing the name of the heavenly father in the bedroom."

"We are not *in* the bedroom."

"Don't be coy, it doesn't suit you."

"Damn it, please I—"

"Such language! I believe you've earned yourself another punishment."

She cried out as he spanked her again, an abandoned sound of raw need. Her nipples pebbled against the cool wood, and her entire body shook with the force of her desire. Shamelessly she arched her back, praying Gareth would see her desperate state and take pity on her.

But he only intensified his efforts, torturing her flesh until it seemed every drop of blood in her body had rushed to the skin beneath his hands—which only increased the torment between her legs. She had read that erotic punishments could intensify one's pleasure, but never realized she could reach such heights of anticipation. Surely her very bones would begin to melt if she wasn't granted respite from this sweet agony.

"Please, husband. Please!" She tugged at the fabric binding her hands, uncertain what she would do if she managed to free herself. Either grasp her husband's cock and guide it between her thighs or tear it completely from his wretched body, one or the other.

"I love you, sweet." He pressed a swift kiss to the back of her neck. "More than I ever dreamed I could love a woman who has fantasies of separating my cockstand from my person."

Rose felt the blunt head of his arousal butting against her entrance a moment later. Finally she did begin to weep with relief as he thrust forward, his thickness shoving inside where she was so very ready, pushing deeper and deeper until he was completely contained within her heat. Her body tightened around him of its own accord, as if her quim had decided to hold him prisoner for his wicked deeds.

"Rose," he murmured, his voice ripe with lust. She could feel his hands tremble as he smoothed warm palms over her reddened flesh, his excitement as over-whelming as her own. "I fear I may not last more than a handful of minutes."

"A handful is all I require." She moaned as she cir-cled her hips, knowing it wouldn't take more than a few thrusts to send her over the edge. She'd been too long from her husband's body. Simply feeling him within her, filling her where she had been so wretchedly empty, was nearly enough to complete her pleasure.

Gareth gripped her hips in his hands, holding her still as he slowly withdrew until only the tip remained in-side her. "No, you require—and deserve—much, much more. And I swear I will do my damnedest to deliver it."

Without another word, he began to move, shallow, languid thrusts that grew deeper, faster, until Rose's fingers ached to claw at the wood beneath her. Higher and higher he took her, slowing his rhythm each time she neared release, as if he knew how near she came and would deny her the pleasure she craved.

Not deny it, prolong it. Can't you feel it, sweet, how the bliss builds with each delay?

Rose moaned and bucked back into Gareth's thrusts, unable to think clearly enough to form a reply to her husband's thoughts, only knowing she must have more of him. More of his cock thrusting within her, more of his kisses at her neck and his teeth dragging along the bare skin of her shoulder, more of his hand fisting in her hair, adding the slightest bit of pain to her pleasure.

"And more of this as well?" he asked, as his hand slid around the curve of her hip, down over her quivering belly, to circle the hard little nub that ached for his touch.

Within moments it became too much to bear. Her entire body shook as her release swept across her skin, waves of delight vibrating from her core to every fingertip. Rose cried out her pleasure, again and again, until her throat was raw and her lips grew numb, yet still the blissful sensations seemed to build.

Just when the pleasure began to fade, Gareth would vary his rhythm or the pressure of his fingers between her legs, coaxing another wave of passion from her clutching sheath. He played her body with the skill of a musician completely dedicated to his instrument, until fresh tears ran down her face and her cries of ecstasy became sobs of complete surrender.

By the time Gareth tore the restraints from her hands and spun her around to face him, her legs would no longer support her own weight. She melted into his arms, staying upright only because his hands gripped her thighs and hitched her up.

"Put your arms around my neck, love," he whispered against her lips, his kiss gentler now, though not lacking the slightest in intensity.

Rose obeyed, managing to maintain her hold as

Gareth spun in a circle and took swift steps across the room. It was only when her back hit the smooth surface of the mahogany-paneled wall and Gareth's arousal once again pressed between her legs that she realized her husband had yet to find his own release, and was as thick and aching as he had been when they began.

"A handful of minutes, indeed." Rose sounded as breathless as she felt.

"Perhaps a few more than a handful." His laugh became a moan as he thrust within her once more.

Her body ached a bit, but momentary discomfort was soon forgotten as Gareth sheathed himself within her again and again, allowing his control to slip as he abandoned himself to pleasure. Rose tensed her arms and held on tight, relishing the feel of his lips against hers, his tongue spearing into her mouth. Though she certainly had a taste for the more wanton couplings, she always preferred to be face to face, to be able to share fevered kisses, to watch her husband's eyes as he neared the edge, to see his features twist with pleasure as he lost himself inside her body.

"Rose, my love. How I have missed you. I want you to-to—" His voice broke, words becoming a groan as he swelled impossibly larger within her. He was close, so desperately close, but still holding back, hoping to take her with him.

"To find my pleasure again?" she asked, tilting her hips so that she met his thrusts with shallow thrusts of her own, bringing her bud into contact with the base of his shaft. Almost immediately, wild tension began to build again. Soon she would shatter, but this time her husband would shatter right along with her.

"Yes, yes," Gareth chanted, fucking her faster,

harder, until there was nothing to be heard but the sound of two eager bodies joining together, and the sharp gasps of two lovers unbearably close to release.

"Gareth!" Rose screamed his name as things low in her body clenched with enough force to color her euphoria with a hint of pain. Her fingernails dug into his bare shoulders, deep and hard, drawing blood she knew her husband would scent on the air. She pulled him as close as two people could get without sharing the same skin, wishing they could be closer still, that she could crawl within him and become a part of his very bones.

Gareth's cry joined hers a second later, his ecstasy as complete as her own if the rapt expression on his face—or the weakening of his legs—was anything to judge by.

"Are you all right, husband?" Rose laughed as she slid down the wall, the result of Gareth falling to his knees. "Shall you survive the pleasuring— Gareth? Love?"

Rose let out a surprised yelp as Gareth's eyes slid closed and he fell heavily upon her. She did her best to steady him, but her awkward position made it impossible. The best she could do was to cushion his head as he rolled onto the ground.

"Gareth? Gareth?" She cupped his face in her hands and gently patted each cheek, but he remained unconscious. Her mind raced in time with the rapid beating of her heart as she struggled to ascertain what had befallen her husband.

At least it was clear he wasn't dead. As a vampire he was technically dead from the instant of his birth, but she was relatively sure whatever had happened was something from which he would recover. If the injury were fatal, he would have begun to turn to dust already. Such was the fate of a vampire's corpse once the spirit inhabiting it had vanished.

However, the fear of losing Gareth was far too fresh for her thoughts to give her much comfort.

Thankfully, a closer inspection of his person reassured her a bit. His flesh was still warm and he had healthy color in his cheeks, though he was alarmingly still, even for a creature of the night.

No matter what he would have her believe, Gareth hadn't been deceiving her. He hadn't possessed the strength to bed his wife—not for the past fortnight and not this evening—and now her foolish dreams and his own jealousy might have done him ill. She should have refused him, or at the very least insisted they return to the comfort of their bed, rather than engage in gymnastics on the library table and against the wall.

If her own carnal abandon and lack of good sense were responsible for wounding him anew, she would never forgive herself.

She raced to grab her nightgown and pull it on. After a moment's deliberation she donned Gareth's robe as well. Better to leave him here in the altogether than for the queen to be seen racing through the keep in nothing but her nightgown. She couldn't waste the time it would take to fetch her wrap from her rooms above, not when fear for Gareth already threatened to steal her breath away.

"I will return in a moment, do not worry," she whispered into Gareth's ear, her hand shaking as she smoothed a stray lock of hair from his brow. Refusing to succumb to the weakness of tears, she turned and flew across the room.

Seconds later she was racing down the empty halls toward the rear of the castle. Ambrose was not in his rooms—she had sensed that much on her way down the stairs—and she knew of only one place the black faerie would be at this time of night.

On an average eve, she would never dare enter the black woods without her weapon in hand, but concern for Gareth banished her trepidation. There was nothing hiding in the night as frightening as the thought of losing her husband. Not even meeting Ecanthar unarmed and alone could terrify her so completely.

THOUGH SHE AND Ambrose spent every afternoon training in the refurbished courtyard, Rose was still out of breath by the time she reached the base of the ravine where Ambrose had enchanted a portion of the river in order to keep abreast of the latest Fey political maneuverings.

High-ranking families among the Fey de la Nuit and the Seelie court had been meeting at her grandfather's home outside London for nearly two weeks, collaborating as they hadn't in centuries. War with the vampires and their new elvish and half-breed allies seemed inevitable, and they had put aside their bickering to outline a plan of defense.

Or attack.

Ambrose refused to tell her what the Fey had decided, whether they would strike first or wait for the vampire high council to launch their offensive before deploying their own forces. He didn't trust her not to share the faerie plans with her vampire husband.

Though the suffering of her newly discovered grandfather and family was hardly something she hoped for,

Rose knew Ambrose was right to keep her ignorant of Fey plans. If the well-being of her husband's people was threatened, she wasn't certain she could keep the secrets she was obligated to keep as a woman in line for the Seelie throne. Therefore, she made certain Ambrose heard her approach, giving him sufficient time to conclude any secret business.

She shouldn't have worried. Ambrose had obviously heard her long before she began shuffling her feet through the leaves. He was settled on a large stone with a cozy fire burning a few feet away by the time she reached the water's edge. His stormy gray eyes could see quite well in the darkness, so she knew the light from the flame was for her benefit, as was the blanket he had folded and placed on the rock beside him.

But Ambrose quickly realized there would be no cozy chat for the two of them this evening, and stood to greet her. All six feet and more of the man stretched up toward the trees in one long smooth movement that seemed it would never end. Not even the ancient residents of the black forest could dwarf Ambrose. He had a way of appearing larger than anything else, of taking up all the air in a room and leaving one dizzy with the need to draw a deep breath.

He no longer frightened her as he had for the first several decades of their acquaintanceship, but neither did he put her at ease. His surly nature and frequent bursts of temper would have ensured that, even if she hadn't known the secrets of his heart. Though, truth be told, it was difficult to believe the man suffered from unrequited love.

Especially when he glared down at her as he was doing now.

"What happened? Where is your weapon?" He bent to retrieve his own sword from the hidden panel in his boot, his long raven braid falling over his shoulder.

For a moment, Rose was transported to a dream she'd had only a few nights before. She'd had that braid fisted in her hand, hanging on for dear life as Ambrose labored above her. The memory made her blush, and she was thankful for the cover of darkness.

Goddess, but this was madness. She must do whatever it took to banish her lustful dreams. She would find a potion or spell. Surely there was something she could do to ensure she was no longer tormented by such wanton thoughts.

"Rosemarie? Your weapon, have you—"

"There was no time. Gareth has—"

"You must make time," he said, his voice laced with censure.

Ambrose often forgot he was no longer her superior and she no longer bound by blood contract to aid the Fey de la Nuit in their fight to control the ogre population. In fact, she and Ambrose would likely have ended their acquaintance entirely if it weren't for the golden magic connecting their life forces as surely as a length of heavy rope. Ecanthar had sought to bind her to him in the same manner, and Ambrose had known no other way to liberate her from the black elf's control.

Rose was grateful for her salvation, but their connection complicated their lives, to say the very least. Though she had learned to control the magic she had gained sufficiently enough to keep from blasting holes in the walls of the keep, she still felt anxiety clutching at her throat if she was too long from his company. It was hardly the basis for a healthy rapport, even if the bond had been the only factor complicating their relationship.

"Your enemies are far too many in number to be wandering outside the castle walls unarmed and—"

"Ambrose, please, there's been an . . . accident." If one could call loving your husband into unconsciousness an accident. "I required your aid most urgently. Otherwise, you can trust I wouldn't have left my chamber without my sword or even a pair of slippers on my feet."

Rose emphasized her words by tugging up the hem of her nightclothes and displaying one small, bloodied foot. The flesh had grown delicate from years of being encased in slippers and boots. She was no longer accustomed to running wild through the forest with nothing at all to protect her from the ravages of sticks and stones or the thorned vines that grew thick near the edge of the river.

"What have you done?" Ambrose knelt before her with a sigh of frustration, encircling her ankle in his warm hand and lifting it toward the light of the fire. The motion disturbed her balance, forcing Rose to drop her hands to his broad shoulders to steady herself.

For a split second she saw specks of golden light floating in the air and felt the unmistakable pull as the magic within her recognized its source. But there was also a pull of a different kind, an awareness that urged her to escape Ambrose's gentle touch as swiftly as possible. She'd always thought it ridiculous that modest ladies went to such great lengths to conceal such a seemingly mundane part of the body, but now she understood the practice completely. From this moment on, she would keep her feet and ankles covered at *all* times.

"I'm fine." Rose scowled as she stumbled backward, nearly falling in her haste. "It will heal, but Gareth is hurt. Please, we must hurry."

"Surely the Seelie court couldn't strike so swiftly." Ambrose fell in behind her on the narrow forest trail leading back to the castle. "The king has assured me Lord Shenley will be granted amnesty for his offenses and welcomed at Manor High as a son of the court."

"Welcomed at Manor High?" Rose asked, her confusion complete. "But I have written to grandfather informing him a visit is quite impossible. There is too much to be done to—"

"He would have us in England before the week is out."

"Before the week is— That's ridiculous! He swore he understood the demands of a fledgling country. He knows I'm needed here."

"He's had a change of heart."

"Well, I haven't had a change of heart, and I won't be—"

"Your Uncle Seamus is dead. Assassinated by a monstrous beast who invaded his safeguarded home. All others in line for the throne have been summoned back to Manor High so that the king might provide for their protection."

"Goddess, the poor man," Rose said, though her mind still frantically sought a way to escape the journey back to England. She barely felt safe here, hundreds of miles from where she had last seen Ecanthar. To know she would be only a few hours' journey from where the giant he sought to raise slept beneath the Thames would drive her mad. "But still, I am only one-quarter Fey. The Seelie would never allow me to rule, even if all those before me were slain."

"There is no argument that will sway your grandfather."

Rose sighed, knowing Ambrose spoke the truth. Even if Gareth couldn't be roused, she could not defy the Seelie king.

She would begin packing at once and they would leave by midday tomorrow. She hoped the elvish steward she had hired would be up to the task of keeping order in Myrdrean while they were away. Even if he were not, there was no other course. It was either risk her country or her life, for none went against her grandfather and lived to tell the tale.

CHAPTER FOUR

May 19, 1750
Port of London, England

Rose stood at the bow of the ship, watching London slowly come into view in the early dawn light. The greenish-black haze of a thousand or more coal fires hung in the air, visible even before one entered the mouth of the Thames. Though she knew it was foolish to read too much into the waste created by such a large city, she took the cloud as an ill omen. From the moment they boarded the Fey ship in Calais and set sail for London, she had been possessed by the certainty that no good would come of their journey back to England.

"Come to take the air, wife?" Gareth's hands gripped the wood railing on either side of her, but even in the circle of his arms she couldn't feel safe.

He hadn't recovered his strength since that night in the library. But even if he were his old self, she knew her soul would still have been uneasy. Supernatural strength and the skill of a great warrior were useless against some enemies. She had learned that lesson before they left London the last time.

"Grew weary of the bickering, I'd wager," Gareth joked.

Bickering indeed. He and Ambrose had been at each other's throats for days. Upon waking from his unconscious state, Gareth had been incensed to find that it was Ambrose who had carried him to his bed, and had been doing his best to punish his half brother for the good deed ever since. But considering Ambrose did little but order them both around like children, lecturing them endlessly on the protocol that must be observed by visitors to the Seelie court, Rose could scarcely blame her husband.

For her part, she'd done her best to ignore them both, and would continue in that vein as long as they refrained from spilling each other's blood.

"Not at all," she demurred, continuing before Gareth could remark on the falsehood. "It simply seemed wise to come enjoy the last of the fresh air. Judging from the direction of the wind, it shouldn't be long before we smell the wretchedness of the capital as well as see its effluence hanging upon the horizon."

"Now, now, love, it isn't all that bad." Gareth smiled, his pleasure at being bound for his home country clear. Of the three of them, he was the only one at all pleased to be making the journey north. "London truly is a singular place. No capital on the Continent is its equal."

"Quite true. The aroma of Paris and Vienna—even on their worst days—could never hope to equal the stench of London's rotting garbage."

"Or the open cesspools and the unwashed bodies of man and beast laboring side by side. And one mustn't forget the bodies decomposing in the paupers' graves." She could hear the grin on his face, though she did not turn to see it. "The first time I journeyed to the city as a boy, the reek of the mass graves made me toss up my accounts all over my new suit. Father was quite displeased, though my nurse said he should have known better than to take a seven-year-old to the theater in the first place."

Rose smiled in spite of herself. "Your sense of humor is diseased, sir."

"But I made you smile." He pressed a soft kiss to her cheek. "Therefore, I must assume I have infected you with my sickness." One of his hands moved from the railing to wrap around her waist, tugging her close to his warmth.

Rose snuggled closer. "If I'd known it was contagious I would have taken steps to protect myself."

"There's no way to safeguard against my fiendish influence. Even your grandfather will be won over in a fortnight, I wager." Gareth muttered the words against the sensitive skin of her neck, making things low in her body twist with pleasure.

The spark of arousal killed the moment of levity as assuredly as if she had leapt overboard and plunged into the icy sea. Gareth's eyes had yet to regain their spark since they'd last lain together, and the limp he'd acquired after the battle with Ecanthar had returned. She felt guilty every time she looked at him, and couldn't bear the thought that she might cause him further damage. Her guilt was such that even their good night kisses had become chaste, closed-mouth affairs more befitting a brother and sister than husband and wife.

"Don't fret, Rose," Gareth said, mistaking the reason for her silence. "Your grandfather is not so very terrifying, and I've heard the banquets at the Seelie court are lavish, decadent affairs. You'll live like a coddled royal *should* live for a few months and then we'll return to drudgery in Myrdrean."

She refused to take his bait. He didn't loathe Myrdrean as he would have her believe. They could be happy there, she was sure of it. If only they had the chance to make it their home without the interference of his brother, her grandfather, and the threat of violence constantly hanging over their heads.

Violence such as the killing of half a dozen noble vampires by agents of the Seelie king as retribution for the death of Seamus, the king's son. The fact that the vampire high council had denied any responsibility for the murder seemed not to matter to Stephen de Feu Vert in the slightest.

The dead bloodmen were all the Fey de la Nuit could talk about during their voyage. They seemed most pleased with the Seelie king's decision and eager to spill more blood. There'd been no threats against her husband as yet, but Rose was glad they were near the port city. Much longer on the ship and she wouldn't trust the king's order not to harm Gareth to outweigh the crew's thirst for vengeance. The black faeries were ruled by the Fey de la Nuit high council, after all, and were not strictly bound to honor the dictates of the golden court's sovereign.

"You should return to the cabin; the sun will be—"

"I have a few more moments," Gareth said. "I would prefer not to leave you in such an agitated state."

"There's no help for it, I'm afraid."

"Come," Gareth said, tugging her away from the rail. "Let us oust the captain from his quarters and I'll find a way to coax you from your melancholy." His smile was positively lecherous, but the fact that he leaned heavily on her for support as they walked didn't allow her to forget his true condition.

"You're not well," Rose whispered, making certain none of the crew could overhear her. "It would be better for you to rest in our quarters. I'll ask Ambrose to leave you in peace while you—"

"I do not wish to be left in peace, I wish to fuck my wife." The hand at her waist dipped lower, grasping her bottom through her heavy skirts.

"Gareth, please." Rose glared at him as she plucked his hand from her ass and positioned it at her waist. "There are strangers' eyes upon us."

"Fey eyes accustomed to much bawdier fare, I assure you. The court of the black faeries is as scandalous as the court at Versailles." His smile was still in place, but Gareth's eyes burned with something that very closely resembled anger . . . or fear. Or perhaps a mixture of the two.

Whatever the emotion, it was scarcely a look she'd dreamed of receiving from her husband. "That may very well be so, but I would prefer to keep such matters behind closed doors."

"You would prefer not to engage in such activities at all, it would seem."

"That is a lie," Rose said, her voice rising in spite of her attempts to maintain control of her temper. "I simply fear for your health. I thought my heart would leap from my chest when you fell to the ground last time. I was afraid for your life."

Gareth's expression softened, his eyes now holding the warmth she had come to expect from her husband.

"Of course. Forgive me. I have been out of sorts. My frustration with my own weakness makes me a bit difficult, doesn't it?"

"Only a bit."

"You're a terrible liar." He smiled and lifted her hand to his lips for a swift kiss. "You really should seek to improve upon the skill before we arrive at your grandfather's."

"Is lying so very necessary at court?"

"Necessary? My sweet, it is an art, or at the very least a treasured form of entertainment. I spent several years in service to Queen Elizabeth when I was a very young man, even by human years. 'Twas quite the hotbed of deceit and treachery."

"It wasn't so when I was a girl. My parents' court was a simple place."

"Your entire country would fit within one of the London parishes. You can scarcely compare the court of an empire with that of a—"

"Do you insult my homeland, yet again?" Rose laughed as she guided Gareth down the steps to their quarters. It was time to seek shelter from the sun.

"Not at all. I adore your homeland. It is as lovely and enchanting as its queen."

"Shameless flatterer."

"Flattery, another highly prized skill at court."

Rose sighed, dreading their journey to Manor High more with every passing moment. "I wish you had stayed behind. I fear for your safety in my grandfather's house."

"I excel at both flattery and lies, Rose. You needn't fear for my sake." Gareth opened the door to their cabin, but allowed Rose to lead the way inside. "Besides, he gave his word. That is still worth something among the Fey."

"The Seelie king is as fickle the English skies, and his promises are scarcely written in stone." Ambrose sat brooding in a chair in the gloomy corner of the room. His temper had obviously not improved since Rose fled the cabin shortly before dawn.

"Call me a madman, but I am a native of our lady Britain and I have not noticed her skies to be fickle in the slightest. They fairly consistently turn to rain," Gareth said in his most mocking tone. "As long as the king's word is one-half as reliable, we should fair well at court. At least for a time."

"You know nothing, vampire, and you would be wise to take my counsel if you hope to live." Ambrose practically growled the words as he vaulted from his chair and began to prowl the confined space. "The leathered flesh of your kind still decorates the walls of the king's chapel to the Goddess. During the last war he had vampires flayed and kept pieces of the skin as decoration."

"Please, Ambrose," Rose said, her stomach turning at the scene he described. For a race that fed upon joy, she found her grandfather's people an alarmingly bloodthirsty lot.

"I speak only the truth, and your *husband* would be wise to hear me."

"You always speak the word husband as if it were the greatest of insults," Gareth said, countering Ambrose's snarls with equally ferocious courtesy. "Yet, I wonder if you would find the term so worthy of scorn if it were applicable to your own self and not the half brother you—"

"Cease your yapping, before I—"

"Please, both of you. Stop!" Rose said, shouting to be heard over the raised voices of the two men. "We must, above all else, refrain from quarreling among ourselves. I have enemies at court, I have no doubt of that. But as I was ignorant of my Fey lineage for so many years I am woefully unprepared to protect myself from those who would wish me ill."

"Which is precisely what I've been trying to impress upon you both since—"

"And we appreciate your guidance," Rose said, interrupting Ambrose before he could begin another lengthy discourse on the rules of etiquette and courtly conduct at Manor High. "And I am equally certain you're correct with regard to the behavior expected of me as a princess of the golden Fey. But I wonder if I wouldn't be better served learning more about the characters in this drama and less about the poses I should strike upon the stage. Surely I'll be forgiven my ignorance of some things as a three-quarter mortal new to the Fey world, but ignorance of other things—"

"Might very well cost you your life," Gareth said, falling heavily into the chair Ambrose had vacated, his weariness clear. "She's right, you know. There are vipers lying in wait who would no doubt relish the death of the half-breed princess."

"Not to mention a creature on the loose that's already killed one Seelie royal." Rose rubbed her eyes, wishing desperately she had slept better on their voyage. She needed her mind clear and sharp for the days ahead. "I fear I will be in more danger at Manor High than if I had stayed in Myrdrean. I appreciate Grandfather's concern, but—"

"Perhaps you should withhold your appreciation. I believe his *concern* is heartily laced with suspicion." Ambrose's voice was soft, as if he were telling a terrible secret, though Rose recognized the truth in his words as soon as they were spoken.

Of course the king was suspicious. She must have known that on some level, though the haste with which they had departed Myrdrean and her own lack of rest had clouded her mind.

Still, she couldn't help but find the idea ridiculous. "He truly thinks I covet the throne? I, who would no doubt be assassinated within a fortnight even if I were to survive the coronation ceremony?"

"Your mother was third in line." Ambrose shrugged. "And there were those who believed she had aspirations. Perhaps your grandfather assumes you've inherited your mother's longing for power."

Rose shook her head, finding it difficult to imagine her mother in such a light. Marionette had been an excellent queen, but far from politically ambitious . . . at least in the human world. "I suspect my mother's perceived longings were largely a product of the king's paranoia."

"It would be wrong to underestimate him, or your own position."

"But the Seelie would never suffer a three-quarter mortal to rule them," Rose said, turning pleading eyes to Gareth for support. "The very idea is absurd."

"Entirely absurd, but within the realm of possibility," Gareth said. "And their contempt for those with human blood is the very reason your life will be in danger."

"It is not the only reason." Ambrose began to pace

again, making it clear his anxiety was genuine. He was usually a creature of great stillness. To see him stalking the floor in such an agitated state troubled her as much as anything she had learned about her grandfather's court.

If Ambrose was worried, there was obviously a great deal to fear.

"Our mother was second in line to the throne of the Fey de la Nuit before the high council replaced the monarchy, and her elder brother has since been slain," Ambrose said, his tone souring only slightly as he was forced to admit he and Gareth shared common parentage. It was a small step in the right direction, but a step nonetheless. "There are those among the black Fey who would relish the return of a king or queen to our people. And if that king or queen also had ties to the golden court . . ."

"The Fey could potentially be united for the first time in over three centuries." Gareth's tone was hushed, as if he had only just realized the truth of this matter. Rose, however, was immediately suspicious.

And then consumed with guilt for her suspicion.

Did she really believe her husband not only had his eye on restoring the monarchy to the Fey de la Nuit, but thought to sit on the throne himself? The deed would only be accomplished through the deaths of several Seelie faeries, and there was little hope for a king and queen such as the pair of them would make. They had no supporters, no allies, and an abundance of contempt from those they would call their subjects.

A three-quarter mortal and a half vampire ruling over a united Fey commonwealth was about as likely to come to pass as a mongrel from the streets of South-wark being sworn onto the throne of England.

"The chances are slim at best," Ambrose said, echoing her thoughts exactly. "But the simple fact that there is a *chance* is enough to win you allies and enemies."

"Allies? What allies would a vampire have in gaining the throne of the Fey de la Nuit?" Gareth snorted, a sound he somehow managed to make elegant. Perhaps it was his clothes that lent dignity to everything he did.

He was once again decked out in his foppish finery, prepared to play the happily married Lord Shenley to any of his human acquaintances they might meet during their brief journey through London. He and Rose were to have been on their wedding tour, so Gareth had insisted on purchasing a new blue silk waistcoat with elaborate embroidery while they were in Paris. The creation had seemed ridiculous in the box, but looked quite fine on her husband.

Rose wished she could say the same of her own clothing. She'd much preferred her deep mauve dress when it was folded in paper instead of draped across wide hoops that made her hips at least three times their usual width. Despite the convenience of hiding weaponry in the oversized undergarments, Rose had little use for the current mode and prayed daily for a shift in the tides of fashion.

"You are not the first in line to the throne, Lord Shenley. I'm nearly three hundred years your elder."

"Indeed, I am well aware of the fact. It is something I struggle to keep in mind when you're boring me to tears with your sermons. After all, one of such advanced age can't be expected to be entertaining."

Ambrose smiled. "And one of so few years can't be

expected to have the sense the Goddess gave a street rat."

"Gentlemen." Rose sighed, weary to the bone with their bickering, and not at all thrilled by the prospect of the upcoming carriage ride.

At least Gareth would likely prefer to remain in the hidden compartment beneath the coach for the first part of their journey, as he must seek refuge from the sun's rays. A brief respite from having both men together in the same tightly enclosed space would be most welcome.

"You're both correct. Ambrose is the first in line to rule, but Gareth is the brother with ties to the golden court." She nibbled at her lip. "Which I suppose means Ambrose must watch his step as well. If there are those who wish to unite the Fey beneath a single rule, they would need your death."

"Not necessarily," Ambrose said, suddenly focused on doing up the buttons of his waistcoat—a dark gray silk no less luxurious than Gareth's, though far less ostentatious. "My inability to honor the marriage contract was not decided by the council, but by you, yourself, Rose. Therefore, there are those among the Fey de la Nuit who believe your marriage to be . . . invalid."

"There are those among the Fey de la Nuit who should be careful what slander they spread, else they find their wagging tongues cut from their—"

"Don't threaten me, vampire. You will regret it." Ambrose's silver eyes flashed, as if a storm brewed in their depths.

"I doubt that, brother. Even dragging one leg behind me, I could best you with sword or pistol. Simply name the day and I shall—"

"If either of you threatens the other again, I will kill you both myself," Rose shouted, her voice echoing off the wooden walls of their cabin. "I've been summoned to my grandfather's side. There is no other course for me, but the pair of you are not similarly bound. If you insist on distracting me from the business at hand, I shall ask you to leave."

"I am your husband, I will stay by your side. It is my right under the law."

"And we are bound by magic. If we are separated for long, you'll feel the ill effects. We will both—"

"Then I will thumb my nose at the law and suffer those ill effects. At the moment any torture sounds preferable to the *pleasure* of your company."

Gareth laughed, making her spin in his direction. "That goes for you as well, husband. If you prove yourself a hindrance, I will not hesitate to invoke my privilege as a princess of the Fey and force you from Seelie lands."

"You threaten me? You dare—"

"I dare because I must. I wish to live to see my country grow and thrive, and that will not happen if I am killed," Rose said, cutting Gareth off before the rage in his eyes could translate into a threat. As her husband he had a certain power over her in the human world, but as a Seelie royal she had power of her own. It would be best for both of them, however, if they never sought to test which power would prove itself superior. "Worrying that the pair of you are at each other's throats troubles my mind, and a troubled mind is an unfocused one. I require all of my focus if I am to survive this visit. I beg you both for your help in achieving that goal."

Rose exited the cabin before either man could speak another word. Best to take their momentary silence as assent and leave it at that. There was no more time for argument. They would arrive at Manor High before nightfall.

CHAPTER FIVE

The sun had set by the time the coach reached the crossing of the Severn river, so Gareth was freed from his hiding place beneath the carriage for the last leg of their journey. After nearly ten hours of jostling along roads ravaged by the effects of an especially rainy winter, neither he nor Ambrose seemed inclined toward conversation as they trundled the last few miles toward Flaxley and the hidden roadway that would lead them to Manor High.

Rose appreciated the silence. It allowed her a few more moments to rest her eyes and gather her inner resources. Though she had slept no more than a few hours in the past three days, she knew her grandfather would expect her at the banquet table come the stroke of ten. The Seelie court was famous for its lavish dinners. The Fey ate well and expected the humans at their table to eat even better. A well-fed human was a happy human, and happiness was the preferred food of the golden Fey.

Which brought to mind a troubling question. "Could the others feed upon me? My relatives, I mean?"

"You're only three-quarters human, so you wouldn't provide as filling a meal as a full-blood, but they *could*." Ambrose smiled faintly. "Of course they wouldn't. To do so would be incredibly rude."

Rose nodded. It was a comforting thing to hear. Whether they dined on misery or joy, faeries did their part to drain the energies of mortals. Ambrose had always refrained from feasting on her emotions, but she wasn't sure if it was because he had known that she was part Fey or that he simply didn't dine upon intimate acquaintances.

"Will you be provided for?" Rose asked, for the first time realizing the difficult position Ambrose might find himself in as the sole black faerie at the court now that the representatives from the Fey de la Nuit high council had returned to Paris. The Seelie dined upon joy and happiness, while the black faeries took their nourishment from the sin and wickedness of the human race.

"There are humans at the court," Ambrose said, as if that decided the matter.

"I know Grandfather and the other members of the court keep human lovers, but they're chosen primarily for their kindness and buoyancy of spirit."

"They are human. I have no doubt I will find all that I require."

In some earlier incarnation of their relationship, the words would have spurred an argument between them. But that was long ago, when Rose still believed the decent outnumbered the evil. She labored under no such delusions now, and in fact felt rather foolish for having asked the question in the first place.

"There's the road. We'll be there within the hour." Gareth no longer sounded as eager to reach her grandfather's home. Apparently her dread was catching.

None of them said a word for the next few moments, only stared out the windows at the darkening fields as it began to rain. Finally Manor High appeared in the distance. The hulking beast of a home crouched upon the land with a vaguely threatening air, its many wings spread out like spider legs across a giant web, its windows watchful, ready to absorb a visitor's secrets . . . and perhaps a bit of his soul as well.

"ELSA TELLS ME you've got your own country in the human world." Mimsy leaned across her lap, treating Rose—and Gareth, who was seated on her other side— to a closer view of her ample bosom.

"Yes. Myrdrean is very small, but I am the last of my father's line so it has—"

"Rose is a queen, and quite an effectual one," Gareth said, interrupting her for the fifth or sixth time since they took their seats for dinner. But she could hardly blame him. The immediate company—composed entirely of her female relatives—was far more interested in what her dashing husband had to say. "The nation was considered a blighted place not fit to loot and pillage a few months past. But now the keep has been restored and cheery-faced peasants litter the landscape like ants at a country picnic."

"Peasants! How charming!" Mimsy clapped her hands and wrinkled her pert nose as if they were discussing a new pair of ribbons, not starving farmers who would risk even the perils of a formerly cursed land in order to eke out a living for their families. "You simply must tell us all about it." She continued to bounce up and down on her chair, causing her bosom to tremble and shake like the marmalade the servants had passed around with the second course.

Rose darted a quick look at Gareth from the corner of her eye to see if he was as riveted by the spectacle as the two men seated three chairs down. Thankfully, he was gazing into Mimsy's blue eyes and not down the front of the young woman's dress. Nevertheless, Rose was acutely aware of her own sad lack of feminine charms and vowed to eat heartily no matter how poor her appetite. Even at her plumpest she could pass for a young boy in the proper clothing, but in her present state she was positively angular.

"Do they truly bathe only twice a year?" Mimsy asked with another delicate quiver as she fluffed her golden curls. Though "out" in Fey Society, she still wore her hair in loose corkscrew curls more appropriate for the nursery. "And do they let their animals into the house at night, to bed down beside—"

"I'm sure you would find tales of the peasants terribly dull." Gareth smiled as he sipped from a glass of red wine. He looked a bit flushed, but the spirits weren't responsible for the color in his cheeks. He had fed from one of the human women of the court earlier in the evening.

Rose hadn't asked which one. She didn't want to know.

"No, I swear I wouldn't," Mimsy said, leaning forward until her bosom was nearly in Rose's lap. "I've never lived among the humans and—"

"But most of us have Mimsy, dearest, and are eager for more stimulating conversation. We tire of human gossip." Beatrice de Feu Vert's voice was as sweet as a song, but her tone left no doubt how very tiring and vile she found everything *human*.

Including her new cousin.

Rose hadn't had a civil word from the woman in two hours, and began to wonder what she had done to offend the faerie. Besides being born to the daughter of a mortal lover of the king, rather than pure Fey nobility, of course.

"So tell us, *Rosemarie*," Beatrice said, the way she lingered on Rose's name vaguely insulting. "Do you find your room satisfactory?"

"Most satisfactory. It's a lovely room." Rose forced a smile. The room she'd been given was scarcely bigger than the maid's quarters and located in the oldest wing of the manor, where a pervasive damp lingered in the air even when the fireplace was lit.

And to add insult to injury, it featured a bed so narrow there was no mistaking that her grandfather intended for her to sleep alone for the duration of her visit. It was customary for married men and women of rank in court to receive their own separate chambers, but Rose had assumed the beds would at least be large enough to accommodate two, should a husband and wife decide to bed down together. Surely she and Gareth weren't the only couple who preferred to pass the night side by side.

There was a chance—since she had yet to view Gareth's quarters—that her husband's room was of superior quality, but she doubted that was the case. If there was one thing worse than being a quarter-Fey princess in the golden court, it was being the quarter-Fey princess's half vampire husband.

"I'm so glad you think so. I chose it myself," Beatrice said, a smile lighting up her pale face. Her amber eyes fairly glowed with spite as she ran a hand through her long, auburn hair, the crowning glory she had inherited from her grandfather, the king. "I thought you'd be more comfortable in something . . . cozy."

"You judged correctly." Rose returned her cousin's smile. "How thoughtful of you to put yourself in my place and imagine what someone of a more *petite* stature might prefer."

Beatrice's scowl was gone almost before it appeared, but the fleeting expression gave Rose a great deal of satisfaction. Her dear cousin had inherited more than a mane of glorious hair from her grandfather—she boasted his giant size as well. Though her head was mercifully in better proportion to her body than that of the Seelie king's—his being nearly three times the size of an average man's—she was still taller than most anyone else at the table. She would have been dreadfully out of fashion in the human world, and Rose had reason to suspect her immensity wasn't coveted in the Fey world either.

"Beatrice always thinks of others." Elsa, a distant cousin possessed of the same slightly wavy, golden locks as Rose, reached over to pat Beatrice's large, though undeniably delicate hand.

"I do my best. It was what father always wanted—for us to think of our guests' comfort before our own." Soon the woman's amber eyes were filled with golden tears that cut silent paths down her cheeks. "He'd have wished that I be of service to Grandpapa now that our home lies empty."

Rose's brief moment of victory was rendered hollow at the sight of Beatrice's tears. Seamus, the uncle she had lost, had been Beatrice's father. Venomous or not, the woman had recently lost a loved one, and Rose should have had been more tolerant of her moods.

"Oh dear. Mummy, Bea's crying!" Mimsy's own bright eyes began to shine and her lower lip to tremble as she shouted down the table to where her mother sat only a few seats away from the king.

Despite her ample charms, the girl behaved like a child, not a young woman of nineteen. Rose had noticed the Fey seemed to lag behind their human counterparts when it came to the business of growing up. But then, when one had hundreds, maybe thousands, of years to live, why rush the matter?

"Hush, Mim, don't attract attention," Elsa hissed. "You know how troubled the king has been. It will do him no good to know one of his favored is in tears at the table."

The willowy blonde snapped her fingers with surprising force. Immediately, there were three human servants at Beatrice's side, cooing and cuddling, doing their best to coax the faerie princess from her melancholy. All the while, merry smiles sat upon their faces and laughter bubbled from their throats like the champagne in Rose's untouched glass.

Finally, after several minutes—and the antics of a raven-haired lad who dared to lick the salty wetness from Beatrice's cheeks—the princess smiled. The ceasing of her tears was met with a collective sigh of relief from those seated around her and a burst of impulsive chatter from Mimsy.

You would think the girl had been near death. Are

*the Seelie always so delightfully theatrical? If so,
I believe I will enjoy our visit even more than I thought.*

Rose turned to whisper in Gareth's ear, not daring to
speak directly into his mind for fear of being overheard. "I can't bear much more of this. I will make my
excuses as soon as the final course is served."

"Would you like me to come with you? I'd love to
see your magnificent room," Gareth said, his words
muted by the wine he brought to his lips.

"The room is dreadful," Rose muttered behind a final bite of stuffed goose.

"But of course it is, darling. Your dear cousin has
taken quite a disliking to you. I'm certain you sleep in
the house only because your grandfather would take
issue with a princess being quartered in the barn with
the horses."

"The barn would likely be a drier place to—"

"Rose, you will come won't you?" Mimsy asked,
her pudgy hand gripping Rose's and squeezing tight.
"It would be so delightful to have someone around who
is even worse at garden cricket than I am."

"Mimsy!" Elsa chided. "Don't be rude."

"Oh! I didn't— I mean— It's only because Rose has
never lived here at court that I thought— The game is
played differently than the way the humans play, isn't
it? I thought I'd heard something to the effect, but I—"

"It's perfectly all right, Mimsy," Rose said, sparing
the blushing girl further explanation. "I'm sure I'll be
quite dreadful at any game we choose to play—human
or Fey. My life until now has provided few opportuni-
ties for merry diversions, but I look forward to frolick-
ing with the best of them."

"The best of them." Beatrice echoed her words

with a weak smile. "It is a phrase I doubt will ever be apt. Not in your case."

Stunned silence fell around their portion of the table as Elsa and Mimsy and the two more retiring young Fey seated on Beatrice's left and Gareth's right darted nervous glances between the two princesses. Rose gritted her teeth to contain the retort on the tip of her tongue. She must remember her cousin was grieving and likely not herself.

Still, the smug expression on the auburn beauty's face made Rose long for the days when the faery sword secreted in her stays solved the majority of her problems. Though it would accomplish nothing, a part of her was sorely tempted to reach back between her shoulders and fetch the comforting length of steel.

Instead she smiled. "I'm sure you're correct. My nature does not lend itself to frivolity. In fact, I am so ill accustomed to entertainment, I find myself quite exhausted. If you'll excuse me, I believe I'll retire to my room."

"Oh don't go, Rose," Mimsy said, the lone voice of protest. "The tumblers will be coming out soon, and they do the most amazing tricks. Sometimes they perform upon the table, bending over backward among the cake and pastry."

"My wife is no doubt exhausted from our long journey," Gareth said, pushing back his own chair. "I'll escort you to your—"

"No, please, stay. Enjoy yourself." Rose met Gareth's eyes then let her gaze slide subtly toward the table. "I'm sure you won't want to miss the entertainment."

"If you're sure." He nodded, making it clear he

understood her signal. He would linger and see what he could learn of her contentious cousin. Rose had obviously acquired a new enemy and as with any foe, knowledge of her could prove most beneficial.

"I'm sure." Rose accepted Gareth's kiss upon her cheek and then fled the room as quickly as she dared, hurrying through the maze of hallways leading to her chamber.

Her grandfather would no doubt be displeased if he saw her leaving. He had made quite a show of pulling her into his arms and welcoming her to court upon her arrival at dinner, but Rose had felt his cold gaze upon her more than once during the long meal. As the servants passed around grapes and olives and pork tongues cured with salt and fried veal sweetbreads with marmalade and a dozen other delicacies, Stephen de Feu Vert had passed around suspicious looks. The guests at his table were also his chief suspects in his son's murder, a fact the entire company realized but graciously ignored.

Except Mimsy. She was one of the only faeries at the table who seemed genuinely at ease.

"A fool's head is merry until the moment it is cut off." Ambrose appeared at her side, as if he'd materialized from the shadows themselves. Even with the bond between them alerting her of his presence, Rose was still startled enough to reach for her sword.

"Goddess, you frightened me," she said, taking a calming breath and firming up her mental shields before continuing down the hall. "I assumed you'd still be at dinner. You were seated much nearer the king than I."

"That cork-brained girl is in as much danger as

any other member of this wretched court," Ambrose continued, as if she hadn't spoken. "None are safe from the king's wrath. Blood will be spilt in payment for the death of his son. And soon. He will not wait to ascertain he has the true villain responsible for sending the creature who slit his favored offspring's throat, but rather take heads first and conduct inquests later."

"You're enjoying yourself already, I see."

"There is no reason for jest, Rosemarie. Our lives are in peril." Even in the dim light provided by the candles on the wall, Rose could see the scowl on Ambrose's face. "I wasn't pleased to see you seated so far from the king."

"Beatrice, who's now second in line to the throne, was seated just across the way."

"Precisely." He ran a frustrated hand through his hair, which hung loose down his back as was customary for Fey men at a formal dinner.

It had been so long since she'd seen it freed from his braid that for a moment Rose longed to reach out and touch it, to run her fingers through the waist-length strands. She wondered if his hair would be soft like Gareth's, or feel as coarse as the horse's mane it resembled.

"A horse's mane?" Ambrose asked, his tone greatly altered from the harshness of a moment before. "If I did not know of your great affection for the beasts, I believe I would be insulted."

"I'm certain an insult can be arranged." Rose blushed and was grateful for the darkness of the hall. Realizing that Ambrose knew of her desire to run her fingers through his hair was embarrassing in the extreme. "Please remove yourself from my mind. I was certain my shields were in place, but obviously I am too weary to control—"

"It is not your weariness that is to blame. Your thoughts were clear to me, and most likely every faerie present at dinner, from the moment you sat down at the table."

"What?" Rose asked, stopping dead as she strove to remember everything she had thought. She'd certainly embarrassed herself, but what if she'd done worse? What if something flitting through her mind had been found incriminating by the king?

"Don't fret. We'll get this sorted. I suspect something within your chamber is spelled—most likely a mirror or some other reflective surface. Such enchantments are often used at court by those wishing to keep eyes and ears upon their rivals," Ambrose said, his large hand settling at the small of her back and urging her forward. "The undoing of the spell is relatively simple, however. I'll work a counterspell and be back at the banquet table before the final course is cleared."

"You'll return then? Perhaps I should as well."

"No, I'll make your excuses to the king. You need your rest."

"And the king needs time to forget all the wayward thoughts he overheard in his granddaughter's mind." Rose cursed herself roundly, feeling the worst sort of fool.

"Your thoughts were above reproach."

"Highly unlikely." Rose did her best to think of nothing at all as they turned the last corner and the door to her wretched little room came into view. "I'm certain I made quite a spectacle of myself."

Ambrose pushed open the door, wrinkling his nose at the musty odor. "Delightful."

"Hardly. But at least someone came to light the candles and turn down the bed." Rose sighed. Even the narrow little mattress looked appealing at the moment. She was bone weary, and craving the oblivion of sleep.

"Soon enough, I already see the focus of the enchantment." He crossed the room in two long strides and began running his hands over the mirror in the corner.

The glass was cracked and scarcely better than the window for gazing at one's reflection, but she'd looked into it before leaving the room. She should have known better. Mirrors were one of the best objects to use when casting a spell from a distance. One glance into the glass and the enchantment was transferred to all who gazed at their reflection.

"You didn't expect your family to be spying upon you."

"You're right. I suppose I'm as cork-headed as poor Mimsy." Rose leaned against the wall near the door, knowing if she went so far as to sit down she would never get up again. She was suddenly so very, very tired, and feeling every minute of sleep she had lost in the past few days.

"No doubt you have cause to be weary, but I believe there's another spell upon the room. Someone wished for you to sleep very well indeed. Even I am feeling the effects of the magic."

"Even the great and powerful Master Minuit? Then it must be a most fearsome spell."

"Your sarcasm shows a decided lack of gratitude."

His tone was humorless, but Rose caught the slight twist of his lips.

"I apologize." She smiled as their eyes met in the mirror. "I would have kept my lips sealed, but as you would have heard my thoughts in any event . . ."

"Indeed. I'm becoming grateful for those shields you've developed. Your cutting little tongue receives enough exercise. Goddess protect me from hearing all your thoughts as well." He returned her smile, his gray eyes dancing with silver light. In that moment, he was as beautiful as any man she had ever seen, all his darkness banished by merriment, all the tension between them melting in the warmth of his grin.

No, not *all* the tension. There was still the pull of man to woman, of—

"Well, get on with it then," Rose said, swiftly turning her mind to other things before her thoughts could betray her. "I would spare you further torment from either mind or tongue."

"Indeed," Ambrose said, the heat in his eyes making it clear he was thinking of the many torments a woman could work with her tongue.

Rose dropped her eyes to the floor, forcing herself to dwell on her shame at dinner, the dreadful stains upon the carpet, the smell of the molding drapes hanging at the window—anything but the man across the room. It wasn't safe for her mind to be so unguarded. She was fortunate that none of her thoughts during dinner had been of the inappropriate variety. After their argument the night before leaving Myrdrean, Gareth would hardly be understanding—

"Are you nearly done?" Rose asked, her voice cracking as she realized how close she'd come to betraying herself yet again. Why hadn't Gareth told her that her thoughts were unprotected?

"Perhaps he didn't notice. He seemed rather busy entertaining your lovely cousins."

Rose ignored the implication in Ambrose's tone, not wanting to distract him from his work. After a time, he began to mutter beneath his breath in ancient Fey, then angled his large body into the small space behind the mirror and whispered for a few minutes more. "One moment . . . Nearly done . . . There." He ran his hands along the frame of the mirror and Rose felt the profound need for sleep fade away. "Quite a complex set of spells. Whoever wished to observe you is no novice."

"Wonderful," Rose said in her driest tone. "Thank you for removing them."

"My pleasure." Ambrose stepped out from behind the mirror as she made certain the shields around her mind were in place.

"I assume my thoughts . . ."

"Sacrosanct. Can't hear a blessed thing."

"Well, that's some small comfort."

"And likely the only comfort you'll find here." Ambrose crossed his arms as he spun in a slow circle, taking in every aspect of the cramped and dingy chamber. "It's even worse than I expected. Surely the king can't know Beatrice chose this room for you."

"I'm certain he knows now," Rose said, burying her face in her hands. "I can't believe the entire Seelie court overheard my every thought. I'll never be able to hold up my head at breakfast."

"Your musings were kinder than mine would have been in your place. You made no enemies tonight, at least none that wouldn't have already been yours to claim."

"I doubt that." Rose searched his face, struggling to read the truth there. "Mimsy must think me wretched. I'm certain I thought several uncharitable things about the girl."

"Mimsy is little more than a child, and likely unable to concentrate long enough to observe the thoughts of anyone save herself." Ambrose's lips twitched, as if he were struggling not to laugh. "And assuming she did overhear, she was probably flattered to know a princess of the Fey envied her bosom."

Rose gasped, shame and mirth warring equally within her. "I do *not* envy her bosom."

"Truly? Not in the slightest?"

"No! Not in the slightest."

"Indeed?" Ambrose brought one hand to his mouth in a contemplative gesture, most likely to hide the grin he was doing such a poor job of suppressing. "I was sure I overheard something about eating heartily so that you might increase the ampleness of your—"

"Do not speak another word," she said, a laugh escaping her lips despite herself. "You are no gentleman, sir."

"No, he is not." Rose spun to see Gareth in the doorway, his eyes glittering dangerously in the light from the lamp near the bed. Despite the fact that she and Ambrose had done nothing wrong, she suddenly felt . . . guilty. "But then we knew as much, didn't we, *wife*?"

Rose flinched at the violence contained in his last word. "Ambrose was only helping me with—"

"Yes, Ambrose is most helpful, isn't he? You've been craving his *help* for some time."

"Gareth, don't," Rose said, hoping he heard the warning in her voice. He would shame them both if he insisted on speaking out of turn.

"If you will give me a moment, Gareth, I'm certain I can—"

"Shut your despicable mouth," Gareth shouted, silencing Ambrose before he turned back to Rose, fairly shaking with rage. "Is this why you urged me to stay behind?"

"Of course not." Rose held out her hands out toward him, beseeching Gareth to listen to her words. He was so upset. Despite his jealous nature, her husband usually maintained control. To see him trembling from the force of his anger troubled her more than she could say. Did he truly trust her so little? "I was intending to return to my room alone, but met Ambrose in the hall—"

"And decided to invite him back to your chamber, for your cunt was itching most—"

"Enough." Ambrose fairly growled the word as he crossed the room, insinuating himself between Rose and her husband.

Dear Goddess, the situation was deteriorating with ridiculous rapidity. Rose tried to speak but Ambrose beat her to it.

"You will not speak to her in that—"

"I will speak to her in any way I wish." Gareth stepped closer to Ambrose, glaring into his face. "She is *my* wife, brother. If you cannot remember that simple fact, I will find a way to impress it upon you."

"I fairly quake with fear." Ambrose sneered, his contempt for his brother clear in the curl of his upper lip.

"If I find you alone in a room with my wife again I will geld you," Gareth said, the cold promise in his tone truly frightening, though not as frightening as the vacant eyes he turned on Rose a moment later. There was no love in his look, no trust, no care, only the fathomless blackness of a vampire's rage. "And you will regret the day you spoke your vows if you ever think to break them. If I smell another man upon you, I will not hesitate to punish your infidelity to the full extent of human and Fey law. I swear that to you, Rosemarie, on my life."

With that softly whispered threat echoing through the room with more force than any shout, Gareth turned and left the room, looking steady upon his feet. Anger seemed to do its part to heal her husband, at least for a time. Though what price he would pay for that momentary strength she had no clue.

"I must follow him and explain." Rose was halfway to the door by the time Ambrose's hand closed around her arm.

"I don't think that's wise."

"We must mend this rift between us, Ambrose, and quickly. It should never have come to this. If you had told him of the spell—"

"Were you not in the same room as I? He wouldn't listen."

She sighed, knowing it was useless to remind Ambrose that of the several times he'd spoken, only once had he attempted to explain himself. "Which is exactly why I must find him and force him to listen to the truth."

"No. He is in a rage, he might seek to harm you."

"Gareth would never harm me."

"Did you not see his face? Hear his threats? He's run mad and—"

"Ambrose, let me go," Rose said, tugging at her arm. "I must—"

"You must do nothing. You—"

Rose wrenched free with a violent twist of her arm. "You are not my liaison anymore, nor are you my husband." She watched Ambrose's face slowly turn to stone. "You will allow me to leave this instant, and you will take your leave behind me."

"As you wish." He stepped away.

Rose gathered up her skirts and raced from the room, following the sound of Gareth's fading footfalls. There was no time to think about the pain she had glimpsed in Ambrose's eyes or the ache in her heart. She must reach her husband and talk some sense into the man. No matter how greatly she cared for Ambrose, it was to Gareth she had sworn her life and future. There was no altering that fact, even if she wished it, which she most certainly did not.

Not true . . . not . . .

She ran faster, until her lungs burned and her muscles ached, refusing to acknowledge the voice she had just heard. It was lack of sleep that had her mind playing tricks. The Mother wasn't real. She didn't exist outside the realm of nightmares.

Still, Rose could've sworn she heard a woman's laughter floating down the hall as she turned a corner and finally spied someone lurking in the darkness.

Unfortunately, it wasn't her husband, but a monster sprung from the depths of hell who waited a dozen feet ahead, its claws extended toward her in a silent, deadly invitation.

CHAPTER SIX

It was as if the night itself had come to life and given birth to a creature of utter darkness. Never in her long history of combating the evil of the supernatural world had Rose seen such a beast. Its great body was made of smoke and shadow that reached nearly to the ceiling and the air where its head should have been swirled black and gray like two paints that refused to be mixed.

The only spot of color on the creature was its eyes, crimson red coals that burned with silent fury as the swirling colors took a more solid form, becoming a set of massive jaws that opened wide as the monster stalked toward her.

"Move no closer," she shouted, her voice ringing through the hall.

There was a chance someone might hear and come to her aid, but it was a small chance at best. She had yet to see another guest in this neglected wing of the estate. For all she knew, it might be days before another person passed this way.

The shadow thing eased closer, its eyes gleaming and its jaws stretching into what almost looked like a smile.

"Clearly terrified of you, Rose," she muttered to herself as she inched away. "Remove yourself from my path, and I will allow you to live." The last she shouted, using her loudest voice, praying Gareth might be close enough to hear his wife's cry.

The monster howled a hideous shriek that Rose suspected was a laugh. Whatever the nature of this beast, it possessed some remarkably human qualities, especially for something that seemed to be lacking a corporeal form. It resembled a wraith or ghost more than any other supernatural being. There were moments when she was certain she could see through its body to the hall beyond, though its head remained relatively opaque.

"Hopefully that, at least, can be damaged with a sword."

Rose's entire being rejoiced as she finally drew her sword from its hiding place. Though her heart raced as the creature closed the distance between them, she couldn't deny that it felt right to have her weapon in hand, preparing to face a foe she could combat with steel instead of words. She was simply not naturally inclined to the business of political maneuvering.

It was ever so much easier to make an enemy bleed.

Goddess, how she hoped this creature could bleed. It would be so disappointing if it couldn't. She desperately missed the hot blood and spray, the bliss that filled her entire body at the moment she knew she had made a killing blow.

Rose had only the briefest second to be disturbed by

the direction of her thoughts before the beast was upon her. She screamed as shadow claws raked across her shoulder, but managed to bring her sword down across one giant wrist before she spun away. The flesh where the creature had struck her burned with a sharp stinging pain, but a quick glance revealed not a speck of blood on the wall she crashed into before backing away down the abandoned hall, preparing for the creature's next attack. There wasn't even a tear in the fabric of her dress.

The monster spun to face her once more, howling though it seemed unharmed. She must aim for its head at the first opportunity. There was no obvious wound on her shoulder, but her flesh still felt as if it had been slashed open in no less than three places. She feared it wouldn't matter if she could see the damage or not, those talons might still be the end of her.

The shadow thing dropped its hands to the floor and bent its knees, reminding her of the tigers she had glimpsed in her travels in the East. She hoped it couldn't pounce quite as swiftly, or even her faery gifts of speed and grace wouldn't protect her.

Seconds later, her enemy was hurtling toward her with its claws extended, each smoky blade growing longer as the beast flew closer. The blasted things could stretch at will! It would be impossible to judge how far she must keep from the creature in order to ensure the relative safety of her mortal flesh.

"Ambrose!" Rose screamed the faerie's name with both mouth and mind, hoping the bond between them might somehow allow him to sense she was in danger.

She waited until the last possible moment before she dove to the floor, rolling beneath her foe, swearing she would beg, borrow, or steal faery clothes from her cousins if she survived to see the morrow. The wretched panniers at her hips were her smallest pair, but they still slowed the speed of her movements considerably. How much faster could she roll across the carpet if she were dressed in a silken Fey gown?

"Much faster." Rose cursed as she struggled to her feet, every second she wrestled with her skirts an opportunity for the beast to catch her unawares.

She had only just lifted her sword and assumed her battle stance when she felt the stirring of air above her head. On instinct, she dropped down once more, but wasn't quick enough to escape her enemy entirely. This time, the wickedly sharp claws caught the back of her head, making her skull feel as if it would explode as she fell to the floor.

No! This was not the agreement!

The voice slammed into her mind, making Rose scream in agony as it crashed through places already ravaged by the creature's claws.

She must not be damaged!

This time the shadow beast's wail joined Rose's anguished cry, as if it too felt the world shatter from the force of the anger vibrating in the Mother's voice.

No, there *was* no Mother. She was simply losing her mind, and her consciousness as well. Black spots swam before her eyes as she forced herself to come to her knees. "Goddess, please," she prayed. Fighting was no longer an option. She must do her best to flee and hope her enemy would not catch her.

Rose's heart beat in her throat and she tasted the goose she had eaten at dinner. Knowing she was only seconds away from retching uncontrollably, she bent her knees and came unsteadily to her feet. Through pure force of will, she kept her supper in her stomach and her grip on her sword as she stumbled to brace her hand against the wall.

The monster crouched no more than five feet away, its claws wrapped around its head, as if it still battled the disembodied voice.

And perhaps it did. There was certainly *something* out there, a being with the strength to break through mental barriers and bruise a mind with nothing more than an angry shout. Perhaps it had even entered Rose's dreams—but she would not believe an ancient myth had come to life without a great deal more persuasion.

Whomever the voice belonged to, she was a formidable woman. Thankfully, she also seemed to want Rose alive . . . for now.

Though her head spun and the ground beneath her rocked like the deck of a ship, Rose hurried as fast as her unsteady feet would carry her down the hall. She thought for a moment to flex her wings free from her body, but found she lacked the strength to manage the deed. Her wounds sapped the vitality from her bones and the sense from her mind. Within moments she was lost, careening wildly from one darkened hall to another.

No longer certain where she stood in the maze that was Manor High, she took the first turn that seemed at all familiar, trusting her instincts, knowing she mustn't slow her step for a moment or risk a killing blow from the beast that pursued her.

It was coming for her now. She could feel it in her very bones. The places where its claws had swept through her skin throbbed with a sickly fever, growing hotter and hotter as the creature shuffled toward her. It was no longer moving with the same swift confidence it had before, but it was as determined to find her as she was to escape.

A pitiful whimpering filled the corridor, echoing off wooden doors locked with heavy bolts from the outside. The sound was so foreign that it took several moments for Rose to realize it sprung from her own lips.

Her courage and her strength were failing her. Though her injuries still remained invisible, she could feel the life seeping from her body as surely as if blood seeped from the wounds. She had felt this way once before, the night her throat had been slit by an ogre near the banks of the Thames. She'd been near death for days afterward and only survived through an infusion of Gareth's blood.

The memory made her wonder if he would do the same for her now, were he to find her before the monster that dogged her steps.

Rosemarie . . . run faster, you are nearly . . .

"No, no," Rose chanted, the hysteria in her voice shocking her to the core. Never had an enemy terrified her as completely as this disembodied voice that seemed to wish for her salvation. Not the ogres, not the wraiths hiding in the ruins of her home, not the wyrms that had blown fire at her back as she walked the catacombs at Faversham Hill. Only Ecanthar himself had even come close to . . .

The red eyes of the beast, so like the red eyes of Ecanthar. Could it be possible?

The Fey de la Nuit's investigations had reported that the black elf could shift his shape, assuming the form of any creature—human or supernatural. But what of a form such as the thing behind her? Could Ecanthar wrap himself in the shadows, becoming a beast invulnerable to harm?

The very idea made the wretched whimpering start again. If only the ogres could see her now, the dread Briar Rose, whining like a frightened child.

"Stop it at once. At once," Rose panted as she neared the end of the hall and thought she caught the faint sound of voices.

Urging her flagging courage to the sticking point, she turned another corner and was finally granted a stroke of luck. At the end of the long hallway, she could see the light of hundreds of candles burning around a giant table still heavily laden with food. It was the banquet room she had left no more than half an hour ago.

So little time, but it felt like an age since she had last walked with strength in her step. She was becoming so terribly weak, stumbling, scarcely able to maintain her hold on her sword, though the enchanted weapon had shrunk to the size of a mere dagger, obviously sensing its mistress's distress.

"Ambrose! Gareth!" She called the names with as much volume as she could muster, but the lush, velvet covered walls in this part of the manor swallowed her frantic cries while behind her, the beast drew near.

It would soon close the distance between them. She couldn't hear its step or even its labored breaths, but she could sense its position. Even more powerful than her connection to her husband, or her magical bond with his brother, was this new awareness of the shadow thing.

Perhaps it had put its mark upon her when its claws swept through her flesh. Or perhaps an unknown poison had been set loose within her veins, a poison that heated the blood and called to the monster, alerting it to where its prey had fled.

Rose risked a glance over her shoulder that sent the world spinning once more. "Ambrose! Gareth! Grandfather! Please someone, help me." Her breath came so quickly she feared she would faint dead away, but still she forced her feet to move, one in front of the other. The beast was still there, no more than ten yards behind.

Though it scuttled along with a hitch in its step and paused frequently, there was no doubt the creature was in better condition than the woman it hunted. The swirling colors at its head now took the form of a giant skull, resembling nothing so much as a demon escaped from the depths of hell.

It must be from hell, otherwise her skin would not burn as it did.

But Ecanthar could also make flesh boil until any torment seemed preferable to the torture of being contained in one's own skin.

It wasn't the stranger's voice this time, but her own thoughts echoing through her mind. But that fact offered little comfort, not when she was now nearly certain it was her old enemy who nipped at her heels. Ecanthar was the one foe who had bested her, who would have killed her if Ambrose hadn't filled her with his magic.

Goddess, if only she had the strength to use that magic now. If only she had the strength to do anything besides stagger toward the light, as weak and frantic as a wounded animal.

"Gareth," she called, breathless with exhaustion and

the drugging effects of the heat burning her alive. Perspiration dripped from her forehead onto her face, stinging her eyes and making the lights ahead dance and blur. But she was nearly there, only a few dozen feet or more, almost, almost—

The creature howled, so close she swore she could feel its breath upon her neck.

"Please, help me!" Rose screamed, the desperate plea bursting from a primal place inside her. "Ambrose! Please—"

Seconds later a great weight hit between her shoulders. Though she knew it impossible, it seemed she fell to the ground as slowly as a snowflake drifting through the air. There was time to mourn that the last words her husband had spoken to her had been in anger, to long for another chance to tell those she loved all that was in her heart, and to bitterly regret coming to Manor High in the first place. She should have known better, should have risked her grandfather's wrath rather than serve herself up to the very beast that had slain her uncle.

The monster that had killed Uncle Seamus—*that* must be what this creature was, and not the black elf at all.

The realization did nothing to quiet the frantic beating of her heart as she continued to fall and fall, dreading the inevitable impact with the ground. For as soon as she was on the floor, the creature would begin to slash and tear at her flesh, shredding her to bits, though none would be able to see the wounds.

Those who found her would no doubt wonder what had killed the Seelie princess. Or perhaps they would know. Perhaps Uncle Seamus's body had been found in a similar state and . . . they would . . . guess . . .

Before her addled mind could reach a conclusion, all thought was snuffed out, like the flame at the tip of a candle.

SHE WAS WALKING through a great white fog. The damp, rank smell of the Thames filled her nose, though it wasn't nearly as awful as the last time she'd run beside the river that served as both London's water source and its sewer.

It must be winter, and a properly cold one, not the oddly warm season the island had recently endured. The smell was always easier to bear when the air was cool and chilled. In the summer, when the heat of the sun baked the waste and refuse floating in the murky water, the stench became a living thing that threatened the very existence of those who dared to breathe it.

Threatened the very existence . . .

Her heart began to race and the fog, which only seconds ago had seemed comfortingly close, became a place where evil could hide. There were things waiting in the mist, things made of shadow that would be upon her before she had time to scream.

Rose spun in a circle, struggling to breathe past the weight that had settled on her chest. "Hello? Who's there?" she whispered, feeling foolish the moment the words were out of her mouth. She knew exactly who was there, or rather *what* was there.

It was the monster that had slain her in the hall at Manor High. She remembered now, remembered the terror as it had chased her through the darkened corridors, the way time had stretched into an infinity of despair as she fell to the ground, to her death. The beast must have found a way to drag her down to hell along with it. Now she would spend the rest of her days wandering the mist, hunted and frightened and alone.

"No!" she shouted, refusing to be afraid of who might hear. She wouldn't meekly play this role. She might have run like a frightened rabbit from this creature once, but she would not do so again. She was not a helpless victim, she was Briar Rose, the woman of many thorns, feared by ogres the world over.

"Yes, the ogres still fear you. But I am not an ogre. Am I?" The voice was more a growl than speech, but Rose understood the words and knew who spoke them.

It was the beast. Its red eyes glowed just a bit to her right, the hellish orbs floating in the mist like two tiny hearts torn still beating from a chest.

"So you speak now?" Rose swallowed the rush of saliva that filled her mouth as she turned to face her tormentor. She would not be ill, she would not show weakness again. "You are finished howling like an animal?"

"I *am* an animal. Thanks to you." It moved closer, its claws clicking on the stone. It seemed more solid now, more substance and less shadow. If she'd had her sword, the realization would have pleased Rose, but her hands were empty and her stays, where the weapon was usually stored, were gone.

In fact, all of her clothes were gone. A swift glance down revealed she was completely nude. And here she'd thought the denizens of hell would be forced to wear constrictive undergarments at all times. Certainly, in her own personal hell, she would be dressed in the widest possible hoops and a heavy wig so poorly made she would sweat like the devil himself for all eternity.

The creature laughed, a grating sound that pricked

against her skin like a thousand tiny blades. "You are not in hell yet, sister. But I assure you, that could be arranged."

"Sister?" she asked, her mouth suddenly dry. "Then it is you, Ecanthar." The black elf had insisted she was his kin from the moment they met. He'd also insisted she become his bride and bear him children, obviously having no care that such a thing was considered an abomination in the human world.

"One man's abomination is another's saving grace." Closer and closer still it came, eager talons drumming the ground and its massive shoulders becoming clearly outlined in the mist. Rose bent her knees ever so slightly, preparing to run. At least she felt stronger now, her vitality returned and her body pain free.

"Don't run. Come to me, dearest. I must take you now, or there will be no sweet release of death for you." The monster moaned, a sound even more pitiful than the whimpers that had escaped her throat in the hall. "She will not allow it . . . not *that* one."

"Who will not allow it?" Rose asked, edging slowly backward.

"She is angry with us both, you know. We are her naughty children, and I the naughtiest of all for trying to take you from her. But I love you too greatly to force you to suffer so."

"Who is angry?" Just a few more steps and she would turn and run.

"No games, sister. You know her name. You know. Now come here to me. I will make it swift and painless, not like her, not like—" The beast broke off with a scream and fell to its knees, writhing in apparent torment on the hard ground.

Rose didn't linger to discover what had wounded it, but turned and fled into the mist. Faster and faster she ran, until the wailing behind her grew faint and the hard stone gave way to hard packed earth, and then to soft grass . . . and then to something even softer, something cool and soothing to the touch that floated away from her churning feet.

Then she was falling again, through the softness, through the white mist, until she hit bottom with a none-too-gentle thud.

"Goddess," she gasped, sucking in a deep breath as her eyes flew open.

Above her hovered half a dozen anxious faces, Ambrose and Gareth's among them. But it was her grandfather's eyes that first captured hers. Perhaps it was the fact that they were glowing a bright gold, or perhaps it was the sadness etching his eternally youthful face with deep lines of sorrow that drew her focus so profoundly.

"She lives!" A Fey man she recognized vaguely from the banquet hall turned to shout the news to those assembled behind him. Relieved sighs and hushed conversations erupted, but Rose could still hear her grandfather's voice clearly above the din.

"Unfortunately, we cannot say the same for my son." The king turned his head, gazing toward the fire burning not far away. It was then Rose realized that she was lying on the floor before the giant hearth of the banquet room, her head cushioned from the stone by someone's coat.

"He was a good man, so very good." A single tear rolled down Stephen de Feu Vert's giant cheek, sparkling in the light like a drop of dew in the morning sun. "I am king. I should have been able to keep him safe."

At first, Rose assumed he spoke of Seamus, but when she followed the direction of his gaze, she saw the body. Flesh had been torn from bone with what looked like giant claws, until all that remained was so much meat. Meat that had once been the king's last living child.

CHAPTER SEVEN

"You're certain you don't need anything else, Rose, anything at all? I plan to insist Beatrice find a more suitable room for you in the morning, but I can attempt to have you moved tonight if you think you'd be more comfortable." Elsa lingered by her bed, rearranging the sheets for the tenth time. Her cousin's deep blue eyes were filled with genuine concern.

Elsa had been among those baptized in Uncle Henry's blood when he was attacked by the very creature that had killed his brother less than a week before. Therefore, she had been absent when Rose was brought back from the edge of death, having been rushed to the baths with the rest of the affected.

Ancient Fey blood could burn the flesh from a human's bones, and was not entirely safe even for other Fey. All those who had been exposed to Henry's were being scrubbed down by servants, which meant there were few maids or valets to be spared. Apparently the murder had been a gruesome event indeed.

If Rose hadn't been running through a terrifying dream mist while her uncle was being mauled, she would have felt blessed to have been spared the sight.

"No, thank you, Elsa. You have already done more than enough. This room is perfectly adequate for this evening," Rose said, a bit embarrassed that she'd needed help dressing from this near stranger. She'd thought to ask Gareth, but then had worried he might be too weak and would feel even worse if he were unable to do such a simple thing as change his wife into her nightgown and lift her into bed. "I wouldn't have asked you to—"

"Please, Rose, it was a comfort to me." Elsa brushed away Rose's concern with a wave of her dainty hand. Her cousin was nearly as thin as Rose herself, but as a full-blooded faerie of nearly two hundred years, she had a strength Rose would never possess. When it had come time to help her into bed, she'd lifted Rose as if she weighed no more than a child. "Poor Uncle Henry. I only wished there had been something I could do . . . but it all happened so quickly."

Elsa's eyes shone with unshed tears. Rose longed to do something to comfort the troubled woman, but she barely had the strength to keep her eyes open. Even lifting her hand seemed a Herculean effort. Whatever spell her grandfather had worked to banish the poison in her veins had taken the last of her vigor along with it.

Words alone would have to do. "Losing one you love to murder is dreadful enough without witnessing the horror of it firsthand."

Her cousin nodded. "I have been so sheltered here.

I realize that now. Manor High has always been such a safe haven, the lone place in the human world where the Fey can truly be as we are in Faerie."

"But we enjoy much better food here, of course. The food in Faerie is so very plain." They were the first words Mimsy had spoken. She'd been so quiet—save for the occasional gasp as Rose's many scars were bared for viewing before Elsa slipped her nightgown over her head—that Rose had almost forgotten she was there.

She truly must be exhausted if she was losing track of such things. Unfortunately, she couldn't rest just yet, not until she spoke to the men waiting outside the room.

"Yes, there is that," Elsa said, smiling indulgently at the much younger woman. "Speaking of food, I will come to fetch you before breakfast, Rose. The king has arranged for the court to dine in the throne room. It is the most protected place in the manor, and he is certain we will be safe there."

Yet not one, but two deadly creatures had breached the spell-defended borders of the property and made their way past the royal guardsmen and women hand picked by the king from the most skilled warriors of the past two millennia. And not only had they gained entry, they'd also escaped without so much as a scratch upon them. The creature that killed Henry had been too fast for Fey swords and seemingly immune to even the king's potent magic, and not a soul save Rose had glimpsed her own attacker. The creature had vanished into the shadows from which it was made, and for all they knew might still be lurking some-where in the mazelike hallways of Manor High.

None of the golden court would sleep well tonight, knowing those disturbing truths.

"Thank you, Elsa. I will look for you on the morrow."

"Good night, cousin." Elsa leaned down to kiss her cheek with Mimsy close behind, the younger girl clearly ready to be finished with her nursemaid duties. "Shall we send the gentlemen in, or insist you need your rest?"

"Send them in, I won't rest until I speak with them."

Ambrose opened the door a moment later. "A wise decision. There is much to discuss."

"You were listening at the door?" Elsa asked, flushing as the black faerie swept into the room with Gareth limping close behind. He didn't look well, but neither did he look worse off than he had before working himself into a fit of anger.

All had been forgiven between them, of course. His rage could not hope to survive the near death of his wife. In fact, he had quickly agreed to Ambrose carrying her to her room and had followed meekly alongside, holding her hand in his as if he would never let it go. It had been no easy task convincing him to let her cousins tend to her.

Now he came to the bed and sat beside her, rearranging the covers Elsa had already fussed over. It made her heart twist in her chest to see his concern—and love—so clear upon his face. Marriage was not a simple or easy business, but there were moments when she could not imagine how she'd made her way in the world without this man at her side. Never before had she felt that her life or death mattered greatly to anyone. It was wondrous to finally feel so treasured.

"Fey hearing is keen and a vampire's even keener," Ambrose said, coming to stand at the other side of her bed, closest to Elsa and Mimsy. "We had little choice in the matter."

"A gentleman might have taken himself farther down the hall to avoid hearing ladies' secrets," Elsa admonished with no real censure in her tone. In fact, the look she gave Ambrose was more intrigued than irritated. She clearly found the black faerie a very appealing houseguest.

Rose ignored the brief flash of jealousy inspired by Elsa's interest in her former liaison. Ambrose was his own man and could do much worse for a companion than her pretty, kind cousin. Besides, hadn't she just insisted no more than a few hours past that the man was nothing to her? The magic they shared would bind them together for perhaps a year or more, but afterward Ambrose would be free to live and love wherever he wished, and she and Gareth would continue alone.

She should be looking forward to that day, but for some reason she was not.

"This is the second time this evening my status as a gentleman has been called into question." Ambrose smiled down at Elsa, and Rose watched her cousin melt beneath his grin.

"Indeed?" Elsa asked, flushing pink across her cheeks.

"It's a sign you must mend your wicked ways," Gareth said, his voice surprisingly light and carefree. She couldn't remember ever hearing him speak to his brother in such a teasing tone. But then, Gareth was no doubt pleased to see Ambrose giving attention to a pretty woman other than his wife.

Ambrose nodded, seeming to seriously consider his brother's words for a moment. "You're right. I've been too long about bloody business to remember my manners. Perhaps I require a tutor?"

Damn the man, he was practically winking at the blushing Elsa. Not only had he forgotten his manners, but he'd evidently forgotten that a man had been killed and she herself nearly shared the same fate. This was hardly the time for courtship or seduction or whatever it was that Ambrose was about.

Forgotten his manners, indeed. She'd never met a more chivalrous man. This entire conversation was ridiculous in the extreme.

"Oh I would be most happy to attend to your tutelage, Master Minuit!" Mimsy clapped her hands with excitement, setting her bosom to shaking as it had at dinner. "I only just finished learning all about the rules of ladies, gentlemen, and the court from Mummy. I will be happy to share all my knowledge. Or at least everything I can remember."

Rose smiled, part of her strangely satisfied to see Elsa's cause thwarted by the younger faerie.

"You are most kind." Ambrose took one of her fluttering hands and brushed his lips across the back.

Mimsy turned a purplish shade of red and giggled madly, while Elsa stood by smiling as if she found the girl's antics amusing. Immediately Rose felt awful for her moment of inner glee.

"And I trust I can depend upon Lady Elsa to fill in any gaps in my education?" As he turned to Elsa his tone became softer, more intimate.

Her cousin met his eyes with a flutter of her long, long lashes. "Of course, Master Minuit. It would be my pleasure."

Her *pleasure*. For such a seemingly proper Fey woman, she could certainly infuse that word with its share of scandalous suggestion. But then, the Seelie were hardly as concerned with propriety as their human counterparts. As soon as Elsa was married and had produced an heir for her husband's family, she would be free to indulge in as many affairs as she desired without censure from family or Fey society. Even now, she could conduct a discreet liaison, providing the proper spells were employed to prevent a child from being conceived.

A child. With Ambrose.

The very thought of Elsa round with his babe made a part of her want to weep. Perhaps it was simple female jealousy—she feared she could no longer bear children, that something within her had been damaged by the birth of the twin sons the ogre had sired upon her as she slept—or perhaps it was jealousy of a different sort entirely.

Rose shook her head. She was clearly in need of rest before she lost what remained of her good sense. "Cousin Elsa, Mimsy, I fear I am weary to my very bones. If I am to speak to Ambrose and Gareth tonight, I must do so now."

"Of course, cousin! You must have your rest. We shall see you in the morning." Elsa and Mimsy took their leave a few moments later, insisting they would be safe until they reached the end of the hall where their armed escort awaited and did not require Ambrose to accompany them to their rooms.

"Quite a fetching young lady, that Miss Elsa."

"Young lady, indeed. I would guess she is several years older than yourself, Gareth," Ambrose said, though his voice held none of the heat it usually possessed when speaking to his half brother. In fact, there was actually a hint of a smile upon his face as he pulled the chair in the corner closer to Rose's bed.

Alone in her room with two men—and she dressed in nothing but a thin nightgown. Surely she should be grateful for the lax rules of propriety governing the Seelie court, not cursing them.

Of course, it was not unheard of in the Fey world for two men to share the same woman, especially in the case of brothers, since the offspring of such a union would inherit the family name and fortune regardless of which man was the father. The practice was more common among the Fey de la Nuit, as black faeries gave birth to far more boy children than girls, but there was at least one such situation among the golden Fey.

It was called *ménage à trois,* a house of three.

As far as she knew, the phrase wasn't even known in the human world. Such an idea was scandalous in the extreme, unheard of in polite society, though Rose knew there were men who paid for such things on the seedier streets of London. She had walked those streets in her boys' clothes and seen gentlemen solicit several bawds to pleasure them at the same time. Of course, she had also encountered men who tried to solicit her, thinking her a pretty young boy yet to grow whiskers upon his face.

There were all manner of perversions to be bought and paid for in the debauched capital.

Though, if she looked into her heart, she wasn't certain she found sharing one's bed with two men to be perverse. It was certainly not a state she would find desirable for her own life, but surely it was an alternative to an eternity spent alone for many Fey de la Nuit. With available women so very scarce, it made a great deal of sense for those who were at peace with the practice to—

"Rose? Darling, are you sure you're strong enough to discuss these matters now? You don't seem as though you've heard a single word Ambrose has spoken."

"Excuse me?" Rose blinked, shocked to find she had nearly drifted off to sleep while pondering such ridiculous things. Two men had been killed. This was not the time for idle thoughts. "I was . . . drifting. Help me sit up a bit will you, husband?"

"Perhaps some water as well," Gareth suggested as he rearranged her pillows and lifted her to lean against them.

His arms felt as strong and safe as ever, and for a moment Rose was tempted to cling to him and never let go. The past few months she had felt on the verge of losing Gareth so many times, and not always because of his failing health. It seemed important to hold on tightly, to cling to this moment when he seemed to adore her as completely as he had when they first spoke their vows.

But instead she let him go. Ambrose was watching and waiting for her to regain her focus. It seemed Ambrose was always watching, and his attention never made things between her and her husband easier.

"Or perhaps some wine to help her regain her color. Her cheeks are alarmingly pale."

"Thank you, Ambrose," Rose said. "But I assure you I am paying attention now, and there's no need to speak as if my ears have ceased to function. Some wine would be lovely."

Ambrose smiled at her tone and made to rise, but Gareth gestured for him to sit. "Stay. I will fetch the wine. You had best repeat your warnings while our patient is still conscious."

"That would probably be best."

They sounded positively cordial. It was nearly enough to convince Rose she should be wounded to the point of near death more often, if the result was such felicity between the brothers. It would be best for all of them if they could put their animosity aside and learn to at least tolerate each other's presence, if not become the friends and allies it would be best for two brothers to be.

Rose watched Gareth cross the room and pour a glass of red wine from the carafe next to the washbasin before she turned back to Ambrose. "Warnings? What sort of warnings? If you mean to tell me to beware engaging in combat with shadow beasts with poisonous claws, I believe you are a bit late."

The brothers exchanged a meaningful look. "So you are still certain that is what you saw, a beast made of shadow?"

"Yes, completely certain," Rose said, troubled by the grave expression on Ambrose's face. Looking at him now, it was difficult to believe he had been smiling and playing the flirt only a few minutes past. "Its body was made of shadow and its head of swirling colors, black and white specifically, with red eyes floating in the middle. The skull could change shape, but it appeared more solid than the rest of it, though I did not have the opportunity to see if it could be wounded with a sword."

"Is that all?" Gareth asked, handing her the wine.

She took a sip, relishing the warmth that spread through her chest as soon as she swallowed. "No, it also had claws that it could lengthen at will. Though they left no mark as they swept through my flesh, the pain of the wounds was intense. I . . . I also think I spoke to it in a dream just before I awoke in the banquet hall."

For some reason, Rose wasn't prepared to tell either of the men about the woman's voice or the possibility that the monster that had attacked her was Ecanthar in another form. She knew she should, but there was something keeping her from it, as if her tongue would cramp and cease to function were she to think of mentioning either the woman or the mad creature that claimed her as his sister.

"But you said it was a beast," Gareth said.

"It *was* a beast and it couldn't speak when I fought it, but in my dream it—"

"You were poisoned. It could have been a hallucination," Ambrose said. "In fact, *all* of it could have been a hallucination."

"What do you mean?"

"He means there might not have been a beast at all. You might have been running from a creation of your own mind." Gareth sighed, as if he were loathe to say more, but had no choice. "Someone put poison in your food, Rose. That's why Ambrose just warned you not to eat or drink anything that has not been inspected first. Your grandfather fears the poisoner might be one of his own court, and has ordered all the rooms searched for evidence of foul play. He swears that if evidence is found, he will deliver the person or persons responsible to the gates of hell himself."

"What?" Rose's mind raced. "But the servants brought out each course. How could anyone have known which plate I would receive?"

"There are subtle ways of administering a poison. One seated near you could have leaned across your plate or slipped the potion into your drink. Or perhaps a servant was bribed—"

"But Ambrose, I swear to you, I felt well until the claws of the beast caught my shoulder. It was only afterward that I—"

"It was deadly nightshade the king summoned from you, Rose." Gareth was clearly of the same mind as Ambrose, both of them convinced her attack was a trick of her mind. "The king is intimately acquainted with the flora of Great Britain and recognized its scent as the toxin floated from your skin."

"Poison from the belladonna plant causes insanity in the Fey if not removed from the blood soon after it is administered. It would not usually cause death, but as you are only a quarter Fey, it nearly proved fatal."

"Goddess, but it seemed so very real. I could feel the claws . . . I could hear the creature's voice so clearly." Rose lifted her cup, but froze as the glass touched her lips.

"The wine is safe. Your grandfather looked it over himself before sending it along with your cousins," Gareth said.

Ambrose nodded. "I also took it upon myself to test the wine. It is safe."

Gareth took her free hand in his and gave it a gentle squeeze. "The king truly does seem to care for your well-being, enough that I may be forced to forgive him his behavior last time we sought his aid. Though his decision to appoint himself executioner of a dozen vampires is unforgivable, I trust he has your best interests at heart."

The first time she had met her grandfather, she and Gareth had been seeking sanctuary from Fey de la Nuit with orders to take them to Paris for torture or worse as their punishment for prophecy interference. Stephen de Feu Vert had turned a blind eye while Rose flew over the wards at the rear of his property, but had insisted on turning his new son-in-law over to the black faeries. That decision had nearly led to Gareth's death, as the officers were not Fey de la Nuit at all, but half-breed Fey working for the black elf, Ecanthar.

"I am grateful to Grandfather for saving my life, but I remain wary of him." Rose took another long sip of her wine, beginning to feel a little stronger as the spirits coursed through her veins.

"A wise decision," Ambrose said. "Despite my earlier certainty that Stephen would seek retribution for the death of his son, I'm finding it difficult to believe the king was so pitifully defended against an attack from this beast. Before we become too grateful, we'll have to see how the rest of the royal family fares."

"Surely you don't think Grandfather ordered the murders of his sons?"

"You said nothing of this," Gareth said, the usual irritation returning to his tone.

"It wasn't safe to speak of such things in front of those who could be his spies."

"Elsa and Mimsy? Spies?" Rose laughed, a short humorless sound. "They are no spies. I can't believe even Stephen de Feu Vert could be so cruel. He loved his sons. His despair was clear on his face."

"Was it? The face of a man thousands of years old is a difficult book to read." Ambrose met her eyes without flinching at the shock he surely saw there. "Why, after all his many, many years upon the earth, did the man only sire three children, one of them a half-breed who barely survived infancy after numerous attacks on her life?"

"My mother was attacked while she lived at court?"

"Poisoned, twice, before she could even toddle through the halls without the company of her nanny."

Rose didn't miss the significance of Ambrose's words. "You think the king wishes to eliminate the heirs to his throne?"

"Perhaps. If so, what better way to achieve his goal than to assemble all his victims under one roof under the guise of protecting them?"

Her head began to pound and the wine glass grew heavy in her hand. "So you would have me believe he poisoned me and then summoned this strange beast to do away with poor Uncle Henry?"

"The beast was indeed strange, but it was not completely lacking in reason."

Gareth nodded in reluctant agreement. "He's right. I reached the banquet hall just as the creature swept down from the rafters. It leapt straight for Henry and tore his head and hands from his body before he began toying with the rest of the corpse."

"It knew how to kill a faerie, and the location of its target," Rose mumbled, passing her wine to Gareth and letting her head drop back onto the pillow with a sigh. "But that doesn't mean Grandfather is responsible. It doesn't mean anyone else is responsible. Could this thing not be acting on its own?" It was the closest she could come to raising the possibility that Ecanthar might have found them.

"The prevailing belief is that the creature is simply a tool for whoever created it," Gareth said. "There's nothing in the entire history of the supernatural world that speaks of a thing half dog, half bird of prey, and half dragon that has a taste for royal Fey flesh."

"Three halves, brother? If such a thing were possible it would surely—"

"Give me peace, Ambrose. It is late and you understand my meaning." Gareth sighed, but did not seem to take any real offense. "My point is, the creature wasn't born upon the earth, but is a tool that will cease to be should the magic fueling its actions cease."

Before Rose could question the feasibility of a magical tool so large or ask for a better description of the creature, Ambrose stood and took his chair in hand. "We shall discuss this more in the morning. You should get your rest."

"I don't want to rest, I want to know if I was poisoned by my own grandfather. It still seems so strange. And what of Beatrice? She is in line to the throne before me. Now that her father and our uncle are dead, she will be queen if—"

"In the morning, Rose. You need your rest. I'll stay here to make certain you're safe while you sleep," Gareth said.

Ambrose turned toward the door, chair still in hand. "And I will be at the end of the hall with the guards assigned to your room."

"I'm not a child to be sent to bed when a man wills it! It is my life that was threatened and I insist—"

The reflection in the small hand mirror Gareth held before her silenced her immediately. Her flesh was a pale, sickly yellow, black circles ringed her eyes, and starbursts of red surrounded her nose and mouth where the poison had caused blood to burst free. She looked like a corpse.

"Sleep will help. You should be much improved by morning," Ambrose said, the pity on his face making her feel even worse.

"Very well." She pushed the mirror away and turned to press her face into her pillow, doing her best not to cry as Ambrose left and Gareth made his way around the room, dimming the lamps and making himself a place to sleep on the floor with extra pillows and blankets she guessed Elsa had brought when she came to tend her.

It would do no good to cry, she must instead find a way to tell Gareth and Ambrose the true story of the beast in the hall. Though evidence of her poisoning was clear, she still believed it was the creature's claws that had tainted her blood, the creature that would come for her again. He would find her no matter where she ran, no matter what guards the Fey sent to protect her life. A thing made of shadow did not fear the weapons of man or Fey. The only thing he feared was *her*, the name Rose didn't dare think in her weakened state.

"Good night, dearest."

"Good night," Rose mumbled, falling gratefully into the sweet oblivion of sleep.

CHAPTER EIGHT

Rose's first thought was that—despite the small size of the mattress—Gareth had joined her in bed. Her entire back was warm from another body's heat and a heavy, male arm was thrown across her ribs. It was a position she usually found comforting, but she was troubled by the feeling that *something* wasn't right.

"Gareth?" she whispered, running her fingertips down his lightly furred arm until she reached his hand. In that instant, she knew what had been troubling her.

It wasn't her husband's arm thrown about her, but someone else's.

The realization made her heart thud in her chest as she gently gripped the man's wrist and lifted, determined to slide out from under him and reach her sword where it lay on the table beside the bed. Now that her eyes had adjusted to the dim light, she could clearly see that the hand was too large and the hair upon the arm far too dark to belong to her husband. A stranger was in her bed, one who had crept into the room and lay down beside her in a manner far, far too familiar.

Even the Fey were not so bold, which meant this man was not one who appreciated the rules of propriety. Which in turn meant he could be dangerous or mad or a frightening combination of both.

Or perhaps he simply felt safe taking what he pleased from a half-breed and didn't feel it necessary to play the gentleman with a—

"I am weary of having my honor called into question." Ambrose's voice was thick with sleep, but there was nothing sluggish about the way he freed himself from her grasp and wrapped his large, muscled arm firmly around her body once more. "I have behaved myself most admirably with you, Rosemarie."

He whispered his words into her hair, making Rose shiver. The warmth of his breath at the back of her neck, the heat of his hard body pressed so intimately to hers, the feel of his arm nestled between her breasts . . . it was not unpleasant, not unpleasant at all. In fact, it was far better than pleasant, a sensation her body had craved from the moment she laid eyes on him that black night so long ago.

Which was precisely why he must leave her bed.

"Ambrose, you must leave at once. If Gareth discovers you here he will do his best to kill you and I—"

"Damn Gareth." Ambrose pulled her even closer, and pressed a soft kiss to where her pulse beat frantically in her throat. "He is a fool who doesn't know what a treasure he has."

"Please," Rose begged, sickened by the arousal rising within her. What sort of wife was she to have her body so easily brought to life by another man? "I cannot betray my vows, to do so would—"

"So now you refuse me even in my dreams." Ambrose's voice held a note of defeat, but he made no move to slide from between the sheets. Instead, his fingers traced a heated trail down the valley between her breasts until his palm rested over the trembling flesh just below her navel. "It is most unfair. I must watch him lay claim to your heart and your body in a thousand torturous little ways every day, but here . . ."

His hand began to glow with golden magic, calling to the same magic within her, making things low in her body twist with a fierce anticipation. Her entire being sang with the sheer rightness of being pressed so close to this man. As the pressure within her built, her breathing grew faster, shallow, until her head spun and she no longer felt ashamed of the slick heat pooling between her thighs.

"Here you can still be mine." He pulled her closer, until she could feel the thick ridge of him against her.

Rose moaned low in her throat and arched her back, wantonly rubbing her bottom against his cock. This was a dream, nothing but a dream. She should have known from the start, for she was no longer in her shabby little chamber at Manor High, but in a room with a ceiling so high she could scarcely make out the rafters above. Velvet curtains hung around the bed, sheltering them from the light of what looked like hundreds of candles.

Still, a part of her was ashamed of how desperately she wanted the man in her dreams. And even more ashamed that it wasn't purely a physical want, but a craving of an even more wicked kind.

"I love you, Rose. I've always loved you, and I'll never stop, no matter that you belong to another man." Ambrose echoed the thoughts she hadn't dared speak aloud, his voice breaking as his hand slid between her legs.

He found her slick heat and plunged his fingers inside with a touch far from gentle. She could feel his every muscle strung tight and the trembling of his hand as he worked in and out of her aching center. The relentless control he exercised in life seemed to shatter in this dream world, taking the last of Rose's reservations along with it.

If there was anything more intoxicating than feeling a man of such strict reserve fall to pieces in your arms, she couldn't name it.

She pulled his hand from between her thighs and spun to face him. His lips found hers with an abandoned sound even as he rolled on top of her, pressing her into the soft mattress. Rose opened her mouth, eagerly accepting the tongue he slid between her teeth, slanting her lips to get even closer to this man who intoxicated her with his every touch. He tasted of cool water from the springs surrounding Myrdrean, of everything dark and calm and utterly irresistible.

"And you taste even sweeter than I imagined," he said, his golden magic dancing in the air around them, shimmering along their skin.

Never had she been so grateful to feel flesh against bare flesh. Every place their bodies fused together was alive with delight, burning with their combined power until it felt as if her skin was too small and too large all at the same time. With Ambrose there was no slow build to the pinnacle of passion—she simply craved him one moment and was certain she would die if he didn't take her the next.

"Ambrose, please. Goddess, please." She writhed against him, parting her legs and wrapping them around his hips.

"There's no need to rush, we have the—"

Rose sobbed against his lips and threw her arms around his neck, tangling her fingers in the long hair that spilled around them. The part of her that was still sane observed his hair was nearly as soft as Gareth's, while the rest of her insisted she convince him to take her before she was burned alive. "The magic is too much, I cannot bear—"

"You've never said so before," he mumbled into the curve of her neck as he dragged his teeth across the sensitive skin, making Rose gasp and buck her hips into his arousal. "Truly . . .'tis an extraordinary dream."

His words made a shiver of apprehension whisper across her skin, but she was too crazed with lust to think upon anything but the man hovering above her. She only knew she must have him, must feel him tunneling into her core before she lost what remained of her mind.

"Please, oh please." She squirmed beneath him, attempting to guide his cock inside her with the movements of her hips. "Please, love."

"Love?" Ambrose pulled away from his work at her neck and smoothed her hair from her face with a trembling hand. The haunted look in his eyes made it clear how long he'd ached to hear that word from her lips. "*Am* I your love, Rose?"

"Always, always," she mumbled, tugging him down to her once more, feeling as if she couldn't live without the taste of him lingering on her tongue. "You're always in my heart."

"Despite the wrong I have done you?" he asked, pinning her wrists to the mattress above her head so she couldn't close the distance he put between them. "Can you look into the eyes that stood by and watched as you were abused and say you feel affection for me? For a coward—"

"You've punished yourself for your sins, Ambrose." Looking into his face, so clearly tormented by the choice he had made so many, many years ago, Rose realized the words she spoke were true.

These haunted silver eyes were not the same eyes that had spied on her during her enchanted sleep, the ones that belonged to a man too fearful of contradicting Fey prophecy to save a young girl from a monster. These were the eyes of a man who loved her, who would risk anything to protect her, and would gladly give up his life if he could travel back in time and undo what he had done.

The final remnants of her anger and bitterness melted away as easily as her body had melted under Ambrose's touch. "I forgive you, dear friend. Completely."

A sound very close to a sob escaped Ambrose's throat. "You can't mean that, you—"

"I do." Rose twisted her wrist until Ambrose set her free, and brought the hand to his cup his cheek. "You are forgiven."

"You do not know how much—"

"Hush." She traced the curve of his lips with her finger. "We shall never speak of it again. Now *please* . . ."

Without another word Ambrose pressed his mouth

to hers, devouring her with a passion that left her breathless, even before his hands urged her thighs wider and the thick head of his cock pressed against her entry. Rose moaned and arched her hips, wordlessly begging for him to love her.

"Always," he said, his voice making it clear he meant the word as a solemn vow. And then, finally, his hips thrust forward, filling every aching inch, banishing the emptiness inside her in a way Gareth never had, never could, because Gareth was a shadow of a man compared to Ambrose, was naught but a sad excuse for a—

"No!" Rose cried out against the thoughts in her head, thoughts that were not her own.

Your thoughts were never your own, you silly child.

"No?" Ambrose's face was twisted with equal parts passion and confusion. "But I—"

"I heard something. Someone else is here," Rose said, still desperately aroused, though she was now just as desperately frightened.

The Mother was here, lurking somewhere outside the velvet curtains. But still the wanton part of her couldn't resist wrapping her legs around Ambrose's hips and pulling his hard length even deeper. She had waited so long to be connected to him in this way. This dream wasn't like the rest, it was achingly real, as real as anything she had ever felt while she was awake.

"There is no one else." Ambrose kissed her softly as his warm hand cupped her breast and his fingers toyed with her nipple. "I've horribly neglected the art of love this first time, Rosemarie." He circled his hips while still buried within her, making her gasp. "But I swear to you I will make amends—"

"Wait," Rose whispered, trembling as she watched a shadow move outside the curtains. "She's here. Please, we must—"

"She?"

"The Mo—"

Do you dare speak my name? The voice was angry now, booming in Rose's ears with enough volume to make her flinch and moan in pain. *Do you know what happens to foolish little girls who dare to speak my name?*

"No, please, I— Ambrose!" Rose reached for her lover, but it was too late. One moment, he was buried within her, his body a comforting weight, then he was ripped from her so swiftly her human eyes couldn't see what had taken him.

It was only when she looked up that she saw *her,* the Mother in all her terrible glory, hovering above the bed like an angel of death. Ambrose lay still as a doll in her giant hand, his eyes closed and his handsome face pale.

Still you insist on seeing with human eyes, denying what you are, making a mockery of the one who made you! There is no punishment too great.

Her features were cloaked by the shadows near the ceiling, just as they'd been the last time, but now Rose could clearly see the rage burning in her ancient black eyes. She was a vengeful serpent who would devour the world, beginning with all those Rose held dear.

"Release him!" Rose screamed, horror in her voice as she watched the Mother bring the limp and lifeless Ambrose toward her open mouth.

You swear you do not want the man for your husband. If you do not want him, then I will have him.

"Please no! I beg of you!" Rose screamed, jumping to her feet on the soft bed, wishing she had her sword, or better yet, a quiver full of poison arrows and a sturdy bow. She would shoot her full of poison and dance on the giant, bloated corpse as she died. The sight of Ambrose so helpless in her huge hand had banished Rose's fear. For what greater evil could the Mother visit upon her than the death of one she loved?

The Mother paused, and a smile stretched her crimson lips. *I knew you would see the truth. You love him, this prince I hold in my hand.*

"I do, very much," Rose said, though a tiny voice in her mind warned her to remain silent. "Please, release him—"

You love him! The mother's red lips began to run as she laughed, turning to blood that leaked down her chin, onto her neck, and fell like rain onto the bed below. *And when there is only he, you will marry him as was planned so many years ago.*

"No, damn you!" Rose screamed, swiping drops of blood from her eyes. The Mother meant to kill Gareth. She could hear his death in her laughter, dooming him as surely as the poison the shadow creature had put in her veins.

The blood rain fell harder and the Mother scowled, obviously displeased at the thought of the monster that had found Rose at Manor High. *He shall trouble you no more, not that one. He has suffered for his sins against the Mother and now must earn my forgiveness with blood—a vampire's blood.*

With a cry of anguish Rose pushed through the velvet curtains, determined to destroy this giant even if she had to start from her enormous feet up. She wouldn't allow her to take the lives of anyone she loved.

But the curtains were heavier than they appeared, and only grew heavier as she fought them. Heavier and heavier, wrapping around her like a cocoon, smothering her, stealing her breath, just as the Mother would steal her breath, leaving her trapped for eternity in a prison of flesh and blood and bone . . .

"ROSE! WAKE UP, this instant!"

"I can't breathe, can't—" Rose broke off with a sob of relief as she realized she was once again in her sad little room in the neglected corner of Manor High. Never had she imagined she would be so grateful to see the musty chamber.

Her breath came in ragged gasps, but already her heartbeat slowed. She was safe. "A dream, it was only a dream." It felt good to speak the words aloud, to feel their truth soak into her very soul.

"Quite a gripping one. It was nearly impossible to wake you. You were weeping in your sleep, you . . ." Gareth sighed, and swept a bit of hair from her face. "In any event, are you all right now?"

"Yes, I'm fine. It was just . . . a nightmare."

"So it would seem." Gareth pressed a soft kiss to the top of her head, but paused before pulling away. He sniffed tentatively, as if he were a hound scenting something suspicious in the air. When he spoke again he sounded decidedly troubled. "Wait a moment, let me turn up the lamp."

"All right." Rose brought a trembling hand to her face, meaning to wipe away a bit of dampness on her upper lip.

"Don't touch it, let's see where you're cut first," Gareth warned as he fetched a cloth from beside the basin and dipped it in water before beginning to turn up the lamps.

Rose's hand froze before her fingers reached her mouth. "Cut?"

"You must have scratched yourself in your sleep. The smell of the blood is what woke me, though your essence has an odd scent this evening. I was so weary I didn't hear . . ." Gareth's words faded away as he turned to where she sat on the bed. She could honestly say she'd never seen him look so shocked, or so at a loss for words.

"You should see your face." Rose tried to laugh, but the sound that burst from her lips was hardly mirthful. "Gareth?"

Her husband shook his head, as if the motion could somehow erase the sight before his eyes.

"Gareth, please say something," Rose said, her voice breaking. "You're frightening me."

"Forgive me, I— In the darkness it wasn't clear. My eyes are no longer what they— I just . . . I don't see how this could have happened."

"See how *what* could have happened?" she asked, growing impatient.

She could feel the stickiness on her face now as the blood began to dry. Whether she had scratched herself or begun to bleed as an effect of the poison she'd had in her veins, she would prefer to know what disturbed her husband rather than stay in bed waiting for him to recover his ability to speak.

"Very well, I suppose I shall have to see for myself." Rose threw off the covers, grateful for the cool air that met her skin. She was decidedly overwarm, and her nightgown stuck to her body as it had the night she dreamed of the Mother in Myrdrean.

"Goddess, Rose." Gareth stumbled backward as she walked toward him, nearly tripping on the rug and barely regaining his feet. It was shocking to see him so affected, but the sight she caught in the mirror as her husband moved away from the glass was more shocking still.

The woman in the mirror parted her lips yet no sound emerged. That was probably for the best. Rose didn't want to hear the sound that would come from such a poor, pitiful wretch, a waif whose white nightgown was covered in blood, whose pale face was streaked with more of the crimson mess, and whose hair had fared not much better.

"Rose? What happened, sweet?" Gareth asked.

The woman turned toward Gareth at the same moment as Rose. It was only then that reality hit her full force. *She* was the blood-soaked waif in the mirror. Somehow, some way, the blood that rained down upon her in her dream had followed her into the waking world.

It was madness to believe such a thing possible, but the hot, stickiness making her gown stick to the curves of her body was very persuasive evidence.

"Are you hurt?" Gareth spoke again, having recovered his ability to form words, though his expression remained vaguely horrified.

"No." Her voice was as small and hollow and frightened as she felt. "It is . . . it is not my blood. I don't think it is, at least."

"Then whose is it? How did this happen?" Gareth

asked. "You haven't left the room for a moment. I slept soundly, but my bed was in front of the door. No one could have come in or out without awakening me."

As if put into motion by his words, the door flew open. Rose turned in time to see Ambrose burst into the room, his eyes wide and wild and his sword already drawn. When his gaze met hers, he nearly dropped his weapon. "Rose, what—"

"I'm not sure," she said, certain she couldn't bear further questioning on the matter. She already felt tears pricking at the backs of her eyes and a scream building somewhere in her chest. It took all her resolve to speak clearly and plainly and to refrain from ripping the bloodied nightgown off and running naked from the room. "I'm not hurt. I was asleep and dreaming and when I awoke I was like this. That is all I know."

"All right, all right. Don't worry, love. The first thing to do is to get you tidied up. I'll tell the guards to summon a maid to bring you a hip bath and hot water. I don't think it would be wise to venture into the communal baths in your present state," Gareth said, striding toward the door in his pants and shirtsleeves, with nothing more than stockings upon his feet. She had never seen her husband leave the bedroom in such a state of undress. The fact that he was willing to do so now emphasized how troubled he must be.

He was afraid for her, maybe afraid *of* her. His energy was difficult to read with her mind so out of sorts. She only knew that she didn't want him to leave her, even for the brief time it would take to venture down the hall to speak to the guards. Tears pooled in her eyes as he reached the door.

"Wait, brother. I will go," Ambrose said. "Stay here with Rose. I believe she's in need of a husband's comfort."

Rose darted a grateful glance his way, but was disturbed by the odd look in his eyes. He was looking at her with such aching tenderness and a strange intimacy. It was as if something had changed between them in the time since she had fallen asleep, as if . . .

"No, no, no," Rose mumbled beneath her breath as Gareth returned to her side and Ambrose spun on his heel and fled the room.

It couldn't be. It wasn't possible. It had been a dream.

"But the blood. The blood is real," she said, plucking at her nightdress with shaking hands. "It's *real.*"

"We'll have you clean in a wink, sweet. Don't torture yourself." Gareth pulled her into his arms, holding her tight to his chest, heedless of the blood that smeared onto his white shirt. He was afraid that her mind had been damaged, she could read that clearly now. She could feel his fear beating against her skin like the wings of a hundred tiny birds.

Just as she could also feel the ache between her legs, where Ambrose had buried himself within her not more than a dozen minutes past. Blood wasn't the only thing she'd brought back with her from the dream world. Now it simply remained to be seen if Ambrose had the same memories as she, if they really had inhabited the same place in the realm of the sleeping mind.

If they had . . . if he recalled what they'd said, what they'd done . . .

The mere thought made her bury her head in

Gareth's chest and cling to his soiled shirt for dear life. "I love you, husband. Don't let me go."

"I won't, Rose. Never."

With every bone in her body, she prayed that the words he spoke were true.

CHAPTER NINE

May 20, 1750

"Don't begin until we arrive at the center! To do so would be cheating!" Mimsy stood on tiptoe, calling to the rapidly disappearing heads of the ladies who had joined them for a morning of gaming in the expansive Seelie gardens.

The maze they walked was the largest Rose had ever seen, and had more twists and turns than the alleys near Ambrose's London home in Southwark. It made her wonder how the lot of them would ever find their way out once they'd marched their way in.

"I'm sure Beatrice will start the batting before we arrive," Mimsy huffed, kicking at a leaf fallen from the shrubbery. "She is the most horrid cheat. That is the only reason she is *always* the victor in any game she plays. No one, even a Seelie princess, can be that naturally gifted in *everything* they—"

"Mim, Rose! A moment if you please!" The women stopped and turned. Elsa arrived beside them a moment later, looking quite flushed and happy for a woman who had spent most of breakfast in tears.

The king had insisted on burning what remained of his son's body in the throne room's giant fireplace that very morning while the entire Seelie court looked on, most of them unable to stomach their tea and cake or carry on a conversation over the chanting of the holy men singing for Uncle Henry's soul. Incineration was the customary method of disposing of a Fey corpse, but usually the burning took place outside amid much pomp and circumstance. That the king had chosen to burn his son in such a common fashion made Rose wonder if the Seelie sovereign *was* behind the murders of his two heirs. It seemed Ambrose could be right in his suspicions.

Ambrose. She didn't want to think about Ambrose.

He hadn't returned to her room last night and they'd assiduously avoided each other at breakfast. She preferred to continue ignoring him and the troublesome matter of their shared dream until there was no other choice.

"Please excuse my tardiness," Elsa panted, still regaining her breath. "I was detained by your black faerie, cousin."

So much for ignoring the man. "He's hardly mine, Elsa."

The other faerie laughed, a gay sound that made the enchanted fabric of her dress glow a brighter pink as her merriment increased. "Of course not, but he is your friend. He cares a great deal for your welfare and made me promise to keep a close eye on you today to make certain you are well."

"He is very kind, as are you. Thank you so much

for arranging for my things to be taken to a new room. It will be a comfort to be nearer to the rest of the court," Rose said, wishing she were as at ease as she sounded. In truth, she was dreading this morning's entertainment and wished she could stay indoors with a book for the entirety of the day.

But hiding wouldn't help her discern who among the Seelie wished to see her dead . . . or at the very least completely out of her mind.

Between the use of a poison known to make the Fey run mad and her disturbingly lifelike dream from the night before, she began to suspect someone would be pleased if she were to succumb to lunacy. She was no longer certain if the Mother and the shadow creature were real or creations of her own fearful mind, born from a mixture of poison and exhaustion. The only thing she *was* certain of was that she must discover what evil was afoot before she truly did become better suited for Bedlam than for the Seelie court.

"It will be a comfort to be out of that miserable little chamber Beatrice gave you, no doubt. What a horrid thing to do to your cousin on her first visit to court," Mimsy said with a snort of laughter. "She is such a petty bitch."

Rose laughed out loud, the first real laugh she had enjoyed in days. Goddess, but she would have to revise her opinion of the young faerie. For all her foolishness, Mimsy was a breath of fresh air.

"You shouldn't say such things, Mim," Elsa said, though a smile tugged at her lips as well. "Beatrice has her spies, and she wouldn't be pleased to hear you speaking so."

"And believe me, you don't want her for an enemy,"

Rose said, then added in a hushed tone. "She might arrange for your other ankle to be broken."

Mimsy laughed as she took Rose's arm and began hobbling toward the center of the maze. Elsa smiled and fell into step beside them, adopting the slow pace Rose and Mimsy were forced to keep due to the younger faerie's unfortunate accident.

Late the evening before, Mimsy had broken her ankle by falling down the stairs leading to her room. Even after being attended by a Seelie doctor, the girl was not quite herself this morning. Rose had eagerly agreed to walk with her, however, as she too wasn't feeling her best.

Sleep had been nearly impossible after awaking coated in blood, and she still felt fragile of mind and body this morning. No doubt it was what the person responsible for the dream wanted.

Fortunately, she had been given a small amount of peace the night before. The human maids who brought her bathwater had become rather chatty once Gareth left the room. The pity was clear in their eyes as they gently washed her hair, telling tales of other odd happenings in the Seelie court of late.

Apparently, she was not the only one to fall victim to dreams of a disturbingly lifelike nature, but the chambermaids would give her no further information beyond that. Even compassion couldn't tempt the humans to tell certain tales . . . which made Rose suspect that other royals, or at least very high ranking faeries were involved. Otherwise, the maids wouldn't be so fearful about revealing the identities of the other victims, or of describing in more detail what nightmarish things had followed the others from sleep into waking.

Still, the knowledge that she was not alone in her torment made her suspect there was magic behind the dreams. There were certainly spells that could inspire night terrors. But could such a spell cause her to wake covered in blood? Surely it must be possible.

But that wouldn't explain the other feeling, the deliciously used sensation that still throbbed between her legs . . .

"You wouldn't mind, would you, Rose?" Elsa asked.

Rose winced inwardly, embarrassed that she had so entirely tuned out the women's chatter. "I must apologize, Elsa, I was daydreaming. What was the question?"

"She asked if you would mind if she and Master Minuit attended the ball together tomorrow night," Mimsy said. "He's already asked her and she clearly wishes to go, but the entire court is atwitter about you and he being magically bonded: I think Elsa is a bit nervous she might be overstepping herself setting her cap at the man."

Elsa blushed. "Mimsy, that is not it at all. Master Minuit is Rose's traveling companion and friend: I wouldn't want to intrude if she has need of his assistance in this admittedly frightening time for royals."

"Ambrose is a trusted friend and advisor, but I don't see that my cause will suffer from the loss of his company for the evening," Rose said, forcing a smile and ignoring the hurt and anger suddenly coursing through her blood. She wished to ignore what may or may not have transpired between them, so why should she care that he wished to escort her pretty cousin to a faery ball?

"Well, I can't say I would feel the same," Mimsy

added in a knowing tone. "I daresay I wouldn't want a man like that out of my sight, even if I was married to an equally dashing man who doted on me as that vampire dotes upon you, Rose. Oh but Gareth is *so* very charming. One nearly forgets he is half blood-man when one—"

"Mimsy!" Elsa chided.

"Well, he is half bloodman. Isn't he?"

Rose only smiled in response, but made a mental note not to underestimate the young and often ridiculous Mimsy. She was far more clever than one would guess upon first meeting, managed to cause her share of trouble with her seemingly thoughtless remarks.

"Finally, the dawdlers have arrived." Beatrice greeted them with an almost genuine smile as they turned one last corner and entered the center of the maze.

The striking redhead sat perched upon the edge of the giant fountain that dominated this part of the garden, swinging her cricket bat lazily to and fro. All around her, the other women of the court gathered roses from the flowering hedgerows. Though the ladies were dressed in the usual flowing spring-colored gowns of the Seelie court, Beatrice looked ready for a hunt in her tightly fitted riding coat and bell-shaped skirt. Even Rose had to admit she cut a rather striking figure. The green wool brought out the brilliant amber of her eyes, while the silver braid trim of her coat complemented her pale skin and auburn locks.

Rose felt positively dowdy in comparison. She'd assumed one of her older dresses would be appropriate for a morning spent running around out of doors, but she should have known better. She'd spent enough years posing as a French comtesse among the humans to realize the rich found no end of excuses for dressing to outdo one another.

"Now that we're all present and accounted for, let us choose teams." Beatrice eased from her perch and began to pace about the stones surrounding the fountain. "Who shall serve as captain of the second team?"

"Oh, I think Rose should be captain," Mimsy said, forgetting her injury and jumping up and down in her excitement for a moment before wincing in pain.

"Oh please, no," Rose said, surprised how frightened she sounded at the thought of captaining some silly game. It was hard to believe she had ever faced down hundreds of ogres with nothing more than her sword and a few dozen trolls at her back. She'd certainly thought herself made of sterner stuff.

"But you must, Rose! One princess heading each team." Mimsy's smile became a pretty pout when she turned and saw the frown on Rose's face. "It is the only thing that makes sense."

"Truly, Mimsy, I would be honored, but I know nothing of the game. I should feel much more comfortable following the lead of one well versed in the sport."

"You shall be on my team then, as I am by far the best player here today," Beatrice said, somehow managing to make the statement seem a matter of fact rather than shameless bragging. "So I choose dear little Rose for my first teammate. Caroline, you shall serve as second captain and I insist you choose our Mimsy first. That way we shall each be put at equal disadvantage."

Mimsy pouted as she broke away from Rose, but Rose simply bit her lip and smiled as Beatrice and

Caroline, another of her distant cousins, chose teams. Within a few moments, two groups of eleven ladies stood on either side of the fountain, separated by streams of water and a few dozen stone satyrs with rather grotesque phalluses protruding from between their legs. For a man who was said to greatly appreciate the female form, the king had made an odd decorative choice for the center of his maze.

"The king allowed me to decorate this part of the garden myself. It was a three-hundredth birthday present," Beatrice said, her crimson lips stretched in a wicked grin. "I have a great appreciation for the *male* form."

"How lovely." Rose returned the smile as she firmed up her mental shields. Damn and blast the exhaustion that had weakened her mental walls and curse her cousin's choice of lip rouge, as well. It reminded her entirely too much of another pair of giant lips.

But then . . . perhaps the resemblance was deliberate. Rose vowed she would watch her cousin very closely as this game progressed, and was grateful for the sword that lay nestled in its sheath between her shoulders. Shadow monsters and night terrors might be invulnerable to her blade, but her Fey cousin was not.

The thought made her smile in earnest.

"So Rose, are you ready?" Beatrice asked, handing Rose a plump rose blossom. "Or do you need me to refresh your memory as to the rules of the game."

"You can't very well refresh what was never there to begin with." Rose cheerfully claimed a cricket bat from the woman next to her. "I will simply attempt to learn from your shining example as we play."

"Perfect. I adore a lady who fearlessly embraces new adventures."

"Well, perhaps not fearlessly, cousin," Rose demurred. "But I can assure you, I never back down from a challenge."

Their gazes caught and held, and for a moment Rose thought she saw a hint of admiration in the other woman's eyes before her lips curled in another mocking grin.

"Oh good, then this should be fun, shouldn't it?" Beatrice held up her bat, gaining the attention of both teams. "The match shall begin at first bat and end when the sun passes high noon. Both teams will meet at the entrance to the maze to calculate points. The team with the highest score at that time shall be the victor, and that shall be the end of it. I can't abide games that drag on for days on end."

Days on end? Rose had had no idea she was committing herself to something that could potentially consume such a great portion of her time and energy. She would have to be more cautious in the future, and remember that creatures who lived for thousands of years often had a different definition of a "brief diversion" than a mostly mortal woman.

"And will there be prizes for the winners?" Mimsy shouted from the other side of the fountain. Elsa, who had also been chosen for Caroline's team, shot the young faerie a sharp look, but it was already too late.

"No, but there shall be punishments for the losers. Punishments are so much more entertaining than prizes," Beatrice said, her announcement greeted by laughter from the ladies of her team, proving once again that the Seelie were terribly spiteful for creatures who fed on joy. "The team with the low score must dress as servants and serve the winners during the formal dinner tonight, eating only the scraps they beg from the winners' plates."

"But I can't serve! I'm practically lame!" Mimsy fisted her hands on her hips and stuck out her lower lip. "And I get terribly hungry by dinnertime."

"Then we must endeavor not to lose," Caroline advised her in an even tone. It was clear from the resigned look in her eyes, however, that she knew her future held a maid's uniform and a night of service.

It was a pity that Rose had somehow found her way onto Beatrice's team. She would have enjoyed a respite from the demands of polite conversation, not to mention being spared the unique thrill of poisoned food. If it was truly nightshade that had undone her the night before and the shadow creature was only a fancy born of tainted blood, she would be better off begging scraps from the plates of those without ties to the Seelie crown.

Rose only wished there was some way to know the truth. The uncertainty of the matter left her feeling alarmingly exposed and ill prepared for the next attack.

And there would be another attack, of that she had no doubt.

"Very well, ladies, Caroline's team shall be white, and we shall be red. Take a few moments to choose your partner in the chase." A wave of her hand and the blossoms each lady clutched obediently transformed to the proper team color. Rose watched as a deep crimson bled from the center of her white rose, until every last one of the petals were the precise color of freshly spilled blood.

She had to fight the urge to hurl the flower to the ground and be rid of it.

"It's only a flower, little cousin," Beatrice whispered under her breath. "And I would think you would be accustomed to the color of blood after your years as a slave to the black faeries."

Rose had evidently dropped her shields again. Lovely. Not for the first time that morning, she wished she had stayed abed with her head under the covers. "I spilled mostly ogre blood, cousin, which is black rather than red. And I was no slave, but paid very well for my work."

"Oh, I see," Beatrice said, the skin between her brows drawing together as if she sought to figure out a great puzzle. "Well, then, you were more like a whore then, weren't you?"

Rose smiled. "No, not at all. A whore fucks men for money; I simply killed them for it and fucked whomever I pleased."

"Charming," Beatrice said, though she was clearly taken aback by Rose's frank speech.

"I would say *mercenary* was an apt term for my work," Rose prattled on, feigning ignorance of her cousin's discomfort. Beatrice had begun this verbal warfare, now Rose would finish it. "Though I did enjoy the business, and plied my trade not only for the coin but for the satisfaction of the task as well. I do so enjoy killing something from time to time, don't you, Beatrice?"

The glare the redhead cast down at Rose was positively venomous, but there was also a hint of real fear lurking in the swirling amber depths of those Fey eyes.

Rose didn't know whether to be pleased or horrified

by her response. She supposed it depended on whether or not Beatrice was guilty of some sin against her—something worse than giving her the most pitiful guest room in the entire manor. Perhaps by the end of their game today, she would have a clue as to the depths of Beatrice's ill will.

Especially if her cousin was to be her partner for the morning's festivities. "Did I hear you say we should be choosing partners? Might I assume you wish for us to be partnered?"

"Of course. If you are to learn from my example, you must be close enough to observe it. And I would rather not have you out of my sight. After your misfortune last night, I am feeling strangely . . . protective."

"I imagine that must be strange for you." Rose smiled.

"Yes, yes indeed it is," the other princess replied, mirroring Rose's smile with one of her own before turning back to the rest of the players. "Game on, ladies! A verbis ad verbera!"

From words to blows.

Presumably of the bat upon blossom variety, but Rose wasn't completely certain Beatrice didn't have blows of a different sort in mind. Nevertheless, she mimicked the other ladies, throwing her flower into the air and striking it with her bat.

Shouts and laughter filled the air as nearly two dozen blossoms soared overhead, darting in all directions with seemingly no rhyme or reason. Rose had watched human men play cricket countless times, but this Fey game resembled the human version not at all. With the exception of the cricket bats they held, Rose couldn't see a single similarity, which was probably just as well.

The mortal game looked terribly confusing and dull. Surely the faery version would be more entertaining, at the very least.

"Come now, Rose. I hope you've recovered your strength, for we must be swift!" Beatrice took her elbow and pulled her toward a hole in the maze. Seconds later, the rest of the company scattered like seeds from a farmer's hand, flying in different directions.

The game was on, and Beatrice was a determined player. She raced this way and that, toward some goal Rose couldn't fathom, but dared not question. She'd witnessed such intensity before—in Fey men during battle—and dared not intrude.

"Here, knock that blossom back the way we came. They won't be expecting it from your bat," Beatrice urged. Rose obeyed, batting the white flower toward the center of the maze and then hurrying to catch up.

"Now that we are alone, I must ask you something, cousin, and you must answer me truly," Beatrice said, not slowing her pace for a moment.

"Of course. I value honesty in myself and others," Rose said, already a bit out of breath. No matter how she'd strived to maintain her physical strength and speed, she was forced to take two steps for every one of Beatrice's and was feeling the strain after her long night.

"I believe that. Your thoughts last night were mostly in accordance with your words. At least more so than I've noticed in others under a watcher's spell."

"The spell you placed in my room?" Rose asked, tailing Beatrice as she made one sharp turn and then another. "We're both being honest, I assume?"

"Quite so. And yes, it was I." Beatrice batted a red

flower over her shoulder, in the general direction of the maze's center. Before Rose could ask if they were to strike the red flowers as well as the white, her cousin explained. "That was Marie Theresa's flower. I can't abide her, can you?"

"I can't say I know who she is. So many introductions were made I'm afraid I can't remember—"

"Well, you must strive to remember if you hope to survive your visit here at court." Beatrice suddenly stopped dead and turned. Rose barely managed to avoid slamming into her. "Marie Therese is third in line to the throne after you. She is an ambitious, inbred cow who can claim ties to both the Seelie court and the throne of the Fey de la Nuit. She is the only Seelie royal who can boast black Fey heritage—if you consider such a thing something to boast about—and that makes her very, very dangerous."

"Why are you telling me this?" Rose didn't like the place Beatrice has chosen for their little talk. It was an isolated corner of the maze, one that looked far more neglected than the rest of the garden. Vines grew from the hedge walls, and beneath their feet weeds burst through the river stones the gardeners had scattered upon the path. It was a fine place for an ambush. Her instincts screamed for her to draw her sword.

"I saw you last night," Beatrice said, her voice hushed as if she feared being overheard, though they were far, far away from the other women. The screams and laughter had faded as she and Beatrice ran, until now she could hear them not at all. "When the watcher spell was broken, I came to see whether you had broken it yourself or had help in the matter. I hoped to gain a better understanding of your control over your magic."

"And?" Rose asked, refusing to answer her cousin's unspoken question.

"And I saw the beast that pursued you." Beatrice's eyes clouded with genuine fear. "It was indeed made of shadow as you said, but seemed very solid as it took you to the ground."

"It was you who alerted Grandfather to my where-abouts?"

"No, a guard found you on the floor while he was chasing after the other beast, the one who killed Un-cle Henry."

"So you left me to die." It took everything within her to keep from drawing her sword. Surely this woman was as much a monster as any creature she had slain.

"I was going to alert the court, but when I returned to the banquet hall Uncle Henry was being torn apart. By the time the creature fled, I assumed it was too late for you to be saved and didn't wish to be blamed for your death. Grandfather is eager to find the one re-sponsible for these murders, and has a habit of seek-ing vengeance first and justice never."

As loathe as she was to admit it, Rose could almost understand the other woman's reasoning. "I've heard some say it is the king himself who is responsible."

"If that is so, then we are both damned," Beatrice said, a haunted note in her voice. "And I will be the next to the slaughter."

"You have yet to tell me why we're having this con-versation, Beatrice."

"You and your men were presumed to be the king's chief suspects. Before you arrived yesterday, there were bets placed as to how long each of you would live. Now it seems the winds have shifted, and the stink of fear drifts through the court as we wonder who will be next to suffer the king's wrath." She turned in a slow circle, searching the blue sky for some unseen danger. "I have come to believe you are innocent of these murders, but there are those who say you poisoned yourself to escape suspicion. The rumor will eventually reach the ears of the king and you'll want to be prepared."

"Thank you," Rose said, still hesitant to believe that Beatrice was an ally, but unable to deny that her information would prove useful. "If there's anything I can do—"

"I think it best for us to bond together for the sake of our lives, but we are not friends, cousin, let me make that abundantly clear. If we both survive to see this beast who hunts our family slain, I will be quite happy to never see your face at court again. I will rule the Seelie eventually, and you will not be welcome when I am queen. Half-breeds are abominations who should never be conceived in the first place, and your sordid history shames our family name."

Rose almost smiled. It was strangely refreshing to hear someone speak her mind so frankly. "I don't agree, but I assure you I have no desire to remain at court a second longer than necessary. I wish only to return to my country and live out my days in the human world."

"Excellent, then we may get along better than I'd hoped." Beatrice thrust her arm into the air and muttered a few words in ancient Fey beneath her breath. Two red roses came flying toward them a second later. Beatrice easily caught them in her massive fist. "Here, take yours and follow me. We shall continue to win this game while I share with you my plan to preserve our lives."

Rose followed the taller woman, already developing a few plans of her own.

CHAPTER TEN

Rose left her room early that evening, hoping to find Gareth still in his chambers and make some suitable excuse as to why he should precede her down to the entertainment before dinner. But her husband was not in his room, nor had he been there all afternoon, according to the valet she encountered in the hall. The servant had been charged with helping several of the less influential male guests dress and was rather harried, but insisted he hadn't seen Lord Shenley since shortly after breakfast that morning.

So Rose was spared the task of ridding herself of her usually attentive husband, but found the bit of luck made her uneasy. After all, Gareth had been adamantly opposed to her leaving his side even to play games in the garden, and had insisted she seek him out as soon as the game of cricket was over.

But she'd been late to luncheon after stopping by her room to change and had therefore been one of the last to learn that the meal had been moved outdoors, leaving no time to seek Gareth out. Seeing as the sun was still high in the sky, her vampire husband was, of course, nowhere to be found on the brightly colored blankets dotting the great lawn.

Unfortunately, the same could not be said of Ambrose.

Mimsy had called Rose over to join her, Elsa, and Ambrose on their blanket, repeating her loud summons so many times Rose could not pretend she hadn't heard the girl. She had passed the meal in a state of supreme agitation as Mimsy prattled on about the unfairness of losing at garden cricket, Elsa and Ambrose exchanged flirtations, and she and Ambrose avoided saying anything at all to each other.

She was beginning to suspect Ambrose was content to ignore her until the conclusion of their visit when he pressed a small square of paper into her hand. It was a note asking her to meet him in the hothouse a half hour before the evening entertainment, for he had information he must share in private.

Now the time for that meeting was at hand, and Rose's stomach was full of knots.

Pushing aside her misgivings, she crept quietly down the stairs, grateful for the sea-blue gown Elsa had loaned her for the evening. Not only was the garment made of a lovely fabric that glistened like the surface of the ocean on a summer's day, it was also the softest thing she had ever worn. The skirts flowed straight to the ground from a set of gathers just beneath her breasts and made not a whisper of sound as she darted down the hall, just barely avoiding contact with a half dozen men and women bound for the throne room. The king had decreed they would dine and be entertained there until the entire banquet hall was redone by his favored designer from the Fey de la Nuit court in Paris.

He seemed to think a change of scenery would banish the horrid memory of what had occurred there, and perhaps he was correct. The Seelie certainly seemed to have recovered quite swiftly from the shock of the murder the night before. Already the manor was filled with laughter and gay conversation, and most hadn't even begun to partake of the faery mead the servants would serve during whatever diversion was planned for the evening.

The relentless cheeriness of the golden Fey made her rather ill, if truth be told.

Rose made her way past the ballroom where human servants were hard at work decorating for the festivities tomorrow night, doing her best not to think of Elsa dancing every dance in Ambrose's arms. Their courtship was none of her concern. She had her own husband to attend to . . . somewhere.

She would have to find Gareth as soon as her meeting with Ambrose was concluded. It was beginning to worry her that he had been so long from her side. After the shocking events of the night before, he'd seemed determined to protect her at all costs. That he was nowhere to be found made her wonder if some ill had befallen him.

Rose slipped out the door leading into the gardens and made a sharp left turn, circling around the outside of the massive estate, enjoying the stroll through the fading light. The spring evening was cool, but undeniably beautiful, and a part of her wished she could stay out in the garden until dinner was over and the rest of the Fey had gone to bed.

"I have become exceedingly fond of hiding," Rose whispered to the flowers that had dared to bloom so early in the season. What had become of the woman who fearlessly threw herself into the fray, who eagerly anticipated the next challenge?

Perhaps it was love that had weakened her, or perhaps it was simply the years that had done their work on her spirit. Despite the occasional longing for the days when she lived by the sword, she craved peace more than ever. Those bloodthirsty desires were simply the final cries of the scourge she had once been dying inside her. Her soul realized it was time for a new Rosemarie to be born.

Unfortunately, the birth of one's self proved harder than she had imagined. Hence the urge to hide from her many challenges, rather than face them or the transformations they would no doubt inspire. It would be so much easier if she knew what she would be when it all was finished, but then, who could know such a thing until the becoming was done?

Just past a grove of fruit trees flush with spring blossoms, the hothouse crouched at the bottom of a shallow dip in the land. The building was deliberately hidden from view and was not often visited by any but the king's servants. The Seelie cared more about enjoying what they were eating than exploring where their food had come from, so Rose had little fear of encountering any but Ambrose as she pushed open the door and stepped into the thick, muggy air.

Ignoring her speeding pulse, Rose searched the hothouse for some sign of the man she was to meet, admiring the loveliness of the place as the setting sun shone through the glass ceiling, casting the entire space in a cozy pink glow. Along one wall various rare and exotic flowers bloomed, while along the other fruits and vegetables not usually available in England in the spring grew with enthusiastic profusion. It was a rather romantic setting, she supposed, but not for a woman alone, or one destined to meet a man who was not her husband.

"You were followed." Ambrose's voice drew a startled sound from her throat. She spun around to see him standing inside the door she had just entered.

He was dressed for a formal evening in a suit of such deep green it was nearly black, with his long black hair flowing freely down around his shoulders. He looked even more handsome than he had that afternoon, and for a moment Rose knew her appreciation shone in her eyes before she shifted her gaze to the ground at her feet.

"Oh?" She was certain she should say more, but words had left her for the moment.

Struck dumb by a man's beauty, a man she had known for nearly one hundred years no less. She was a sad case indeed.

"It was naught but a curious young faerie hoping for an assignation with a Seelie princess, no doubt. I sent him on his way. Still, I'm surprised you didn't sense you were not alone."

Rose took a deep breath and blew it out through pursed lips. "I am surprised as well. I—" She turned back to the hothouse interior with a frustrated curse. "No, I'm not surprised, not at all. I haven't been myself."

The truth was out before she had time to think better of it, but she didn't regret it. No matter how much she dreaded this meeting, Ambrose had always been one she could turn to in times of trouble. Perhaps not for comfort, but always for sound advice.

"How so?" he asked, joining her beside the strawberry vines. Together they surveyed the bright, cheery fruit, both of them seeming to sense it would be easier to converse without looking at one another directly.

"I have been more inclined to fear, for myself and others. My first instinct is often to run rather than to fight, and I have been altogether more . . . feminine in my behavior."

"Heaven forbid." There was a hint of laughter in his voice that made her smile in spite of herself.

"I am a great appreciator of the various talents of the female race, but they have their weaknesses as well, weaknesses that before now I have never claimed as my own." Rose let her fingers roam over the plump berries, finally choosing one and plucking it from its vine. She rolled it between her fingertips, enjoying the texture—rough, like a cat's tongue. "Last night, as I ran from the beast that chased me, I called for help like a woman who had never faced death, not a trained killer who'd stared it in the face four dozen times or more."

"Perhaps you have grown a bit soft in our months in Myrdrean. It is nothing to be ashamed of," Ambrose said, his hand brushing hers as he reached for his own berry. "I rather enjoy the softness of women . . . and this new softness in you."

Rose's heart beat even faster and she was acutely aware of how close they were standing. There was no denying the spark that leapt between them, or the anxiety in her heart. She shouldn't have taken him into her confidence. It was madness to encourage any further intimacy between them. "Ambrose, I—"

"I have learned information I believe will prove useful," he said, cutting her off as if he sensed what she was about to say and would prevent the words from spilling from her lips. "There's a small group of Seelie who plot your death."

"Indeed?" she asked, rather cheered by the realization that learning her life was in danger soothed her nerves rather than jangled them.

"Indeed. And not your death only, but the deaths of all those who stand in the way of Marie Therese taking the Seelie throne and, if they have their way, reclaiming the Fey de la Nuit crown as well. You are of special interest to these assassins, however, as you also have ties to the thrones of both courts through your marriage. If my informant is correct, you will be their first victim."

"Beatrice warned me Marie Therese was an ambitious inbred cow," Rose said, biting into her strawberry with decided ferocity. Ambrose's laughter startled her into a smile, making a bit of juice run down her chin, which she swiped with the back of her hand. "Well, she did. Only this morning, in fact." His eyes lingered on her lips, making Rose wonder if there was still red on her face.

"So Beatrice befriended you? I would be wary of her friendship. It may prove as deadly as her contempt."

"She's already warned me I will not be welcome in her court when she is queen, due to my low and despicable birth, but I believe she will honor the bargain we struck while in the garden." Rose briefly explained Beatrice's plan for the two of them to meet later that evening and work a spell to determine who dared invade their dreams. "Beatrice has also suffered from the same sort of dreams as I had last night. She awoke two night's past with deep scratches down both of her legs as if a wild animal tore at her while she slept, and the doctor called to her room summoned a toxin from her blood. He was uncertain as to the nature of the poison, but I'd wager it was the same nightshade coaxed from my blood last eve."

Ambrose ate his berry in one bite, leaves and all, and chewed contemplatively. There was something incredibly sensual about his devouring of the fruit, something Rose did her best to ignore. "The spell to determine the location of your tormentor would require three victims of the curse, a triangle of power. Two would be insufficient."

"Well, perhaps—"

"And exactly how did she discover you were visited by such a dream? To my knowledge, neither Gareth nor I told a soul. Have you—"

"Of course not, but I'm certain she has her spies." Rose plucked another berry from the vine, a bit frustrated with Ambrose's obvious distrust of Beatrice and her own judgment. "I assure you, I don't believe my cousin wants the best for me and I am determined to proceed with caution, but when we spoke of the dreams I felt her fear. It is that fear that has driven her to find an ally in a relative she would prefer to pretend did not exist."

"Perhaps. Or perhaps this is a trap she has set to get you alone and defenseless. Her magic is strong. Once you've bonded to her for the spell, she could control you completely and use that control to send you walking into the nearest fireplace or—"

"Do you trust me not at all?" Rose threw the remains

of her berry back into the vines from whence it came. "Admittedly my instincts may not be what they once were, but the fact that I am alive when so many who hunted the tribe are dead is a testimony to my ability—"

"You were rarely alone in those days," Ambrose said, his dark brows arching over his silver eyes as he noted her stormy expression and yet chose to keep speaking. But then he had never been overly troubled by her anger. At times, he even seemed to enjoy it. "I was there to watch over you, to correct your mistakes."

Rose laughed. "Correct my mistakes?"

"Of which there were many."

"Goddess, you are the most pompous—"

"Perhaps, but at least I'm not a coward," he said, stepping closer, until only a few inches separated them. Rose's first instinct was to take an equal step back, but instead she stood firm and lifted her chin to look him straight in the eye.

"I thought you admired my new softness. Yet now you would criticize?"

"Your hesitance to engage in battle is not why you are a coward."

"I am no coward," she whispered, refusing to flinch when he leaned down, bringing his face so close she thought for a moment he meant to kiss her.

"Then why do you refuse to speak of last night?" His breath was warm on her lips and smelled lightly of tobacco and mint and . . . Ambrose. Simply Ambrose, the man who had intoxicated her from the moment they met. "At first I too thought it was a dream, but when I awoke—"

"Please, stop," Rose said, her hands coming to his

chest. She meant to push him away, but as soon as her palms were pressed against the solid heat of him, she wanted only to pull him closer. "I don't know what you're talking about."

"Don't lie to me. The smell of you was all over my skin," he said, his voice thick with a need that called to her own. "I could taste your kiss on my lips."

"And how would you know the taste of my kiss?" she asked, calling on her anger, gathering the strength to pull away. "The one kiss we shared, that night in Ecanthar's ballroom, took place in my mind. It was no better than a dream, no—"

"So you admit you dreamt of me last night?"

Rose sucked in a breath, cursing herself. "I said no such thing."

"You don't have to say it." He grasped her just below her shoulders and pulled her closer, his fingers digging into her arms until she winced. "I was still hard as stone when I awoke."

"Surely you aren't the first man to awaken in such a state." Her voice was breathless, belying her harsh tone. She could deny their meeting last night forever, but she could not deny how aware she was of his lips hovering above hers, of the hard planes of his body only inches away from her own.

"No," he said, a cruel smile on his face as he released her with one hand and reached into his pocket, pulling out a few strands of blond hair and holding them before her face. "And I am sure I am not the first man to awaken with golden strands of dream hair tangled in his fingers either. But that is much rarer I would think. Wouldn't you?"

Rose swallowed hard, knowing she had been caught,

but a perverse part of her still praying he would let the matter go if she denied it vehemently enough. "Perhaps it is Elsa's hair. You certainly seem to long to run your fingers through—"

"And perhaps it was the slickness of Elsa's body still hot and wet upon my cock," he said, his anger clear in the way he emphasized every word. *Hot. Wet. Cock.* The violence in his tone should have frightened her, but it didn't. She didn't want to admit what it did to her to hear him say those words. "But I did not bury myself between Elsa's soft thighs last night, did I, Rose?"

His voice gentled, as did his hands, loosening his viselike grip on her arms to smooth down her back until they lingered just above the curve of her bottom. Rose stared at his chest, not daring to look into his eyes, not daring to speak, afraid of what she would do, what she would say.

"It wasn't Elsa's hands that fisted in my hair." His hands slid even lower, until he cupped her bottom in his wide palms. "Or Elsa's voice that broke as she begged me to enter her, to fill her where she ached." His grip abruptly tightened as he tugged her up the length of his body. She gasped, her feet no longer touching the floor as she was forced to twine her arms around his neck to steady herself. "Do you ache now, Rose? I confess I do." His lips were at her ear, his breath warm against her neck, his whisper snaking through her very blood, making her entire body burn. "I ache."

Rose's eyes closed and her breath rushed from between her lips as Ambrose pulled her hips more tightly to his, letting her feel the hard ridge of his erection through the thin fabric of her dress. Her breasts flattened against his chest and her hands tangled in his hair as a shudder of desire ran through her in spite of her-self.

He had never dared touch her in this fashion. Never. He had never dared to so much as touch her hand, and for a moment it didn't matter what he had done in the dream they shared. Rose was overcome with the thrill of finally feeling Ambrose holding her close, and like-wise consumed with shame.

She betrayed her husband every moment she stayed thus, not pulling away, not telling Ambrose they would never share more than they had in that dream.

When he spoke again, his whisper was as rife with pain as with need. "It is true, dreams are strange places. I vow I would not have behaved as I did last night if I'd thought it was not simply a dream like any other." He paused, and his mouth moved so close she could feel his lips against her neck. "Tell me you regret the things you said, the things we did, and I will never speak of this again. But I will have the truth, not whatever lies the human part of your heart insists you must tell."

It was the closest she had ever heard Ambrose come to begging. Even on that day in Myrdrean, when his eyes had pleaded for her to forgive him for keeping the secrets of their entwined pasts, he had never spoken words like this. His desire was for more than her body—though the hard length so hot against her spoke clearly of physical hunger—it was for her forgiveness, her care, for all the things she had given him so freely when they both believed they were safe within a dream.

But those were things she couldn't give, not here, not now. Not when she clung to her self-control by the thinnest of threads.

"I cannot give you what you seek," she whispered, her lips brushing against his tight jaw as she spoke and tears threatening to spill down her cheeks. "Forgive me, Ambrose, but this is no dream. I cannot forget my husband, nor do I wish to."

He pulled her closer for a moment, so close she was certain she could feel the ache of his heart echoed in her own flesh, before he set her slowly back on her feet.

Or perhaps that was her own heart twisting mournfully inside her.

He eyes trained resolutely on the floor, Ambrose stepped away and turned back to the strawberry plant they had attempted to make their distraction. They should have known better than to put their faith in a thing with fruit the color of sin itself—the color of the Mother's lips.

That thought made Rose long to tell Ambrose that Beatrice had also been visited by the Mother—though she had called herself by another name—and to ask him whether he thought that might be a clue to the identity of the one who cast the spell.

But she dared not speak. Pain and regret hung in the air between them, thicker than the sweet fragrance of the flowers blooming not far away.

Besides, if she asked him about the Mother, she would also have to confess that she, or whoever was invading her dreams, wanted the pair of them wed. Though it was something she was certain Ambrose should know, she couldn't bring herself to speak of it. Not now. Not yet.

"This did not proceed as I'd hoped," Ambrose said, his voice once more under control, so much so that he sounded as if he spoke of losing at a game of darts.

"But we have still have had a most beneficial meeting." He turned back to her, his eyes cold and guarded, not a hint of affection or hurt in their silver depths. "We have confirmed that we were both bespelled last eve, and I can therefore aid you and Princess Beatrice in your work tonight. I will speak with her myself and arrange to serve as the third in the spell."

"Very well," Rose said, wishing there was some way to refuse him. "We plan to meet in the banquet hall when the clock strikes two."

He frowned. "You can't be certain you'll live until then. Your uncle was killed as he took a second helping of dessert." His tone was still so dispassionate, as if he spoke of the weather, not the death of a woman he'd held in his arms a moment before. "I brought you a journeying stone." He pulled the bauble from his pocket and thrust it into her hand. "You should have been wearing one since the moment we last left London. Do you remember how to—"

"Yes," Rose said, continuing when it became obvious Ambrose expected more. "I clasp the stone in one hand and trace the runes of liberation with the other. It should transport me to the lower Fey realms, to the villages, I believe you said?"

Ambrose nodded. "Even being a quarter Fey is enough to take you there, though the higher lands will remain closed to you. Of course, I'm certain Gareth has apprised you of that fact, as he's seemed rather eager to journey to Faerie himself of late."

Rose said nothing. She had made the mistake of asking Ambrose if Ecanthar's claims that Gareth would perish if he did not visit the Fey lands before his two hundredth birthday could be true. He had seriously doubted a half vampire would ever require a visit to

Fairie to ensure his survival. It was true their mother had perished after being denied entrance to the enchanted Fey lands when she was cast out, but she had been pure faerie, not a half-breed.

Still, Ambrose seemed rather pleased by the idea that Gareth may have deceived her and that his brother's life could be in danger.

"Use the stone at the first sign of danger. Do not wait to see if you can fight this beast. I saw it last night, it moves faster than anything I have ever encountered."

"I will. As I said, I have little difficulty running from a fight in recent days."

Ambrose nodded and turned to go, stopping only when he reached the door to the indoor garden. "You will tell your husband of this meeting?" he asked, not turning to face her.

Rose sighed, realizing she should feel obligated to confess all to Gareth, but for some reason . . . she did not. "No. It would only hurt him, and it won't happen again."

"No, it will not." And then he was gone and she was alone with the flowers and the fruit and a bellyful of regret.

CHAPTER ELEVEN

The first person Rose saw upon returning to the manor was Gareth himself. He was standing at the entrance to the ballroom, watching the servants continue their preparations for the ball with a pensive look. Though she had been eager to see her husband only a short time ago, now she longed to flee back into the garden before he saw her.

Instead, she forced a smile and waved.

"There you are. I have been looking everywhere. I was worried something had happened." All the words were true, but for some reason they came out sounding like lies.

Thankfully Gareth did not seem to notice. He turned to her, a wide smile on his own handsome face. "Didn't mean to worry you, sweet. I got lost in a book and time escaped me. I assume you passed the afternoon in an entertaining fashion?"

"Lost in a book?" Rose asked, a frown furrowing

her brow. "But I looked for you in the library. I was trying to make mental contact all afternoon."

"Ahh, well, you've caught me." He grinned that rakish grin she had seen on so few occasions of late, then offered her his arm. "There may have been more napping than reading accomplished during my time there. It's your grandfather's fault for making the sofas entirely too comfortable."

"I'll be certain to advise him to replace them with some firm-backed chairs," she said, allowing Gareth to guide her toward the throne room, ignoring the odd feeling that her husband was hiding something.

It was *she* who was hiding things, after all, and the suspicion that Gareth was being dishonest was most likely a product of her own mind. What better way to ease the guilt one felt over her own indiscretions than to imagine someone else to be equally steeped in deception?

"I heard your team was the victor in this morning's game. Congratulations," Gareth said. "You must be eagerly anticipating being served by the members of the losing team."

"Actually, I would have preferred to be among the losers." Rose sighed, vaguely troubled by the fact that Gareth stared straight ahead rather than turning to look at her as he usually did. "At least then I could be certain my food wasn't laced with poison."

Guilt raised its ugly head once more. She hadn't told Gareth about her chat with Beatrice or that she felt certain it was the shadow monster that had poisoned them both, not something slipped into her food. She had intended to tell him this afternoon, but now it seemed better to keep the truth to herself. If she was to keep

Gareth ignorant of the dream she had shared with Ambrose, she couldn't risk him accompanying her to her secret meeting tonight.

Which meant she would have to find some way to convince him to sleep in his own room and not bed down in her chamber. It wouldn't be easy, especially considering her new rooms were decidedly lavish in comparison to his small apartment, and he obviously felt a husbandly duty to watch over her as she slept.

"Don't worry, sweet. I have a brilliant plan. We shall exchange plates. I've already dined twice today and find I have little appetite for solid fare."

He'd dined twice, had he? Normally the thought would make a wave of jealousy rise within her, but not this evening. She was in no position to be jealous of Gareth's food after what she'd done. Not to mention all she planned to do. Her lies for this evening were not all told.

"Brilliant, though I must admit I've not much of an appetite myself." She brought her hand to her head, rubbing her fingertips into her temples. "I've had a headache threatening all day and fear it is only getting worse. I may be forced to retire early for a second night in a row."

"Just say the word and I will make our excuses." He patted her hand in an absentminded fashion, his eyes still searching the hall ahead of them for something or someone, though what or who, Rose couldn't imagine. He knew no one here at court. Did he?

"It would probably be best if I slept alone tonight. With this headache I would be poor company and it's silly for you to go to bed so early on my account. After all, it rather goes against your nature."

"I don't mind at all, Rose. I want you to be safe."

"My new room is secure and the court doctor has given me a powder he assures me will keep away troubling dreams. I am certain I'll be safe enough on my own." They turned the last corner before the entrance to the throne room. "Please, you should stay and enjoy yourself and keep watch on the assembled company. Then you can inform me of all I missed over breakfast."

"If you're certain . . ." His words trailed away as he seemed to spot whatever it was he had been looking for. "Save me a seat beside you, love, I'll join you in just a moment."

Without waiting for her response, Gareth released her arm and hurried off into the crowd. Rose had assumed she'd be late to the entertainment after her meeting with Ambrose, but apparently tardiness was the mode for the Seelie court. The press of bodies hurrying to find seats upon the cushions spread before the stage was a bit overwhelming.

But not so overwhelming that she couldn't catch a glimpse of blond curls nodding at Gareth before both he and his mystery woman vanished from sight.

Perhaps she was not the only one testing the boundaries of her marriage. The thought made her stomach burn and she tasted again the earthy sweetness of the strawberry she had stolen from the king's hothouse.

How could this be? Gareth had seemed so sincere in his devotion. All three months of it.

Rose let herself be carried along on the tide of Fey bodies—all so much taller than she—toward the stage. Had she been a fool to think her wedding could be a true lifelong love match? The betrothal between their two families had been arranged without their knowledge, let alone their consent, and she herself had been tempted . . .

"Tempted, but I didn't succumb, at least not knowingly," she muttered beneath her breath, certain her expression was far stormier than a performance of *A Midsummer Night's Dream* actually warranted.

Though she *was* dreadfully tired of Shakespeare. Was she the only being alive—human or Fey—who thought the poet tiresome? For all his grand emotion and attempts at comedy, he still seemed to be a man overly impressed with his own wit.

Much like another man she could name.

She turned back to the doorway at the sound of Gareth's laughter, but could no longer see her husband. All she could see was the giant steel doors swinging shut behind the last of the faeries streaming into the throne room—a precaution the king had insisted upon to keep the Seelie merriment from being interrupted by beasts hungry for royal blood. Until the end of the entertainment, when the doors would once again open to allow stragglers in to dine, there would be no one coming in or going out.

And her husband had just disappeared with another woman. Even if she were an admirer of the bard, Rose knew she would not be laughing at his clever words tonight.

"I DON'T SEE why I must wear this ridiculous thing," Mimsy said, somehow managing to flounce toward the rows of tables arranged before the king's throne despite her injury. "I look a positive toad."

"You do not resemble a toad in the slightest. The

green actually looks lovely with your complexion. Not many women could say the same." Rose found the table where she and Gareth had been seated for breakfast, but her husband was still nowhere to be seen. The play had concluded nearly a half hour past and the doors been reopened, but if he did not hurry they would close again before he made his way inside.

"Well I feel like a toad, no matter how I look." Mimsy leaned down to claw at her legs through the bright green material of her servant's dress. "I vow these petticoats are made of sackcloth. I have never felt anything so horrid. I shall have a rash before the evening is through."

"You are simply too accustomed to wearing silk," Elsa said, appearing at Mimsy's other side, slightly out of breath. Her cousin was forever dashing here and there.

It made Rose wonder what obligations kept her so terribly occupied. There wasn't a single other lady of the court who seemed to have anything more pressing to take care of than deciding whether she would pass the afternoon playing the harp or dancing through the trees surrounding Manor High. Even the king's advisors had far more leisure time than the busy Elsa.

"Yes, I am quite spoiled and prefer to remain that way." Mimsy stuck her pert, upturned nose in the air and added a bit of a bounce to her flounce. "I shall never forgive Beatrice for this."

"Ah, to be nineteen again," Elsa said, catching Rose's eye and lifting her gaze toward the heavens. "I wouldn't go back again for all the world. It's a time when passions run entirely too high. Wouldn't you agree, cousin?"

"I honestly wouldn't know," Rose said. "I slept through my nineteenth birthday, and when I awoke my passions rather justifiably ran toward rage and vengeance."

"Well, of course. Quite so." Elsa looked uncomfortable.

It was the response Rose had intended, but for some reason she still felt dissatisfied. A part of her admired her sweet, helpful cousin, the only lady in court who had truly attempted to befriend her, but the other part of her did not care for the faerie at all. It was probably only jealousy over Elsa's obvious interest in Ambrose, but Rose was still grateful she would be spared the other woman's company during dinner tonight.

Elsa was also dressed in a green servant's uniform and would be busy tending to the needs of the ladies who had won the game of garden cricket.

"Rose, you will take an extra bun or two, won't you?" Mimsy asked, as if she hadn't noticed the awkward silence between Rose and Elsa. "I'm famished, and if we are truly only to have what food we are passed from the victors' plates, I fear I will starve to death. Beatrice and Marie Therese will not think to save anything for their hungry slaves."

"I will certainly save food for both of you, if you're sure you trust what will be placed upon my plate. After all, I was poisoned last night, Mimsy," Rose said, rather amused at the young faerie's obvious misery.

No matter what she'd said to Elsa, she could completely understand her cousin's angst. She remembered the days when being forced to study French rather than be allowed to run wild with her brother through the Myrdrean woods was simply the most tragic thing in the entire world. She would not be that girl again for anything, even if it would spare her the suffering she had endured. She enjoyed the perspective she had gained in her long life, and relished being a woman rather than a girl.

The thought made Rose hopeful that she might also relish this new person she was becoming, this creature whose first instinct was not to reach for her sword.

"Oh pish, I'm not at all worried. You weren't poisoned, at least your food wasn't," Mimsy said, the surety in her voice striking Rose as strange.

"You sound awfully certain. Do you have some knowledge you haven't shared with Rose?" Elsa asked, a concerned look on her face. "If so, you must tell us at once. Her life could depend upon it."

"No, I have no special knowledge." Mimsy shrugged. "But none of the servants fell ill last night, and they certainly would have if Rose's plate had been poisoned. She scarcely touched any of her food, and you know how the servants are. They would rather steal goodies from our table than eat whatever Cook makes for them. You remember the time my chambermaid took ill after stealing my old beef during my last visit, don't you, Elsa? She turned that terrible shade of greenish white and then clutched at her throat, her tongue lolling out of her skull like a—"

"I do, though I'd rather not discuss it in such detail, Mim." Elsa looked a little green herself.

"That's very clever of you, Mimsy," Rose said, meaning every word.

It was rather amazing the things this girl noticed, and even more amazing she herself had not thought to check and see if any servants had taken ill. She had spent several months posing as a young page in the home of a wealthy ogre in Venice and had done her share of pilfering from the plates of the more well fed among the household.

"You really think so?" Mimsy's round face positively beamed with pleasure.

"I do."

"Mother says I am by far the most foolish child she has ever had the misfortune to be entrusted with raising." She laughed, obviously pleased with her ability to torment her mother. "She despairs of me ever finding a man willing to endure my frivolity, even if my dowry is larger than any other Seelie Fey in her first one hundred years."

"Well, I think your mother may be forced to reconsider her opinion. I'll be certain to tell her what a help your keen observations have been to me in the few days since I have arrived at court."

"Thank you, Rose!" Mimsy hugged her impulsively, and for a moment Rose was engulfed by the taller girl's ample bosom. "You are just the dearest little thing."

"So happy to see you making friends here at court, Rosemarie." Stephen de Feu Vert's voice was the only thing Rose had witnessed thus far that was capable of wiping all expression from Mimsy's face. In fact, the girl was pale and solemn as she released Rose and sank into a deep curtsy.

The king looked quite grand this evening in an elaborate gold robe shot through with ribbons of red the same color as his auburn hair. The robe emphasized his great height and the broadness of his shoulders, managing to make his giant skull seem almost proportional to his body. Almost.

Rose thanked the Goddess she was no longer under the watcher spell. It would do her no good to have the king realize she found the sheer size of his head intensely disturbing.

"The Fey style suits you. I can't say I've ever seen you look lovelier." He smiled benevolently, obviously pleased with the offspring of his offspring this evening.

"Thank you, Grandfather." Rose curtsied as well, though not as deeply as Elsa or Mimsy. Ambrose had been certain to impress upon her that as a princess of the court, she should never dip lower than any woman aside from Beatrice, who was ahead of her in line to the throne. "And thank you for all you did last night. Without your aid I surely would have passed into the Summerland."

The king's smile vanished, and Rose cursed herself for bringing up the unpleasantness of the night before. She should know better than to introduce a fretful subject to the king of joy and pleasure.

"That is precisely why I must have words with you, dear. I am glad you spoke of it or I might have forgotten. This old mind isn't what it once was."

Of course. And her eyes were no longer the same shade of blue.

The old fox's mind was as sharp as the blades used to harvest wheat in his abundant fields. What was he about that he would have her think him a doddering old man?

"If you will excuse us." The king didn't wait for Mimsy and Elsa to murmur their assent; he simply took Rose firmly by the hand and led her toward the raised dais where his throne and the presently unoccupied throne of the Fey queen sat.

He hadn't remarried since her Uncle Seamus and

Henry's mother died nearly four hundred years before. Some said he still grieved the loss of his one true love, while the more pragmatic swore the king had simply learned he did not like sharing his rule with anyone, even a queen who was given very little power.

Rose did not know enough of court history to offer her own opinion, and at the moment couldn't seem to form a clear thought at all. All she knew was that she hadn't felt so very young and small since she was a child not yet big enough to ride her pony without the groom at her side. Her grandfather's hand did not merely engulf hers, it consumed it. Her small, sweating palm was completely surrounded by his warm dry flesh, as if it had been swallowed whole and was now in the belly of the beast.

It was all she could manage not to tear her hand free. The sensation was too similar to her dreams of the Mother, in which she was consumed by the ancient creature.

"Sit next to me, Rose." Stephen gestured to the smaller throne—thankfully releasing her hand to do so—and relaxed into his own, much larger seat. Immediately servants surrounded him, arranging his robes, smoothing his long hair behind his shoulders, and fetching him a great goblet of faery mead. "Fetch my granddaughter mead as well, a smaller glass, for she is a wee thing."

As if the attendants could not see for themselves her size. Even compared to the human servants in residence at Manor High, Rose was petite. Though she had been small her entire life, she still loathed hearing others discuss the fact, so it was with a rather sour expression she accepted her glass from the servant at her elbow.

"I would like to discuss your marriage. Or rather this farce you insist is a marriage."

Rose's expression grew sourer still. "Pardon me, Grandfather, but I thought you wished to discuss my poisoning last eve."

"Yes, I do. I believe . . ." He paused, as if he were an actor giving a dramatic speech and knew an entire audience hung on his every word.

Rose cast a quick glance toward the tables at their feet, realizing that at least the first several rows of seats very likely *were* hanging on the king's every word.

"I believe the two matters are connected," he finished, narrowing his eyes at her over the rim of his glass as he took a great swallow.

In one gulp he consumed more than enough to have her completely intoxicated. Faery mead was not only one of the sweetest drinks on earth, but also one of the most potent.

"My Lord?" Rose asked, knowing her confusion was clear on her face.

Stephen lowered his cup and explained in the slow, tolerant tone one employed when speaking to very small children. "I believe your husband is the one who slipped that deadly nightshade into your food. He means to have you dead."

"I don't understand. How did you come to this conclusion?" Rose did her best to rein in her anger. It would serve neither her nor Gareth's cause for her to offend her grandfather, but what he suggested was ludicrous. "My husband is my greatest protector and champion. We are—"

"You are wrong, Rosemarie. I am your family and your king. It is I who am your protector, and you would be wise not to forget that truth."

She nodded, shivering at the unspoken threat in his words. If she were to forget, he would be more than willing to provide a painful reminder.

"Of course, Your Majesty. Forgive me," Rose said, unable to keep from thinking of the day she had first met this "protector" seated next to her, the day he had been all too willing to turn her over to men who wished her dead.

"You are forgiven." He held out his hand and Rose kissed it obediently.

"Thank you, Grandfather. But I would beg you to believe that my husband and I are a love match, though our marriage was arranged so many years ago by our parents."

"No marriage was arranged between you and a bloodman." The king's scowl smothered all the chatter and laughter in the room. When the king of joy and mirth was displeased, it was a displeasure felt throughout the Fey world. "You were meant to wed Ambrose Minuit, a man with ties to the Fey de la Nuit throne. Though his mother was an outcast, his father is one of the finest men on the high council."

The king leaned closer, so close Rose could see the beads of mead clinging to his beard, and continued in a softer voice. "He will lead the council one day very soon, and on that day he will have the power to decide whether the faeries of the night shall keep to this foolish new method of rule by the many, or return the rightful power of the monarchy to their people. On that day you could very well be queen, for I have it on good authority that the elder Master Minuit does not wish to see the council continue or to rule in his deceased wife's stead, but will instead pass the crown to his eldest son."

She took a sip of her mead, hoping the cup would hide her troubled expression. Ambrose had said nothing of this, even when he had warned her and Gareth of the political implications of their marriage the day they sailed into London's harbor. Perhaps he knew nothing of his father's plans, but then, perhaps he did. And perhaps he wished for a wife with connections to the Seelie court.

Not that it mattered what Ambrose or her grandfather wished. She was a married woman, and had no intention of being bullied into foreswearing her vows.

"I shall not be queen," Rose said, striving for a soft, deferential tone even while she hoped she made her resolve clear. "The Fey de la Nuit would not wish to be ruled by a king whose wife had tainted blood. And whether it pleases you or not, Ambrose is not my husband. Gareth is my husband by law and by choice, and I will remain his wife."

"Even if he's tried to kill you? Use your common sense, girl."

"Grandfather, please." Rose felt a leap of fear in her chest as she watched Stephen's expression grow darker still. "If Gareth wanted me dead, why would he wait until we arrived here, with my dear family here to protect and preserve my life? Would he not have simply smothered me in my sleep while we were still in Myrdrean? Or found some other way to do away with me in a fashion no one would guess was foul play?"

For a moment, Rose thought the king had seen the logic in her argument, but his next words offered no comfort.

"He is a fool, no doubt, and hoped to cast the blame upon one of my court." He took another contemplative drink of his mead as he turned to survey the faeries seated before him, all of them striving to appear merry for his sake. "I have no doubt I am correct in this matter. I have been visited by the spirits of my ancestors in a dream, and they have warned me that the bloodman is a disease that will steal first my granddaughter's life and then my own. They insist I shall not suffer the princess's husband to live."

"But Gareth is no match for your strength and he is very ill, I cannot see how he could—"

"Your duty is not to see, child. Your duty is to obey." Her grandfather turned back to her, his resolve clear in his ancient eyes. "I will tell you what must be done and you shall do it."

"Please, sire. I swore to obey my husband on the day of our marriage." Rose was begging now, but she couldn't help herself. This conversation had spiraled toward lunacy all too quickly, and she felt as if the very ground were being pulled from beneath her feet. "I must honor my vows to him or I—"

"You must prepare yourself to don widow's weeds, Rosemarie. That is all you *must* do."

Rose felt the weight of his words crash down upon chest, knocking the breath from her body.

"Please, Grandfather." There were tears in her eyes as she threw herself at his feet. Her glass clattered to the ground, mead spilling across the shining gold tile. She could feel every eye in the court turn to stare, but she didn't care, could not bring herself to care about anything but forcing the king to revoke his death sentence. "He is not guilty of any crime against me or this court. I swear it was a beast made of shadow that poisoned my blood. Ask Princess Beatrice if it is not so.

She saw the beast last night and was even attacked by the creature in her dreams."

The king simply stared at her, not a shred of curiosity or pity in his eyes.

"Please, I swear I am telling the truth. If you would only call her to us now, I am certain she will clear my husband's name." She was sobbing, her words nearly unintelligible through her tears. "Please, Your Majesty."

"If what you say is true, I can only assume the vampire poisoned Princess Beatrice as well. I should have been wiser than to seat such a monster so close to the heirs to my throne."

Rose scrambled to her feet, her tears drying as she backed slowly away from the king.

"Return to your seat and eat in peace, Rose. The vampire is being dealt with and will not threaten your life again."

A strangled laugh burst from her throat. Only a man with an ancient, cruel heart could order a wife to eat heartily while she knew her husband was being murdered somewhere within the very same walls. Frantically she searched the room for an avenue of escape. She must get to Gareth and they must both flee this wicked place.

But the great doors were tightly closed with faerie guards pacing before them, and there wasn't another entrance to the room. It had been designed as a fortress to protect the king. There weren't even any windows near the ground, only two great panes of glass near the ceiling, glass that looked as thick and impenetrable as the steel door itself.

Still, she must try to break through. It was her only chance. Gareth's only chance.

Flexing that newly discovered muscle that freed her wings from her body, spiriting them through both flesh and clothes, Rose flew toward the ceiling. She had her faery sword drawn and was nearly to the glass before she heard the guards take flight behind her. They would be upon her within moments. She would have only a few seconds to shatter the glass.

As she swung her sword with all her might, Rose prayed the enchanted steel would once more serve her well. Her husband's life depended upon it.

CHAPTER TWELVE

Rose burst through the thick glass like a bullet, sending razor-sharp shards raining down upon the men behind her. She heard a man's shout and then a frightened gasp rise from the court at large, but didn't dare pause to see the consequences of her actions.

There was no time to spare.

Flying as swiftly as her small wings could carry her, she circled back toward the roof of the mansion. A glance over her shoulder revealed two Seelie warriors in pursuit, their swords drawn and their palms already glowing with the contained force of their magic. They would cast a spell upon her soon, and then there would be no salvation for her or her husband. Her own magic, even when bolstered by Ambrose's energy, was no match for warriors handpicked by the king for their strength and power.

She needed to be out of their sight, and quickly.

Before she had the chance to second guess the instinct, Rose flew straight into the chimney of a nearby fireplace. The space was a tight fit even for her relatively small frame, so she was certain the men could not follow. She had no idea where in the great house she would emerge once she reached the bottom, but thankfully the lack of smoke curling from the chimney top proved a trustworthy signal. The coals she landed upon were stone cold.

Unfortunately, the fire hurtling toward her from above wasn't.

Rose flung herself onto the floor just as the hearth burst into flame. The wretched guards had tried to burn her alive! The king must have given the order she was to be stopped at all costs, with no concern whether his granddaughter was returned to the throne room dead or alive.

"And so he proves once again he is my fiercest protector," Rose muttered as she leapt to her feet and surged toward the closed door of the small sitting room. It didn't look as if the chamber had been used in years, so she hoped the warriors would not know where she had landed.

A quick glance down the hall revealed she was still alone, but it wasn't a condition that would last for long. Her grandfather wanted Gareth dead, and she along with him if she dared choose her husband over her king. He had no doubt dispatched a goodly portion of his guard.

Despite her half-breed status, Rose knew the king would not make such a decision lightly. He must truly believe his ancestors had visited him while he slept, and that he would die if he did not slay Gareth.

A dream. A horrible certainty rose in her chest as

she slipped out the door and ran down the hall away from the throne room. She and Beatrice had both been victims of a spell that allowed someone to enter their dreams.

Could that same villain have invaded the dreams of the Seelie king, a man nearly as old as time itself? The very idea was terrifying. If the caster of the spell possessed that kind of power, it would be futile to struggle against it. If it could break through the mental walls of one of the oldest living supernaturals . . .

Rose couldn't even bring herself to carry the thought to its natural conclusion. It was too horrible to be believed, and for now she must concentrate on saving her husband's life. She would come to terms with the fact that it was more and more likely it was the true Mother who meddled in the future of the Seelie court *after* she and Gareth were safely away.

Though what place would be a safe haven from an all-powerful goddess-like creature, she could not say.

She raced down one candlelit hall and then another, instinctively turning toward the first room she had been given. If she were the king, and planning to have a man killed, she would do so in the least traveled corner of the estate. Though the king would not fear retribution for the murder, even he would not wish the children to see such a thing. And he would consider not only the little ones still in the nursery but also Fey with not quite two decades to their name, like Mimsy, children in need of protection.

Damn him, but he most likely considered her herself, a woman who had slept away eighty of her two hundred years of life, to be not much more than a child. But she was not a child and she would not sit meekly by and allow one she loved to be slain, no matter what man gave the order.

"This way. I hear a heartbeat too swift to be Fey." The deep voice was distant, but not nearly distant enough.

Curse her wretched heart and curse her foolish mind for consenting to bring Gareth here in the first place. She should have left him in London after learning of the vampire assassinations. This wasn't a safe time for a vampire to roam the faerie courts, even if that vampire was married to a Seelie princess and had faerie blood in his veins.

Realizing there was little need to keep her mind closed now that the guards knew her whereabouts, Rose let her shields collapse and reached out for her husband's thoughts with every last bit of her strength. She must make him hear her, no matter how far he might be.

Gareth! Please, where are you? Grandfather has ordered—

Rose! Goddess, Rose, hurry! His thoughts burst into her mind with a power born of pain and desperation. For a moment the connection between them was so intense that she could see through his eyes as if they were her own.

She was nearly too late. The guards —two, maybe three of them—had Gareth trapped in a dark, dusty room. He was already hurt, and blood flowed down his arms and onto the rocking horse he gripped in his hands like a weapon. His swords had been knocked to the floor and lay in a pile of blocks toppled over in the opposite corner.

He was in a nursery, or someplace where children

had once played, though not for some time by the looks of the tattered curtains. She ran faster, certain now that Gareth fought somewhere in the abandoned wing of Manor High. Within a few moments she would pass her old room, then surely she should be able to hear—

Rose! Gareth's cry rattled her very bones as she caught another glimpse through her husband's eyes. A Fey warrior crept ever closer, smiling as he lifted his sword over his head, his certainty that this would be the killing blow clear on his face.

Then suddenly the vision was gone and she was left frighteningly alone in her mind. "Gareth! Gareth!" She screamed his name as her wings once more burst through her flesh. Using her wings would weaken her more than using only her feet, but it wouldn't matter how strong she was if she arrived too late.

"There she is! Gryffud, use your bow!"

Rose risked a quick look over her shoulder to see three Fey warriors closing in on her with alarming speed. Their great wings were nearly twice the size of her own and they showed no sign of growing fatigued as they surged toward her, two with swords raised and the third stringing his bow with a black arrow.

Black arrows were composed of poison and designed to immobilize even a purebred Fey within seconds. Rose would be down on the floor before she had the chance to cast a final prayer to the Goddess, and have her head and hands severed from her body moments later—most likely while her eyes were still open to observe the blade descending upon her neck. Though she was only a quarter Fey, the warriors would not risk leaving the job unfinished.

Frantic, she began to weave back and forth as she

flew, refusing to give the man behind her an easy target. The first black arrow whizzed by her hip, just between wing and flesh, but she knew it was only a matter of time before the archer's arrow found its mark.

Rose! Gareth's voice, weaker this time, but at least he was still alive.

She wouldn't be able to say the same if she didn't find some way to delay the men behind her. Even if she managed to elude the black arrows until she reached Gareth's side, they would then be outnumbered five or six to two and surely perish regardless.

There was only one thing she could think of that might gain her a bit of time and distance from the king's brutes.

All that remained was to wait for the right moment. A glance behind her revealed the archer and the other two men drawing closer, and closer, until only a dozen feet or more separated them from their prey. But still Rose waited, knowing there would be only one chance for her scrap of a plan to work.

Closer and closer still, until she could see the different colors of their eyes and count the buttons upon their coats. One more second, two—watching the man with the bow pull it taut—three, four.

"Blast!" With a curse and a howl of pain, Rose hurled herself to the ground, landing on her back as she aimed her palms toward the ceiling. She slid along the aging carpet, the delicate tissue of her wings burning as it tore, but she refused to acknowledge the pain. Instead she concentrated every bit of her being on the golden magic within her and abandoned all the hard-won control she had gained in the past few months.

The explosion was immediate and impressive. The ceiling above the Fey crumbled down upon them as if a giant had taken his hammer to Manor High. And as long as Rose continued to channel her power through her hands, more rubble cascaded down, burying the men in the ancient stones. Finally, when the ceiling began to turn to dust, Rose shut off the power as best she could.

But even as she gained her feet and turned to run, she could feel the magic bubbling away inside her, eager to be free now that it had been given new liberty. Assuming she survived, she would have to petition Ambrose for aid in putting the golden power he had given her back under her control. Considering the frightfully large explosions caused whenever she relaxed that control—which *had* proved useful in the days when she and Ambrose were burying the hundreds of dead upon their return to Myrdrean—Rose didn't trust herself to put the magic to further use.

"To your left!" This time Gareth's cry was made with his mouth, not his mind. Just ahead a door stood ajar.

Rose drew her sword as she burst into the room, determined not to think about the ghastly odds of survival as she took in the two men who had her husband backed into a corner. Gareth swung at them, meeting each sweep of their swords with the battered rocking horse in his hands, but his time was nearly at an end. The men he fought surely realized that and were merely toying with him for their own entertainment, drawing out his death with sword and mace when they could have ended his life with magic a good time before.

These warriors were as highly trained as the ones

who had pursued her and had been in the business of ending lives for centuries. A quarter-faerie princess and a wounded half vampire were no match for them in physical strength or magic.

So we must use cunning. Fly to me, Rose, with your hands upon the stone.

Rose obeyed without hesitation, knowing the other men had no doubt heard Gareth's mental command as well. They had only a few seconds, maybe less, before the Fey warriors dispensed with formalities and dealt them both a killing blow.

Besides, Gareth was right. Flight was their only chance, and what better place to flee than into the lower Fey villages where so many thousands of half-breed faeries lived? They could disappear amid the multitudes and perhaps never be found. At the very least, they would have a few hours to plan their next move in the deadly chess game their lives had become.

One of the warriors reached for her as she flew by, but Rose twisted in the air, eluding his grasp. She crashed into Gareth and seconds later felt his arms wrap tightly around her waist. As far as she understood, physical connection was all that was required for her to pull another of Fey blood into Faerie along with her. So she didn't hesitate, gripping the stone tightly and tracing the runes of liberation with her other hand.

Tensing her muscles and tightening her grip on her sword, she steeled herself for what magic might come, not knowing at all what to expect. Though she had known of her Fey heritage for months, she hadn't yet made the journey to the enchanted lands that existed parallel to the human world . . .

And it looked like she wouldn't be making the journey this evening.

"Again, Rose. Try again!" Gareth urged, his arms still tight around her.

Rose frantically retraced the runes, paying special attention to each, ensuring she was precise and correct in each movement yet still . . . nothing.

The two warriors looked down upon them for a moment—one in confusion and one with obvious amusement—before lifting their swords above their heads once more.

"Wait! Goddess, don't you see what this means?"

"Ambrose," Rose gasped, his name as close to a prayer as anything she had ever uttered. She could safely say she had never been so happy to see the man. He stood just inside the doorway, his sword drawn, though he made no move to advance upon the two Seelie warriors.

"This is none of your affair, Master Minuit," said the man with the fire red hair and a scar on his cheek shaped like a crescent moon.

Of the two men charged with killing her husband, he was by far the more fearsome looking. The other, with his golden hair and cruel blue eyes, took too much pleasure in his work. He would be easier to kill than the passionless Fey who used both sword and mace with such ruthless precision. Rose hoped Ambrose would see that truth and take the scarred man's head first.

"If you don't disarm yourselves this instant I will kill you both," Ambrose said, his voice filled with enough menace to make a human man bleed, but neither faerie seemed intimidated. "You are charged with killing an innocent man. Once I explain to the king what has happened here, I am certain he will grant both Rosemarie and her husband a reprieve."

"Oh you're certain, are you?" The blond man all but sneered the question, obviously pleased to have the chance to lord his authority over an older, more powerful faerie. "Well, I am certain the king knows who he wants killed before he issues a command. Leave us or we'll see you charged with treason."

"Please, the king has been deceived. I'm sure of it," Rose said, hoping to draw attention to herself and give Ambrose the chance to rush the Seelie men.

But he only stood there, a strange sad look in his eyes. "Put your swords down. This is your last chance. You will look foolish if you continue this mission."

"I don't take orders from the black Fey, or a half-breed princess."

"She is not a half-breed. She is not Fey at all," Ambrose roared, the rage in his tone making the very walls tremble. "The journeying stone did not obey her command."

The two men only stared at him, their weapons not wavering an inch. If either of them were to step forward a pace or two, they would be in perfect position to slide their blades into Rose's heart and then into her husband behind her. Their lives were completely dependant upon Ambrose's power of persuasion.

"You saw her trace the ruins with your own eyes and yet still you are blind to the truth?" Ambrose asked. "She is not Fey. If she had a drop of faerie blood within her, the stone would have transported her and the vampire to Faerie, no matter that he is an exile and cannot command a stone with his own hands. I gave her the stone myself, you can be sure it's of the highest quality."

The hard warrior turned back to Rose with a grim expression on his face and after a long moment, let his sword and mace fall.

"No, Ackley. We have our orders, man!"

"Master Minuit is correct. We should share this news with the king before proceeding," Ackley said as he sheathed his blade.

"And give them the chance to escape? You're mad." The blond-haired warrior was clearly distressed to learn he wouldn't be killing anyone this eve—at least not in the next few moments—but nevertheless lowered his sword after a stern look from his fellow officer.

Rose knew she should be grateful their lives would be spared for the time being, but her mind couldn't seem to think of anything but Ambrose's words.

She wasn't Fey, not even the slightest bit. The realization made her entire body feel numb and cold, and she suddenly found it very difficult to pull herself to her feet. She leaned on Gareth's arm when he offered it, despite the fact that he was far worse off. He had been in a weakened state even before his battle and now bled freely from several wounds. His face was a ghastly shade of white, yet still he looked as if she were the one whose life might hang in the balance.

"You'll need to feed soon, or I fear for your health," Rose said, her lips strangely stiff, as if they had forgotten how to form words.

She wasn't Fey.

The horrible thought came again as she watched Gareth's lips move but couldn't seem to force her ears to understand his meaning. A second later his arms were no longer around her, but even the loss of his comforting touch couldn't penetrate the haze surrounding her mind.

Surely there must be some mistake. She *must* be a child of the Seelie court. If not . . .

"No," she mumbled as her sword fell to the ground, her fingers incapable of clinging to the hilt. If what Ambrose said was true, then she could not be her grandfather's heir, or her mother's child.

She was not her mother's child. She was not Rosemarie Edenburg. If that were true, then . . . who was she?

"Rosemarie? Come you . . . Stay . . ." Ambrose was in front of her now, his gray eyes filled with concern and fear and something else. Regret perhaps? Surely that was it. Regret, for thinking himself in love with a woman whose entire life was a lie.

"But what of my wings? How can I possess wings and not be at all Fey?" she asked, too cold inside for the tears pressing against the backs of her eyes to fall.

"I do not know."

"What sort of *thing* am I? What sort of strange creature?" Her voice broke with despair, but still no tears fell, which was probably for the best. She was dimly aware of the two Seelie warriors standing behind Ambrose, looking very uncomfortable to be witnessing such a moment. Surely they would reconsider taking her head if she dared to begin weeping.

"We shall discover the truth. I swear it to you," Ambrose said, gripping her arms as he had in the hothouse only a few hours before. Goddess, but that seemed like a lifetime ago, when she still had a family, a history. "But you must strengthen your resolve. You cannot face the king as you are now—and face him, we must."

"I . . . cannot." She shook her head slowly back and forth, preferring to stare at his chest rather than view his pitying expression. For surely he felt sorry for her now, whatever manner of thing she was.

"Rose, look at me. Look into my eyes." Slowly she obeyed, though it felt as if her head weighed a dozen stone. Once she met that silver gaze, however, a bit of that weight lifted. It wasn't pity she read in his eyes, but resolve.

When he spoke again, it was in a whisper so soft she was certain only she could hear it. "I will not leave you. I have been at your side nearly a hundred years, and I will not leave you now. I will be there beside you when you face the king."

"But what if—"

"There is no swaying me." He leaned closer, until his face was inches from hers. "I do not care what you are. No name anyone could give you could frighten or repulse me. I am bound to you, through magic and more."

She had never loved him more than she did at that moment. A part of her wanted nothing more than to throw her arms around his neck and hold on for dear life, but instead she stepped back and dropped her gaze to the floor, struggling to recover herself. Ambrose was right; she must prepare herself to face the king and her uncertain future.

Speaking of her future . . .

She had all but forgotten Gareth was in the room. It would do no good for her husband to see the look in her eyes, for she surely betrayed the divided nature of her heart with every glance.

Of all the people in the world, Gareth was perhaps the only one she trusted—besides Ambrose—to still care for her now that she was not the child of a king and queen or the granddaughter of the most powerful Seelie faerie in the world. She had seen into the depths of her husband and knew his love was not based on such earthly things. Besides, he was an earl in his own right and possessed sufficient finances to buy and sell her tiny country two times over.

"All right," she said finally, pleased to sound a bit more like herself. "Then we shall face the king."

Rose turned, seeking her husband behind her, but found him already across the room, hovering near the door. It was then she realized that perhaps she shouldn't have taken his unswerving loyalty for granted.

"Gareth?" Her fear and despair were clear in her voice. Surely she was wrong, and the expression on his face was not that of a man who felt nothing so much as . . . trapped.

"Yes, of course, sweet. We shall face him, we three together." His expression smoothed like linen under a hot iron, but it was too late. She had seen his panic. Gareth Barrows, the third earl of Shenley, was not merely distressed to learn his wife was not the woman he thought, he was positively sickened by the news.

CHAPTER THIRTEEN

May 21, 1750

It was nearly morning by the time their trunks were loaded onto their carriage and prepared for the journey back to London. As the groomsmen hitched the horses and Ambrose and Gareth attended to their final arrangements, Rose retreated behind the lavish Seelie stables.

It was the first moment she'd had alone since the shattering discovery the night before.

In the pale gray light of dawn, with the cool air seeping through her brown wool traveling dress and the road to Manor High winding calmly through the mist, it was hard to believe so much had changed. She still felt the same. Her skin was the same pale white flesh that had held her bones together for nearly two hundred years, her mind the same slightly addled place where thoughts continuously warred with one another for supremacy.

But her blood was a different matter altogether.

She couldn't guess the origins of the essence flowing through her veins, and neither could anyone else.

Even the king appeared baffled by the news that his granddaughter could not, in fact, *be* his granddaughter. He'd forced her to attempt the voyage to Faerie with no less than half a dozen journeying stones before he'd reluctantly admitted she was no kin to him, and therefore her husband no threat to his life or throne.

He'd bid the three of them a cordial farewell from his court, and offered them the everlasting friendship of the Seelie should they succeed in their quest to find the real Rosemarie Edenburg, the true princess of Myrdrean. Assuming she was still alive and well after all these years.

Not even Rose's name was hers to claim for certain. Not anymore. The realization still had the power to make her throat ache and her eyes sting. She had no family, no country, no birthright, no name, and perhaps soon . . . no husband.

Gareth had spoken no more than a dozen words to her since she'd risked her life to save his the night before and hadn't seemed overly troubled to hear the king muse that their marriage might, in fact, be invalid. If she was not Rosemarie Edenburg, then she was not the woman betrothed to one of Agatha Minuit's sons.

His kiss before leaving her to attend to his packing had been as sweet as ever, and he had professed his intention to do anything in his power to aid her in sorting out her past, but she was not convinced all would be as it had been between them. His energy was more troubled than she had ever felt it. So much so that, were she to awaken one morning a few days hence and discover Gareth had vanished, she would not be surprised.

If she were wrong, then she was not worthy of her good husband's love. If she were right, she was a blind, trusting fool who had been deceived to the depths of her very soul.

Neither option was terribly appealing.

"I am not too late, then. Good, I should have hated for you to leave without a proper farewell. This slinking off into the dawn is hardly proper now is it?"

Rose turned to see Beatrice easing around the corner of the stables, her delicate cream silk skirts gathered high in one hand to avoid being dragged through the mud. She looked a vision in the predawn light, her skin so pale and unearthly she seemed a marble statue come to life, or some ancient goddess of the moon.

Though not as ancient as the creature they might have located last night, if the events of the evening had taken a different course.

"Our meeting in the banquet hall," Rose said, cursing beneath her breath. She knew she shouldn't be surprised she had forgotten her appointment with the princess, but she was. No matter how fraught with danger and intrigue her life had been when she lived as executioner to the tribe, she had never failed to honor her social or supernatural engagements.

"Yes. I was rather distressed to find you absent until I heard of the great drama taking place in the throne room." Beatrice took a few more dainty steps, until she stood at Rose's side, directing her gaze out toward the pastures.

"Please forgive me."

Beatrice waved her hand, as if brushing Rose's concern from the air. "No matter. If you are not of faery blood there is a chance the spell would not have worked in any event." She paused, and Rose felt the other woman's curious gaze upon her but did not turn to look. It was easier to face the mist than another pair of delightfully scandalized Fey eyes. "It is true then? You are not Marionette's daughter?"

"Apparently not," Rose said, the words still cutting her to the core.

Of all the relationships in her life, she had treasured her affinity with her mother above all others. Marionette had been more than a mother, she had been a friend and kindred spirit. Her maman's goodness had comforted Rose in those times when she worried her soul grew perilously close to blackness. After all, surely she could not be beyond redemption when she had been born of such a truly good woman.

Now there was no such comfort to be had.

Beatrice shrugged in that frustratingly casual way only the French and the Fey had completely mastered. "Perhaps it is for the best. You will surely be spared many attempts on your life. Just this morning the girl who tests my food fell over dead from something a would-be assassin had slipped into my chocolate."

Rose said nothing, but sent up a silent prayer for the girl's soul. Such a low member of the golden court would not even warrant a funeral service. Her body would be burned and the next poor human girl of no family, whom no one would miss upon her death, would be brought in to take her place.

"Besides, now you have a great undiscovered world ahead of you. Who knows what delightful secrets you might uncover as you pursue this mystery to its conclusion?" The touch of Beatrice's fingers was surprising, but not as surprising as the tightly folded parchment she pressed into Rose's hand. "Surely you shall turn out to be something more interesting than a mostly mortal woman. Perhaps even something of sufficient interest to gain you an open invitation to my court when I rule the Seelie."

"Might I ask—"

"Do not speak of it. Slip it into your coat pocket and wait to read it until you are far away from Manor High and the reach of prying minds." She pointed one elegant finger out to the far pasture, as if drawing attention to the herd of cows ambling toward their pen for the morning milking. "Can you keep your mind shielded for the next few moments?"

"Yes," Rose said, sensing now was not the time to mince words. No matter what Ambrose thought of the princess or how unkind she had been since Rose's arrival, she truly believed Beatrice sought to aid her cause, as long as it aided her own in some way.

"The room I initially chose for you was once your grandmother's. She and your mother were exiled to that dreary little corner of the manor for their own protection soon after your mother's third birthday."

The princess's voice dropped to a whisper, as if she feared what ears might overhear her tale. "The wing was sealed off with a great brick wall and a magical barrier, and none but the king and a few trusted servants were allowed in or out. They said your grandmother eventually ran mad and begged to be released from her prison, but her request was denied by the king. She killed herself a few months later and your mother was sent to live with friends of the Seelie court in Paris. They were Fey de la Nuit, and well connected with the black faerie's high council. I believe your mother turned to them for aid again, some years later, after her father swore he couldn't lift the curse from her infant daughter. They are still living."

"Thank you." It was not a name or even a guaranteed source of information, but it was more than she'd had a moment ago. It was a place to start, a thread of hope to cling to as their carriage trundled toward London.

Beatrice did not acknowledge her thanks, only leaned closer and spoke even faster. Apparently their time was nearly at an end. "It was only a few years ago that the barriers were lifted. I believe the king thought to have the rooms redone for his latest mistress, but she fell from favor before the renovations were completed. I had hoped to cause my dear grandfather some degree of pain by housing you there. You are the very image of your grandmother, you see. The same blond hair and human delicacy the king so treasured for a time. But now I wonder . . ."

"That's hardly a wise decision, inciting the wrath of the king."

Beatrice smiled, a mirthless stretch of her lips that made her look every one of her hundreds of years. "If I were wise I would not live in this court, where even my own family can't be trusted not to slip a knife between my ribs. A part of me envies you. To be free of all this would be a blessing in a way."

Silence fell between them, punctuated only by the sound of the birds beginning their morning song and the snuffles of the horses awakening in the barn behind them. Comforting sounds, but they offered no solace today.

"You believe the rooms may hold some clue to my past?" Rose finally asked, when it seemed Beatrice would say no more. "How is that possible when no one has lived there since my grandmother passed away? My mother couldn't have been more than thirteen when she left the Seelie court, for she was married to my father not long after her fifteenth birthday."

"I never said it held a clue to your past, little Rose, but I believe the mirror in your first room may reveal a few interesting things about your *present*." She turned to go, picking her way delicately through the mud, tossing her words over her shoulder. "Ambrose disabled two of the spells I placed upon the object, but there was one he missed. Look into the mirror and trace the ruins of remembrance and you shall see what I saw last night, what your dear husband was about before his unfortunate encounter with the king's guard."

"Perhaps you could simply tell me this news yourself?"

Beatrice paused, and cast a glance back at Rose. "No, I think not. I prefer not to be the bearer of bad tidings when it can be avoided." For a moment her eyes softened and Rose could have sworn it was true empathy she read in the other woman's expression. "Be careful, my former cousin. I know not what darkness hunts you, but there is death in your future, I can feel it with every bit of magic within me. Whether it will be your own or one dear to you is the only thing that remains to be seen."

Rose watched the princess disappear into the mist still lingering in the garden, and marveled at the hollowness of her skin and bones. It was as if all the matter had been scooped away, leaving nothing but a terrible emptiness. She could not even seem to summon the trepidation usually associated with hearing words such as Beatrice had spoken.

In fact, she was remarkably calm, her heart beating at its usual steady pace, as she turned and hurried back toward Manor High, determined to make one last visit to the neglected wing of the mansion before taking her leave. If Gareth had played her false, she would prefer to know sooner rather than later. After all, it would be no easy task to take vengeance on one she loved, and she would need time to steel her heart for what must be done.

For if he had betrayed her . . .

Before they married she had teased him that it would be no small matter to do away with one vampire husband should he displease her—now she was not entirely sure the words had been spoken in jest.

ROSE ENCOUNTERED SURPRISINGLY few people on her way from the grand entrance hall to the abandoned wing she had called home her first hellish night at court. On a usual morning, there would have been a dozen or more faeries lounging in the lavish sitting room just to the right of the foyer.

The sideboard there was laden with a wide variety of fruits, bread, and cheeses, and was continuously refreshed by the busy human servants of the court. The Seelie were notoriously fond of a little something between meals, hence the popularity of the parlor and the gaming room just beyond, where the faeries fed upon the joy of the humans who played there.

This morning, however, only one young woman lingered in the sitting room, reclined on a plum-colored couch with a bowl of strawberries and fresh cream. It seemed the rest of the court had stayed abed later than usual. But then it was hardly any surprise after the night they'd had. It wasn't every evening the king tried to kill his son-in-law and his granddaughter who then turned out *not* to be his granddaughter after all.

Spying on the proceedings in the throne room would

have kept the majority of the Seelie alert until at least three, and the resulting gossip was worthy of another few hours of chatter over wine in the various master suites throughout the manor. In fact, Rose wouldn't be surprised to hear many were just now taking to their beds.

The result of the eventful night was a tomblike silence once she entered the portion of the great home containing the sleeping quarters of the court's many residents and guests. The soft shuffle of her skirts as they swept across the thick carpet was the loudest sound to be heard, making Rose wish she had accepted Elsa's offer to make a gift of the blue dress she'd worn last night. Fey clothing was so much more appropriate for slinking about, which was no doubt part of the reason for the fashion.

Still, even with the rustling to contend with, she reached the hallway leading to the neglected corner of Manor High unnoticed. The rooms she passed were as quiet and seemingly abandoned as ever, which struck Rose as strange somehow in the light of all that had happened the night before. Surely there should be some sign that two people had nearly been killed in this very hall.

But even the rubble from her magical explosion had been cleared away and the hole in the ceiling mended, leaving nothing but a slight bit of dust on the carpet and the smell of paint in the air.

A bit farther on, the door to her old room stood ajar, saving her the effort of using a liberation spell to gain entrance without a key. She suspected Beatrice had done her the favor of leaving the room unlocked, but still drew her sword before she pushed the door open with the toe of her traveling boot. After the evening she had passed, she was hesitant to drop her guard simply because the king had declared her a friend of the court.

Carefully, she checked each corner of the room and every inch of the ceiling as well—when dealing with creatures that could fly one couldn't be too careful—but found herself quite alone. Alone, except for the reflection of her pale face in the mirror. Rose was startled to see how weary she looked, as if she had finally begun to age, and had done a decade or more of the business in one night.

Dark blue circles lay beneath her eyes and thin lines marked the once smooth expanse of her forehead. Upon sheathing her blade and moving a bit closer, she realized she could count several more small lines about her eyes and one deeper groove between her brows. She looked like a woman who frowned often.

The realization made her frown again, deepening the most disturbing furrow.

"Then I shall simply endeavor to smile more, and frown less," Rose announced to her reflection, forcing a merry grin—after all, if one had to bear the marks of age, it was better to give testimony to a cheerful life than to a tragic one. But her smile possessed a decidedly grim quality that made it far more disturbing than any frown.

She let all expression fall with a sigh.

She was stalling, putting off what had drawn her to this room in the first place. Still, she could not help but wish she possessed faery blood. The Fey ability to cloak their physical defects with magic would certainly appease her vanity. If she were a faerie she would simply imagine the wrinkles smoothing away from her face and—

"Goddess!" Rose leapt away from the mirror as if serpents had suddenly sprouted from her head.

For a moment she was convinced she had imagined the transformation, but a closer look revealed her flesh to be as smooth as the day she had taken to her enchanted bed on her eighteenth birthday. The smudges beneath her eyes remained, but her skin was revitalized, practically glowing with health and vitality.

Which made her wonder.

Ignoring the racing of her heart and the feeling that she was somehow engaging in a forbidden thing, Rose focused on the dark smudges, imaging them fading away bit by bit, leaving her looking as if she had enjoyed a full night's sleep. Within a few moments the troubling circles were gone, leaving even more questions in their wake.

What had she done? And more important, how had she done it? Was this some side effect of the magic Ambrose had set to work within her, or an ability she had always possessed?

In the past few months she had learned to read thoughts, sprouted a pair of wings, and now somehow managed to alter her appearance using the power of her mind. It was clear some previously dormant power was awakening within her blood, but she still could not guess what sort of blood that might be. She knew of no supernatural creature possessed of this curious mix of gifts.

And she could employ the rune-based magic of the Fey. Though some mortals could say the same— mostly those with some trace of faery blood far back in their family line—it was a rare enough thing that she should take the ability into account.

"Not only take it into account, but employ it." Her reflection looked stern now, unamused with her needless delay of the business at hand. "Show me Gareth Barrows, the third earl of Shenley."

She quickly traced the runes of remembrance, not allowing herself the luxury of fretting over what she might see. As far as she knew, there was no way to enchant a mirror to make it reveal anything but what had actually taken place before its smooth glass. Whatever she saw, it would reveal some truth about her husband.

The mirror grew cloudy for a moment, then cleared just as suddenly. Now, however, instead of her own face staring back at her, Rose watched as Gareth burst into the room their first evening at the manor, his face twisted with rage and hurt as he spotted her and Ambrose in the midst of some shared joke.

"Next, please," Rose said, her throat tight. That evening seemed so very long ago. But then, everything before last night was distanced from her present reality. She knew from this moment on her life would always be divided into the time before and after she learned she was not her mother's daughter, the events separated by a great, painful chasm.

The mirror cleared again and now she watched Gareth and Ambrose putting her to bed and Gareth petting her hair until she fell asleep. "Next."

How could the man who touched her so tenderly have betrayed her? It was impossible to believe, but she did not doubt that when the mirror next cleared she would be cut to the core by whatever Gareth had done. Beatrice was no fool, and would not have sought Rose out if what she'd seen in the mirror wasn't genuinely troubling.

Though whether the princess truly wished to help her or was merely intrigued by her situation and amused at the thought of making trouble between a husband and a wife remained to be seen.

For the third time, the mist floating in the mirror vanished, but this time Rose witnessed a scene she was not a part of. In it, a blond woman and Gareth were speaking with their heads very close together. The woman's back was to the mirror, so Rose couldn't be certain of her identity, but her husband's face was clear.

He appeared intensely interested in what the woman had to say—so interested that his face kept drawing closer to hers. And closer. Until it seemed he would bestow a kiss upon her upturned lips.

Instead, the woman stood on tiptoe and whispered into Gareth's ear.

"Blast," Rose cursed, wishing the mirror had trapped sound as well as image.

Not that she would be able to hear what was being said in any event. The woman had her face pressed tightly to Gareth's neck. Rose's only clue to the nature of the woman's whisperings came from her husband's expression, which grew progressively more horrified as the petite blonde continued to speak.

The light faded from his eyes until it seemed not a spark of humanity remained within them. He became the feral beast he often resembled in battle, the cold, ruthless killer who had no pity for any who dared cross him.

Rose held her breath for a moment, fearing he would tear into the lady's neck and rip her head from her body, but he made no move to touch her when she finally pulled away. He merely stared straight ahead, as if he no longer saw anything beyond whatever ghastly image the woman's words had painted in his mind.

Judging from the way her artfully arranged curls bounced up and down on her head, Gareth's new confidante spoke once more. Then she reached into her pocket and pulled out a stack of papers tied together with a scarlet ribbon. As the bundle was handed to Gareth, Rose could see that there was writing on the pages. The scrawl was oddly familiar, even from a distance, but she couldn't quite place where she'd seen it in the time it took for Gareth to shove the entire package into his coat pocket.

Once the papers were safely stored, Rose watched her husband sag, as if the very will to live had been drained from his body. The woman reached up to touch his cheek in a gesture of comfort, but Gareth blocked her hand with one of his own, the expression on his face making it clear the thought of her touch sickened him to the core.

He was no longer playing at being the charming, foppish rake who had guided the woman into the room for a stolen moment safe from the prying eyes and ears of the court. Whatever information he needed, he possessed, and now he was done with the chit.

Seconds later, he strode from the room as if fleeing the gates of hell itself. The mirror grew cloudy once more, making Rose curse as the image faded just before the mystery woman turned. Without knowing the wretch's name, she could not demand the mirror show her more, and without a clear look at the other woman's face, she would be hard-pressed to discover her identity.

There were dozens of women with blond hair living and visiting the Seelie court.

"But very few who are shorter than my husband," Rose muttered to herself, remembering how the woman had to stand on tiptoe to bring her mouth to Gareth's ear.

She had seen no more than a dozen such women at court, and none of them were of Fey blood. Faerie women were invariably tall, so she could be certain she sought a human woman who had been entrusted with delivering a message for her master or mistress. Even Mimsy, one of the more diminutive pure-blooded faeries, was still several inches taller than Rose herself.

Rose thanked the Goddess for that fact, as it allowed her to see the girl in question—and the knife she held—in the mirror behind her before dear little Mim had the chance to bury her blade deep in Rose's back.

CHAPTER FOURTEEN

Rose spun on her heel and seized Mimsy's wrist before the girl had the chance to gasp in surprise. There were advantages to being gifted with grace. One hundred years of fighting experience wasn't anything to scoff at either.

She shifted her grip, digging her thumb deep into the center of the young faerie's wrist, causing her fingers to become stiff and useless. The knife fell to the carpet with a dull thud. Rose kicked it away, careful to avoid the tip of the blade, which was black and sticky with some sort of poison.

"Ow! You're hurting me!" Mimsy screamed, clawing at Rose's hand with her free fingers. "Let me go!"

The girl's nails tore at her flesh, drawing blood, but Rose only tightened her grip. A keening whine burst from the back of Mimsy's throat as she fell to her knees. "Please, please. My hand!"

"I believe you intended much worse for me, Mim,"

Rose said, her voice as cold and passionless as it was during battle. "To be fair, I should take your life, but I might be persuaded to make do with a hand. I hear there are powerful magics to be worked with the severed fingers of a faerie."

"The king will have your head, even if you are his granddaughter! You wouldn't dare to take the life of a pure-blooded—"

Rose leaned down, bringing her face only inches away from Mimsy's. "I am not the king's granddaughter and I most certainly *would* dare. The number of people I have killed is greater than you are capable of counting, you stupid little girl."

Mimsy whimpered, her blue eyes growing wide with true fear. "But I-I was only— It was Marie Therese who told me I must take your life or she would disgrace my family and ruin my chances of marriage. Please, I didn't want to do it!"

"And why would Marie Therese wish me dead?" Rose asked, intensifying the pressure on Mimsy's wrist when she paused for a second too long.

"Ow! Please, I—"

"Answer my questions and I may spare your hand."

"Y-You and Beatrice. You both have to die or Marie Therese will have no chance at the throne."

"What?" Rose asked, completely baffled. Had the fools somehow missed the news that Rose was no longer the king's heir?

Misunderstanding her question, Mimsy hurried to explain herself. "She sent me to kill you. She knew we had become friends and thought you would let down your guard. I was supposed to have killed you two nights past, but when I reached your room there were too many people about and you were awake. I was afraid the guards would see me, so I ran. That was when I twisted my ankle."

So Mimsy had been playing her false friend since that morning in the garden. She was a horrifyingly good actress, and as wicked as any Fey three times her age. "So you returned to finish your work this morning? Did you forget I'd been given a new room?"

"No, I followed you from the stables. Marie Therese said she'd seen you go outside and sent me to take your life. She had already slipped poison into Princess Beatrice's breakfast." She paused, the excitement clear in her eyes. Despite her earlier words, it seemed Mimsy was rather thrilled to be part of the assassinations. "Her maid should discover her body any moment now."

"The princess is quite well," Rose said, giving Mimsy's hand one last vicious squeeze before flinging it away from her. The girl fell to the carpet with a sob, rolling into a ball and clutching at her wounded arm. "It will take a great deal more cleverness than either you or Marie Therese possess to do away with Beatrice. And I am no longer a princess of the golden court."

"Wh-what? *Why?*" Mimsy asked from her place on the floor.

She clearly did not intend to continue this fight, which made it difficult for Rose to draw her own sword. She did not wish to kill this foolish girl, no matter that Mimsy had been prepared to take her life.

"It has been proven, beyond any shadow of doubt, that I am not the king's granddaughter. I do not, in fact, possess any faerie blood at all."

"So you are not . . . But how is that possible?"

"I do not know. But it is the truth, and if you had succeeded in killing me, it would not have furthered Marie Therese's goals in the slightest." Rose sighed and bent to retrieve Mimsy's poisoned blade. The least she could do was remove this instrument of death from the fool's hands.

"But I didn't succeed," Mimsy said, her eyes wide with fear as she watched Rose approach with the knife in her hand. "Please, I beg of you. Spare my life. I have but nineteen years to my name, and—"

"And are already a completely vile creature with not a care for any life save your own." Rose paused above her, holding the blade near the girl's throat, part of her still toying with the idea of killing the faerie.

There was little doubt in her mind she would regret leaving such a budding monster alive. Mimsy wasn't the sort to take a lesson from another's mercy. She would not alter her course, but would simply grow more cautious when it came to the business of treachery and deceit.

"Please, please." Mimsy's breath caught on a sob. "I swear to you I will no longer aid Marie Therese's cause. I will suffer the scandal she will unleash upon my good name, and know that I deserve to lose my chance to make an impressive match. I have been naughty. I know I have and—"

"Naughty?" Rose laughed in spite of herself. "A soft word to describe attempted murder."

"Wicked, then. I have been wicked, but I promise I shant be again. I will be the princess's champion and ally. Beatrice will not want for a better friend."

"What care have I for the Seelie princess or her friends?" Rose moved the blade closer to Mimsy's trembling flesh. "It is my favor you must curry. So tell me, little Mim, what shall you do for me?"

The girl's blue eyes went wide with fear, but it was clear her busy little mind worked to find something she might offer her. At another time Rose might have drawn out her suffering a bit more, simply to ascertain she had made an impression upon the chit, but she had already tarried too long. Ambrose and Gareth would be wondering where she had gotten off to. It was time to end this game, and hopefully gain her cause a valuable spy.

"You will be my eyes and ears here at court. You shall report to me weekly via the enchanted waters. I shall expect to be appraised of any further attacks by the creature that killed the king's sons, and I will want news of any attempts made by the king to find his true granddaughter—"

"But someone might overhear! The waters are not always safe."

Rose pushed the knife closer, until the poisoned blade rested against Mimsy's slim throat. "If your reports are not punctual or do not contain accurate intelligence, I will come for you and finish what I neglected to finish today."

"Please, you can't really—"

"But you won't sleep through your death. I will allow you to experience the agony of having your hands cut off before I grant you release from your torment by slitting your wretched throat."

Mimsy's breath came in desperate little pants so swift Rose feared she might faint dead away before they concluded their business. "You—you are sincere."

"Utterly, my sweet." Rose smiled and in that moment knew she looked as terrifying and merciless as the Mother herself. "Have we come to an understanding, then?"

"Y-yes." Mimsy nodded gingerly, highly aware of the weapon at her neck.

"Excellent." Rose stepped away from the cowering faerie and wiped the blade free of poison using the coverlet on the bed. It was a hideous, mildewed thing and would not be worse off for a little poison on its edges.

Behind her, she heard Mimsy struggle to her feet, but she kept her back turned, making it clear she knew she had nothing to fear from the girl. "May I go now?"

"You may," Rose said. "No wait, there's one more thing. There is a woman whose name I must learn as soon as possible." She briefly described the blonde she had seen speaking with her husband.

"As small as you? She must be a mortal, then. You are the only half-breed who's been allowed at court in centuries," Mimsy said, sounding calmer now that she was at a greater distance from the knife in Rose's hand. "I should be able to discover her identity within a day, maybe two at the most. Even if she lies about meeting with the vampire, I will be able to read the truth in her thoughts."

"When you have the name, send it by messenger to Master Minuit's home in London."

"So I shouldn't use the waters?"

"No, I prefer to receive that news by letter," Rose

said. She depended upon Ambrose to relay messages from the enchanted waters, and she didn't wish for him to know she suspected Gareth of betrayal. At least not yet.

She would give her husband the chance to deliver the pages in his possession first. For they were her rightful property. Sometime during her conversation with Mimsy, Rose had realized why the scrawl upon the papers had seemed so familiar. It was her father's uniquely cramped and slanted hand, and the pages were precisely the same size as those torn from his journal. How the blond woman had come into possession of them was unclear, but perhaps it wouldn't be for long.

Hopefully, Gareth would see fit to share both the pages and the troubling news given him by the mystery woman in the very near future. It was understandable that he may have forgotten after the events of last night, but if he kept silent for much longer . . .

"I will send the news as soon as I am able," Mimsy said, edging toward the door with a panicked look in her eyes. "But please, there is someone coming, I can hear a swift step in the hall. May I leave? I do not wish to be discovered alone with—"

"Go." Rose dismissed Mimsy with a wave of one hand as she drew her sword with the other.

She had just tucked Mimsy's dagger into the empty sheath in her boot and lifted her sword to the ready when the owner of the swift step burst into the room. Fortunately, it was one of her own who came for her. Unfortunately, the news he bore was more troubling than the appearance of a half dozen bloodthirsty Fey.

"Gareth is gone," Ambrose said, with not a trace of satisfaction in his voice. He seemed genuinely troubled, as though he couldn't believe his brother would desert them both, no matter how often he had expressed his contempt for the vampire.

"Gone?" Rose's mouth went dry, and her heart raced in her chest.

"His trunk still sits in his bedchamber, but many of his clothes and both of his swords are gone. The stable boy said he heard a single rider leave well before sunrise, but the child was too sleep addled to remember the exact hour."

"The rider could have been anyone," Rose said, knowing she was being foolish even as the words left her mouth. In her heart she knew Gareth had been the man fleeing Manor High, just as she knew he never intended to give her the pages from her father's journal. "Perhaps Gareth is simply—"

"A battalion of vampires has been sighted no more than three leagues from here. They wear the black armor they use to fight when the sun shines, and are marching toward Manor High."

So the vampire high council had finally decided what to do about the assassination of the six high-ranking vampire nobles. The timing couldn't be worse.

"They've likely been observed by mortals," Rose observed, understanding the implications of such a thing even before Ambrose spoke.

"No doubt. Though the ravings of a few peasants will not undo centuries of secrecy, they still violate Fey law with their actions. It is clear they mean to challenge the established order."

"But surely they do not mean to attack Manor High itself? It would be suicide." She couldn't bear to ask the other question plaguing her mind.

Had Gareth had some part in this? Could her husband have been a spy for the high council from the very beginning? More than anything she longed to believe he was innocent, that he wouldn't risk their lives in such a fashion, but his hasty departure let dirty fingers of doubt make their mark upon her heart.

"The manor's perimeter is well protected, and its magical fortifications strong, but after the events of last evening, the king's warriors are ill prepared to face such a large, well-armed force. If the scout is to be believed, the vampires number in the thousands. These are not merely Great Britain's bloodmen, but many from the Continent as well." Ambrose crossed the room in two steps and took her arm. "The scouts rush to wake the king even as we speak. We must hurry if we hope to take our leave—"

"Before the king decides to detain us here and charge us both with treason."

"Or simply take our heads and hands and be done with it."

Rose cursed beneath her breath as she allowed Ambrose to bustle her from the room.

If Gareth had been aware of the coming attack, he had knowingly put his wife's and brother's lives at risk when he rode out of Manor High. Even if he hadn't known, his flight in the middle of the night was highly suspect.

What was he about, and why did she have the horrible feeling that whatever it was would be the end of their marriage, and perhaps the end of his very life?

If he had betrayed them, Ambrose would do his best to see Gareth dead . . . if she herself didn't accomplish the deed first. The thought made her chest ache and tears threaten at the back of her eyes, but she would slay him if he had put his allegiance to the vampire cause above his concern for his wife's well-being. There was nothing of higher importance for her than her loyalty to those she loved. She wouldn't tolerate any less from her husband.

If he had wronged them, she would see him dead, though it would kill something within her to do so. She had never loved as she loved Gareth. For all his faults, for all they still had to learn about one other, he was the only man who had ever touched her so deeply.

So much so that even the suspicion that he hadn't loved her made her want to tear every silky hair from his head. Or collapse to the floor and weep for a year or two. Perhaps both.

"Rose? Do you attend me?"

She swallowed with some difficulty and tried to lock away her rage and anguish. Now was not the time to lose her head. "Forgive me, I didn't—"

"Put away your blade and assume a more leisurely pace before we reach the front parlor. We will only attract attention if we seem to be fleeing."

Rose sheathed her weapon and forced herself to slow down, though her fingers could not help digging into Ambrose's arm, clinging to what seemed to be the last sane being in the world. "Then the attack is not known to all?"

"The scout went straight to the king after delivering his horse to the stable. If I hadn't been awaiting you and Gareth near our coach, I wouldn't have overheard the news myself. For the moment only you and I, the scout, and the groom are aware of the approaching threat."

"Thank the Goddess." Rose's breath rushed out between her parted lips, which she then curved into a smile for two young men wandering toward the front parlor.

"Do not give thanks just yet," Ambrose whispered. "We haven't yet reached our coach."

"Is it wise to take the coach? Would we not reach the city quicker upon horseback?"

"We could no doubt move more swiftly, but it would look rather odd for the newly married Lady Shenley to arrive in London on horseback, bedraggled from hours of hard riding, and without a single change of clothing to her name."

"It shall no doubt look even stranger for the newly married Lady Shenley to arrive in London without her husband, on the arm of another man, and without a female companion." Ambrose had once possessed enough magic to make himself appear to be a woman to the human eye, but had lost the ability upon sharing his power with Rose a few months past.

"There is no help for that, I fear." Ambrose's voice was grim. "'Tis a pity the vampire spread the news of your marriage throughout England before our departure for Myrdrean last February. If he hadn't . . ."

"If he hadn't I would be an unmarried woman traveling alone with an unmarried man, which would be even worse. Even with the length of your hair disguised with glamour, you have always been a mysterious figure. Society doesn't know exactly what to think of you."

"I ceased to care what human Society thought of me centuries past, Rosemarie." Ambrose nodded to a group of whispering women near the front entrance and then guided Rose out the door into the dim morning light. They were nearly there, and it was hellish to keep their pace to a stroll. "I am concerned now only because wagging tongues will draw unnecessary attention to us at precisely the moment when discretion is imperative."

Fifty more feet and they would reach their carriage. The trunks were already loaded and the driver was standing at attention near the hitched horses. If their luck held they could be on their way in a few minutes and reach the end of the road leading to Manor High in a quarter hour.

"I begin to care little for discretion. Let the English talk. All I wish is to return to Myrdrean and . . ." Rose swallowed the lump that rose in her throat. She'd forgotten that Myrdrean was no longer hers to claim. As of last eve, she had no home, no country. In fact, her identity as Lady Shenley might be the only thing she could legitimately claim.

Ambrose was silent as he helped her into the coach, motioned to the driver, and then climbed in beside her. Within a few moments, the wheels were set into motion and they began the seemingly interminable journey down the enchanted road to Manor High. Rose turned to catch a glimpse of the great house through the window, knowing she would not feel truly safe until they were back on human roads, headed toward London.

Assuming, of course, that they were not detained by vampire soldiers.

"Did the scout say from which direction the vampire forces were advancing?" Rose asked, keeping her voice low, though their driver was human and incapable of hearing anything said within the carriage. But as long as they were on Seelie land, she couldn't be certain who might be listening. "Perhaps we should direct the driver to take an alternate route to London."

"No, they come from the north. The southern routes should be clear, at least for now. If the vampire generals are wise, they will send a portion of their force to guard the entrance to the enchanted road, but they have not done so as of yet."

"There's one thing to be thankful for." Rose sighed, but her chest remained tight.

Ambrose was quiet for a moment, but when he next spoke it was as if he had read the troubles written upon her heart. "If she no longer lives, Myrdrean will still be yours." Ambrose brought his hand to rest lightly upon hers. Even through the leather of their gloves, Rose felt the comforting warmth of his touch. "There's no reason to abdicate your throne for a ghost. After all you have done to restore the country—"

"She is one quarter Fey, surely she still lives," Rose said, determined to be realistic, no matter how she longed to hold onto the hope Ambrose offered. "I am duty bound to find her, though I fear locating the true Rosemarie Edenburg may be quite a challenge. She surely has no notion of her true identity. There's no other explanation as to why she hasn't come forward to claim what is rightfully hers."

"Perhaps she is a sensible woman who loathes the idea of becoming both human and faerie royalty and prefers to remain safely anonymous."

Rose smiled. "Yes, women are notoriously averse to increasing their social standing."

"She will also increase her chances of winning her way into an early grave." Ambrose's fingers curled intimately around her own, becoming more distracting than comforting.

Even in the midst of fleeing for her life and fearing her heart would break, Rose discovered that Ambrose could still cause desire to creep into her blood. In fact, it seemed her fear that Gareth had never truly cared for her only made the longing for Ambrose's touch even more powerful. She craved the comforting embrace of an old friend and the oblivion of passion more than ever.

And what reason was there to resist falling into Ambrose's strong arms when her husband had likely abandoned her?

Ambrose leaned his head closer to hers, so that his next words slipped seductively into the shell of her ear. "I confess a part of me rejoices to see you out of this danger."

"Even though the very nature of my being is now in question?" she asked, staring at where their hands were entwined.

What would it be like, to be as they had been in their dream, to feel Ambrose's bare skin sliding against hers?

"I meant every word I spoke last night. I care not

what you are. I know *who* you are, and that will not change, no matter how strange or unusual your parentage."

Rose smiled, though tears pricked at the back of her eyes. "Perhaps not, but it will most certainly alter the course of your future. If the true princess of Myrdrean lives, she is your betrothed."

"Then it would be she who the prophecy foretold shall kill her intended." He sounded entirely too cheerful for a man discussing his own death. "Which means it would then fall to your husband to marry the woman."

"And I would be ruined once he cast me aside."

"I am certain there would be several men who would vie for the privilege of your hand in marriage, no matter what scandal was attached to your name," Ambrose said, trying to make light of her potentially dire situation. "Besides, you are quite a wealthy woman in your own right, even without your holdings in Europe, and there are always penniless nobles and young rakes with gambling debts in need of wives with deep pockets."

"Please, stop, your flattery shall undo me."

"There's no need to pander to your vanity. You know you're one of the loveliest women in the world. Men would kill to have you on their arm for only one night, let alone an entire lifetime."

"But not you, of course, as you will be dead," Rose said, wincing inwardly as soon as the words left her lips. Neither of them were ready for that type of jest, not now, perhaps not ever.

Ambrose was silent, but didn't pull his hand away from hers. Rose wondered if he was thinking about the moments they'd shared in the greenhouse, wondering if her response would have been different had she known her husband would abandon her without so much as a fare-thee-well as soon as he learned she was not the Fey princess he had assumed.

No. For you would love Gareth still, you fool. Her own inner council cut her as deeply as the haunting voice of the Mother.

But she was correct on both accounts. She was a fool, and she did still love her husband. For all that it looked as if he had played her false, her heart still ached to think of him far from her side, to imagine that she would never hear his voice again, never feel the brush of his lips against hers or bask in that singular grin.

Lusting after Ambrose didn't change what was in her heart, and bedding the faerie wouldn't keep it from breaking if her husband had indeed betrayed her. The only thing that could prevent that was the man himself, the man who still deserved her loyalty and fidelity until his guilt or innocence was proven.

"We cannot arrive in London soon enough." Rose pulled her hand away from Ambrose's under the pretext of adjusting the pins in her hair. "I am eager to begin unraveling this mystery."

"As am I," Ambrose said, pretending not to notice her discomfiture as he turned to the window. They had finally reached the end of the road to Manor High and turned left onto the human highway. Their safety was still not a given, but already Rose could breathe a little easier. "It will be most gratifying to begin answering the many questions that have arisen."

Whether he meant the questions of her birth, the

identity of the true Rosemarie Edenburg, or the location of her errant husband, Rose did not ask. After all, there were some questions that were better left unanswered.

CHAPTER FIFTEEN

May 22, 1750
Burton Mews Road
Mayfair, London

Rose placed her tuppence on the scarred bar before her, careful to withdraw her hands before the boys to her left caught a closer look at her soft, white fingers. She'd smeared dirt and ash from the ruins of her Berkeley Square home under her nails to complete her stable boy's disguise, but prolonged inspection would make it clear hers were not hands accustomed to engaging in hard labor.

"Porter, mum." Rose kept her words soft and her pitch low as she ordered, but quickly realized she needn't have bothered.

The rosy-cheeked woman behind the bar had clearly been in her cups for some time and hardly spared a glance for the skinny little boy with the oversized cap perched on the smallest chair at the bar. She simply plunked down the cup of ale, snatched her two pennies, and returned to the clutch of ruddy-faced men at the far end of her L-shaped domain. The gentlemen seemed to be regulars and favorites of the proprietor, if the loud guffaws sounding from that direction were anything to go by.

Rose couldn't remember feeling as welcome anywhere as those simple laboring men obviously felt here at the Bald Duke. The thought only deepened the sense of melancholy that had haunted her the entire day.

She tipped back her cup, taking deep pulls of the thick, smoky ale, feeling the brew coat her belly like a second serving of mutton pie. If she was to be tormented by sour emotions, might as well add a bit of liquor to the mix. Nothing like heavy English ale on an empty stomach to make one truly maudlin.

"Careful, little breeches, or you'll be undone before the sun is set." The old man leveraging his bulk onto the chair next to Rose resembled one of the older bucks huddled round the table near the fire, dividing their attention between their drunken game of draughts and leering at the maids who served them, but Rose knew his true identity immediately.

"Caspar. Good of you to come," she said, then took another long drink. If she was to win any information from this man, she would have to prove she could handle not only her drink, but her sword and her magic as well.

Harmless-looking Caspar, with his yellowed fingers and sagging brown skin, his rheumy black eyes and mouth blessed with fewer teeth than Rose had fingers on one hand, was, in fact, the most ancient and sought-after seer in the British Isles. Some said he was the son of a faerie who had been raped by one of the ancient gods when they still journeyed in the mortal realm.

Others insisted he was a human foundling raised by golden dragons and infused with their fortune-telling magic, and still others said the man was nothing but a gypsy, though the oldest gypsy ever to wander the earth, a man who'd made a deal with the devil himself to keep his aging carcass above the earth's surface rather than below.

Humans and supernaturals in desperate need of guidance had been seeking him out for at least seven hundred years and possibly more, if some of the stories were to be believed.

The only truth Rose could find in the tales was that one must be desperate to work the spell to summon Caspar the Wise, for the man nearly always demanded quite a price for merely appearing to a supplicant in need, and an even more fearsome price if he were to speak his wisdom.

Ambrose would have chained her to the wall in the dungeon beneath his Southwark residence if he had guessed whom she was to meet only a few blocks from her old Berkeley Square home. He would have been livid to know she risked herself in this way, but she knew she had no other choice. After what they had learned from the letter Beatrice had slipped into her hands before leaving Manor High, Rose was willing to take any risk necessary.

Beatrice had done her the service of revealing the name of the Fey de la Nuit family that had sheltered her mother in the years before her marriage to the king of Myrdrean. Ambrose had contacted them via the enchanted waters only to learn that every last one of them was dead, slain by the same shadow creature that had hunted Rose and attacked Beatrice in her dream.

A creature that had also taken the form of a strange dog-dragon-hawk beast, if the servants at the family's home were to be believed. They swore the creature had shifted from man to shadow monster to beast and back to a man again before finally sweeping out of the estate.

It was Ecanthar, there was no longer any doubt in her mind, and Ambrose seemed inclined to agree with her. But how could the black elf have known she was aware of the family's existence unless he was somehow in league with Beatrice and had seen the letter before it was given to Rose?

But if that were true, and the princess worked against her, why would Beatrice give her the letter with the names in the first place? And why would she have been attacked in her dream? Even if she had lied about the dream attack, what did a Seelie princess have to gain from Rose, a woman who was, for all practical purposes, no one?

In the end, Rose was certain of only one thing— that her ignorance posed a greater danger to her life than Ambrose's anger. So she had lied, telling him she meant to search the ruins of her Berkeley Square home in hopes of finding her mother's lost diary.

"A wise decision." Caspar grinned, proudly displaying three slanted teeth jutting wildly from the front of his mouth. "What the black faerie doesn't know won't hurt him, but it will hurt you, little breeches. Oh yes, it will."

Then he *could* read her thoughts. She shouldn't be surprised. It seemed nearly everyone could these days. Her mental walls failed more often than not, and there was never time for the rest she required to rebuild them with the proper strength. She might as well abandon the attempt and save both her and the man seated next to her the effort of dissembling.

Rose finished the last of her drink in one long swallow, grateful for the soothing effect of the brew upon her nerves. Making certain to project her thoughts, she wondered what the man meant by his last remark. Was he confirming her suspicions? Or was the statement a thinly veiled threat?

"No threat, child. When I threaten ye, ye shall know it." Caspar smiled again and reached for her empty mug.

Before Rose could offer him pennies for ale, he had crushed the tin in his withered hand and placed the entire ruined remains into his mouth. Then, despite his lack of teeth, he chewed and swallowed with relish.

"Oh." She stared at the man's lips, oddly transfixed. "Well, that is . . . comforting."

Was it truly? She wasn't sure, but she suddenly found herself not knowing what to say. How did one respond when the man you'd come to for guidance had just finished eating your cup?

"You tell old Caspar what you need," he said, reading either her face or her thoughts. "Then Caspar tells you the price."

Rose took a deep breath and—after a quick glance around to make sure no one attended them—explained the situation in which she currently found herself. She told Caspar of her false life and her recent discovery that she was not her mother's daughter or of Fey lineage. She told him of the black elf who claimed her as his sister, of the shadow creature that had attacked her at Manor High and claimed to be that same black elf when she encountered him in a vision, and of the troubling dreams of the Mother that had tormented not only herself and her former liaison, but a true Fey princess as well.

For some reason she could speak the name of the Mother to Caspar without that horrible clutching sensation at the back of her throat. Before, when she and Beatrice had described the monster in their dreams to one another, it had been all Rose could do to hint at the creature's identity, and she had yet to gather the courage to ask Ambrose if he'd seen the giant who had plucked him from their dream bed a few night's past.

No matter how she longed for knowledge and aid in this matter, a part of her was terrified to mention the ancient beast for fear her words would somehow summon more dreams.

"I have seen these things." Caspar nodded kindly before turning to the boy next to him and plucking the ale from his hand. "But there is more."

Rose leaned forward, thinking to apologize to the boy and make some excuse for her senile grandfather, when she noted the youth's strange stiffness. Neither his face nor his body moved at all. It was as if he'd been frozen without the benefit of ice, and it seemed the same fate had befallen the rest of the public house. Every last patron, from the proprietor caught midlaugh, to the old man by the fire with his hand paused over his draught piece, was as still as a painting in a museum. Even the fire was still, its flames caught in midleap toward the chimney.

"Goddess," she mumbled beneath her breath. How

had she not noticed the sudden silence that had fallen over the room? Now the unnatural quiet seemed to press in all around her, threatening to smother her the way the Mother's flesh had done at the conclusion of each, terrifying dream.

"She is not a goddess, but the Mother sees and hears much," Caspar said before consuming first the beer and then the cup he'd stolen from the boy beside him.

Rose strove to keep her mind closed to the man, concealing her elation at having one of her most pressing questions answered without even having to ask. So it *was* the Mother who haunted her dreams, not one who merely sought to assume the identity of the all-powerful being. Though hardly a comforting realization, it was vital to know what they faced. Now she would be able to go to Ambrose with facts, not suspicions, and together they could seek a way to best the woman.

Assuming, of course, that she *could* be bested.

"Perhaps," Caspar mused, "but she is powerful, indeed. Even a bubble like this will not keep her out for long. You'd better tell me the rest, girl, and I will ask the fates if there is aught to be done for a thing such as you are."

"A *thing*?" Rose asked, her throat so tight she could barely speak the word. "What do you mean? What sort of thing am I?"

Caspar snorted and his black eyes grew cold. "I know not; I've never seen such a thing as ye. No aura surrounds you, not a speck of soul's light."

"But why? Do you mean to say I haven't a soul?" Surely the man was wrong. How could she ache as she did if she didn't have a soul? A woman without a soul would not be capable of love, or of suffering.

"It is a question I could perhaps answer, but it is not what you came for." His voice became a whisper, a soft warning that chilled her flesh. "Be careful, little breeches. For such difficult knowledge, I would demand a price I am not certain you would wish to pay."

Rose swallowed with no small amount of difficulty. Her mouth felt very dry despite the beer she'd just consumed, and she longed for a cool drink of water from the springs of Myrdrean. Goddess help her, but she longed for Myrdrean, for her home to be hers once more, for her place in the world to be assured and she herself no longer an outcast.

That was what she had come here for, help in finding the one whose identity she had assumed when she was naught but a tiny girl. Surely finding the true Rosemarie Edenburg would also lead her to the truth of her own past, hopefully before anyone else was killed.

For some reason the Mother and Ecanthar did not wish for Rose to discover the truth. They were willing to kill to protect the secret that began nearly two hundred years ago, when one little girl was exchanged for another. But why?

Finding the real Rose would no doubt aid her in answering that question as well.

She turned to Caspar with renewed resolve. "You are right. I have come for aid in another matter. If the true Rosemarie Edenburg still lives, I must find her."

Caspar nodded, obviously pleased with this question.

It was almost as if he had been expecting it—which she supposed he had, if he were truly as skilled a seer as purported. "And find her you shall. In fact, she is closer than you imagine."

"She is? You mean she is here? In London?" Rose asked, a spark of hope warming her more than the swiftly downed porter. With such a wide world to wander, what were the chances that the woman she sought would inhabit the very same city? Perhaps she was experiencing a bit of luck at last.

The old seer laughed until he began to choke, then choked until he brought up a twisted piece of tin, which he placed upon the bar. "You do beat all, little breeches. Such innocence in one of your age and experience is a treasure, indeed."

"So she isn't in London, then," Rose said, her mood souring. She should know better than to expect this matter to be simply solved.

"No, she is. Most assuredly."

"But her presence here is not a stroke of good fortune?"

Caspar toyed with the piece of tin he'd coughed out, using it to pick his teeth, though how any morsel of food could be stuck between things so very far apart Rose had no idea. "Well then, that depends upon what you consider good fortune, sweet."

His last word made her blood freeze in her veins. It was what Gareth had called her from the day they'd met, and he'd uttered it with the same rakish jolliness as her absent husband—who had yet to attempt to contact her in any way.

"Yes, there you are," Caspar encouraged. "Now hurry, tell me the rest of your tale. *She* begins to wonder why she can no longer see you. Soon she will discover our little hiding place and our dance will be done."

"But I'm not certain what to tell," Rose said, desperation clouding her thoughts. Or perhaps it was the porter. Maybe the old man was right and she had drunk too quickly for one who wore "little breeches."

"Very well." Caspar shifted on his chair, leaning closer to Rose. "Then let me lay the touch upon you, child. We can't be wasting time, not now."

When he placed his gnarled hands upon either side of her ears and tugged her head forward to touch his own, Rose felt no urge to pull away. Despite his disturbing appearance and even more disturbing smell—a mixture of dried urine and a deep filthiness acquired only through many years spent in the same clothes—there was something comforting about being near Caspar the Wise. His firm hands and gentle fingers reminded her of the man she had assumed was her father, of the way he had held her upon his shoulders as he walked about the yard observing his knights at their swordplay. She had always felt so safe there, secure in the knowledge that her father would never let her fall.

I mean you even less harm than that man, little breeches. Now open your mind and show me those secrets you keep.

Rose gasped and tried to pull away, but it was already too late. The very bones surrounding her mind had suddenly melted away, burned to ash by the searing heat of Caspar's thoughts. He swept inside her like a tidal wave, poking into every crevice, raping her memories, pawing through the wispy threads of her soul with a merciless efficiency that left her too weak to even hold up her head by the time the seer's mental presence departed.

She collapsed to the floor in a boneless heap, her skull pounding and her muscles aching as if she'd fought an epic battle. The pain throbbing through her was so intense she couldn't even lift her face from the filth upon the floor, so overwhelming her mouth lacked the strength to moan, let alone ask the man what he had seen.

"May the powers preserve you," Caspar muttered, stumbling from his stool and backing away from Rose as if she were a monster, not a completely helpless woman prostrate on the ground before him.

Calling on the last of her strength, she reached a hand to the seer in supplication. "Please . . . Tell me." He couldn't leave now, not before sharing whatever it was he had found while rifling through her mind. "Who is—"

"Her name is Hughes, Hannah Hughes." Caspar licked his cracked lips, then darted a fearful look over his shoulder, as if he expected the Mother herself to appear at any moment. "But you were never she, never birthed to human or supernatural—never birthed at all."

Rose longed to ask him what he meant, to demand an explanation of his cryptic words, but at that moment the interior of the public house began to glow. A bright crimson radiance shone upon them from an unseen source, casting the bar and all its inhabitants in the ruby red light of hell.

The seer shuddered and his eyelids began to flutter like paper blown by a spring breeze. "Beware the secrets of man and beast, beware the coming of the cold fire. It is eat or be eaten, there is no other choice, no other hope for any who have wronged the womb that bore us all. So have the fates decreed."

The vision—if that was what it had been—departed as swiftly as it had come, leaving Caspar looking even weaker. The red glow vanished as the man sagged visibly and braced himself on a nearby table. Seconds later, the rest of the bar patrons resumed their motion, bursting back into the world with an audible popping sound.

With no small amount of effort, Rose pushed against the floor, struggling to sit upright. She couldn't afford to draw attention to herself. If anyone here took a closer look, he would discover she was a woman in disguise.

Through pure force of will and no help from her trembling limbs, she made it to her feet just in time to see Caspar fumbling for the door handle. She reached to him with her mind, knowing she would never get to him in time to ask her question with her lips.

Wait! I do not understand, what—

I can say no more. His mental voice was so much stronger than her own that it echoed painfully through her skull, making her wince.

But please, I have yet to pay your price and—

When the seer turned back to face her, he was silhouetted in the open doorway, casting his face in shadow. *There will be no price unless you dare contact me again. If so, I will have no choice but to deliver you to the one who hunts you, little piece.*

And then he was gone, moving with a speed seemingly impossible for one of such advanced age. Rose weaved toward the door, knowing better than to chase after the man, but suddenly craving a breath of fresh air—fresher air than could be found indoors amid the press of unwashed bodies.

"Scuse me, sir," she mumbled when she bumped into first one man and then another, deliberately slurring her speech. She hoped they would think she had simply had a bit too much to drink and ignore her.

Finally she reached the door and hurled herself out of the tavern, sucking in a deep breath, oddly comforted by the smell of manure wafting toward her from the street. It was an earthy smell, something base and safe and sane.

Rose stumbled a few more paces and leaned against the brick wall of the pub. She was still weak as a kitten, but recovering quickly. In another minute or two, she would be fit enough to begin her journey back to Southwark, where she hoped to find Ambrose returned from his own afternoon errand.

An errand that would have proven unsuccessful, Goddess willing.

There was no longer time to waste by seeking out Gareth or the truth behind his disappearance. They had much greater challenges to face than a wayward husband or brother, bigger problems even than the vampire and Fey war that loomed on the horizon.

The Mother was no faery story. She was real and had declared herself an enemy to all her children, if her words in Rose's first dream were to believed.

"The time for love has passed. Death to all who set themselves above the Mother," Rose whispered aloud to herself.

Combined with Caspar's warning that all who had

wronged the womb that bore them would "eat or be eaten," the Mother's words were enough to convince her that the world as the supernatural community knew it was about to change. Forever.

CHAPTER SIXTEEN

Rose strode up the stairs to Ambrose's office without bothering to change out of her boy's clothes.

Ambrose had always found her tendency to dress against her gender distasteful. Wishing to keep the peace between them, she usually tried to humor his sense of propriety, but the furious beating of her heart would not allow her the luxury of donning feminine attire.

The sense of urgency that had descended on the road outside the Bald Duke had only increased as she made her way across the bridge and back to one of the poorer parishes in London. Despite his great wealth, Ambrose chose to make his home far from fashionable Mayfair and the streets where the rich and influential typically set up house.

Few supernaturals and not a single human soul—save his servants—knew the position of his four-story Southwark brownstone. For supernaturals, various concealing enchantments protected Ambrose's privacy; for humans, the mere location was quite enough. There wasn't a hostess in London who craved the presence of the mysterious Ambrose Minuit sufficiently to risk sending her invitation deep into a section of town composed mainly of workhouses and crumbling tenements—no matter how rich the gentleman was rumored to be.

And the rumors were true. Just the books lining the walls of his office were worth several thousand pounds, priceless first editions and rare finds that would send any London bookseller into apoplectic fits.

Ambrose was pacing the floor in front of said books as she burst through the door and turned to greet her with an expression both outraged and relieved. "Where the devil have you been? I drove through Berkeley Square three hours past and you were nowhere to be found."

"Maman's— Marionette's journal did not survive the fire, so I sought alternate means of intelligence," Rose said, still out of breath from her race through the city streets.

"I see." Ambrose's eyes narrowed, as if he truly did see and most certainly did not approve.

"I fear what I've learned is most dire."

"Not likely one-half as dire as what I have discovered. Sit down. You'll not want to be upon your feet when you hear this news."

Rose propped her hands upon her hips and stood her ground. "No, sir, perhaps *you* should sit down. I swear to you there is no chance on the Goddess's green earth your news can be half as distressing as my own."

"Your former cousin, Elsa, has betrayed the Seelie

court," Ambrose said without further argument. "She deactivated the wards of protection at the rear of the grounds, allowing the vampire forces to enter without impediment."

"Why on earth would she—"

"Apparently, she'd taken a vampire lover some years ago. The man was one of the nobles killed by the Seelie king's order. She sought revenge for his death. Nearly fifty Fey were slain as a result of her actions, and twice as many of the vampires' invading force. She herself barely escaped with her life, and now seeks sanctuary here in London."

Rose blinked. The information was startling, but she failed to see how it related to their situation.

Ambrose sighed. "She seeks sanctuary *here,* in my home."

So *that's* why Elsa had been so eager to make friends with Ambrose, and to a lesser extent, Rose herself. Her plan must have already been laid and she knew she would need friends outside the Seelie court when the time came.

"And you wish to help her?" Rose asked. "We have just escaped from Manor High with our lives, and you would invite the king's wrath once more? I do feel a certain amount of pity for Elsa, but—"

"She claims she has information that will benefit the Fey de la Nuit. Proof of the Seelie King's plan to assassinate the Fey de la Nuit high council and claim the throne for his own heir."

"For Marie Therese." Rose cursed colorfully while Ambrose looked on with disapproval. "So the king *is* behind the deaths of his own children?"

"It would appear so. Marie Therese is his dead sister's grandchild and the only Seelie who can claim direct ties to both thrones. Her grandfather was my mother's uncle."

Lineage. Such a confusing thing. For her part, she was beginning to think the world would be better off if no one kept track of where he or she came from. "But how will this benefit the king himself? Surely Marie Therese has no—"

"She would be crowned princess of the combined courts, not queen. As she claims barely three hundred years, she has agreed to allow her great uncle to rule until she attains greater age and wisdom."

So the king wished to rule the supernatural world. For that was effectively what would happen if he had control of both Fey courts. The faeries were the most powerful of the Mother's children and, as such, had always governed the rest—no matter how many times the lesser beings sought to defy their rule.

Until now, the power of the Fey had been held in check by the vastly different natures of the two faery courts. The Seelie and the Fey de la Nuit could never seem to agree, and therefore never achieved total control of those they considered their inferiors.

"And Elsa has proof of this? Something that will convince the high council?"

"She has stolen the original document signed by the king and Marie Therese, agreeing that he shall rule in her stead for at least one thousand years or longer, should it take more time for her to achieve the wisdom needed."

Rose shook her head in silent disbelief. "It is a bold and dangerous plan, even for a king."

"It is madness. The Fey de la Nuit will see him dead for this."

"If Elsa lives to share her evidence with the high

council," Rose said, completing Ambrose's thought. "We must give her sanctuary."

He paused, looking deep into her eyes. "I feel there is little other choice. It is my duty to protect Elsa and the document until the council can send an emissary from Paris, though I am loathe to put you in further danger. Perhaps we could secret you away in another Fey de la Nuit's home, as a servant or some such thing. Given your taste for dressing as a penniless whelp, we might find a position in someone's stables."

"No, I won't run with my tail between my legs. What is the wrath of one ancient king, when I have already earned myself a far greater enemy than my former grandfather?" She hesitated, not eager to tell the tale of summoning Caspar the Wise.

"Caspar is not your enemy." Ambrose walked back to his desk where he collapsed in his leather chair.

"Wha— How did you know? My mental shields are firm, I am certain of it."

"Your forehead. Take a look in the mirror above the fireplace. The star is his signature."

A few steps took her to the mantel. A deep black star marked her forehead, a delicate web of lines that reminded her of the puckered top of a blueberry. She scrubbed at it with her hand, but the marking did not so much as smear.

"Blast," she muttered beneath her breath.

"No use scrubbing. The mark is permanent. You are lucky that is the only mark you bear and that you survived to walk away from the man." Ambrose sighed that weary sigh that never failed to communicate how disappointed he was with her. For a man who seemed to care for her like a lover, he often behaved more like a disapproving father. "You can be certain you're safe, at least until you are foolish enough to summon him again."

"I received the answer I sought, so perhaps I was not so foolish." Rose continued to scrub at the star, determined to prove Ambrose wrong. The seer had said nothing of marking her with his touch. Surely he wouldn't do such a thing without making her aware of it. "I learned that the true Rosemarie Edenburg currently goes by the name Hannah Hughes and resides right here in London."

"And what price did you pay for this intelligence?" Ambrose asked, a hint of real fear in his gray eyes. "Do not think Caspar will forget what is owed. If he hasn't taken the fee yet, he will come for it when you least expect him. He takes great pleasure in claiming his payments."

"He did not seem as cruel as all that." Odd, yes, but not particularly evil.

"I knew a man who spent a year in the seer's cave near the sea. Every day, the monster would visit him and take a single bite of his flesh, then leave his wound to bleed and fester. It took over three hundred days for Caspar the Wise to consume the man's arm. He kept the wretch alive with his magic for the duration, but when his feast was through, he abandoned the man to an infection of the blood. He died three days later, his last words screams for mercy that could be heard for miles."

Rose's mind flashed upon an image of the seer devouring the tin cup that had held her beer. She had never known Ambrose to lie about such a thing as this. She'd had no idea what she risked by summoning the man. If whatever he'd found inside her mind hadn't frightened him, there was little doubt she would be missing an arm or a leg or perhaps something even worse.

A shiver worked across her skin, raising the hairs on her arms. "Then I suppose I must thank the monster who has haunted my dreams. At least she spared me from paying a gruesome price. Caspar fears her, and refused to ask for payment, though he did vow he would deliver me into her hands should I summon him again."

"What monster is this?" Ambrose asked, leaning forward and motioning for her to take the chair opposite his.

And now she had an answer to one of her questions. Ambrose hadn't seen the Mother the night of their shared dream. It was disappointing news, for a part of her desperately wished he could truly share her terror.

"The Mother, the first womb . . . She's visited me twice in my sleep and I'm certain I heard her voice the night Ecanthar attempted to kill me at Manor High." Rose winced slightly as she said the Mother's name, but pushed away her uneasiness.

There was no other choice now. Even if speaking the name served as some sort of summons, she must take that risk. Ambrose must know what she faced— what they both faced—for the Mother clearly had her eye on the black faerie as well.

"*What?*" Ambrose rose and crossed the room to stand beside her at the fire, as he seemed to sense she wouldn't be claiming her own chair. She couldn't sit down, not now, not when anxiety rushed through her veins like some devilish spirit, leaving her with the feeling that the ground beneath her could give way at any moment. "But surely she is no more, if she ever truly existed in the first place. I was always told she was a myth, a story to aid the uneducated in understanding their origins."

"As was I, but she is no myth. She is real, and she has turned her ancient eyes toward Myrdrean and our entwined fates."

Quickly Rose told Ambrose of the Mother's desire for her to wed him instead of his brother, of her attempts to turn Rose's affection and loyalty away from the vampire, and of her threats to kill Gareth in order to ensure a union between Rose and her former liaison. "That is why she drew you into my dream. I believe she thought if we . . . shared a bed, I would be more easily persuaded to betray my vows."

"But why would a goddess wish for such a thing? Surely she has more important business in the world than the union of a faerie man and a woman of uncertain blood." Absently he took the poker and stoked the fire, clearly having difficulty believing Rose's tale. "And she certainly knows you are not the true Rosemarie Edenburg. If this really is the Mother who visits you, then she is all-knowing."

"Caspar said she is not a goddess, but I believe you are correct in that she knows far more than anyone else who walks the earth. She knows the secrets of my birth, but for some reason does not wish me to know them. Ecanthar is in her employ and does her bidding. We know he was responsible for slaying my mother's friends in Paris before they could tell their secrets, but I believe he also killed the king's sons. And I think the Mother visits the king in his sleep and fills his head with perverse ambition, though to what purpose I cannot imagine."

"Then why did Ecanthar try to kill you?" he asked. "If the Mother wishes you to wed, and he is truly under her—"

"He was disobeying orders that first night at Manor High. He told me he had come to kill me with swiftness and mercy rather than force me to suffer the torment the Mother had planned."

"Marriage to me is such a torment?"

Rose crossed her arms and had to fight the urge to stamp her foot in protest. This was no time for jest. She must find some way to make him believe what she now knew to be true. "Ambrose, please, I am serious. The figure in my dreams is more frightening than anything I have ever seen. I vow, even Caspar the Wise, this monster you fear, was terrified of her. Yes, she wants me to marry you, but that is not the end of it. She wants something else . . . something awful. Why else would she meddle with the Seelie king?"

"You cannot be certain of that. Just as you cannot be certain it isn't someone pretending to—"

"I feel it in my heart. I believed Ecanthar when he spoke to me in his shadow beast form. Mad though he might be, he truly thought he was saving me unspeakable torture by claiming my life before the Mother could take control of it."

"So the creature would have you think it a friend?"

"I know not what Ecanthar would have me think, but he called me sister and swore he loved me too much to see me fall into the Mother's hands."

"This man's 'love' caused him to rape and impregnate half a dozen women. He nearly claimed you as his mate, though his power caused a fever of such heat your mind would have been irreparably damaged. If this truly is Ecanthar who's taken these other forms—"

"I thought we had agreed it had to be—"

"Then his notion of saving you may very well be preventing you from finding favor with one who will—"

"Please, I beg you." Rose took Ambrose's hand in hers and gazed up into his eyes, pleading with her entire being for him to trust her. "The Mother doesn't mean to grant me a boon. She will destroy me or worse. Believe me, and help me fight this creature. I cannot bear the thought of facing her alone."

"You will face nothing alone as long as I am alive and drawing breath." Ambrose's gaze softened and his free hand moved to cup her cheek. "If you believe she wishes you ill, I will do whatever it takes to banish her from your dreams and your life."

"Thank you." She fought the urge to press a kiss to his palm. They had put that impulse behind them on the road to London and it would serve no purpose to stir that particular pot. "You can't know how that eases my mind."

His gaze grew darker as he gently pulled away, stepping back as if he must put space between them or be tempted to do more than touch her. "Believe me, I would ease your mind even further if I could. Instead, I fear what I must tell you will only agitate it further."

"If it is about my husband, I don't wish to know," Rose said, meaning every word. "Whatever information you gathered from your vampire friend, you may keep it to—"

"I learned nothing from Sebastian, save that Gareth had nothing to do with the attack on Manor High. He was, in fact, deliberately kept ignorant of the battle plans for fear he would betray the cause to his new wife's people. His deep love for you is something the rest of the vampire nation cannot seem to understand."

"Deep love." Rose laughed, a sharp sound that cut through her chest. "Such deep love that he would abandon me in the middle of the night and neglect to send word of his whereabouts."

"You shall receive no argument from me. I simply wished you to know that he has convinced his blood brethren that his love is true." Ambrose took a deep breath and Rose could feel his reluctance to speak his next words, but speak them he did. "But if the letter young Mimsy sent this morning is to be believed, he has certainly strayed from the path of a faithful husband."

Rose took the letter Ambrose pulled from his pocket, cursing the trembling of her hands as she unfolded the missive. Only moments ago she had been certain no news of Gareth could affect her, not when she was fighting for her life against an ancient monster of unspeakable power. Yet here she was, shaking like a girl in her first Season fearing the slight of some favored beau.

Mimsy's hastily scrawled words did nothing to ease her nerves.

The woman who spoke to the vampire in the mirror is unknown to any at court. (And I asked absolutely everyone, I swear it!) But I have learned from a reliable source that your husband's destination is London,

and that he goes to meet a woman there for an assig-
nation. (And this source is very, very reliable. I swear
to that as well!)

> *Yours in utter secrecy,*
> *The Mysterious M*

"She is obviously taking some pleasure in her new duties as spy." Rose carefully refolded the paper in her hands, though a part of her wished to crumple it into a ball and throw it into the fire.

Destroying the letter would not affect its contents.

"I can't believe you would trust the little fool to keep at this without being found out. She will certainly forget to be discreet and be slain for treason against the king."

Rose shrugged. "Perhaps, but that is not my concern. Though I will say she is far more clever than most give her credit for. She certainly had me fooled into thinking her a simpleton who offered her friendship to someone new at court."

"The minx is a talented actress. Lies fall from her lips with alarmingly alacrity for someone so very young."

"Yet . . . you think she tells the truth?" Rose held the letter up between them.

"I am certain she tells the truth. The Fearsome still owe me their allegiance for the years I worked the illusion spell to aid them in hiding from humanity. They know I will aid them again, as soon as my magic is recovered."

"Of course." Rose trusted that the Fearsome were loyal to Ambrose. The troll forces had saved her life at least once, proving more helpful than her own family when the tribe organized against her. Though admittedly strange creatures, they had their crude sense of honor.

"Two hours past, I received a visit from a troll messenger. Gareth was spotted near the Jewish rag market, walking into a rooming house with a blond woman on his arm. The pair of them looked very cozy, according to the report." To his credit, he didn't look pleased to be delivering the evidence of her husband's infidelity.

"The Jewish rag market?" Rose asked, the location seeming strangely relevant.

But then, perhaps she was simply trying to focus on any element of his words other than the distressing knowledge that her husband was an utter louse.

"Yes. And he is still there. The Fearsome stand guard outside, and have vowed to alert me as soon as he departs the rooming house."

Rose took a deep breath, then turned and threw the letter into the fire. "It is no concern of mine."

"Surely you can't—"

"I must prepare myself to face the Mother. Though I have not seen her in my dreams since that night at Manor High, I can feel her eyes upon me. She hasn't abandoned her plans for my future—whatever they may be."

"We shall discover those plans. There are excellent Fey scholars of ancient history located right here in London who can tell us everything known about the Mother. I will contact them directly," Ambrose said, stepping closer, until she could feel his heat warming her back even as the fire warmed her front.

"Thank you, that will prove valuable."

"As will the name of the true Myrdrean princess. I'll

set my sources to work discovering her location at once, and when she is found, she'll be placed under guard. No creature shall harm her until we learn all that she knows."

"Whatever that may be. I fear she may be as ignorant as I. Our parents obviously didn't wish either of us to be aware of the bargain that had been made."

"She will know enough to lead us to the secrets of your birth. I have no doubt of that," he said, as if he sensed her need for reassurance. "But for now, there is little we can do that we have not done already. I wonder if it would be best to take steps to clear your mind and heart so that you might focus on the greater mission at hand."

"I do not want to see him, Ambrose." Rose's voice broke despite her attempts to retain control. "I fear I will do something . . . rash if I find him with another."

"An understandable urge." His hands came to rest on her shoulders and immediately she felt a bit calmer. Since the day they'd been connected by magic, it had always been thus. Despite the passion Ambrose could stir within her, when he touched her he summoned a certain peace deep within her soul.

"Caspar said I lacked a soul," she whispered, ashamed to say the words aloud. "Do you suppose that could be true?"

"I cannot say. But I *know* you have a heart, a very kind heart." He pressed a soft kiss to the top of her hair, the gesture so tender it nearly brought tears to her eyes. "And you must use that heart now. Consider, Rose. If there's an ancient supernatural attempting to separate you from your husband . . . might she not have some hand in his present behavior?"

She could no longer resist turning to gaze into his eyes.

Was this truly Ambrose Minuit standing before her, urging her to reconsider her harsh judgment of his brother? The brother he had always loathed and resented for his presence in Rose's life?

"I cannot bear to see you wounded so deeply," he said. "Though my half brother is not all I wish for you in a husband, I can see that you love him, and how happy he's made you even in the midst of great trial."

"Is this happiness? The feeling I will shatter apart?"

He continued with a smile. "And I can see how greatly he cares for you. It wasn't with a false heart that he spoke his vows. Despite his supposed betrayal, I believe his love for you is real, and that it would destroy him to lose your regard."

"Truly?"

"Truly."

"Thank you." There were tears flowing down her cheeks now; she couldn't help herself. She hadn't realized how desperately she'd needed to hear those words until they were spoken.

But Ambrose knew, and he had spoken them. For her. That one action spoke to the depths of his affection in a way nothing else ever had.

"I am a very lucky woman to have such a friend," she whispered, aching to stand on tiptoe and press a kiss to his lips, even as another part of her was wild to race to Gareth's side without delay.

It was because she wanted them both. Goddess help her.

She didn't want to choose between her strong, stalwart faerie and her merry, clever vampire. She wanted them both—in her life, in her heart, and in her bed.

The very idea would have shocked her to the core even a few weeks past, but that was before she realized how precarious life could truly be. She had faced death a hundred times or more during the years she fought the tribe, but what—and who—she fought for had always been clear.

Now she knew she had spent a hundred years fighting for a cause that was not her own, living the life of another woman. She was no longer sure what was real and what was fantasy. The only thing she knew for certain was that her adoptive mother and father had loved her—and that she had loved them in return. Deeply, with unwavering devotion.

But even that love couldn't compare to what she felt for the two men in her life. Gareth and Ambrose were buried deeper in her heart and soul than even those who had raised her as their little princess. In a world that suddenly seemed so terribly changeable, that was, at times, all that kept her sane.

She loved them both, and would continue loving them no matter what course their lives took in these tumultuous times—even if the three of them ended up traveling in very different directions.

It was a sad thought, but an oddly comforting one as well.

"Are you ready?" Ambrose asked.

She nodded. It was time to begin the work of sorting out her life, and what better place to begin than with the man who had claimed her as his wife?

"I'm ready. Call for the carriage when it suits you." Rose hurried toward the door, already debating which dress she should don for this sort of errand. What did one wear when rushing to confront a wayward husband? "I will change and be down shortly."

"Then you shant be rushing to the rag market in your breeches."

Rose paused in the doorway, Ambrose's taunting tone not lost upon her. "I am a sensible woman, Ambrose, but not that sensible."

"No call for sensibility in a situation such as this," he said. "You should wear the navy silk with the white ribbon."

"Isn't that rather plain?" she asked, turning to glance at him over her shoulder.

"Not when you wear it."

Such simple words, but one of the most heartfelt compliments she'd ever received. "Thank you."

"If you thank me one more time I'll have to do something rash in order to protect my reputation as a scoundrel." He scowled before stalking toward his desk, presumably to write the letters that would set in motion their plan to track down Hannah Hughes. "Now hurry, let us attend to this errand and be done with the matter. We have more pressing business to attend to."

"Yes, we do." She fled up the stairs without another word, amazed at how much stronger and more capable she felt after hearing the word "we."

She could still claim Ambrose as one of her allies, and she hoped Ambrose was right about Gareth. Perhaps there was a perfectly reasonable—if you considered the supernatural interference of an ancient monster reasonable—explanation for his strange behavior. Perhaps the Mother had been whispering evil words into his ears while he slept, maybe even going so far as to convince him Rose had betrayed her vows.

If the Mother had accomplished that, she knew her husband would not be above seeking his revenge. Gareth had many excellent qualities, but his taste for vengeance was not among them.

In fact, she wouldn't put it past him to make certain his location and the debauched nature of his activities were known to the supernatural community at large. If he had deliberately set out to castigate her, it would hardly be an effective punishment if she were unaware of what he was about.

The realization made her shiver as her maid helped her out of her filthy clothes and began scrubbing her clean with a cold rag. If Gareth had planned for her to seek him out, there was no doubt that whatever position she found him in would be very compromising and hurtful indeed.

It was nearly enough to make her rethink placing her sword in its usual position in her stays. Perhaps it would be better if she wasn't armed for this particular errand. For no matter what he had done, she truly didn't wish to kill her husband.

CHAPTER SEVENTEEN

It was half past six by the time Rose and Ambrose exited their carriage at one end of rag market, but the area was still bustling with activity. The Jews of London had claimed the entire street for their own several decades past and on market days there was no chance of making one's way down the thoroughfare except on foot.

Carts overflowing with brightly colored scraps of material of various lengths and quality crowded every inch of available space. And in those few corners where one of the worshippers of the older incarnation of the human god didn't hawk his wares, other vendors had set up shop, selling warm buns with chunks of cheese and beer.

The smell of spilled ale and unwashed bodies assaulted Rose's nose as she took Ambrose's arm and set off through the market. Despite their fine clothing, the cloth sellers did not hesitate to pull out bolts of their choicest material to thrust toward the couple as they

walked by. Rose had heard tales of recently impover-
ished nobility seeking out the scraps of their more priv-
ileged neighbors here.

There had been quite a scandal several years past
when the seventh daughter of a penniless duke attended the first ball of her Season in a gown fashioned
from the leftovers of three different dresses recently
commissioned by a wealthy merchant's daughter. To
hear the gossips tell of it, the merchant's daughter had
all but clawed the garment from the young lady and
both had ended their debuts in disgrace.

The entire story made Rose rather glad she'd never
had a Season. It seemed a brutal thing to put young
women through at such a vulnerable time in their lives.

"And you are positive you used no cosmetics?"
Ambrose asked for easily the tenth time since she descended the stairs at his home.

Damn her own vanity. If she had left Caspar's
wretched mark upon her forehead instead of doing her
best to work her new power upon it, she could have
avoided Ambrose's scrutiny.

"You may rub at the spot with your glove if you'd
like, Ambrose," she said, trying not to read too much
into the faerie's fascination with her new gift. It was a
strange magic, no doubt, but surely there had to be others like her somewhere in the supernatural world. "But
I swear to you, it was precisely as I said. I simply
looked into the mirror and thought of the mark fading
away and so the business was done."

"I will send another missive to the scholars straight
away, as soon as we arrive home this evening. In the
future, you must share any new developments in your
power with me immediately."

"Yes, of course." Rose ignored the spark of irritation inspired by his domineering tone.

She had known the man for more than a hundred years. He would always attempt to take the lead, and she would always resist. It was what they were both accustomed to and there were times when the push and pull amused them both.

But not today. Nothing was amusing her today. She was ready to be done with this errand and proceed to the business of finding the woman whose life she had stolen when she was but three years old.

"Just a few doors down. It's on the third and fourth floors, and shares a common entrance with a grocer," Ambrose said, as he guided her gently away from one of the more passionate hucksters.

"A grocer?" Rose lifted her skirts, dodging two stray dogs racing through the busy street, and wished she had donned something a bit more practical. At this rate, her hem would be in tatters by the time they arrived.

"Did you expect a rooming house in the rag market to be fashionable?"

"I expected it to have its own entrance, at the very least." She walked on tiptoe, hoping to catch a glimpse of where they were bound. "At this rate, I begin to doubt it is a rooming house at all."

Ambrose laughed softly beneath his breath. "You needn't worry. The address is not a scandalous one. Though according to several gentlemen of my acquaintance, there are ladies living just down the street who specialize in flagellation and other, more exotic diversions. Perhaps Gareth acquired his companion there."

"If my husband wished to be whipped, I could have

managed the act myself." Her words emerged with far more heat than intended, and for the thousandth time she urged herself to remain calm. No good would come from losing her temper.

"There are some men who prefer to be serviced by strangers," he said, relishing the opportunity to disparage Gareth's character. Rose supposed he felt his obligation to treat his brother fairly had been concluded with his words of caution before the fire. "But the women living near here charge a guinea or more, and are likely free of the worst of the diseases. Should you decide to take your husband back to your bed, you can be relatively sure you wouldn't—"

"I would prefer to discuss these matters with one person, and one person only."

"Of course. Your husband," Ambrose said, infusing the last word with his usual disdain. "Shall we set about finding the man, then?"

He urged her down the steps leading into a very tidy grocer's shop without waiting for her reply. Rose paused just inside the door, allowing her eyes to adjust to the dim light while Ambrose strode straight across the room, past a shop boy who had fallen asleep with his cheek upon the counter and a pair of young girls sorting scraps of ribbon. Without further ado, he rang a tiny silver bell set upon a small table near the rear of the store. A few moments later, a severely dressed woman of nearly forty years hurried down the steps.

Ambrose exchanged a few words with the dark-haired proprietor—who darted a nervous look at Rose once or twice during the brief conversation—and then returned to fetch her from the doorway.

"Mrs. Clabber says she has one free room that may

suit your purposes, sister." Ambrose took her arm and guided her toward the darkened stairwell where the woman was already disappearing.

"And what purposes might those be?" Rose tried to ignore the speeding of her heart as she realized she was only moments away from seeing Gareth again.

"You're a young widow looking for a respectable place to stay until you can find a position as a lady's companion to one of your elderly acquaintances," he whispered as they mounted the stairs. "Not that it truly matters. I've entered the woman's mind and found her easily swayed to another's will. She will show us to her free room and then depart on a previously forgotten errand. We should have several hours until she returns."

She hoped their errand would not require more than a few minutes, let alone hours. What in the world did Ambrose think they would be doing in this place?

Rose was afraid to ask, so she kept her silence.

As predicted, the woman unlocked the door to a very small but clean room on the third floor and then immediately made her apologies and rushed to fetch her wrap, begging their pardon for her sudden departure. Ambrose and Rose waited until they heard her descend the stairs before starting their search.

Beginning on the third floor, they paused before the door to each room, Rose seeking her husband's mind and Ambrose using his superior hearing to listen through the surprisingly thick doors.

But as fortune would have it, there was no need for supernatural hearing to locate Gareth and his companion.

Rose heard a woman's gay laughter in the stairwell

leading to the fourth floor, and soon after the low rumbling of her husband's voice. He sounded positively lighthearted, far merrier than she had heard him since before they had spoken their marriage vows. It seemed this new woman gave him reason to be his cheerful, rakish self, while she brought him only misery and infirmity.

"Close your mind, Rose. If I can hear you, your husband will certainly be able to do the same." Ambrose took her elbow just as they reached the door to the woman's room, holding her still before she could reach for the handle.

"I plan on speaking my mind. Shields are immaterial." Rose pulled away from his calming touch.

She didn't wish to be calm. She wanted to cling to her anger, and hope that rage would be enough to hold her together should the scene within the room prove as distressing as she believed it would be.

There was a hint of resistance as she pushed the handle down, but it gave with a slight increase in pressure. It couldn't have taken more than a second or two to open, not nearly long enough for Gareth to fight his way free of a compromising position if he had been of the mind to do so.

It seemed, however, that he was not.

He lay upon a green and gold settee, his stocking feet propped upon one arm of the couch and his head in the lap of a striking young woman. Her long golden hair and bright blue eyes were incredibly similar to Rose's. She seemed to be a bit taller, but it was difficult to tell when she was seated.

Seated with her long, elegant fingers tangling in Gareth's unbound hair . . .

Rose's eyes landed upon those fingers and could not seem to move away, even when her mouth went dry and her ribs felt as if they would explode from the pressure building within her.

His head was in another woman's lap.

It was not nearly so awful as she had imagined, nor half as scandalous as the scene they could have burst in upon. But the ease with which this woman touched her husband and the almost feline relaxation evident in Gareth's pose left little doubt this was not the first time these two had met. Nor was this simply a carnal assignation. No, there was real affection between her husband and his mystery woman. Maybe even love.

It was that realization that threatened to take her breath away, and cause her heart to die a painful death within her chest.

"Ambrose, Rose, what a pleasant surprise. I was glad to hear you'd made it free of Manor High before the vampire forces arrived." Gareth's smile wavered only for a moment, and he made no move to lift his head from his lover's lap. His eyes were deeply shadowed and his skin alarmingly pale, but his ill health could not soften her heart. Not this time. "I assure you, I hadn't the foggiest notion what my fellow bloodmen had planned."

His wife was in the doorway, and yet he made no move to leap to his feet and conduct himself with anything resembling propriety. His behavior was so baffling that for a moment Rose could do nothing but stand there and stare at the pair of them, anger and pain and disbelief warring for supremacy within her breast.

"Miss Hughes, I'd like to you to meet my half brother, Ambrose Minuit. He is of the Fey de la Nuit, the dark Fey I've been telling you about."

"Miss Hughes." Ambrose nodded slightly, the barest acknowledgment to the introduction.

"They're the ones who will be out for my new grandfather's blood once they realize what he has been about?" the woman asked, her voice thick with an accent Rose couldn't quite place.

"Precisely." Gareth chuckled, as if Miss Hughes hadn't just snubbed his brother by refusing to acknowledge Ambrose's nod with any gesture or words of her own. "And this is Rosemarie—or so the lady has been called all her life—the woman I believed to be my betrothed."

Then, for the first time since she entered the room, his green eyes finally met hers. The moment their gazes connected, Rose felt the ground beneath her fall away and a silent scream rose in her throat. She couldn't bear this, couldn't look into the eyes that had stared into her very soul as they made love and see nothing.

It was as if all the memories they had made together had been stolen away from him, and now his sunken eyes saw her as nothing but a stranger, some woman he had mistakenly married in a moment of confusion.

She wanted to fly at him and tear the calm look from his face, to scream that she was not simply his mistaken betrothed, but his legal wife, but found she could do nothing. Nothing save stand there and gape as the world crumbled around her, burying her alive.

"Ambrose, Rosemarie," Gareth said, still holding her gaze, as if daring her to do something to stop him from completing his introductions, "this is Miss Hannah Hughes, my true intended and heir to Myrdrean's throne."

Someone made a sound of disbelief, but Rose honestly couldn't say if it was her or Ambrose. All she could focus upon was the rush of the blood in her ears, a sound that quickly became so overwhelming it seemed her heart was bigger than the entire rest of her body combined. It was a giant monster that would crowd everything else from the room, from the world.

It most certainly crowded everything else from her mind.

She couldn't seem to care that the woman she sought sat before her, ready to be questioned, most likely in possession of answers that would change the course of Rose's life. She couldn't seem to care that her husband was obviously eager to end their marriage and claim his true bride, or that her dearest friend had witnessed her shameful abandonment by the one she loved. She couldn't seem to care that her right to claim Myrdrean was now most certainly forfeit, or that the Mother still searched for her, or that Ecanthar might very well try to take her life again. The heavens could have rained fire upon the earth and she doubted even *that* would have captured her full attention.

There was nothing but that horrible beating, that rushing in her ears that would surely drive her mad if she didn't escape it. And soon.

At the moment Rose stumbled backward, Ambrose stepped forward, extending his hand toward Miss Hughes, thankfully clearing the way for her escape. She was through the door and down the stairs before anyone in the room could say a word—not that she would have heard any protests regardless.

There was still only the drumbeat of her heart chasing her as she burst out onto the crowded street and fought her way through the press of bodies and hucksters' carts. More than anything she longed to exercise the gift of grace she'd been given by the Fey, to run flat out, as she had run from the wyrms in the catacombs at Faversham months ago, but there were too many people out and about.

She could feel hands clawing at her as she hurried by, doing their best to hold her in place until the wretched pounding could take her over completely, until she became nothing but an empty shell suited only to the containment of that ravenous heart.

"No!" Rose screamed as her wings burst through flesh and clothing without her consciously summoning them forth.

The change was upon her before she could even think to control it—as sudden as a summer storm. She stumbled under the weight of her wings, which felt so much heavier than they ever had before, while all around her the poor people of the market gasped in shock and fear. Many of those closest to her turned to run, but a select few fell to the ground at her feet, crying out for mercy as if she were some heavenly messenger sent to pass judgment upon them.

And perhaps that's what the humans thought her— an angel. With her pretty face and blond hair she would certainly fit in nicely with the golden men painted on cathedral ceilings and portrayed in church glass. It was really too bad for the men and women laid prostrate at her feet that she was no holy creature blessed with the power to heal or destroy. She was simply a woman in pain, as lost and desperate as any mortal upon the great wide earth.

With a sob, Rose took to the air, flying low over the crowd, grateful to hear their shouts and cries if only because they seemed to drown out the furious beating in her head. Softer it grew and then softer still. The farther she flew away from her faithless husband and his new love, the more peace she gained within her mind.

By the time she reached the end of the market, she was able to think clearly enough to realize she should find someplace to hide before the chaos below her attracted the wrong sort of attention. The last thing she needed was to be taken into custody by the Fey de la Nuit for violating supernatural law by displaying her true nature openly in front of a crowd of mortals.

Upon reaching the end of the road, she made a sharp turn to the right, leaving Rosemary Lane for a much quieter street.

"Rosemary Lane," Rose whispered to herself as she sought an ally where she might steal a private moment to draw her wings back within her body.

She now realized why the location of the rooming house had seemed important. The rag market was located on *Rosemary* Lane. Surely it was no accident that the street where she learned she had been replaced as the princess of Myrdrean bore nearly the same name she had claimed as her own for two hundred years.

Her husband must have planned it deliberately. Perhaps he found it perversely amusing. Gareth had always taken pride in his rather twisted sense of humor. Rose usually enjoyed it as well, but that had been when his jokes were merely inappropriate and outrageous, not cruel. And what he'd done *had* been cruel. That he'd planned her humiliation so thoroughly cut her to the quick—as he'd surely known it would.

Despite her best efforts to hold them at bay, tears filled her eyes by the time she found the sort of place she searched for.

The deserted little alleyway stretched back far enough from the street to offer privacy, stopping dead at an ancient brick wall and a pile of putrid garbage. It was a suitably wretched place to end her flight from one of the bleakest moments of her life. Only finding her parents and brother dead and rotted upon their thrones could compare.

"Not my parents, not my brother." Her voice echoed hollowly off the crumbling bricks as her feet touched down upon a relatively clean patch of ground. Would her stubborn mind never accept the truth? She was nothing now, and those she loved had never been hers to claim.

"They were yours. They loved you, no matter that you weren't their true child." Ambrose's gentle words made her wince, the kindness in his tone only intensifying the ache within her.

"Leave me," she said, grateful the tears flowing down her cheeks couldn't be heard in her voice. If she kept her back turned, perhaps she could save herself any further shame. "I want to be alone."

"So I gathered. I assume you are aware that you broke the law nearly a hundred times over. It's a separate charge for each human who witnessed your transformation. Only one charge would be enough to keep you in chains for a dozen years or more."

"I don't care." Her voice caught, betraying her weakness.

Damnation. Surely Ambrose thought her the worst sort of fool. After all, hadn't he warned her from the very beginning not to trust Gareth?

Ambrose sighed, and she could hear him walking closer. She vowed she would take flight again if he dared draw too near. No matter how she tried, she couldn't seem to summon her wings back within her, so she might as well make use of them a second time. "I doubt the Fey de la Nuit high council would care either. Not once they saw what you made of yourself." His words grew soft, hushed, and if she hadn't known better she would have said he sounded almost fearful. "What have you done, Rose, and how have you done it?"

"I am not Rose. I do not know who or what I am." She swiped her tears away with the back of her gloved hand.

"Don't be ridiculous. You have been Rosemarie for two hundred years and more and you are Rosemarie still. That little fool Gareth discovered doesn't change that. Nor does it change what you are becoming. You are coming into great power, a power unlike anything I've heard of before."

Rose said nothing. No matter what strange talents she claimed, she had never felt less powerful. It seemed everything was beyond her control, and that fear plagued her more than ever.

"Truly, these are magnificent," Ambrose said. "You could outdistance any Fey born in the past five hundred years."

"Don't." She flinched as she felt his hand upon one extended wing, and spun around to face him, further protests dying on her lips as she caught a glimpse of her new wings.

Gone were the small, lightly feathered gray things she had first discovered a few months past. In their place were giant leathery wings as black as night. They resembled nothing so much as the wings of a bat and were so immense the tips would extend ten feet across if stretched to their full width.

"Goddess." She reached a timid finger toward the tightly stretched flesh, and was shocked to find the thin skin soft to the touch.

She was even more shocked to feel the echo of her caress within the wing itself. It was almost impossible to believe these great, powerful things belonged to her. They were intimidating, to say the least, almost frightening in their darkness.

"I rather enjoy darkness." Ambrose was reading her thoughts, but Rose found she didn't care. In fact, rather than firming her shields, she abandoned them altogether, letting him sweep into her mind like a cool breeze.

Immediately she felt a certain calm descend upon her, banishing a bit of her despair.

"I look like a bat . . . or a devil." She flexed the muscle she had once used to pull her small gray wings within her, but to no avail. It made her wonder if she would be cursed to remain thus for the rest of her life.

"There are worse curses. Though these will make it difficult to walk unobserved among the mortals."

"They are . . . strange," Rose said, a shiver working through her as she spied the tiny clawlike projections at the end of each wing.

"They are beautiful. The perfect dark foil to your golden loveliness." Ambrose stepped closer, until only a few inches separated them.

Rose tipped her head back, looking up into his silver eyes, and was taken with the strange urge to wrap her great wings around them, to cloak them as the night would cloak two lovers in the shadows beneath the trees at the Vauxhall Pleasure Gardens.

Is that an invitation? His thoughts curled intimately

into her mind, twining with her own, the mental touch as erotic as a finger traced upon bare skin.

Lust and despair surged within her, urging her to take the solace she craved from the willing man in front of her. But for some reason she hesitated, pulling away from him and forcing her lips to form a reply. "I am in no place to offer any sort of invitation. I am . . . broken."

"You are nothing of the sort." His hands cupped her face, the usually cool fingertips hot, burning her as he drove them into her hair, ruining what was left of her carefully arranged curls. "That waste of flesh who calls himself a man could never break you."

Rose sucked in a breath, striving to keep the fresh tears pricking at her eyes from spilling down her cheeks. "I loved him, Ambrose. I loved him so much."

"And he is a greater fool than even I would have thought possible to have squandered such a gift." He leaned close as he spoke the words, his breath soft and warm against her lips. "I would not be so foolish."

She wanted to taste him, to drive her tongue into his mouth and finally know the true flavor of Ambrose. The real Ambrose, not some lover in a dream, but the flesh-and-blood man here before her.

Then taste me, Rose. Devour me if you will, I will make no protest. His lips were so close she could feel them warming her own, making her burn with the need to do precisely as he asked.

I think I would prefer to be the one devoured. Her arms were around his neck and her breasts pressed tightly to his strong chest before any conscious decision could be made. Her body had taken control and no longer cared for the opinion of her mind. It wanted to feel something other than despair, to drown in the pleasures of the flesh, in the bliss of man and woman connected at their most primal. *Consume me, Ambrose. Make me forget.*

When we are finished you won't remember his name, I swear it. And then his arms were around her waist, pulling her impossibly closer, melding their bodies as his lips met hers.

CHAPTER EIGHTEEN

Rose moaned as Ambrose laid claim to her body without a moment's hesitation. His lips angled against hers and his tongue swept inside her mouth with a fervor that left no doubt how desperately he wanted her.

Want is too pale a word for what you do to me, Rosemarie. One arm tightened about her waist as his other hand drove into her hair and fisted there, pulling her closer, until their teeth pressed together through their lips and Rose could feel her mouth beginning to bruise.

The hint of pain made her moan again as she dug her fingertips into his shoulders, wishing his coat and shirt were gone and he could feel her nails scoring his back. She wanted to tear at his flesh until he cried out, until he dispensed with the last of his gentleness and took her with all the raw need she could feel simmering beneath his tight control.

You would have me take you here? In this place that reeks of rot and filth? His mouth left hers, and his lips trailed down the length of her neck, kissing and biting, the feel of his teeth raking across her sensitive flesh taking her breath away.

I would have you take me against that wall like a common whore. She let her teeth find his throat and return the favor, biting down until he growled and spun them both toward the wall.

The back of her head hit the bricks hard enough to make stars dance behind her closed eyes, but the momentary dizziness only made her lust spiral higher. She wanted Ambrose to touch her everywhere, all at once, to be free of every wretched article of clothing that separated their eager bodies. She couldn't bear to be so covered for another moment.

With a trembling hand she clawed at the ribbon at her bodice, pulling at the fabric until it tore and then tugging at her stays until her breasts spilled free into the cool evening air. Her nipples were already tight and aching and the cold only made the sensation worse. Never had she been so desperate to feel a man's hands upon her, to feel him suckling at her tender flesh.

Goddess, woman, you are *wicked.* Ambrose's lips found one tightly puckered tip a moment later, tugging her into the wet heat of his mouth until she screamed from the force of the pure pleasure coursing through her.

"Ambrose!" Her head fell back against the wall as she arched shamelessly toward him.

He moaned against her breast. *Your skin is even softer than I imagined.* Strong hands encircled her ribs, holding her captive as he abandoned one breast for the other.

Her fingers drove into his hair and pulled him closer,

urging him to suck her harder, deeper. *Yes. Please, yes.* Wet heat ran shamelessly down her thighs in response to his rough use, and there were tears in her eyes by the time he moved away, bringing his lips back to hers.

But this time they were tears of pleasure. It seemed like decades since she had felt so deliciously free, so consumed by anything other than fear or pain.

I would never bring you any further pain. I would sell my very soul to ensure your happiness. His hands were trembling as he cupped her face and pulled away from their kiss, his breath coming fast against her swollen lips.

"I love you, Rosemarie. I cannot remember a time when I did not love you," he said, his eyes shining as if he too would weep. "If you say you care for me even a little, I would—"

"Show me," she begged, fingers fumbling with the close of his trousers, her breath coming faster as she felt the thick bulge of his sex beneath the wool.

Goddess, but it seemed she would die if she had to wait another moment to feel him buried inside her, pumping between her thighs until they both shattered apart. "Make these clothes vanish and show me the force of your love."

He seized both her wrists and pressed them into the rough brick above her head. "Give us shelter. I wish no other to see what is mine."

A spark of anger flared within her, but she wrapped her wings about them as he had commanded. "I am not yours. I am nothing and belong to no one."

"You are far from nothing." Seconds later, their clothes disappeared in the wake of some hastily whispered Fey words and Ambrose stood nude before her, his hot, bare skin only inches away from her. He was so beautiful it made the ache within her swell until it was nearly unbearable. "And you will be mine, Rose. I will not share you with another."

Before she could speak a word of protest he seized her thighs in each of his strong hands, lifting them up and out, then pinning her to the wall with his hips. The rigid, swollen length of his cock pressed against the slick heat of her sex, making her moan and writhe against him, wild to feel him where she needed him so desperately.

"Please," she begged, her arms wrapping around his neck and her lips pressing feverishly against his. "Please, Ambrose. Love me."

"Always," he whispered against her mouth as he guided the tip of his shaft to her entrance. "I will never stop." And then he pushed forward, his cock tunneling deeper and deeper, until she was completely filled with the man she loved.

Loved. She did love him—despite their past, despite the fact that part of her heart was still breaking, mourning the loss of her husband's affections—she loved Ambrose.

So you admit your love, here in the waking world?

I have always loved you, even when I feared you. She kissed him, her tongue spearing into his mouth as her legs wrapped even more tightly around his waist, pulling his cock to the very end of her. Goddess, but he felt even better than she had imagined he would. It seemed impossible to get close enough. She wanted to crawl inside him and never find her way free. *How can you doubt it?*

Do you know how many years I've dreamt of hearing those words? His fingers dug into her as he fought for control—not that he need have bothered. She was so near the edge it seemed the slightest shift of his hips would shatter her completely.

Do you know how many years I have dreamed of this? Her breath caught as he began to move ever so slowly, withdrawing until only his tip remained within her, then driving back inside, making every inch of her body sing with delight. *Of your skin bare against mine? Of your body buried—*

You will undo me, woman. You already have me feeling as artless as a boy. Golden light danced through the air, flitting from his lips to hers and back again, teasing them both into a near frenzy. Her wings suddenly vanished into thin air as the magic within them called to one another, but Rose couldn't bring herself to wonder at the strange disappearance or care that anyone walking by could see them. She shamelessly relished the fact that they were bare as the day they were born on the streets of London.

You are far from artless. Rose moaned into his mouth as his thrusts grew faster, deeper, tightening the fist of tension coiling low in her body until she knew it would only be seconds before release claimed her. *Please, love, join me. I want to feel you lose yourself, I want to—*

Goddess, Rose. He groaned and fucked her even harder, faster, until she had no choice but to succumb.

She screamed as she came, her quim gripping Ambrose where he swelled between her thighs. He joined her seconds later, his cock pulsing within her, his arms holding her so tightly to him she could scarcely breathe, but she didn't miss the air. What use was air when there was such a man, clinging to her as if she were the most precious thing in the world, truly banishing her despair in the warm glow of the golden magic that danced around them?

"Rose?" The voice was raw, dripping with pain. Rose's eyes flew open, meeting Gareth's over Ambrose's bare shoulder. He stood at the end of the alleyway, clutching his chest as if he had been shot through the heart. If she hadn't known better she would have said his was the face of a devoted husband who had witnessed the worst possible betrayal he could imagine. "What have . . ."

He looked even worse than he had an hour past, as if there was a poison rotting him from within. As he moved slowly down the alley, his limp was so pronounced she wondered if he would be able to stay upright or crumple to the filthy ground before he reached their position. Part of her wished to see him fall, while the other part ached to take him into her arms and offer him what comfort she could.

But he didn't deserve comfort and her arms were already full. She stayed as she was.

"On the *street*? You were that desperate to fuck my brother?" he asked, rage and misery mingling in his eyes.

"Leave, Gareth. Who Rose takes to her bed is no longer your concern," Ambrose said, making no move to turn around or withdraw from where he was still buried between Rose's legs. He was making it clear, in the cruelest way possible, that he didn't consider his brother a threat.

"She is still my wife!" Gareth roared, his shout the only thing that seemed to have retained any shred of his old strength and vitality. The rest of him was in a sorry state indeed. He'd been forced to brace one hand against the brick wall of the alley for support and was scarcely able to move one foot in front of the other. "You are my wife, Rose. You are my *wife*!" His voice broke, and it seemed he would sob his very heart out.

Still, Rose didn't say a word, only wrapped her arms more tightly around Ambrose's neck and pressed her lips into his bare shoulder. His flesh was slightly damp and salty, and tasted of pure carnal pleasure. She hoped Gareth was listening to her thoughts and could sense how thoroughly Ambrose had loved her, how, even now, her entire body felt aglow with satisfaction.

Her husband's face fell, and he leaned heavily against the wall. When he spoke again, it was in a whisper so soft, she could barely hear him. "Rose . . . please . . . I know I deserve no better after what I did back in that room. If I could undo it all, I swear to you I would. Please . . . just let me explain."

Again she said nothing, but it was not easy to look upon one she loved in so much pain and remain cold. She was tempted to untangle herself from Ambrose's arms and go to him, no matter that he had done his best to shatter her heart into a dozen sharp, cutting pieces.

"I swear to you, it was not what I wanted, it was what— What I mean is, I couldn't do it, even for—" He broke off once more, a growl of frustration ripping from his throat as he drove a hand through his loose hair. "Damnation! There are things I cannot—"

"Leave us, vampire. I will give you a minute more," Ambrose said, every muscle in his body tense. "Then I will claim your head as I have claimed your wife."

Goddess, why? Couldn't he have said something else? *Anything* else?

As Rose could have predicted, Gareth's face

turned nearly purple with rage. Anger seemed to revive him as it had in days past, and suddenly he was on his feet, standing tall, pure menace vibrating from every inch of him. "Not if I claim yours first, you smug bastard."

"Gareth, no!" Rose shouted as Ambrose quickly set her on her feet and spun around to face his brother. Seconds later, their clothing reappeared, as did Ambrose's sword, which he pulled with decided relish. He'd been waiting for this chance, and wouldn't hesitate to kill Gareth.

If Gareth didn't kill him first.

"Please, both of you. Don't do this!"

"This is between my brother and me. Do not interfere, Rose," Ambrose said, moving her behind him protectively before stalking slowly toward where Gareth stood.

"I love you, Rose. Never doubt I love you more than anything, more than this black-hearted faerie could begin to comprehend." The passion in Gareth's voice was real, as were the swords he pulled from the hidden sheaths in his boots.

Rose's heart pounded as she watched them advance toward each other, swords at the ready, each wearing the cold expression they donned in battle. They were going to fight to the death, there was no stopping them—unless she somehow managed to injure each of them enough so that they couldn't destroy the other.

No sooner had the thought entered her mind and her hand began reaching for her blade, then her stays—and the Fey sword secreted within them—vanished. The bodice of her dress grew tighter as her ribs expanded to draw a full breath.

Blasted magic! "Return my sword to me! Damn you, Ambrose, I swear I will—"

"I love you dearly, Rosemarie, but I will not be dissuaded."

"Love? What do you know of love?" Gareth asked. "You, who watched an ogre steal her innocence while she slept. You, who lied to her for a hundred years."

Ambrose raised his sword, ignoring the vampire's words. "I will not suffer this rogue to live."

"No! Please, I—" Before she could finish her plea, the men rushed at each other, swords colliding in a clang of metal.

Gareth thrust one blade forward as the other circled around Ambrose's head, prepared to move in as soon as Ambrose's weapon was otherwise engaged. Ambrose deflected first one blow and then the other, but barely avoided taking a third blow to his stomach as Gareth's first sword returned.

He leapt backward, but Gareth gave him no quarter, pushing forward with blades flying, driving his brother against the brick wall behind him. Rose had never seen Gareth move so quickly. It was as if he had fought with half his speed and skill before, only now revealing his true artistry with his blades. Ambrose parried with his usual grace, but for once he seemed no match for his brother. This battle would not be a long one.

"Don't kill him, Gareth. I swear to you, this will not mend what is broken."

"But it is a start," he said, his words for her but his eyes all for the man who had fallen to his knees before him. "When he is gone your heart will no longer be divided. You will finally love me, and *only* me."

"I will hate you for this!"

He paused for half a second then continued his

deadly advance, swords flying so quickly it was all Ambrose could do to deflect them, let alone prepare an attack of his own. "That is a chance I fear I must take, though I am loathe to cause you pain."

"Goddess, please, I—" Rose broke off with a gasp as Ambrose flung himself to the ground and Gareth caught his thigh with the tip of a blade as he rolled away. He made it to his feet, but just barely, and Gareth's swords were close behind, giving him not a second to recover. "Gareth, I vow I will kill you myself if you—"

"Cease pleading for my life, woman," Ambrose said, the effort it took to fight his brother clear in his voice. "If I die, it is because I chose this death." He grunted as he leapt over a pile of refuse and did his best to push Gareth into an unfavorable position. "Because I have finally found something worth dying for."

"It is an easy thing to die, it is not so easy to *live* for the one you love," Gareth said as he slipped to one side, easing free of the corner Ambrose would have forced him into. "To show her she is all that makes the trial of such a long immortal life bearable."

"You have certainly done a piss-poor job of it, vampire." Ambrose cried out a second later, and a thin red line appeared just below his jaw.

"If I were you, I would cease attempts at conversation." Gareth smiled. "Unless you wish to die more swiftly, of course."

"Stop this!" It was all Rose could do to keep from pulling her hair out. These fools insisted on their idiotic rivalry, too senseless to see it was their lives they played with while acting like roosters vying for control of the henhouse.

Well, this hen wouldn't tolerate this fatal game a second longer.

Seizing a rotted piece of wood from the garbage at the end of the alleyway, Rose dashed to where the men were coming to increasingly vicious blows. Without waiting for a break in their battle, she strode between them, bringing her piece of wood down in a swift arc, deflecting Ambrose's blow and knocking one of Gareth's weapons from his hand before the wood splintered into useless pieces.

"Damnation, Rose, I could have—"

"You could have been killed, you foolish—"

"No, *you* are the fools," Rose said, silencing their protests. "I swear to you on my life and on the lives of every innocent babe who sleeps in London, that I will kill whichever of you still lives at the end of your ridiculous battle. I am not a prize to be won by the man with the swiftest sword."

"Surely you don't—"

"And if you think I speak false, Gareth, then you cannot truly love me." Rose looked slowly between them, making certain they read the message clear in her eyes. "The man who loves me will understand that I am a woman who strives to tell the truth in all things, and my heart will be won by the same. By truth and by deeds that reveal genuine affection and regard— nothing less and nothing more."

All was silent for a moment, save for the sound of swiftly drawn breaths and her own slowing heart. Now that she had said her piece, she could feel herself gaining control once more. If these two insisted on their fight to the death there was nothing more she could do save honor the promise she'd made and destroy them all.

She wasn't certain she could live without the pair

of them. Even if magic hadn't bonded her to Ambrose and marriage bonded her to Gareth, she would have still felt the same. Such was the weakness of love.

"It isn't weakness," Ambrose said, throwing his sword to the ground with a shake of his head. "It is a gift to be so vulnerable to another. I did not wish it to be so."

"Killing Gareth will not keep you safe from pain," Rose said, her voice softening a bit. For all his hundreds of years, Ambrose was nearly as new to love as she herself, and Goddess help her, but she knew how terrifying that vulnerability could be.

"Yes, but it would keep you from running back to this fool now that he comes crawling on his belly, penitent for his misdeeds." Ambrose glared openly at Gareth, who stood no more than three feet away, his sword still in hand. "But I see now that you speak truly. You are the mistress of your own destiny. You always have been, no matter what bargains you've made in the dead of night. I was a fool to think I could win your love with a sword."

Before Rose could think of what to say, Gareth stepped forward and positioned his blade directly beneath the taller man's chin. "Then I am also a fool. Unfortunately, I find it cannot be helped."

"No!" Rose screamed as Gareth thrust his arm forward, the horror of seeing cold steel pierce the sensitive flesh at Ambrose's throat making her gorge rise.

He had done it. He had truly killed his brother.

She was moving before her mind could discern her body's plan, seizing a splintered piece of wood from the ground and aiming it where she knew it would do the most damage. A faerie could survive a stake through the heart, but not a vampire. What she did now would kill him, would cause those merry green eyes to close forever.

Still, she didn't hesitate, though a sob ripped from her throat as she plunged her weapon home.

"Rose!" Her name was the last word on his lips before he fell to the ground.

Time began to move as it had that night at Manor High, each second stretching into an eternity as she watched Gareth fall. She had time to see the shock and regret twisting his features, to feel her heart lurch painfully in her chest as he brought his fingers to where the makeshift stake protruded through the front of his coat, and to note the graying of his skin that foretold the transformation from flesh to ash.

Finally, he hit the ground with a groan—eyes flying even wider for a moment, hands clawing at the dirt beneath him as if it offered some escape from his fate. His back arched as one last terrible jolt of pain ripped through his body before he sagged back to the ground, the life gone out of him, his spirit fled from the eyes that stared vacantly up at the darkening sky.

He was dead. Her husband was dead.

And she had killed him.

Her knees gave out and she hit the ground in a puddle of ruined skirts. A low, wretched moan vibrated through her every cell, yet it seemed the sound came from somewhere outside herself. Or perhaps it was she who was outside herself, her soul hovering outside of her body, reluctant to return to the scene of such devastation.

"Rose . . ." Ambrose's voice was soft, but made her flinch as if he had shouted. She turned toward him, crawling on her hands and knees to where he had fallen only a few feet away from his dead brother.

"You live. Thank the Goddess, you . . ." Her words broke off in a choked sob as she saw her dear friend's face. His flesh was pale and blood ran freely both from the wound at his throat and from between his parted lips. He looked exactly like what he was—a man moments away from death.

"Don't . . . fret. 'Tis easily . . . mended." Ambrose seized the trembling hand she reached toward his wound.

Golden magic flared between them once more, but this time there was pain accompanying the streams of light rather than pleasure. For a moment, Rose could feel the agony of the wound at Ambrose's throat, could sense how horribly close Gareth had come to severing his head from his body, and then the feeling was gone, replaced by a hollowness that was the absence of Ambrose's gift.

"The bond has been weakening quickly in the past few days," Ambrose said, his wounds mended and his voice strong, though he made no move to rise from the ground. "I could have summoned my magic back to me without ill effect at any time, but I was loathe to give up my reason for staying by your side."

"You are my oldest, dearest friend," Rose said, cupping his cheek softly in her hand. His pale face swam before her as she strove to keep her tears from falling. "You do not need any other reason to stay by my side."

"Thank you. For that and for my life. I regret—"

She held up her hand, effectively putting a stop to his words. "I can't. Not just yet. Please. I need a moment with him before . . ."

Before he turns to ash and blows away, before there is not so much as a single white bone lying upon the street to prove Gareth Barrows, Lord Shenley, ever existed, before the man she loved was nothing more than dust swept through the streets of London.

She couldn't finish her sentence aloud, but Ambrose seemed to sense her meaning. With obvious effort, he rolled to one side and rose unsteadily to his feet. "I will await you on the street, and ensure your privacy."

Privacy. Yes it would be a good thing.

Tears began to pour down her face in earnest, and wrenching sobs filled the alleyway, echoing off the bricks that watched her with the same cold detachment with which they had watched Gareth die.

CHAPTER NINETEEN

Tears rolled down Rose's cheeks as she gazed into her husband's lifeless face. She wanted to reach out and take his hand, to throw herself on his chest and absorb the heat of his body, to catch the scent of him one last time, but she didn't dare lay a finger upon him—not even to close the lids of his eyes.

Vampires turned to ash soon after their death, and from the gray tinge to Gareth's skin, he was well on his way to becoming the stuff that filled cold fireplaces all over London. She feared he would disintegrate and disappear at any moment. It was best to simply sit by his side and look upon him, memorizing his every feature before he was taken from her forever.

And all his secrets with him.

He'd followed her here to tell her something, to beg for forgiveness and perhaps explain why he had behaved as he had in that rooming house. Now she would never know what he would have told her, or whether it would have made a difference.

Could his words have mended the rift between them?

"Not the murder of your brother. It could never have survived that," Rose said, swiping at her damp nose with her silk sleeve.

She'd done the only thing she could do. Now she would never know what madness had driven Gareth to lift his sword against an unarmed man. She would never know why he had lain with his head in another woman's lap, or why he had chased herself into the city streets.

But she might still learn what had inspired his flight from Manor High.

Her father's journal pages had been in Gareth's coat pocket when he'd left the Seelie Court, and if she knew her husband, he would have kept the pages upon his person rather than risk another discovering the secrets they contained.

With trembling hands, Rose gently worked open the buttons of his coat, careful not to put pressure upon the body beneath. She was not prepared to see pieces of her husband float away just yet.

As if she would *ever* be prepared for such a thing.

She found the journal pages in his left coat pocket, folded tightly and secured with a simple length of brown twine. Rose tucked the small parcel into the repaired bodice of her gown. Ambrose's magic had mended the tear when he'd summoned their clothing back into the earthly plane. She should have realized then that his magic was stronger than it had been in recent months.

Ambrose had been keeping secrets from her as well, but she wasn't truly surprised. If there was one thing she had come to depend upon, it was the men in her life keeping important information from her. It was something she'd hoped would change with time, once they learned that they could neither protect nor control her by concealing matters she deserved to be made aware of.

"Now nothing will change," she said, fresh tears rolling down her cheeks and falling onto her skirts, staining the silk. Gareth was dead, and Ambrose . . .

She still loved him, perhaps more than ever, but couldn't imagine sharing her life with him now that her husband was dead. Too late, she realized why the two men had always been at each other's throats. It was almost entirely her fault.

They must have both known she couldn't be content with only one of them. She wanted them both, needed them both, and would have eventually put forth the idea that the three of them come to some sort of arrangement—perhaps a house of three such as other Fey de la Nuit brothers often had with the woman of their choosing. It was only a matter of time. Ambrose had put down his sword because, on some level, he had been open to such a thing. Gareth had killed his brother because he would not, could not, share her love.

But why?

Rose fumbled with the twine around the journal pages, doubting her father's words would shed any light on her husband's motives, but needing something to distract her from the man lying inches from her. There was at least some chance these pages would reveal why Gareth had come to London, and how he had found the woman she searched for.

The woman she must return to speak with. Soon.

"Tomorrow is soon enough," Rose whispered beneath her breath as she lifted the papers to the last of the fading light. It would be dark in less than an hour and she couldn't imagine doing anything else but crawling into her bed in Ambrose's guest room and crying until the sun rose once more.

What she read upon the pages, however, quickly changed her mind.

Hannah Hughes is the name Marionette has given our sweet Rose. It is a common name, one that will not attract attention in the human or supernatural worlds—and that is of utmost importance. We must make certain she remains hidden. The creature with which I have struck my unholy pact is terrible, and I fear she will seek to do our daughter harm someday, should it serve her purpose.

Our agreement expressly forbids such an action, and I have paid dearly to win the witch's signature. But now I am left to wonder . . . what good is the mark of a witch?

I am loathe to reveal to my dear wife the true nature of the little one I have found to take Rose's place, or what bargains I have made to secure this child from her mother. I have told Marionette only that the new Rosemarie is a good, biddable girl who bears a remarkable resemblance to our own babe.

We plan to meet in secret at the estate of Marionette's Fey de la Nuit friends just outside Paris. She will take the new Rose and return to Myrdrean to await my return. I will take our child and secret her in some remote corner of the world, hopefully with good people who will love her as we do and raise her to be all that we would wish our beautiful little princess to be.

I will miss her. Even as my heart softens toward this Fey child who watches me across the fire with her big blue eyes, it also breaks . . .

A mother should never be forced to exchange her child for another in order to spare her child's life. And a man should never be forced to go to such lengths to see the pain and suffering fade from his good wife's eyes.

Sometimes I wish I did not love Marionette as I do, then perhaps I could take Charles's advice and simply—

Rose dropped the papers to her lap and sucked in a breath past the giant hand that seemed to be fisting around her heart. The terrible creature, the witch from whom her father had claimed a child to replace his own . . . It was too dreadful to be believed, but at the same time it explained so much.

"It was there all the time. The truth, right there before my eyes." The Mother had called her *daughter* in her dreams. The ancient had never tried to conceal what she was from the child she had sold to the king of Myrdrean.

Goddess. Her true mother was a monster. Rose had sprung from the loins of the most wicked, horrible creature she had ever had the displeasure to meet— and lord only knew the identity of her sire.

She wondered if Gareth had known—if that truth had in any way informed his decision to leave her at Manor High and seek out this Hannah Hughes. It seemed a distant possibility, at best. Gareth knew what it was like to have evil blood on at least one side of his family. His mother had been a Fey de la Nuit exile and the very woman who cursed the Myrdrean princess in her cradle. He wouldn't judge her so harshly.

No, there had been some other reason Gareth felt he must find his true betrothed. Perhaps it was Fey law that drove him, or maybe it was a faerie wife that he had required all along. If he truly had needed someone to transport him to Faerie as Ecanthar had said . . .

Ecanthar. He *could* be her brother. If she was the Mother's daughter, there was no reason he could not be the Mother's son. If he possessed the same shape-shifting abilities as he it would certainly explain her wings and the new powers she'd discovered in the past few days.

The very thought that he was her kin made her want to retch, though nothing could match the horror of the body growing cold before her. Her husband was merely a body now, a lifeless thing that would soon disappear entirely.

"Forgive me, my love," she whispered, bracing her hands on either side of Gareth's shoulders and lean-ing as close as she dared, wishing she could give him one last kiss. "You will always be in my heart."

More tears. It didn't seem possible, but down they poured, falling onto Gareth's graying flesh, turning each place they touched a muted obsidian. In horror, Rose watched the damp black patches spread until they covered his face and poured down across his clothes. Soon he was encased in the black ooze, which hardened before her eyes, transforming into a shining shell, like that of a giant insect.

A shell that began to bubble and snap.

Rose scrambled backward, hobbled by her heavy skirts. Her hands fell into stinking muck—but she didn't pause to swipe the fluid away. The shell was boiling now, popping and crackling like a vat of oil.

Every few seconds, she spied a hint of movement beneath the blackness, as if some man-sized creature struggled to be born.

She had never heard of such a thing. Vampires turned to ash upon their death, even half vampires. Whatever was happening to Gareth was not natural.

What if her tears had somehow done this to him? What if the horrible powers she had inherited from her mother were taking a new and awful form, and something evil emerged from that rippling shell? Would she have the strength to kill Gareth a second time, if he had somehow been resurrected as a soulless beast?

"Ambrose!" Rose tried to scream the faerie's name, but the sound emerged as a whisper, her voice stolen from her as a hand burst through the blackness. It was her husband—the garnet ring upon his finger confirmed it.

Gareth was alive, or at least not quite dead.

With a strangled sob, Rose pulled herself to her feet and searched the ground for Gareth's discarded sword. She must arm herself. There was no way of knowing what state of mind her husband would be in after this strange rebirth—if he was possessed of a mind at all. The walking dead were mindless things, intent on feasting upon the flesh of the living. If Gareth came back as such a creature she would have no choice but to slay him once more, to hack him apart limb from limb and bury each piece in a separate grave.

Finally she spied the shining hilt of his weapon and leapt upon it, spinning around to face the shell just as it split in two.

Gareth burst from between the two halves, vaulting into a seated position with a great gasp. His hair was soaking wet and sticking to his scalp, as if he had just emerged from the sea. His clothes were in a similar state and his skin—restored to its usual pale cream color—glistened in the fading light.

"Damnation," he whispered, the curse followed by a fit of coughing that ended with what sounded suspiciously like laughter.

Rose gripped the sword in her hand until her knuckles turned white, her mouth opening and closing as her baffled mind struggled to think of what to say, what to do.

"I am . . ." Gareth shook his head in disbelief, a smile spreading across his face. "My heart . . . A stake through my blasted heart . . ."

There was no doubt about it, the man was laughing. Laughing his fool head off, as if being staked through the heart was some great joke. She didn't know whether to throw herself at him or slap the ridiculous grin from his face. Or perhaps she would simply fall to the ground and weep some more.

If there was anything more baffling than having the man you loved come back from the dead right before your eyes, Rose could not name it.

"Rose!" He turned to her, as if he had only just realized he was not alone. He was on his feet in seconds, striding toward her, looking fitter than he had since the day she had first made his acquaintance. The man practically radiated health and vitality.

It was oddly terrifying, and she took several hasty steps away from him. "Stay where you are." She held up her hand, not her sword, but she hoped her warning would be taken regardless.

"How can I stay so far from you when I am dying to take you in my—"

A desperate laugh leapt from between her lips. "No, you are not *dying*. You were dead. I killed you myself." Every muscle tensed, ready to defend herself should Gareth decide to seek retribution.

His smile faded. "So you did. And I suppose I deserved it, but I vow to you—I swear—I had no idea." He began to pace back and forth, his excitement clear in his every move. "Everything pointed to Hannah, but when you left the rooming house I felt— Goddess, I can't describe it, but I *knew* I had made a horrible mistake. There was no way she was the one to break the spell. She is hollow inside. She is a pitiful candle and you, my love, the sun."

"A rather deadly comparison." It was a cold thing to say, but she wasn't ready to speak about Hannah or anything else. A part of her still found it impossible to believe Gareth was truly standing before her, alive and well, and that this wasn't some trick of her mind.

Perhaps Gareth was a dream she was having after fainting dead away. Even now she could be lying in the filth of the alley, oblivious to all.

Gareth stopped dead, and turned to her with a pleading look in his eyes. "I am not a dream, sweet. You are awake, as am I." He stepped closer, but Rose countered with another step back. Now she was pressed against the wall where Ambrose had taken her only an hour past, where Gareth had discovered them and this evening had become a true exercise in pain.

Too late she realized her thoughts were unguarded.

Gareth's face lost the last of its merriment. "It killed me to see you with him."

"As it killed me to hear you speak of me as your mistaken betrothed."

"Words. Merely words."

"Words can destroy as surely as any weapon," Rose said, not quite able to put her whole heart into her argument. After all, he was right in a way, and she was far too grateful that he was alive to allow her rage and indignation to take control.

"Which is precisely why I arranged for you to kill me. I knew I'd never gain your forgiveness otherwise." He grinned and closed the distance between them, bracing his hands on either side of her head and leaning closer. "My plan worked perfectly, wouldn't you say?"

"Don't." She closed her eyes. "You nearly killed your brother. If I hadn't stopped you in time . . ." She shuddered at the very thought of Ambrose dead on the ground beside Gareth. "It is not funny, not in the least."

"I know it isn't," he said, his voice as sober as she had ever heard it. "I chose my own life over my brother's. I have loathed the man for years, but such a choice was not mine to make. I will beg his forgiveness and yours if it will make a difference."

"There was no *choice,* Gareth. Ambrose had laid down his sword. He was no threat to you."

"Not at that moment, but I was certain the love he felt for you, and you for him . . . *That* was the threat I sought to . . . It was wrong, but I swear to you there was a reason for my madness. If you will only let me explain." One hand reached out, smoothing her wild hair away from her face. "Look at me Rose. Please."

Her lids slid open, but she stared at his chin rather than at his eyes. She wasn't ready to look him full in the face, not yet. "Wounding my brother was wrong, but hurting you was the worst thing I've ever done. I cannot describe what it did to my heart to see you in the doorway, looking as if I cut you to the quick with every word I spoke. It was far worse than a bit of wood through my chest, I can assure you."

"Then why in the Goddess's name—"

"I had no choice. My two hundred years were nearly complete, and my mother's spell made it clear that I must win the heart of the princess of Myrdrean and have her claim my heart in return before my two hundredth year if I was to survive. I don't know if it was simply that her power was fading by the time I was born, or that she wished for me to take Ambrose's place at your side so badly she was willing to risk my life, but her magic would have kept me whole for only so long."

"After that, only your love could preserve my life. I feared Ambrose had stolen your heart away from me, and I . . . I took the coward's way of eliminating my competition for your affections. I pray someday you will be able to forgive me for that, and . . . the rest of it."

Rose shook her head, struggling to make sense of his rambling, but found herself at a complete loss. "This was all caused by your mother? Another one of her curses?"

"Not a curse, not for her son. She was not quite that evil." He paused, his next words obviously difficult to say aloud. "I was born . . . wrong, my heart infirm and my body twisted and deformed. I was so monstrous the elvish midwife who later became my nanny said it looked as if my mother had mated with a frog, not a man. My father would have thrown me from his keep the day I was born if Mother hadn't worked the spell she did. It made me whole, strong."

"But there was a price."

"Yes. If I hadn't appeased the magic, I would have begun to transform back into that thing I once was. My heart was already weakening and my leg twisting, so that I walked with that wretched limp. You witnessed the beginning of the end, Rose. I wouldn't have lived long once the transformation was complete."

"Then I suppose I am happy for you. No matter what you have done, I find myself unable to wish you ill," Rose said, resisting the urge to pull him into her arms. His story was awful indeed, but he freely admitted he had behaved horribly, nearly becoming a murderer in the quest to preserve his life.

Besides, it seemed he'd claimed his happiness as well as his life.

Hannah Hughes must love him, and he love her in return. Otherwise, the spell wouldn't be broken, or Gareth be standing in front of her so elated to be alive.

His hands, strangely warm for a vampire who hadn't recently fed, cupped her cheeks. "But don't you see, it isn't Hannah. No matter what your father's diary says, she is not the true princess of Myrdrean. You are, Rose! You and only you. I sensed it back in the rooming house, and it seems for once my instincts were correct."

"I found the journal pages in your coat, Gareth. I've read the truth with my own eyes, so please, do not attempt to—"

"This is not some pretty lie. I tell you the truth." The excitement animating his features was real. "There's only one woman who has ever claimed my heart. First, she won it with her goodness, her bravery, and her beautiful spirit."

Tears threatened for what seemed the thousandth time that evening. Rose did her best to pull away, but Gareth held her fast.

"Then she pierced it with a wooden stake." He waited, seeming to know it would take a few moments for her to realize the import of his words. "Knowing my mother, I should have realized it was a more deadly 'claiming' she referred to, not something from a romantic novel."

"Then I—" Words abandoned her for a moment. "You mean, I didn't truly—"

"You didn't end my life, you saved it," he confirmed with a wry smile. "You, the princess of Myrdrean, *claimed* my heart. The wording of the spell was very clear."

Rose sucked in a deep breath, suddenly needing more air, slightly dizzy with the possibility. If what Gareth said was true, then perhaps all of this had been some horrible mistake. Her father's journal might very well be a clever forgery, made by whoever wished to take her place as ruler of Myrdrean and become heir to the Seelie throne.

"But wait." She shook her head, forcing away the giddiness that had consumed her while she briefly clung to the hope Gareth offered. "I can't make the journey to Faerie, and I attempted the voyage with no less than a dozen journeying stones. I am not the princess of Myrdrean."

"I would disagree. If you weren't the true princess, I would not be standing here." His hands smoothed away from her cheeks, fingers skimming down her throat to rest lightly on her shoulders. The touch sent shivers of awareness through her entire body. She could feel the vitality radiating from his very fingertips. He was her strong, capable husband once more, with nothing to prevent him from taking her to his bed.

Nothing, save the fact that she had betrayed him with his brother, and he had betrayed her with Hannah. Though she could understand now why he had sought out Hannah Hughes and felt compelled to win her heart, she wasn't sure she could forgive what he had done—either in that rooming house or here in the street.

If only he had simply told her the truth, they could have faced this trial together.

"I couldn't. I was prevented from telling anyone of my curse by the magic itself."

"So now you agree it was a curse, not your saving grace?"

"If it causes me to lose your love, then it was a curse indeed." His lips fell to hers, dropping a soft, aching kiss upon them before she could think to pull away. "I love you, Rose. More than anything in the world. I could have died for that love, true, but I wanted to live. I hoped, once the spell was broken, I could win your forgiveness and tell you why I was forced to turn to Miss Hughes."

"So you would have broken *her* heart instead?" This time Rose succeeded in pulling away from her husband and ducking under his arm. "You would have used her for your own salvation and then discarded her when she was no longer convenient?"

"No, I— You don't understand." He cursed as he spun to face her. Full dark had fallen and now all she could see of him were his catlike eyes, shining in the dark. It made it easier, somehow, to think clearly.

"I understand completely. And I think you should return to Miss Hughes and make good on your betrothal to her. Fey law demands one of the Minuit line marry the woman, and it seems you have already formed an attachment to her."

"She is not my betrothed. She is not the princess of Myrdrean, you are. Have you not listened to a word I've—"

"I *have* listened. It is you who refuse to hear the truth. I am not the princess. I have no Fey blood in my veins. I am *not* my mother's daughter."

"No, you're not, but you very well may be your *father's*. Don't you see? The throne of Myrdrean is inherited through your father's side, not your mother's."

Rose was silent for a moment, wishing she could see more clearly. She would love to see Gareth's face, to know if at least *he* believed he was telling the truth. Seconds later, as if summoned by her thought, Rose felt her eyes begin to reshape themselves, the very mechanics of sight reforming to suit her unspoken desire. Within a few moments she could see as well as any creature made to walk the night.

That was all the convincing she needed. She wasn't Fey, but neither was she merely human. If forced to decide one way or another, it seemed more likely that she *was* the offspring of an ancient monster than that she was not. She would bet her life that it wasn't a witch her father had bargained with, but something much worse.

Something that might have been capable of giving him a daughter much more swiftly than the months required by a human or Fey woman. Rose had read nothing in the diary to make it seem he'd lain with the witch, but there was a chance—a horrible chance.

And if he had indeed fathered a child with the Mother, could the king of Myrdrean have sacrificed one daughter for another? He wasn't a cruel man, but to ease his beloved wife's breaking heart . . .

For that, Rose feared he would have done just about anything.

"I must speak with Ambrose and have him contact his scholars," she said, brushing past Gareth and striding down the alley with purpose. "We must see if such a thing is possible, and if there is some record of the contract Father signed with my true mother."

"Your true mother? The witch he wrote of?" Gareth asked, falling into step beside her. "I believe Hannah has some knowledge of her, though I couldn't pry it from her mind. We could return to the rooming house—or perhaps I could go alone if you feel I would be more able to gain the intelligence we need."

Rose declined to answer. "You should leave. I fear Ambrose may try to kill you a second time once he sees you alive, and I wouldn't blame him for it. You earned a sword in the belly when you attacked him while he was unarmed."

"I will risk it. I will not leave you again. I am committed to your cause, to helping you—"

"I don't need your help."

As they reached the street, Ambrose stepped from

the shadows at the end of the alley. "Unfortunately, that is not so. We shall require all the aid we can muster if we are to fight the Mother."

Gareth froze a few feet away from his brother, obviously unsure of the reception he would receive. "There. See, Rose? Ambrose is willing to be reasonable." He risked a smile and a slight bow. "Please accept my apologies, brother. I confess I felt I had no choice but to—"

"I heard your reasons." Ambrose stepped closer, danger vibrating in every tense line of his body. "And you will have to accept my apologies, for I find myself not at all pleased to see you among the living."

"Except for Rose's sake, of course."

"Except for Rose's sake," he repeated, before adding in a deadly whisper. "But once the threat to her life is dealt with, *I* shall be dealing with you, Gareth." He spun on his heel a moment later, stalking down the street toward the carriage parked at the end of the lane.

It was the only time Rose could remember hearing Ambrose speak his brother's given name, and she knew she didn't want to hear him say it again. Never had one word been so filled with contempt or menace, or caused her spirits to sink so profoundly.

There would be no peace between them anytime in the near future.

"Don't worry, sweet," Gareth said, as they hurried after Ambrose. "If this witch is as terrible as all that, we may not live long enough for Ambrose to seek his vengeance."

Rose sighed. She could always depend upon him to offer comfort in a time of crisis.

"I swear, you *can* depend upon me. Be certain of it. Now that I am finally free of—"

She ran to the carriage, certain of nothing but that she needed a large glass of faery mead as soon as possible.

CHAPTER TWENTY

Less than an hour later, Rose was once again climbing the steps to the rooming house. But this time she was alone, and for the first time in the past several months, she was glad of it. She needed a respite from the two men in her life.

No matter how grateful she was to have both of them alive, she'd found herself supremely uncomfortable in their company. She was grateful Ambrose had insisted on paying a personal visit to his scholar associates and Gareth thought himself best put to use searching Miss Hughes's room after Rose had drawn the woman out for a chat.

A midnight chat. Rather odd timing, but none of them felt the matter could be put off until morning. If *they* knew where Miss Hughes was staying, it wouldn't be long before the rest of the supernatural community learned the news as well. Then she would become a person of supreme interest to a great many people and the three of them would be lucky to gain a glimpse of the woman, let alone an audience.

And they must discover what she was hiding—and soon.

Another note from Manor High had arrived while they were out, this one from Princess Beatrice herself. She warned Rose that the king had once again been visited by his ancestors in a dream. A dream in which his great-grandmother told him to send the princess to lead the battle against the vampire forces regrouping in the dark forest outside the magical boundaries of the Seelie court.

Unfortunately, the grandmother the king described bore a striking resemblance to the wicked creature who had haunted both Rose and Beatrice in their dreams. The princess feared the woman sought to bring about her demise by convincing the king she could lead the Seelie to victory against the bloodmen.

Therefore, she too sought sanctuary in London, determined to throw her lot in with the Fey de la Nuit rather than risk death or worse by obeying her sovereign's mad order to arm herself and ride into battle. She would arrive in less than a day's time, as she would take a shortcut through the Faerie realms in order to escape the Seelie court. The king had reinforced the magical boundaries guarding his home, this time making certain they allowed no one in and no one out.

Luckily, Beatrice had managed to retain her journeying stone when the rest of the courts' were confiscated. Now that small deception might very well save her life.

Ambrose had spoken to the princess through the

enchanted waters and assured her that she would be guarded as fiercely as her cousin Elsa. She hadn't seemed pleased to share a guard with the woman who had betrayed the Seelie to the vampires, but fugitives from the king's wrath couldn't afford to be particular in their company.

Rose couldn't wait for the other women to arrive at Ambrose's home. The longer she was alone with Ambrose and Gareth, the harder it would be to keep them from reading the secrets of her heart. Now that she realized what she wanted from the pair of them, it seemed impossible not to think upon it and she feared one or both would overhear her wishful thinking.

"Your utterly *foolish* thinking. They would kill each other before they would suffer such an arrangement," Rose whispered aloud, taking a bit of comfort in the sound of her own voice.

She'd thought the rag market rather eerie this late at night. But the empty street, littered with scraps of fabric blowing along the cobbles like tiny ghosts, seemed positively cheery compared to the interior of Mrs. Clabber's rooming house. There was something . . . wrong here, something she hadn't sensed during her first trip up these steps, but that now seethed from the very walls.

It was too quiet, too still, as if nothing living remained within 57 Rosemary Lane. Out in the street there had still been the usual London noises—soil men sweeping the remains of thousands of chamber pots into the sewers leading down to the Thames, lamplighters trudging along on their stilts, drink-addled men and women arguing in their homes or seeking a companion in the darker corners of the city streets.

But within the rooming house—not a sound.

Even when Rose willed her ears to hear as well as any faerie or vampire, she couldn't catch so much as a soft snore or the shuffling of sheets as a woman tossed in her lonely bed.

"Perhaps they're all out."

Or perhaps a pack of ogres descended and devoured Mrs. Clabber and all who roomed here.

Ogres were unique among supernatural predators, in that they devoured the entirety of their victims, bones and all. And they *did* prefer to feed upon humans who wouldn't be missed—women such as widowed and spinster ladies forced to board with a stranger rather than find welcome in the house of a family member or friend.

But Rose hadn't seen a single member of the tribe since she and Ambrose arrived in London. The ogres had fled the British Isles after their failed attempt to kill Rose and raise their ancient ancestor, and they most likely wouldn't return for a hundred years or more.

Once frightened, ogres remained so for quite some time. Rose wouldn't be surprised if the other Fey de la Nuit assassins led lives of complete leisure for a decade or more. The ogres would be hiding in their secret sanctuaries beneath the earth, feeding upon what animals they could drag into their lairs, too terrified to hunt for human flesh in any but the most remote locations.

So whatever had happened here, an ogre wasn't to blame, but something else entirely. Something she would be wise to arm herself against before continuing on to Miss Hughes's door.

Rose tugged her sword free of the sheath in her boot,

feeling a bit calmer as she watched the blade extend to its full length. She was grateful she'd taken the time to change into her boy's clothes. Life seemed sufficiently challenging of late without an additional struggle with heavy skirts and awkward hoops.

There were fourteen steps leading from the third to the fourth floors, but whatever small peace she gained from having her sword in hand faded before she reached the landing. The malevolent feeling in the air returned with a vengeance, making her skin grow damp despite the cool night temperatures. The closer she drew to Miss Hughes's door, the worse it became, until her very bones were vibrating with evil energy.

The urge to run was nearly overwhelming, but instead she laid her hand on the door handle and pushed. The time for running had passed. No matter what dark force lay on the other side of the door, she must face it, and draw strength from knowing she was not alone. Her husband lurked outside Miss Hughes's window, stronger than he had ever been before, and ready to come to her aid should it become necessary.

Still you place such trust in him, after all he has done. You are a fool, and I do not suffer fools to live.

The Mother's voice hit her like a physical blow, knocking Rose into the wooden planks of the wall behind her. It was the first time she had heard her so clearly while still awake, and for a moment she feared the evil that had birthed her was actually here in the flesh.

Not yet, but soon . . . very, very soon. Her laughter made the entire house rattle and shake, and awakened a pounding in Rose's head.

She gasped for breath and struggled forward, managing to take hold of the door before it slammed shut once more. She had to get inside before it was too late, before the woman writhing on the bed, bloodstains spattering her cotton night shift, lost her life.

"Hannah! Wake up!" Rose screamed. The Mother couldn't kill her if she was awake. For now, the ancient beast could only wield such power while her prey was asleep.

Rose could feel that truth in her very bones, as if she were rifling through the Mother's thoughts. That was why she had sent Ecanthar to fetch Rose at Manor High. She couldn't come for her daughter herself; she was trapped somehow. Held prisoner in a high, lonely place, a place where—

Rose, you begin to surprise me. The small mental portal through which she had stumbled into the Mother's thoughts slammed shut, making her wince. *I was becoming so accustomed to your human idiocy.*

"But I'm not human, am I, Mother?" Rose asked, the last word leaving foulness in her mouth. In her heart, she would only ever have one mother—Marionette Edenburg.

You have finally discovered the truth.

Goddess. The creature's words confirmed her worst suspicions. She was the daughter of this evil thing, a vengeful beast older than the Christian god, nearly as ancient as the goddess who had created the earth.

"I also know you poison the mind of the Seelie king and threaten the lives of his heirs." Rose allowed herself a brief moment of celebration when she felt a ripple of surprise run through the Mother's energy. So

Princess Beatrice was right. For some reason, the Mother wanted her dead and the king set upon the united Fey throne. "Cease your evil work, or I will not hesitate to destroy—"

The Mother's laughter filled the room. *I am terrified. Truly, little bug.*

"Perhaps you should be," Rose said. "Who better to destroy you than one sprung from your womb? I do not know my full potential yet, Mother, but be assured I will discover it. And when I am strong, I will come for you, and there will be no mercy in my heart."

You think yourself rather clever, don't you, Rose? She was angry—truly angry—which gave Rose more hope than she had possessed in weeks. For the first time she felt she and her allies might stand a real chance against the ancient. *But not clever enough or swift enough to gain the secrets you came hunting for this night. She is mine now.*

Hannah began to buck and thrash upon the bed. "Leave her be! You swore to her father you would not hurt her!" Rose couldn't be certain she spoke the truth, but the pages from her father's journal had said the witch vowed never to hurt his child, and that he had bargained dearly for that promise.

I swore I would not kill her. I made no other promises.

"Hannah! Hannah, wake up!" Rose fought her way across the room, shoving against an invisible wall of resistance. With all her strength, she pitted herself against the fierce wind that filled the room. Her cap flew from her head and her hair tore free of the pins that held it, but still she pressed forward.

This was the worst the Mother could do to her at

the moment, and she couldn't be killed by wind. Hannah, on the other hand, looked seconds away from death. Blood leaked from between her lips and invisible claws rent her night shift and the delicate flesh beneath. She bowed up from the bed, her heels digging into the mattress and her eyes fluttering wildly behind her closed lids. No matter what the Mother said, Rose feared the other woman would perish if she didn't reach her soon.

The sound of shattering glass was more welcome than she could have dreamt possible. Gareth landed in a rather undignified tangle on the floor, but was on his feet in seconds, fighting his way across the room to stand beside her.

"Run! Down the stairs, find Ambrose and have him summon the trolls, I—"

"No!" She fought him as he did his best to guide her toward the door. "We must wake her, Gareth! Please, help me. Wake her or I fear she—"

"Blast it all! Then guard the window. I was followed, though I do not know by what," he shouted over the roar of the wind before fighting his way toward the bed where Hannah still bucked and writhed in agony.

Rose spun toward the hole Gareth had made in the glass, sword at the ready. Her hair flew into her face, tangling before her eyes, but she didn't need her eyes to know what had followed Gareth into this small room. She could feel the oily presence of the intruder thick upon her skin.

Ecanthar. He slipped through the window as swift as a shadow, though he was in his dark elf form and far larger than the man who had come before him.

"Rose. So glad to have found you," he said, the power

of his aura nearly knocking her off her feet, though he stood across the room.

Her newly discovered brother was far stronger than he had been the night she faced him in his beast form at Manor High. Power and magic throbbed in the air around him and the Fey sword he held glowed with new life, as if it had just been pulled from an enchanted forge. He was prepared to do battle, and he hadn't come alone.

Outside the window, dozens of wings filled the narrow space between the rooming house and the brick building behind. Sharp claws flashed in the dim moonlight, and the screams of enraged women rent the air. Ecanthar had been joined by a flock of harpies, the most ancient of the sky predators, predating even the few dragons still prowling the corners of the world.

"She didn't trust me to come alone with the new power she has given me. She knows what a soft place I have in my heart for you, my sister." He smiled, teeth alarmingly white against his dark blue skin, his long black hair swirling around his shoulders.

But it was his eyes that truly made her blood chill within her veins. There had been a time when she feared those bright red eyes would be the last thing she'd ever see. Without Ambrose's aid, they very well might have been. Ecanthar's speed and strength had nearly allowed him to triumph over half a dozen of the Fey de la Nuit's most gifted warriors.

She was not ready to face him. Not yet, and certainly not alone.

"Gareth, your swords!" Rose screamed, knowing Hannah would have to wait. "It is Ecanthar."

"Thank you," Ecanthar said, smiling as he lifted his

sword. "It is he who I have come for. Mother's sisters will be your escorts."

"Her sisters?" Rose asked, cutting a swift glance at the window where one crone-faced vulture clawed at the window frame, struggling to make the hole large enough for her to fly inside. "Our aunties?" Her family tree kept growing more and more repulsive with every passing moment.

"She has grown tired of waiting," Ecanthar said, ignoring her question. "If you had only done as she wished, you would have had more time. Still, the end would have been the same. There is no help for that." His smile faded completely, and the sheen of unshed tears appeared in his eyes. "My poor sister. It is a fate none should be forced to endure. And someday, I fear I may join you there."

"Stand back, Rose. Let me take care of this wretch." Gareth appeared at her side, a sword clenched in each fist, his rage palpable in the air around him. Ecanthar was the one responsible for nearly bleeding the life from him that night down by the bank of the Thames, and he was obviously ready to take his revenge.

"What fate? Join me where? What does the Mother have planned for me?" Rose asked, moving between Ecanthar and Gareth, though every part of her screamed to get as far away from her brother and the harpies behind him as possible.

This might be her only chance to discover what the Mother wanted. If she lived to see another morning, she would need that knowledge. Without the understanding of what the monster desired, all attempts to protect herself and the ones she loved would be ineffective at best.

"The harpies will tell you," Ecanthar said, pulling himself together with obvious effort, swiping the unshed tears from his eyes. "It is a three-day flight to Mother's tower, and the crones do enjoy telling a good tale. You'll find them far more amiable once you deliver yourself into their keeping. They were some of my favorite companions when I was a boy."

"She will deliver herself into no one's keeping." Gareth shouldered his way in front of her. "Now run, Rose, or perhaps flight would be a better option if what Ambrose tells me of your new trimmings is true."

Flight! Goddess, why had she not thought of it herself? Her new wings. Ambrose had sworn she would be able to outdistance any Fey presently living, and surely the harpies couldn't fly any faster than an ancient faerie.

This only proved what she had been feeling for the past week—she needed a respite, just a few days in which she could pull her mind and spirit together and regain some much-needed focus. Too bad the only vacation in her future seemed to be a one-way trip to the Mother's tower.

A tower. *She was hidden in a tower three days' flight from London.* It was not the information she sought, but it was something, and more than they had known before.

"I will find Ambrose and return as swiftly as I can," Rose said to Gareth, backing toward the bed where Hannah now lay quiet, though the other woman was still unconscious.

She sheathed her sword and then with swift, sure motions, fashioned a sling of the sheets and tied the end around her waist, ignoring the outraged screams of the harpies and the fierce scrabbling of their claws at the window.

"It is too late!" the elf shouted. "There is no way out, sister."

"You are quite the voice of doom, aren't you, Ecanthar?" she asked, refusing to call him brother. "I would encourage you to take a more positive view of the world. My acquaintances among human Society swear anything less is bad for the skin."

Rose managed not to grunt and groan as she tugged Hannah from the bed to the floor. She would be forced to drag the girl for a short distance, but it couldn't be helped. Better bumped and bruised than dead, after all, and she couldn't bear to leave the other woman here, not when it seemed she was the only one who knew the secrets of Rose's past.

And not when she might very well be her half sister.

Foolish though it may be, she was loathe to lose the one relatively normal family member who still remained among the living—even if she was a complete stranger.

"Forget her. Run!" Gareth shouted as the first harpy burst through the hole it had made. The creature's wings seemed enormous in the small space, and its sharp claws were long enough to wrap around Rose's waist.

Still, if it had been alone, she would have stayed to fight. But the crone's sisters were already on their way through the window. At this point, the best thing she could do for Gareth was to lead the harpies away from the rooming house, and call for the reinforcements they so desperately needed.

Moving as swiftly as she could while dragging another's weight behind her, Rose darted behind Gareth, aiming herself toward the door. The harpy would have to make its way around Ecanthar before it could reach her position. She prayed that would delay the beast the few seconds she needed to slam the door shut behind her.

"It is no use. The Mother enchanted the doors and windows. There will be no escape. Good journey, sister. I fear we will not meet again." Ecanthar raised his sword and rushed at Gareth just as the harpy launched itself at Rose.

Then I shall not use the doors or windows. The walls were made of brick, but with a little help from her sword, it would not be impossible for her to create her own way out of the building.

Rose drew her blade and summoned her new wings from her body with a cry, praying the fear and rage coursing through her blood would aid her in coaxing the great wings into existence once more.

In an ideal world, she would have preferred a bit of practice before wagering her life upon the strength of her new gift. But if her past had taught her anything, it was that the world was very seldom anything close to ideal.

Thankfully, her raven-colored wings burst through skin and clothing with ease. But unfortunately for her and Hannah, she had neither the space nor the time to build up the momentum necessary to take flight. The harpy was too swift, and the distance across the room far too short.

"Damnation," Rose cursed, the word ending in a groan as her sword collided with the harpy's claws.

The blasted things were made of some sort of metal, and easily deflected her blow.

With each successive parry, she sought to catch the beast higher on its gnarled limbs—hoping to sever its claws completely. But the creature was surprisingly adept at keeping the proper distance from her sword, all while hovering in the air before her like some giant mosquito escaped from the marshes of Essex.

Across the room, she caught flashes of Gareth and Ecanthar likewise engaged in battle. Her husband was holding his own against the larger, swifter elf, but it was only a matter of time before Ecanthar gained the upper hand. The room they battled in was hardly conducive to evasive tactics, and Gareth couldn't last if not allowed a single moment's respite from Ecanthar's brutal attacks.

She had to find a way out. But how? The Mother had set a clever, if rather simple, trap.

"Simple," Rose muttered beneath her breath even as she renewed her efforts with her sword, struggling to deflect the flashing claws of the first harpy and the second that joined the battle on Rose's right.

The manifestation of her new wings had been a simple matter—so simple she hadn't even known her thoughts had channeled themselves into massive instruments of flight until Ambrose had brought the matter to her attention. The erasure of Caspar's mark and the improvement of her eyes had been equally simple matters. Effortless, as if she were born to shift her shape, to become whatever it was she wished to be, her various forms limited only by her imagination.

Hadn't the Mother herself said that Rose was being held back by her human upbringing?

Her brother, who seemed to have been raised by the beast that bore them, clearly had no such limitations. He easily shifted from one form to the next. At Manor High he had been both a shadow monster and the other beast, the one that had killed her two uncles.

And yet here he was now, once again the black elf she had first met that bleak night in February.

If they truly shared the same gifts, there was no reason for her to fear becoming something else, something more. She could presumably shift back into her own form when the battle was done—but only if she could keep that form from being torn apart by the crones snapping their claws at her flesh.

She must become something strong, invulnerable—something capable of defending not only herself and the woman at her feet, but hopefully of protecting her husband from Ecanthar as well.

There was only one thing that immediately came to mind.

Rose didn't stop to second-guess her instinct. There wasn't time to debate, to wonder at the limitations of her gift or the consequences of becoming something so very different than the body she had inhabited for two hundred years. She was quickly running out of choices. She must evolve or be destroyed.

The first wave of the transformation was as simple as the unfolding of her wings, but then the pain hit. It was a horrible, searing agony that consumed her, as if her insides were struggling to make their way out and would flay her skin from her bones in the process. She dropped to the floor beside Hannah, a liquid scream gurgling from between her parted lips.

The harpies fell upon her a second later, their claws

extended and their toothless mouths open wide, eager for a taste of what would soon emerge from her flesh, to consume the woman they had come to fetch for the Mother and bring her home to their sister safe in their starving bellies.

CHAPTER TWENTY-ONE

Two large hands, as blue-black as the midnight sky, reached up and seized the harpies around their throats. Their claws caught her new flesh and tore at her newly-tight boy's clothes as she rose to her feet, but Rose scarcely noticed the pain. It was a trifle compared to the anguish she had suffered to create the form she now inhabited, and she put an end to their struggles soon enough.

The sickening soft thud of skin and bone colliding filled the air as she crushed the harpies' skulls together, transforming their screams to tortured moans. Gray and white liquid flowed from their wounds, down into their filmy blue eyes.

Rose dropped the pair of them to the floor some distance from Hannah. They were not yet dead, and it wasn't wise to take chances with supernatural creatures. One never knew just how quickly or thoroughly they could recover from their wounds.

She had half a second to bend and recover her sword—which felt strangely small in her new hands—before another crone was upon her. The creature howled into her face, outraged by the damage Rose had done to her sisters.

"I've heard your type can speak," Rose said, surprised to find that her voice sounded the same as it always had, despite the change in her outward appearance. "But thus far, I do not believe it."

"I will speak as I rip you limb from limb, child," the harpy screamed, lashing out with her claws.

Rose's sword whipped through the air with such speed it made the air around it sing. The harpy's claws fell away from its legs in a spray of gray blood, and its body fell to the floor a moment later. "You will tell me what you know when this battle is finished. If the story is a useful one, perhaps you will live."

Very human tears leaked down the old woman's face as she writhed on the boards at her feet, but Rose wasn't moved to pity. She felt incapable of such a soft emotion in this body, as if all the feminine weakness had been crushed from her soul and her heart had hardened along with her new muscles.

In fact, a part of her felt she would enjoy bringing her boot down on the harpy's neck and slowly suffocating the life from the beast's body. She couldn't imagine anything more satisfying than feeling the woman buck and thrash beneath her as she fought for her life. She would relish the creature's death, allowing her a desperate breath now and then, just enough to resume her struggling, to draw out the murder to its very fullest.

"Rose! Behind you." Gareth's voice pulled her from

her cruel imaginings. She turned just in time to find two more of the harpies bearing down upon her, claws reaching for her neck.

Her sword flashed and the crones screamed in agony. Their strangely grayish-white blood splashed onto Rose's face, hot and thick, running down her neck into the collar of what remained of her boy's shirt, making her throw back her head and laugh. There was truly nothing in the world as glorious as the dealing of death. Just a taste of the slaughter made every cell in her body ache to continue her bloody business. She wanted to run out into the street and tear apart every creature she encountered, to open them with her sword and reach inside their warm bodies and seize their still-beating hearts, to feed upon their sweetmeats as greedily as the Seelie king fed upon the fruits of his enchanted gardens.

The king . . . even *he* had been consumed by the Mother's power. He was easily the most ancient being she had ever met in the flesh, and yet he had been as effortlessly deceived as a boy in his thirteenth year. She was a fool to think she would be any different, to think she could triumph over the one who had made them all, over a being older than time itself.

Rose shook her head and stumbled as she ducked to avoid the claws of yet another harpy.

The lust for blood and death and the doubt plaguing her mind, they were the Mother's doing, she was certain of it.

But in this form it was impossible to tell her thoughts from those placed into her mind by another. She was lost, adrift in a primal sea where there was no space between her and the creator, the destroyer, the monster who would soon swallow the entire world. Her mind was the Mother's mind, her skin the Mother's skin, her soul the Mother's soul. There was no such person as Rose. There was only the pounding heart that summoned her home to her source, to the place where she would finally find peace, buried deep inside the flesh of the one who had formed her.

Someone screamed, and then someone else shouted. A man, it was a man's voice, but she couldn't understand the words he spoke. She was beyond language.

But thankfully, she was not beyond hunger or thirst. The appetite for blood was stronger than ever, so strong she didn't care who it was she attacked with her sword. The body was warm and moving closer with every second—that was all she needed to know.

She swung wildly, lacking the focus to think of such things as strategy or technique. It was pure luck that her sword connected with his and nothing more. But it was enough. The clang of metal meeting metal, the trembling of her muscles as she clung to the hilt of her weapon—they were enough to bring her back from the edge of oblivion.

"You wear this body well, sister," Ecanthar said, his bright red eyes alight with excitement and madness.

It made her wonder what she would see if she looked in the mirror. She had taken the shape of a black elf in the hopes of matching her brother's strength, but it seemed she was near to matching his madness as well. She must dispatch him as quickly as she was able and return to her true form.

"What immensity you've achieved. You're bigger than your beaux now, aren't you? I can't say I've ever seen arms that large on a female."

"The better to kill you with, brother." She slashed at him, forcing him back two paces.

"*Petit Chaperon Rouge,* one of my favorites." He laughed even as he lunged forward, bringing the point of his blade perilously close to her stomach. "If only we could have been raised together as brother and sister, we could have lain at Mother's feet and heard the tale of the Little Red Riding Hood together."

"Shut your wretched mouth and fight," she said, her voice emerging as little more than a growl.

Never had she felt such unadulterated rage while in the midst of battle. On most occasions, she was as calm as the center of a storm, no matter how dire the odds or how hated the enemy she fought. There was no room for emotion in the theater of war, not if one wanted to live. It was the first lesson she had learned from the Fey de la Nuit.

But she couldn't seem to rein in the hate coursing through her veins. She didn't want to simply kill this monster who was her brother; she wanted to torture him until he died from pure pain. She wanted to hack apart his body and perform sacrilegious acts upon the pieces. She wanted to tear his flesh from his bones with her teeth and scream her fury into his wicked red eyes while his blood still dripped from her fangs.

"The fever is so fresh the first time, isn't it?" He easily avoided two rather clumsy swipes of her sword and landed his first blow. "There is nothing quite like it."

Rose cried out, clutching at the shoulder he had slashed, willing the skin to close and the blood to cease its flow. The wound healed quickly with the use of her new talents, but the pain remained, slowing her sword-play, though it seemed to sharpen her mind.

She could hear sounds filling the room again, under-stand words other than those uttered by the man she fought.

"Take his head, Rose. Take his head and be done with it. We must flee this place," Gareth urged from across the room where he struggled to keep any more of the winged horde from flying in the damaged window.

There seemed an endless number of harpies doing their best to push their way inside. Gareth was right, they couldn't remain here and hope to live. She must disable her brother first, and worry about killing him later. From what she knew of Ecanthar, his death would not be easy. She had watched him be torn limb from limb by Fey warriors who swore they had se-cured the separate pieces of him to the four corners of a London rooftop, and yet still he lived.

"Yes, sister, take my head. Take it home with you and place it beneath your blankets and I will wake you in the night with sweet kisses between your pretty, white thighs."

Rose gritted her teeth and renewed her efforts with her weapon, driving Ecanthar toward the bed against the far wall, determined not to let his words force her mind back into the mad land of rage and bloodlust.

"Brother knows what you crave." He darted to the left, moving closer to the open door. "My lips and tongue will still be able to service you when the rest of my body is gone. Such is the gift of the Mother. Even in pieces we shall live . . . until *she* would have us.

And she would not care if I tasted you. All of us are one to her."

She followed him, willing her thoughts to be calm and passionless. Her brother must fear he was losing this fight if he had resorted to horrifying her with threats of his amorous attentions. She must retain her focus, concentrate on the task at hand, or she would lose what little control she had gained over her new mind.

"I've seen how you enjoy a good poke," he said, one hand running down his stomach to grip his cock even as he renewed his efforts with his sword. "I saw the faerie fucking you in the street. I should have attacked you then, but I couldn't help myself. I wanted to watch, to hear you cry out as your tight little cun—"

"Silence!"

"And you did cry out, your sweet face twisted with the force of your passion. Mother help me, but I wanted to be the one buried inside you," he said, his breath coming faster as he stroked himself through his breeches. "Instead I had to content myself with my own hand, imagining how you would kneel at my feet one day and beg me to baptize you in my seed."

"Not if yours was the last cock on the face of the earth!" Rose screamed, recklessly swinging at Ecanthar's head, hoping she would slice out his wretched tongue.

Instead, he easily dodged the blow. Her sword lodged in the wood of the door, allowing her brother a clear shot at her left flank. He took full advantage of the unguarded moment, sliding his blade between her ribs, nearly reaching her heart before Rose managed to spin away, leaving her weapon behind and herself defenseless against the man advancing quickly toward her.

"Goddess!" she screamed as she stumbled backward, striving to heal the horrible wound Ecanthar had dealt her even as she dodged his new attacks.

The pain was excruciating, even worse than what she had suffered to assume a black elf's body. It would have been enough to prompt a shift back into her human form in the hopes that transformation would heal some of the damage, if she had been granted the time or opportunity, but Ecanthar gave her no quarter.

Ruthlessly, he chased her from one end of the room to the other, bearing down upon her with his sword, lust for her flesh replaced by the lust for her blood. She had a few minutes at most before he finished what he had started, and Gareth couldn't come to her aid without allowing a flock of murderous harpies into the room and condemning them both to death by razor-sharp claws.

She must deal with Ecanthar herself. She had to think of *something,* anything to—

"You may be able to survive in pieces, brother, but are you quite certain I can do the same? If you kill me, your life will be finished, for you know the Mother wants me delivered to her alive. You have said as much yourself." Rose ducked just in time to avoid having her head severed from her body by Ecanthar's sword.

Thankfully, she was swifter in her dark elf form, or he would have killed her for certain by now. He moved so quickly, her human eyes would have been unable to perceive it, let alone dodge his quick sword.

"You will survive. You are the Mother's daughter, as I am her son. The gifts and curses of our lineage are yours to bear, just as I have born them for—"

"But what of our fathers, Ecanthar? Surely we were not sired by the same man," she said, dashing beneath his arm and fleeing toward the bed once more. She was getting stronger with every moment, recovering far more quickly than she would have imagined possible. If she could only distract him long enough to reach her sword . . .

"Our blood is not the same." She inched to her left, making sure she did not so much as glance toward her discarded weapon. "There is a chance you will kill me."

The elf laughed, as if what she said were the most humorous thing he had heard in an age. "You are endlessly amusing, sister. How I wish we could have known each other better. Your ignorance is adorable. It makes me feel quite the older brother, though you were Mother's firstborn."

"Was I? Are you sure?" Rose asked, not knowing what she would say next, struggling to think of something that would distract Ecanthar from his single-minded purpose. "I have heard of another, a brother as old as the sea that the Mother searches for but cannot find."

"What?" Ecanthar asked, his smile fading and his sure step faltering for a moment.

"It is *he* she will ask to join her on her throne." Her voice lilted slightly, as if the words were part of a song. What had begun as pure falsehood now held the unmistakable ring of truth. There *was* another somewhere, and she did search for him.

As before, Rose found her thoughts overlapping those of the Mother, somehow making the journey to wherever the monster was imprisoned and reaching into her maker's mind. Never would she have dreamt herself capable of mental connection at such a great distance, but then neither would she have imagined that she would transform herself into a great beast of an elf before the night was through.

The only certainty in her life at the moment was that everything was uncertain, and she would be a fool to limit herself with any preconceived notions.

"It is not possible. I am the only male heir." Ecanthar's face reflected the rage brewing within his heart. He was losing his resolve, swiftly being consumed by the tumultuous emotions that were so close to the surface in this form. "I am the only one capable of fathering the world as the Mother will re-create it."

"No. It is the *other* who will rule when the humans are cattle once more, and the children slaves who live only to serve the Mother's will," Rose said, her mind clearing a bit as she drew closer to her sword. The connection to the Mother was fading, but it was too late now. She had already learned all she needed to know to thoroughly undo her brother. "She will never allow you to live as her equal."

"You know nothing. *Nothing!*"

"I know she will never allow you between her thighs." Rose smiled, deliberately taunting Ecanthar as she prepared to reach for her blade. "She will not have you. And neither will I."

He howled in pain and rage as he lunged for her, but Rose was already on the move. She reached for her sword, grasping the hilt and pulling the blade free even as she kicked at Ecanthar with her boot. His momentum, combined with her urging, sent him sprawling to the floor. She was on his back a second later, bringing her sword down upon the thick sinews of his neck with all the power in her new arms.

By the time his scream of agony escaped from his lips, her brother's head was already severed from his body and rolling out into the hall. Ignoring his tortured moans, Rose swiftly kicked his skull down the stairs before running back to where Gareth still battled the harpies. Retrieving his head should keep Ecanthar occupied for a while, at least long enough for her, Gareth, and Hannah to make their escape.

"Gareth! Follow me to the end of the hall," Rose shouted, scooping the still-unconscious Hannah from the floor and throwing her over her shoulder. This elf form would continue to prove useful this night. In her own body, she could never hope to carry a woman larger than herself and run from a flock of harpies at the same time.

Still, the opportunity to return to the body she knew could not come soon enough, a sentiment obviously shared by her husband.

"Goddess, Rose, what the devil have you done to yourself?" Gareth followed her out of the room, slamming the door behind him. As the harpies had claws instead of hands, it would be difficult for them to grasp the handle and open the door, hopefully buying them a few precious moments to escape. "You look like a sailor. A blue sailor, no less, and I can't say the look agrees with you."

"You are a shameless flatterer, as always," Rose said, setting Hannah down when they reached the end of the hall. She would be able to put more force behind her blows if she wasn't holding the other woman. "But there are times when utility is of more importance than vanity."

"You surely don't mean to—" Gareth's words ended in a wince of pain as he watched her slam her fist into the plaster of the wall, but he didn't try to stop her. They required an alternate route of escape and she was providing that with speed and effectiveness. Within a few seconds, she had pounded her way through the bricks, creating a hole large enough for the three of them to fit through.

"As I said, utility." Rose turned to retrieve Hannah from the floor, only slightly out of breath from her efforts.

"Indeed," Gareth said, eyeing her bloodied knuckles with what looked like pride. Though his aesthetic was clearly offended, he seemed able to appreciate her new talents—especially when they were put to use saving his life. "I shall go first. You toss her out to me and then follow. It will be safer for you both than if you carried her down."

Rose nodded her agreement, stepping back to let Gareth leap through the hole she'd made. He landed with the grace of great cat, then turned and looked up. Rose shifted Hannah in her arms, preparing to drop her down to where he waited thirty-five feet below. She was loathe to toss the woman about like some oversized doll, but there was no other choice.

Behind them, the harpies' claws scrabbled at the door and Ecanthar's head wailed his location to the empty house, presumably attempting to communicate with the lower portion of his body. Soon the winged creatures would be upon them and her brother would find a way to make himself whole once more. They must be away from this accursed place well before then if they hoped to survive.

Ambrose had surely been told of the battle they fought, as his trolls kept watch from their hiding places in the rag market, but it would be best if they could avoid any further confrontation with the Mother's forces. They needed time to build their army, and to prepare to combat this enemy so unlike anything they had faced before.

"What has . . . ? Oh dear, my head." Hannah shifted in Rose's arms, bringing her delicate hands to her forehead. "I fear I have—"

Her words ended in a scream as her eyes opened and she saw what it was that held her. It was a piercingly feminine response, but Rose could scarcely blame her. She had yet to see her new image reflected in a glass, but she was certain it was far from a comforting sight.

"Please, I am a friend. Don't be afraid," Rose said, doing her best to hold onto the other woman, though Hannah began to struggle fiercely for her freedom. She couldn't allow Hannah to go running back to her death simply because she presently resembled a monster. "I am Rose, the woman you met earlier this afternoon. My husband is below, waiting to—"

"Put me down. At once!" Hannah's tone was imperious, but she ceased her struggling, proving she was not a completely irrational woman.

"As you wish, but please, you must believe me." Rose set her on her feet, but remained poised to recapture her if needed. "Our enemies have found us. We must flee this place at once if we hope to live."

Hannah's blue eyes narrowed, as if she sought to see through Rose's exterior to what lay beneath. "You are Rose? The woman who took my place and suffered the curse placed upon me at birth?"

"I am, and I wish to help you."

"And why would you wish to do that?" Hannah backed slowly away, looking as if she would flee back down the hall at any moment. Rose followed her, ignoring the sound of Gareth calling to her from below. She couldn't take her attention from Hannah for a moment, not now, not when they were so close to gaining their freedom. "I've come to take everything that is yours. Your kingdom, your property, your family . . . even the man you call your husband."

"He *is* my husband. We were married according to the law."

"He is my betrothed now, and I will not allow him to remain with the woman who has stolen my birthright for a hundred years and more."

Rose gritted her teeth, forcing back the retort on the tip of her tongue. Being raped by an ogre and awakened from an enchanted sleep by the pain of childbirth was a birthright she would have eagerly bequeathed to the ungrateful woman before her. But there would be time to adjust Hannah's thinking later, when they were not both on the verge of certain death.

"I wish to help because I believe we may share more than a common past," Rose said, refusing to acknowledge the rest of Hannah's words. "I believe your father was also my father, that he lay with my mother—"

"You believe my father lay with a witch?" she asked, clearly horrified.

"I can't say for certain, but yes, I believe so. Which makes us more than two women who've walked in each other's shoes," she said, casting a frantic look over her shoulder. They were quickly running out of time. She had to convince her half sister of her sincerity or they would both be killed. "It makes us sisters."

"Sisters?" To say Hannah's expression was doubt-filled was an understatement.

"You must admit there's a resemblance between us," Rose said, her sword falling from her hand as she began the painful shift back into her true form.

Hannah could flee this place on her own two legs now that she was awake, and at the moment it seemed the only way to convince her of their shared bond was to remind her that they each boasted their father's cornflower-blue eyes and pale blond curls. Marionette had possessed the same hair color, but hers had been as sleek and smooth as a mink, and hadn't curled wildly around her face after a rain. It was from their father that she and Hannah had both gained their hair and their identical sharp little noses. Surely even the stubborn woman before her would see that now.

"The resemblance, it cannot be denied," Rose said, her voice thin from the effort of shifting her form while still staying on her feet. She leaned back against the wall behind her, needing a bit of support while she regained her strength.

Hannah smiled, an oddly triumphant look. "It is true. It's almost like looking in a mirror. Or gazing into the face of the fool I would have been, had I not lived the life I was forced to live."

The woman had Rose's sword in her hand before Rose could do so much as draw breath. Hannah was remarkably fast and skilled with a weapon for a woman. She wasted no time positioning the tip of the blade at Rose's chest and shoving the point through her breast bone, directly into her heart.

Rose felt her eyes open impossibly wide as a new sort of pain exploded from her wounded heart to every inch of her poor, aching body. The unbelievable pressure in her chest was unlike anything she'd ever felt before, agonizing, yet at the same time strangely muted, the pain held apart from her in some way. It was as if her body and soul had been divided, as if some part of her had already stepped outside the boundaries of flesh and bone, determined to escape the torturous business of death.

For that was what this was—her death.

She had come so close so many times, but never had she known without a doubt that she would die. Never had she been forced to look into the eyes of the one who had taken her life, to see horror and triumph in the woman's expression as she backed slowly away from the murder she had committed.

But now she did, and found herself unable to take her eyes from Hannah.

"It was you or me," she panted, gripping Rose's sword tightly in her trembling hand. "The blue creature said he would help me, that he would deliver the pages he had stolen and summon my betrothed. And he did— even going so far as to take the form of a woman to do so if Lord Shenley is to be believed."

"Please . . . Do not . . ."

"But then *she* came to me in dreams again, and she

was no longer the sweet mother I'd always longed for. She wanted me dead, so that you might take everything that was mine once again," she shouted, her eyes wide with madness. "But I have taken what is *hers* first. You will die so that I might live—finally live as I was born to."

Rose could no longer summon the strength to speak, but simply watched as her half sister disappeared through the hole she had made in the brick wall. It was impossible to speak, even if she'd known what to say. Her throat was filled with warm liquid that spilled from between her parted lips.

Blood. Heart blood that would never find its way through her veins again. It was over. Her long life had finally come to an end in this dingy little hall, stolen away by one she sought to save. Betrayed again. If there was one common theme threaded throughout her existence, it was betrayal.

But at least she could take comfort in knowing this betrayal would be the last.

Her knees buckled and she slid slowly down to the floor. Before her, the faded flowered paper on the wall swam, each pink and peach petal blending into a pastel blur. A blur that seemed to pull her into its hazy depths, easing the last of her pain, taking her to a place where there were no more battles to be fought, no more heartaches to endure.

She would finally be at peace, a state of being she'd longed for throughout most of her life.

A part of her was grateful for that, even as the last of her human soul shattered under the weight of her grief, mourning the life she would never live, and the dream of two pairs of strong arms at the close of each day, two men whose love she had been blessed enough to win for eternity.

It was a pretty dream. So pretty. Her lips curved into a soft smile even as her eyes slid closed, shutting out the world for the very last time.

CHAPTER TWENTY-TWO

The afterlife was not at all what she'd expected. Neither heaven nor hell, it was instead a fragmented place, filled with strange visions framed by a great blackness that came and went as it pleased. Sometimes the darkness was a mere fringe at the edges of the scenes she beheld, sometimes it was so complete she couldn't see a thing at all.

In those moments she often succumbed to a sleep deeper than anything she had ever known, even in those eighty years under a black faerie's enchantment. Each time she sank into that sweet oblivion, she was certain it would be the last. That she would never see or hear again, at least not with her human eyes or ears.

Yet time and time again, her mind would swim up from the depths, break the surface of the world and gaze—at least for a moment—at all she had lost.

She saw Gareth, his face bloodied by what looked like a set of small claws. He crouched above her, tears streaming down his face. Had she ever seen him cry? She couldn't seem to remember, but it was a heart-breaking sight. It made her want to hold him, to rock him like a child until the tears were gone from his shining green eyes, but she couldn't move. She could only watch.

Seconds, or perhaps days later—it was difficult to judge the passage of time in this strange place—she gazed up at the watermarks on the ceiling of the rooming house as Gareth scooped her up in his arms and leapt from the fourth floor. She felt the odd sensation of the earth rushing up to meet them even as a pair of harpies bore down on them from above.

The blackness came again soon after, making Rose wonder if the crones had perhaps plucked out her eyes. There was no pain, but then she experienced no sensation at all in her present state—no pain, no pleasure, not even the awareness of her own flesh. If her body still existed she was certainly not contained within it any longer. Of that she had no doubt. And yet . . .

Later, there were more visions. Trolls waddling down abandoned streets, a small army of Fey de la Nuit joined by the Seelie princess herself, their wings unfurled and their swords held at the ready, though there were still humans about—mortals running in terror, screaming from open windows as harpies flew into their squalid homes and flew out with babes still in swaddling clothes. Some great battle was being fought, one so great the Fey had violated their most sacred law, keeping the supernatural world secret from the mortal one.

She was granted a brief glimpse of Ambrose, his face set in a fearsome mask of rage and pain, but then he was gone. He didn't stop to look at her where she lay upon the ground, but Rose didn't blame him. There was a chance she was not there at all, that she was simply a ghost haunting the earth for a time, a remnant that would soon fade from the world entirely.

More blackness then, followed by more mundane visions—the London sky growing dark before a rain, the inside of a carriage, the canopy of a bed that seemed oddly familiar, a stretch of ocean and an unfamiliar dock, the inside of a teacup made of delicate pink porcelain. The last would have made her laugh if she'd had the ability. It made her remember something Gareth had once told her, a story of how the word "porcelain" had come from a Latin phrase meaning "pig's cunny," and of long-ago farmers who had done their fair share of exploration into the private places of their poor animals.

The bawdy tale had led to a long afternoon of lovemaking on one of those rare afternoons in Myrdrean when Gareth had been feeling himself, when the effects of his curse and his wounds hadn't been so heavy upon him.

Only her husband could have managed to arouse her with something so base. He had a gift for unusual seductions, there was no doubt of that. It made her wonder how long he would mourn her before finding another woman to warm his bed, and if he would eventually wed the woman who had killed her.

And what of Ambrose? He was a far more passionate man than he would have most believe. He would eventually find another lady to pin his amorous attentions upon. Perhaps Elsa would tempt him from his melancholy over Rose's death and they would heal each other's broken hearts. She was a beautiful woman, and fiercely loyal once her affections had been won. After all, she had betrayed everything she'd known to avenge the death of her vampire lover. Surely she would come to love Ambrose with an equal passion. He was an irresistible man—both him and his brother.

Her musings summoned the blackness once again. This time she was glad of it. She didn't want to think anymore, didn't want to feel the ache that accompanied thoughts of her husband or Ambrose in another woman's arms.

But oblivion was not to be hers. In fact, the next time she awoke, she found the soft edges of the world had sharpened and her soul and body seemed to have been thrown back together once more.

Immediately she longed for the sweet separation to return. Pain came sweeping back into her mortal form, a ruthless wind that set her skin on fire. She wanted to scream, to thrash, to run until she found some deep water to throw herself into and sink to the bottom, but she could scarcely move. Even the slight movement of her lips brought new explosions of torment up and down her spine.

"Please . . ." The word rasped from her raw throat. She sounded five hundred years old—one thousand— and felt every bit as ancient.

Why was she here, trapped in this body that had obviously fulfilled its duty and should have been allowed to rest? Why was she—

"She speaks. Goddess, at last she speaks." Gareth's voice was thick with relief. The hands he smoothed down her bare shoulders offered some comfort, but it wasn't enough. "Rose, can you hear me, sweet?"

She wanted to answer, but instead of words a sob

emerged from her lips. The pain was too much, too great to allow any gratitude into her heart. She wanted to rejoice that she seemed to be alive, but she couldn't summon the strength to open her eyes. The world was full of hurt, and even the soft sheets beneath her seemed to cut her flesh in a hundred different places.

"Draw closer. The spell is not yet complete." It was Ambrose's voice, so close she could feel his breath stirring the hair on top of her head.

"I am close, I swear it," Gareth said, though he did indeed move his body nearer to hers, so near she could feel his groin against her bare bottom and his stomach trembling against her back. "Perhaps you should draw closer. It is your magic at work. I have nothing to give, but I can feel her pain and it is . . . horrible. I fear she will run mad if we don't—"

"What we feel is merely the echo of her agony," Ambrose said, his pain clear in his tone. "Rose, love, nod your head once if this makes it worse."

Soon he was closer as well, his large hand moving behind her knee, drawing her leg up and over his hips so that he could glue his front to hers. His softened member pressed between her legs and his chest against her breasts. Almost immediately, her skin began to cool, as if she had leapt into one of Myrdrean's lakes on the hottest day of summer.

The relief was profound, making a sigh of pure pleasure escape from her parched lips. As long as she remained pressed between them, she sensed she would be spared further pain. Of course, if that were true, then they would all have to remain abed forever.

The possibility was not so disturbing now that her

skin didn't feel as though it had been flayed off the bone. She even managed a small smile.

"Better. So much . . ." Her eyes slowly slid open even as her tongue moved restlessly in her mouth. She was so thirsty. She felt as if she hadn't had a sip of water in years. "A drink. Could I—"

"Fetch the mead, Gareth, but take care not to sever the connection," Ambrose said, relief making his voice catch in his throat. Strangely, Gareth obeyed his brother's order without a word of protest. Rose felt him reaching to the side of the bed, but his flesh never separated from hers for a moment. "Goddess, Rose. We feared—"

"We feared you were lost to us forever, trapped in that strange little body of yours."

"Strange and wondrous. You were without a heartbeat for nearly a fortnight," Ambrose added, shaking a bit as he cupped her face gently in his hands, as if he must touch her to believe she was real. "Yet your flesh was warm and your eyes would open, so we were certain you had not passed on to the Summerland."

"But you didn't respond as one alive. You seemed so empty." Gareth brought the pink porcelain cup between her lips, and Rose drank greedily of the faery mead within. "If I ever see you thus again—"

"You never will," Ambrose said, the resolve in his voice almost frightening in its intensity. "What we do here tonight will ensure it. If Rose is ever injured so again, her soul will be granted its freedom. Being bound to two mortal creatures will ensure it."

"Neither Ambrose nor I are truly immortal. Not in the same way you are, love," Gareth said, as if sensing her confusion. "I wasn't sure this was what you would want, but there seemed no other way. We feared you would never be coaxed from whatever darkness you inhabited if we didn't act soon, and the Mother's creatures have—"

Gareth fell silent when Ambrose shook his head sharply. "Now is not the time, vampire."

Every muscle of her husband's body tightened against her back, but he didn't pull the cup away from her lips. "Bonded brother or not, I will cut open your throat a second time if you continue to name my kind as if it is the gravest of insults. I will not tolerate your imperious, arrogant—"

"You are right," Ambrose said, shocking Rose to her very core with the sincere apology in his tone. "Forgive me."

Gareth's body relaxed. "Forgiven." Rose could hear the smile on his lips though she couldn't see his face. "See there, we may yet prove a very happy pair. I can see us in years to come, dandling our children upon our knees while we share a glass of port and debate which of us fathered the little—"

"Do not test my patience. Not now," Ambrose said. Gareth fell silent with a soft laugh.

Rose wrinkled her forehead, a thousand questions flitting through her mind, but she didn't stop drinking until the cup held to her lips was empty. Nothing had ever tasted quite so fine as the golden, honeyed mead flowing down her throat. At this rate, she'd be in her cups in no time, but she didn't care. Being a bit drunk seemed wise, better to guard against the pain should it return.

And better to avoid the many questions that needed to be asked. Such as, what was the bond Ambrose spoke of? What had the Mother's creatures been doing while she was trapped in a prison of her own flesh? And why were the three of them in this bed together, as naked as the day they were born?

"I'll answer the last question," Gareth said, his breath hot against her neck as placed the cup beside the bed then swept her hair carefully to one side. "We decided it was best to give the lady what she desired."

His hand moved slowly down her body, smoothing over the curve of her waist, coming to rest possessively on the swell of her hip. His hips shifted forward, letting her feel the telltale swelling of his cock against her bare bottom. Tiny shivers of excitement swept across her skin, coursing away from each place he touched like ripples along the surface of the water.

It was shocking to feel her body come alive with the familiar ache of longing when only moments ago she couldn't imagine being beyond pain, let alone adrift in pleasure.

The only thing more shocking was the feel of Ambrose growing long and thick between her thighs. Her eyes widened and her heart began to race in earnest as his fingers traced a searing trail down her throat and over her bare shoulder, continuing along her arm until he took hold of her hand in a gesture that was somehow more intimate than the feel of his arousal pressed against where she was swiftly becoming slick and damp.

"Your pleasure is mine. Now and for as long as the three of us shall live," he said, his words holding a warning she didn't fully understand. "You will not be rid of us, Rose. The spell is cast and within the hour will be complete. Then we will truly be a house of three. No other man will have you once it is known you are one of a Fey de la Nuit ménage à trois."

"You've got two husbands now, sweet. I hope that won't trouble you too greatly," Gareth said, a teasing note in his voice that couldn't disguise his doubt. He was afraid she would be angered or even repulsed by what they had done. "We knew no other way. Even with this we—"

"I wasn't certain it would bring you back, but we felt bound to try." Ambrose dropped his head, bringing his lips to hers. His kiss was as sweet as she remembered, stealing her breath away, making every cell in her body sing with delight.

"Weak men that we are, we didn't think we could live without you." Gareth's lips pressed softly against her throat even as Ambrose's tongue slid along the seam of her mouth, demanding entrance. One of them would have been enough to overwhelm her, but together their kisses were almost more bliss than she could bear.

But still, she wondered what had brought about this dramatic change. How could two men who had literally been at each other's throats not too long ago now be content to lie in the same bed, and share the woman each desired for his own?

The world without our Rose was a cheerless, shadowed place. How could we cling to our contempt when our accord was the only way we might have you with us again? Ambrose couldn't conceal his longing from her when he spoke within her mind. The fear and despair he had known while she was lost and the overwhelming joy he felt now that she had returned to the world of the living filled her until she felt she would burst.

*Say you will be ours, love. You will make two
wretched men happier than you could ever dream.*
When Gareth's thoughts slipped in to join Ambrose's,
the dam within her burst.

There were suddenly tears everywhere, on her
cheeks, on her lips, slipping into Ambrose's mouth,
smearing onto Gareth's hand as he brought his fingers
down to wrap around her and Ambrose's joined hands.
It seemed impossible one woman could create such a
flood, but the proof was on Ambrose's damp face when
he finally pulled away from their kiss.

"For shame, Rose. They are not only yours. Do you
think I am too old to weep?" He looked like a boy just
then, with his gray eyes shining and his face so full of
hope and uncertainty.

He wanted her to say the words as much as Gareth
did, but he would never ask. Rose knew she would
never make him.

"I know you're not." She shifted her grip so that her
fingers wrapped around both of theirs. "If the pair of
you can get along this beautifully, I see no reason we
should not live quite happily together. Or at the very
least, far happier than we would live apart. You know
I love you both."

"I know. I think perhaps your first husband will need
some convincing," Ambrose said, the relief on his face
belying his confident words. "He feared he wasn't forgiven for all his recent sins."

Rose shifted slightly so that she could look into
Gareth's eyes. "I can't say that you would have been . . .
before. But dying has quite altered my perception of the
world. I find a great many things forgivable at this
moment."

"I hope that forgiveness does not extend to the bitch who plunged your own sword into your heart." Gareth moved even closer, nestling his cock between the cheeks of her ass in a gesture that was both arousing and strangely comforting at the same time. "I killed her. I cut off her hands and head and threw them to the harpies. The rest of her I tossed into the sewer for the rats."

"I can't say I will mourn her." Rose kissed Gareth softly on the tip of his nose. "But whatever secrets she held inside that head would have—"

"I doubt there's much she could have told us that we didn't learn upon a thorough search of her room," Ambrose said. "She possessed a document signed by the king of Myrdrean and a woman named Naomi who we believe to be the Mother. In it were outlined the terms for the exchange of one daughter for another. As it turns out, Myrdrean was always yours to claim. Your father wished for you to rule as payment for what you would suffer in his daughter's stead."

"You *are* the true princess." Gareth smiled a bit sheepishly. "Which explains why my spell was broken when you took my heart that day in the street."

Rose's forehead wrinkled. "But Hannah told me she had—"

"She was a liar and hardly the lady she pretended to be. She'd spent the past twenty years serving in the British royal navy, disguised as a man, until a handful of Seelie fools managed to locate the wretch." Ambrose's tone left no doubt how repulsive he found the former Miss Hughes. "They would have used her and then killed her, simply to make certain the Seelie throne was never occupied by any but a pure-blooded Fey."

"You are once again in line to said throne, by the way," Gareth said.

"How can that be? I haven't a drop of Seelie blood in my veins."

"Marionette claimed you as her third heir, after her true daughter and son, though you were not of her blood. We found those papers among Miss Hughes's things, and there is a copy in the Fey de la Nuit hall of records. It is not a forgery. Your adopted mother loved you well." Ambrose pulled his hand away from hers, bringing his fingertips to play along the bare thigh he had draped over his hips, tugging her a bit closer to where his cock pulsed, thick and heavy, between her legs.

It seemed someone was growing tired of explanations.

Ambrose smiled. "Not at all, I will gladly tell you everything I know. But perhaps a bit later . . ."

Rose struggled to think, but the combination of faery mead and warm, aroused bodies made it insanely difficult. If she hadn't been a bit nervous as to how this business of loving two men at once would work, she would never have been able to resist succumbing to the passion simmering between the three of them. "But what of Ecanthar and the harpies? One of you said something about the Mother's creatures. What creatures? I have vague memories of some sort of battle, and children being stolen. What has she—"

"As Ambrose said, this is not the time for war stories." Gareth feathered soft kisses down her neck, ending with a nip of his teeth at her shoulder.

"We're safe for now." Ambrose's hand slid down her belly, teasing at the tuft of hair between her legs as his lips found her once more. *And don't worry, love. Your husbands are well aware of how this should work.*

Precisely. Gareth's hand slipped between Ambrose and Rose, finding Rose's breasts and cupping her in his hand. His fingers rolled an already taut nipple, making her moan into Ambrose's mouth.

So you are both experienced in sharing your bed with more than one person? Rose captured Ambrose's lip between her teeth and bit down even as she arched her back, rubbing Gareth's swollen length with her hips. *I don't know whether I should be scandalized or—*

Grateful. Simply be grateful. Gareth pressed forward, moaning as he slowly fucked the valley between her cheeks.

And prepare to scream two men's names instead of one. Ambrose's hand dipped lower, over her nub and into the well of heat between her legs. He plunged deep, first two fingers and then three, dispensing with the last of his gentleness when she dug her nails into his back hard enough to bring blood rushing into the cuts she had made.

Goddess, I meant to keep the promise I made . . . Seconds later, Rose cried out as Gareth's fangs slid cleanly into the soft flesh at her neck.

The slight sting of pain was soon banished by the rush of euphoria only a vampire's kiss could bring. It had been far too long since she'd known that particular bliss and it was nearly enough to force the tension spiraling within her to the breaking point.

Her head spun and her eyes slid closed as she was consumed, quickly drowning in pure sensation. Gareth's bite and Ambrose's kiss, Gareth's hands at her breasts and Ambrose's fingers between her legs, the feel of two aroused males pressed so tightly to her it seemed the three of them would merge into a mass of writhing, aroused flesh—it was swiftly becoming enough to drive her mad if she didn't find relief.

Take her, brother.

Rose wasn't sure who had spoken, but judged it must have been Gareth, for seconds later, Ambrose's fingers between her legs were replaced by the blunt head of his arousal. Without a moment's hesitation, he shoved his thick length inside her. She screamed at the fierce pleasure accompanying his invasion and clung to his shoulders, suddenly uncertain what to do next.

If she and Ambrose— Then what would Gareth— Would he be angry? Hurt? How did this work when she was but one woman and—

Relax, sweet. There are no worries here. Gareth's hands joined Ambrose's on her hips and with a slow, easy confidence they began to move her, back and forth, as if this were the thousandth time they had shared a woman and not the first.

After one last moment of hesitation, Rose gave herself up to their direction, growing accustomed to the feel of Ambrose driving deep inside her as her hips tilted forward and Gareth's cock sliding between the mounds of her ass as she tilted back. All too quickly, familiarity became delight, and delight, desire.

A desire so profound she became a wild, abandoned

thing, a wanton who bucked between the two hard bodies on either side of her, her lips, teeth, and tongue tangling with whichever man found her mouth, her hands desperate to touch every inch of them all at once. She delighted in the primal smell rising from their skin, in the low, throaty moans of the two men who took her. Any last remnants of shame or uncertainty vanished as the ecstasy building within her became too much to bear.

She did indeed scream both of their names as she shattered apart, her body clamping down around Ambrose, triggering a rush of heat between her legs and a wild cry from his lips as he lost himself within her. Gareth's cry joined his brother's a second later, the hot, sticky evidence of his pleasure smearing into her back as he wrapped an arm around her waist and pulled her close.

They continued to move as the waves of bliss abated, sweat-slick skin sliding against sweat-slick skin, the three of them writhing together until they were even closer than they had been before. When they finally grew still, Rose found her face buried beneath Ambrose's chin and Gareth's cheek pressed tight to the curve of her shoulder, his lips idly playing over the wound he had made.

Her limbs had never felt so heavy or her soul so at peace in her own skin. This was where she belonged, no matter how strange the idea of two husbands would have once been, no matter how much the three of them had yet to face. She was more content than she'd have dreamt possible after such upheaval and was, in fact, halfway to falling asleep when a sharp knock came at the door.

It was only then that Rose noticed the sparseness of the room they presently occupied. Though the bed was as soft as any she had lain upon, the walls of the chamber were rock and there wasn't so much as a single chair placed before the primitive-looking fireplace in the corner.

"Our circumstances have been a bit reduced," Gareth said, clearly still rambling around in her private thoughts.

The knocking came again, harder this time, triggering a weary sigh from Ambrose. "We shall be out momentarily."

"The sooner the better. If the three of you are finished with your spell, there are important matters to discuss." It was Beatrice's voice, as chilly and imperious as it had been before she learned Rose wasn't a threat to her throne.

The princess laughed. "You aren't a threat now, you silly thing. I will be queen far sooner than even I assumed, and you shall be safe on your little throne in Myrdrean doing your best not to cause any more trouble."

"From your mouth to the Goddess's ears," Rose said aloud, though she made no effort to shout to be heard through the heavy wood door. The princess was privy to her thoughts as long as she neglected to guard them, a fact that didn't seem so distressing at the moment. Let the world be aware of what she was thinking. She no longer had anything to hide.

"Excellent. I envy you, little Rose." Beatrice's tone was softer, almost affectionate when she spoke again. "And I am most pleased to feel you back among the living. Your lovers were quite impossible while you languished like some living corpse."

Rose laughed, a genuine sound that made her entire body shake. "Thank you, Beatrice. Eloquently put."

The other woman sniffed. "There is little reason for eloquence in times such as these. Now get dressed immediately or I shall have no other choice but to hold our conference in your bedchamber with the three of you in the nude."

Rose heard the rustle of skirts as Beatrice moved away from the door. "I suppose we ought to get dressed then. I assume I have been brought something to wear?"

"Ambrose's home was burned to the ground, but Elsa has agreed to share what clothing she managed to bring with her. You are nearly the same size." Ambrose made no move to roll out of bed. "I will fetch something from her in a moment."

"I believe the princess is sincere in her threats." Rose smiled and pressed a soft kiss to Ambrose's throat and then turned to capture Gareth's lips. "We should dress."

"She is most sincere, that's what my brother is afraid of," Gareth said, sitting up with obvious reluctance. "She means to force the pair of you into some rather dangerous spell to locate the Mother. Some business about your dreams has her convinced she, you, and Ambrose will be able to find the beast before she can finish whatever black work she is about or before—" The window into his mind snapped closed as he slid from the bed and began pulling on his stockings.

"Before what?" Rose asked, already knowing she

didn't wish to hear the answer. If only they could have stayed abed a bit longer, she might have felt more up to the business of hearing bad news. Perhaps a month or two tangled in the sheets would have sufficed.

"Never. A year at the very least." Ambrose kissed her deeply, as if a part of him feared it would be the last time.

After a few moments she reluctantly pulled away. "But we don't have the luxury of even a day." She stared into his troubled eyes, willing him to tell the truth about what new challenges they would face.

"No, we don't." He sighed again, and for a moment looked every one of his many years. "The Mother calls for you to be delivered to her. In exchange, she swears she will stop her attacks."

"Every major city in Europe has been beset by harpies. They are stealing human babies by the thousands," Gareth said. "At this rate there will be no more humans left to grow up."

"And nothing left for supernaturals to feed upon in thirty or forty years' time." Rose nodded, understanding the look on the vampire's face. "It's a wonder no one has turned me over to her yet. The Seelie king is mad as a hatter, and surely such a threat to their very existence would sway the Fey de la Nuit—"

"Most have the sense to realize that whatever the Mother wishes with you, it will likely prove worse for the supernatural world if you are delivered to her than if you are not. She means to destroy or enslave us all." Ambrose finally rose from the bed and made swift work of his own clothes. "Every Fey scholar from Britain to the dark expanses of the African continent agrees that she is finally seeking her revenge for her imprisonment so many thousands of years ago. She will not be appeased by something so simple as having her daughter returned to her side."

"You said *most* realize." Rose sat with the sheet tugged around her breasts, more for comfort than for modesty. She felt the need to cling to something now that she was alone once more. "Then there are those who would see me given to the beast?"

Gareth smiled. "And so we hide from them. Nothing to fear, sweet. I rather enjoy a nice long stay underground. It's so refreshingly dark, don't you think?"

"We have many allies here. Neither we nor they will allow you to be taken." Ambrose came to stand beside his brother. For once there was no tension between them. They were united, and it was for the love of her.

Rose had never felt more fortunate. Even in the midst of the greatest challenge any of them had ever faced, she felt like the luckiest woman in the world. There was no guarantee that the entire lot of them— her, her husbands, and their allies—would not be crushed beneath the Mother's will, but first they would give the creature a fight she wouldn't soon forget.

"You've been spoiling for a fight, don't try to deny it." Gareth smiled the mischievous grin she remembered from their first days together, bringing an answering smile to her lips.

"I have." And for the first time in weeks, she felt ready to face her many enemies. "So will one of you fetch me those clothes I was promised? I prefer to meet our allies wearing something other than a sheet."

"Giving orders are we?" Ambrose raised his

eyebrows even as he moved toward the door. "It seems the Briar Rose truly has returned."

"She has," Rose said, every inch of her warming as she realized the truth in the words. "I truly believe she has."

TOR
ROMANCE

Believe that love is magic

Please join us at the website below for more information about this author and other great romance selections, and to sign up for our monthly newsletter!

www.tor-forge.com